ALL OUR
YESTERDAYS

Books by Natalia Ginzburg

All Our Yesterdays

Family Sayings

The Little Virtues

The City and the House

The Manzoni Family

Valentino and Sagittarius

*Family: Family and Borghesia,
Two Novellas*

Voices in the Evening

NATALIA GINZBURG

ALL OUR YESTERDAYS

Translated from the Italian
by
ANGUS DAVIDSON

ARCADE PUBLISHING • NEW YORK

Originally published in Italy under the title Tutti I Nostri Ieri

THIS ARCADE PAPERBACK EDITION 2015

Arcade Publishing books may be purchased in bulk at special discounts for sales promotion, corporate gifts, fund-raising, or educational purposes. Special editions can also be created to specifications. For details, contact the Special Sales Department, Arcade Publishing, 307 West 36th Street, 11th Floor, New York, NY 10018 or arcade@skyhorsepublishing.com.

Arcade Publishing® is a registered trademark of Skyhorse Publishing, Inc.®, a Delaware corporation.

Visit our website at www.arcadepub.com.

10 9 8 7 6 5 4 3 2 1

Library of Congress Cataloging-in-Publication Data

Ginzburg, Natalia.
 [Tutti i nostri ieri. English]
 All our yesterdays / Natalia Ginzburg ; translated from the Italian by Angus Davidson. -- Arcade paperback edition.
 pages cm
 ISBN 978-1-62872-508-7 (pbk. : alk. paper) 1. Italy--Social conditions--Fiction. 2. World War, 1939-1945--Italy--Fiction. I. Davidson, Angus, 1898-1982, translator. II. Title.
 PQ4817.I5T813 2015
 853'.914--dc23
                                        2015014050

Cover design by Carin Goldberg
Cover photograph by Marcia Lippman

ISBN: 978-1-62872-508-7
Ebook ISBN: 978-1-62872-072-3

PART ONE

THEIR mother's portrait hung in the dining-room : a woman seated on a chair, wearing a hat with feathers in it, and with a long, tired, frightened face. She had always been weak in health, suffering from fits of giddiness and palpitations, and four children had been too much for her. She died not long after Anna's birth.

They used to go to the cemetery sometimes on Sundays, Anna, Giustino and Signora Maria. Concettina did not go, she never set foot outside the house on a Sunday ; it was a day she detested and she stayed shut up in her room mending her stockings, wearing her ugliest clothes. And Ippolito had to keep his father company. At the cemetery Signora Maria would pray, but the two children did not, because their father always said it was silly to pray, and perhaps God might exist but it was no use praying to Him, He was God and knew of His own accord how matters stood.

Before the time of their mother's death Signora Maria did not live with them but with their grandmother, their father's mother, and they used to travel together. On Signora Maria's suitcases were hotel labels, and in a cupboard there was a dress of hers with buttons in the shape of little fir-trees, bought in the Tyrol. Their grandmother had had a mania for travelling and never wanted to stop, and so she had run through all her money, for she liked going to smart hotels. Latterly she had turned very nasty, so Signora Maria said, because she could not bear having no money and could not make out how in the world this had happened, and every now and then she forgot and

5

wanted to buy herself a hat, and Signora Maria had to
drag her away from the shop-window, thumping the ground
with her umbrella and chewing her veil with rage. Now
she lay buried at Nice, the place where she had died, the
place in which she had enjoyed herself so much as a young
woman, when she was fresh and pretty and had all her
money.

Signora Maria was always pleased when she was able
to talk about the money the old lady had had, and when
she could tell stories and boast about the journeys they had
taken. Signora Maria was very small, and when she was
sitting down her feet did not touch the floor. For this
reason, when she was sitting down she used to wrap herself
round with a rug, because she did not like it to be seen
that her feet did not reach the floor. The rug was a
carriage rug, the one that she and the old lady used to
spread over their knees twenty years before, when they
drove about the town in a carriage. Signora Maria used
to put a little touch of rouge on her cheeks, and she did
not like to be seen early in the morning before she had
put on her rouge, and so she would slip into the bathroom
very quietly, holding her head down low ; and she started
and was very angry if someone stopped her in the passage
to ask her something. She always stayed quite a long
time in the bathroom, and everyone would come and knock
at the door and she would begin to shout that she was tired
of living in that house, where no one had any respect for
her, and she intended to pack her bags at once and go to
her sister's in Genoa. Two or three times she had pulled
out her suitcases from underneath the wardrobe and had
begun putting away her shoes in little cloth bags. The
only thing to be done was to pretend nothing had happened,
and then after a little she would start taking the shoes out
again. In any case everyone knew that the sister in Genoa
did not want her in her house.

Signora Maria would come out of the bathroom fully
dressed and with her hat on, and would then run out into

the street with a shovel to collect dung to manure her rose-trees, moving very swiftly and taking good care that nobody was going past. Then she would go off with her string bag to do the shopping ; and her quick little feet in their little shoes with bows on them were capable of carrying her all over the town in half an hour. Every morning she ransacked the entire town to find where things were cheapest, and she came home dead tired, and was always in a bad humour after doing the shopping, and would get angry with Concettina who was still in her dressing-gown, and say that never would she have believed, when she was sitting in the carriage beside the old lady, her knees nice and warm under the rug and people greeting them as they went by, that one day she would have to go toiling round the town with a string bag. Concettina would be very slowly brushing her hair in front of the looking-glass, and then she would put her face close to the glass and look at her freckles one by one, and look at her teeth and her gums and put out her tongue and look at that too. She combed her hair and knotted it in a tight roll at the back of her neck, with a ruffled fringe on her forehead, and this fringe made her look exactly like a *cocotte*, Signora Maria said. Then she would throw open the door of the wardrobe and consider which dress to put on. In the meantime Signora Maria would be throwing off bedclothes and beating carpets, a handkerchief tied round her head and her sleeves rolled up over her dry, withered arms, but she would run away from the window if she saw the lady of the house opposite appear on her balcony, for she did not like to be seen with a handkerchief round her head, beating carpets, remembering that she had come to the house as a lady companion—and look at the things she had to do now !

The lady of the house opposite had a fringe too, but it was a fringe that had been curled by the hairdresser and then put into a graceful disorder, and Signora Maria said she looked younger than Concettina, when she came out in the morning in one of her fresh, bright-coloured wraps, although it was known for certain that she was forty-five.

There were days when Concettina could not manage to find any dress to put on. She tried skirts and blouses, belts, flowers at her bosom, and nothing pleased her. Then she would begin to cry and complain what an unlucky creature she was, without a single pretty dress to wear, and with such a bad figure into the bargain. Signora Maria would shut the windows so that no one in the house opposite should hear. " You haven't a bad figure," she would say, " it's just that you're a bit heavy in the hips and a bit flat in the chest. Like your grandmother ; she was flat-chested too." Concettina bawled and sobbed, throwing herself half-undressed on the unmade bed, and then all her troubles would come out, the exams she had to pass and the difficulties with her *fiancés*.

Concettina had so many *fiancés*. She was always changing them. One of them was always standing in front of the gate, one who had a broad, square face and wore, in place of a shirt, a scarf, fastened together with a safety-pin. He was called Danilo. Concettina said she had given him up some time ago, but he had not yet resigned himself to this and walked up and down in front of the gate, his hands behind his back and his cap pulled down over his forehead. Signora Maria was afraid he might come in all of a sudden and make a scene with Concettina, and she went to Concettina's father to complain about all the troubles the girl had with her *fiancés*, and drew him over to the window to look at Danilo with his cap and his hands behind his back, and wanted him to go down and send him away. However Concettina's father said that the street belongs to everybody and one has no right to drive away a man from a street ; and he pulled out his old revolver and put it on his desk, in case Danilo suddenly climbed over the gate. And he pushed Signora Maria out of the room, because he wanted to be left in peace to his writing.

He was writing a big book of memoirs. He had been

writing it for many years, he had in fact given up his work as a lawyer in order to be able to write it. It was entitled *Nothing but the Truth* and it contained fiery attacks upon the Fascists and the King. The old man used to laugh and rub his hands together at the thought that the King and Mussolini knew nothing about it, while in a small town in Italy there was a man writing fiery remarks about them. He was telling the whole story of his life, the Caporetto retreat in which he had been involved and all the things he had seen, and the gatherings of Socialists and the March on Rome and all the fellows who had changed their shirts in his own little town, people who had appeared honest and decent and the shady, dirty things they had afterwards done—" nothing but the truth ". For months and months he wrote, ringing the bell every minute to ask for coffee, and the room was full of smoke, and even at night he sat up writing, or called Ippolito to write while he dictated. Ippolito would tap hard on the type-writer, and his father would walk up and down the room in his pyjamas as he dictated, and nobody could get to sleep, because the house had thin walls, and Signora Maria would turn over and over in her bed, trembling with fear lest someone in the street should hear the old man's raised voice and the fiery things he was saying against Mussolini. But then all at once the old man lost heart, and his book no longer seemed so fine to him, and then he said that the Italians were all wrong but that you certainly could not change them by means of a book. He said he would like to go out along the street shooting off his revolver, or else that he did not want to do anything at all, just to lie on his back and sleep and wait for death to come. He no longer left his room ; he spent his days in bed and made Ippolito read *Faust* to him. And then he would call Giustino and Anna and tell them how sorry he was that he had never done the things a father usually does, he had never taken them to the cinema or even out for a walk. And he called Concettina and wanted to know about her

exams and about her *fiancés*. He became very kind when
he was sad.   He woke up one morning and no longer felt
so sad ; he made Ippolito massage his back with a horse-
hair glove, and he wanted his white flannel trousers.   He
went and sat in the garden and asked them to bring him
his coffee there, but he always found it too weak and gulped
it down with disgust.   He would sit in the garden all the
morning, his pipe between his long, white teeth, his thin,
wrinkled face screwed up into a grimace, and it was
impossible to make out whether this was because of the
sun or because of his disgust at the coffee, or because of
the effort of holding the pipe in his teeth alone.   He made
no excuses for anything to anybody after he had stopped
feeling sad, and he used to flog the rose-trees with his cane
while he was thinking afresh about his book of memoirs,
and then Signora Maria would be distressed about the
rose-trees which were so dear to her heart, and every morning she made the sacrifice of going out into the street to
collect dung in her shovel, notwithstanding the risk that
someone might see and laugh at her.

The old man had not a single friend.   Occasionally he
went out and walked all over the town, with a contemptuous,
hostile air, and he would sit in a café in the centre of the
town looking at the people passing, in order to be seen by
those whom he had once known very well, to show he
was still alive and meant them to be angry with him.   He
would come home well satisfied when he had seen one of
the ones who had once been Socialists like himself and
were now Fascists, and who did not know the things that
were written about them in his book of memoirs, about
the time when they were honest and decent people and
about the shady, dirty things they had afterwards done.
At table the old man would rub his hands together and
say that if God existed, He would let him live till the end
of Fascism, so that he could publish his book and see
people's faces.   He said that in that way one would know
at last whether this God existed or not, but he himself

thought, on the whole, that He did not exist, or again, possibly He did exist but was on Mussolini's side. After the meal the old man would say, " Giustino, go and buy me a paper. Make yourself useful, seeing that you're not ornamental." For there was nothing kindly about him when he was not sad.

From time to time big boxes of chocolates used to arrive, sent by Cenzo Rena, who had been a great friend of the old man's at one time. Picture post-cards also used to arrive from him, from all parts of the world, for Cenzo Rena was always travelling, and Signora Maria would recognize the places where she had been with the old lady, and she stuck the post-cards into her dressing-table mirror. But the old man did not like to hear Cenzo Rena's name mentioned, because they had been friends but had then had a terrible quarrel, and when he saw the chocolates arrive he would shrug his shoulders and snort with rage, and Ippolito had to write secretly to Cenzo Rena to thank him and to give news of the old man.

Concettina and Anna had piano lessons twice a week. A timid little ring would be heard, Anna would open the gate, and the music-master would walk across the garden, stopping to look at the rose-trees, for he knew the story of the dung and the shovel, and also he hoped that the old man would pop out from some corner of the garden. At first the old man had paid him a great deal of attention and had imagined that this music-master was a great man ; he had sat him down in his own room and given him his own tobacco to smoke, and had tapped him hard on the knee and told him over and over again that he was an exceptional person. The music-master was engaged in writing a Latin grammar in verse ; he copied it out into a little exercise-book and every time he came he was anxious that the old man should hear a few new stanzas. And all of a sudden the old man had become terribly tired of him ; he did not wish to hear any more new stanzas of the grammar, and when the music-master's timid little ring at the gate was heard the old man could be seen escaping up the stairs to hide where best he could. The music-master could not resign himself to being no longer welcomed in the old man's room, and he would talk in a loud voice in the passage and read out his stanzas, looking this way and that all the time. Then he grew sad, and used to ask Concettina and Anna whether he had perhaps offended their father without knowing it. Neither Anna nor Concettina played well. They were both sick of these lessons and wanted to stop them, but Signora Maria was unwilling because the music-master's was the only face from the outside world that was ever seen inside the house. And a house is really too gloomy, she said, without a few visitors now and then. She herself was always present at the piano-lessons, with her rug over her knees and her crochet-work. And afterwards she used to carry on a conversation with the music-master and listen to his new stanzas, and he would stay on till it was quite late, still in the hope of seeing the old man.

The music-master was in very truth the only stranger who came to the house. There was indeed a nephew of Signora Maria's who put in an occasional appearance— the son of that sister of hers at Genoa ; he was studying to be a veterinary surgeon and at Genoa he always failed in his exams, and so he had come to study in this little town where the exams were much easier, but even so he failed from time to time. In any case he was not a real stranger because everyone had seen him constantly ever since he had been a child, and Signora Maria was always on tenterhooks when he arrived, for fear the old man should treat him unkindly. The old man did not want anyone about the house, and even Concettina's *fiancés* were not allowed to enter the gate.

In the summer they all had to go to Le Visciole, every year. Each time Concettina wept because she wanted to go to the seaside, or else to stay in the town with her *fiancés*. And Signora Maria, too, was in despair, because of the *contadino's* wife there, for they had quarrelled one day when the pig had eaten some handkerchiefs. And Giustino and Anna, too, who as children had enjoyed themselves at Le Visciole, now wore cross expressions when they had to go there. They hoped their father would let them go one summer to stay with Cenzo Rena in a kind of castle he possessed, for Cenzo Rena wrote every year to invite them. But their father did not wish them to go and said that in any case it was an ugly castle, a wretched thing with poor little towers ; Cenzo Rena only thought it beautiful because he had spent money on it. Money is the devil's excrement, said their father.

They went to Le Visciole by a little local train. It was near, but departure was a complicated business, for the old man gave no one any peace during the days when the packing had to be done ; he flew into rages with Ippolito and with Signora Maria and the trunks had to be packed and unpacked a hundred times over. And Concettina's *fiancés*, who had come to bid her good-bye, hung about the gate, and she cried because she was filled with a tremendous rage at having to stay for so many months at Le Visciole, where she grew fat from boredom and there wasn't even a tennis-court.

They left early in the morning, and the old man was in a very bad temper throughout the journey, because the little train was crowded and people were eating and drinking, and he was afraid they would soil his trousers with wine. Never once did he fail to start a quarrel in the train. Then he would get angry with Signora Maria, who always had numbers of little bundles and baskets and her shoes in cloth bags stuck about all over the place, and in her string bag a wine-flask of coffee and milk ; the old man was particularly disgusted at this flask, to him it seemed revolting to see coffee and milk in a wine-flask ; and he said to Signora Maria that he quite failed to understand how the old lady could have wanted to take her about with her on so many journeys. But when they

arrived at Le Visciole he was content. He sat himself
down under the pergola and took in deep, strong breaths,
breath after breath, and said how good the air tasted, it
had such a strong, fresh taste that he felt he was taking a
drink each time he breathed. And he called the *contadino*
and greeted him warmly, and called Ippolito to see whether
he didn't think the *contadino* looked like a Van Gogh picture ;
he made the *contadino* sit with his face supported on his
hand and put his hat on his head, and asked if he didn't
look like a real Van Gogh. After the *contadino* had gone,
Ippolito said he might indeed be a Van Gogh, but he
was also a thief because he stole grain and wine. The old
man flew into a great rage. He had played with this
contadino as a boy, and he could not allow Ippolito to start
pouring contempt in this way upon the things of his childhood, and it was much worse to pour contempt upon the
childhood of one's father than to keep back a few pounds
of grain when you needed it. Ippolito made no answer,
he held his dog between his legs and stroked its ears. As
soon as he arrived at Le Visciole he used to put on an old
fustian jacket and high boots, and he went about dressed
like that the whole summer, and he was shockingly dirty,
and besides, he must be bursting with heat, said Signora
Maria. But Ippolito never looked hot, he did not sweat
and his face was always dry and smooth, and he used to
go about the countryside with the dog in the hot noonday
sun. The dog ate the armchairs and had fleas, and Signora
Maria wanted to give it away, but Ippolito was mad about
this dog, and once when the dog was ill he had kept it in
his room at night, getting up to make bread and milk
for it. He would have liked to take it with him to the
town, instead of which he had to leave it at Le Visciole
with the *contadino* who did not look after it and who gave
it bad food, and Ippolito was always much distressed in
the autumn when he had to say good-bye to the dog, but
his father agreed with Signora Maria about the dog and
would not hear of having it in the town. So Ippolito

would have to wait patiently for him to die, his father said, and really, perhaps Ippolito did hope very much that he would die soon, perhaps this was his pet dream, to be able to go for a walk in the town with his dog.

Ippolito listened in silence when his father spoke unkindly to him, he never answered back and his face remained quiet and pale, and at night he stayed up to type out the book of memoirs, or to read Goethe aloud when his father could not sleep. For he had the soul of a slave, Concettina used to say, and camomile in his veins instead of blood, and was like an old man of ninety, with no girls whom he liked and no desire for anything, all he could do was to wander about the countryside alone all day with the dog.

Le Visciole was a tall, large house, with guns and horns hung up on the walls, with high beds and mattresses that rustled because they were stuffed with maize-leaves. The garden stretched down to the high road, a big, uncultivated garden full of trees ; it was no use trying to plant rose-bushes or other flowers because in winter the *contadino* would certainly not look after them and they would die. Behind the house was the courtyard, with the farm-cart and the *contadino's* cottage, and the *contadino's* wife who came to her door from time to time and flung out a bucket of water, and then Signora Maria would shout out that this dirty water made the courtyard stink, and the *contadino's* wife shouted back that it was clean water, quite good enough to wash Signora Maria's face in, and so the two of them would go on quarrelling for a bit. All round, as far as the eye could see, stretched fields of corn and maize, and in the middle of them stood scarecrows, waving their empty sleeves ; vineyards and oak-trees started at the foot of the hill, and every now and then a shot would be heard from that direction, and a cloud of birds would rise and Ippolito's dog would be heard barking, but Concettina said it barked from fright, not from a desire to catch any-thing. The river was some distance away, beyond the

road, a bright, far-off streak amongst bushes and rocks :
and the village was a little beyond it, about ten houses or so.

In the village were the people whom the old man called
" the humbugs "—the local Fascist Secretary, the Superintendent of Police, the Secretary of the Commune ; and
the old man went every day to the village so that the
Humbugs might see him, that they might see he was still
alive and that he cut them dead. The Humbugs would
be playing bowls in their shirtsleeves, ignorant that they
too were in the book of memoirs ; and their wives would
be sitting round the monument in the little square, knitting
and suckling their babies, with handkerchiefs over their
breasts. The monument was big and made of stone, a big,
stone young man with a badge and a fez : the old man
would stop in front of it and stick his' eyeglass in his eye,
and look and smile sarcastically, he would stay there for a
little, looking and smiling sarcastically : and Signora Maria
was afraid that some day or other the Humbugs would
arrest him, and she would try to pull him away, as she
had once done with the old lady in front of the hat-shop
windows. Signora Maria would have liked to talk to the
wives of the Humbugs, to have learnt new stitches and
taught them some as well : and also to have told them that
it would have been a good thing if they had washed their
breasts with water that had been boiled before suckling
their babies. But she never dared go near them because
of the old man.

In the summer, freckles and places where the skin had
peeled were to be seen on the old man's bald, shiny head,
because he went out in the sun bareheaded ; and Concettina's legs went golden brown, seeing that there was
nothing else to do at Le Visciole except sunbathe, and
Concettina sat all day long in a deck-chair in front of the
house, with dark glasses and a book that she did not read ;
she would look at her legs and take care that they got
nicely sunburnt, and then she had the idea that if she kept
them sweating in the sun they might grow a little thinner ;

for Concettina, besides being heavy in the hips, was heavy in the legs as well, and she used to say she would give ten years of her life to be slimmer from the hips down. Signora Maria would arrange her clothes about her as she sat under the pergola, her extraordinary clothes cut out of old curtains or bedspreads, with a hat made out of a newspaper on her head and her feet crossed on a footstool. Far away, on the brow of the hill, Ippolito could be seen going backwards and forwards with his gun and his dog : and the old man would curse the stupid dog and Ippolito's mania for wandering about the countryside, when all the time he needed him to give him his injection and do some typewriting, and he would send off Giustino to chase him.

2

It was at Le Visciole that the old man felt ill for the first time. He was taking his coffee, and all of a sudden the hand that held the cup started trembling, and the coffee was spilt on his trousers, and his body was bowed down, and he was trembling and breathing heavily. Ippolito went on a bicycle to fetch the doctor. But the old man did not want the doctor and said that he felt a little better ; he said the doctor was a humbug and he wanted to leave for the town at once. The doctor came, a humbug of the most insignificant kind, hardly taller than Signora Maria, with fair hair that looked like chickens' feathers, and big baggy trousers like a Zouave and check stockings. And all at once he and the old man made friends. For the old man discovered that he was not a humbug at all, and that he hated the local Fascist Secretary and the Superintendent of Police and the stone young man in the village square. The old man said he was very pleased he had been ill, because in that way he had discovered this little doctor, a person whom he had believed to be a humbug whereas he was really a fine fellow ; and every day they used to have a chat and tell each other all sorts of things, and the old man was almost inclined to read him some bits out of the book of memoirs, but Ippolito said better not. Ippolito could not now go roaming over the countryside, but had to sit all day long in his father's room and give him injections and drops and read aloud to him : but the old man no longer wanted Goethe, he now wanted detective stories. Luckily there was the little doctor coming all the time, and the old man was perfectly contented : only he had told him to stop wearing those check stockings, because they did not suit him and were rather ridiculous.

They left, as usual, at the end of September : however Giustino and Signora Maria left earlier, because Giustino had to sit again for his examination in Greek. In the town the old man began to be ill again, growing thin and coughing, and a doctor came to see him, a doctor who was entirely different from the little doctor with hair like chickens' feathers, a doctor who did not sit and chat with him, who did not listen to him and who treated him badly. He had forbidden him to smoke : and the old man gave Ippolito his tobacco-pouch and told him to lock it up in a drawer and keep the key ; but after a short time he wanted the tobacco, he wanted just a little of it, and Ippolito paid no attention to him and stood there with his hands in his pockets, and so then the old man said how ridiculous Ippolito was, who took everything literally and was lacking in commonsense, lacking a touch of commonsense and imagination, and the world was ruined by people like that, by people who took everything literally, and he couldn't get over having produced such a ridiculous, stupid son, who stood there with a stony face and kept tight hold of the key : and it was a great grief to him to have a stupid son, a grief which did him more harm than a little tobacco. Until finally Ippolito gave a sigh and threw down the key on the desk : and the old man opened the drawer and took the tobacco, and started to smoke and to cough.

Then one day, while they were all at table, they saw the old man come into the room, in pyjamas and slippers, with a bundle of papers in his arms.   It was the book of memoirs : and he asked whether the stove had been lit, and it *had* been lit because it was already cold : then all at once he started stuffing the sheets of paper into it, and they all looked at him open-mouthed, only Ippolito did not appear surprised. Big flames came up from the open stove, and the book of memoirs was blazing, and no one understood anything : but Ippolito did not appear surprised, he had got up and was looking at the flames, smoothing back his hair very slowly, and with the poker he pushed into the stove a few sheets that were not yet burned : and then the old man rubbed his hands together and said, " I feel happier now. It will have to be written all over again. It wasn't going right."   But all that day he was very jumpy, and would not hear of going back to bed nor of dressing himself either, and he walked up and down the room and bullied Ippolito with the usual story about his tobacco : he was very angry with Ippolito and finished by sending him out of the room, and insisted upon Concettina reading aloud to him : while she was reading he held her hand and stroked it and told her that she had beautiful hands and a beautiful profile, a really beautiful profile : but then he began saying that she read badly and in a singsong kind of voice, and made her stop.

He went to bed and was now unable to get up again. He grew slowly, steadily worse, and was dying, and everyone knew it, and certainly he himself knew it too but he pretended there was nothing wrong—he who used always to talk of death before he fell really ill ; he spoke less and less as the days went by, gradually he came only to ask for what he needed ; Giustino and Anna were forbidden to enter his room and saw him from the door as he lay flat in the bed with his thin, hairy arms lying on top of the coverlet, his nose getting whiter and whiter and sharper and sharper; sometimes he would make a sign to the boy and girl to come in, but then he would say nothing that was intelligible, only confused words, and would rumple up his pyjamas on his chest with his arms, and tremble and sweat. There was a smell of ether in the room, and a red rag tied round the lamp, and the old man's long, pointed shoes stuck out from under the wardrobe, and you knew he would never walk again, because soon he would be dead. Anna and Concettina had not started their piano-lessons again since the summer, but the music-master still came in order to ask for news, only he did not dare to ring the bell and would stand in front of the gate and wait for Signora Maria to come out into the garden and tell him if the old man had been able to get a little rest. And Danilo, too, would almost always be at the gate, leaning against the wall with a book, and Signora Maria said it was really shameless of him not to leave Concettina in peace now that her father was so very ill; and when Concettina went out for a moment to do some shopping, he would put his book under his arm and walk behind her, and Concettina would throw fierce glances at him every now and then, and would come home very red in the face, with her fringe all untidy.

The old man died in the morning. Anna and Giustino were at school and Signora Maria came to fetch them, a tiny little black handkerchief tied round her neck; she kissed them gravely on the forehead and led them away. To kiss them she had had to rise on tiptoe, because they were both much taller than herself; it had been in the corridor at the school and the headmaster was there watching; usually he was rude but he was very kind that morning. They went up to their father's room: Concettina was kneeling there sobbing, Ippolito on the other hand was standing still and silent, his face thin and white as usual. Their father was lying fully dressed on the bed, with his tie on, and shoes on his feet, and his face now was very beautiful, no longer trembling and sweaty, but composed and gentle.

Then Signora Maria took Anna to the house opposite, for the lady there had sent over to suggest that she might be left with them for the whole day. Anna was frightened because there was a dog there. Not a dog like Ippolito's, curly-haired and stupid, but an Alsatian tied up with a chain ; and hung on a tree in the garden was a notice : *Cave canem.* And she was also frightened because there was a ping-pong table. Through the hedge she had seen a boy playing ping-pong with an old gentleman. And so she was frightened that the boy might ask her to play and she didn't know how to. She thought of saying that she knew how to play but didn't want to because at their house at Le Visciole there was a ping-pong table and they did nothing but play at it all the summer. But if later all of a sudden she and the boy made great friends, it might perhaps be necessary to invite him to come one summer to Le Visciole and then he would realize that there wasn't a ping-pong table there at all.

She had never been in the house opposite. Through the hedge she had looked at the boy and the old gentleman and the dog. The lady with the fringe who appeared on the balcony in her dressing-gown, and who looked so young, was the old gentleman's wife. Then there was a red-haired girl, who was the daughter of the old gentleman and of another wife whom he had had before. On the other hand the boy, and also another bigger boy who must be about Ippolito's age, were the sons of this present wife, the one with the fringe. Signora Maria said they were very rich people, for the old gentleman was the owner of the soap factory, the long red-brick building on the river, with chimneys that were always smoking. They were very, very rich people. They never boiled up their coffee-grounds a second time, but gave them to certain monks who came to ask for them. The red-haired girl, daughter of the old gentleman's other wife, came out in the evenings with a broom and swept the whole garden, muttering all the time and working herself up into a rage. Signora Maria, too, had very often looked through the hedge, for she was inquisitive and much interested in rich people.

Signora Maria left Anna with the maid who came to open the door, recommending that they should make her put a scarf round her neck if she went out in the garden, and then she went home again. The maid led Anna to a room on the floor above and told her to wait there, and in a moment Signor Giuma would come and keep her company. Anna did not know who Signor Giuma was. From the windows she saw her own home—quite different when seen thus from this side, low, small and old, with the dried-up wistaria on the balcony and, on one corner of the roof, Giustino's ball, torn and rain-soaked. The shutters were closed in her father's room : and she remembered suddenly how he used to throw open the shutters with a clatter and lean out to look at the morning, soaping his chin with the shaving-brush and stretching out his thin neck, and would say to her, " Go and buy me some tobacco. Make yourself useful, seeing that you're not ornamental." And she seemed to see him going out into the garden, with his eyeglass, in his white flannel trousers, with his long legs that were slightly crooked because he had done so much riding as a young man. And she wondered where her father was now. She believed in hell, in purgatory and in paradise, and thought that her father must now be in purgatory, repenting of the unkind things he had so often said to them, particularly when he bullied Ippolito about the tobacco and about the dog ; and how surprised he must have been to find that purgatory existed, when he had so often said that almost certainly there is nothing for the dead, and it is better so because at least you can sleep at last—he himself being such a bad sleeper.

The maid came to tell her that Signor Giuma had now arrived. It was the boy, the one who played ping-pong. He came running in, whistling, his hair over his eyes ; he

threw down his books, which were tied together by a
leather strap, on the desk.   He seemed surprised to see her ;
he gave a little cold, shy bow, stooping his shoulders slightly.
He started looking round the room for something, whistling
as he looked.   From a drawer he took an exercise-book
and a pot of glue, and stuck some things into the book :
they were big faces of film actors, cut out of a magazine.
It appeared to be very important to stick them in, and
very tiresome too, for the boy panted and snorted, throwing
back his hair from over his eyes.   Beside the desk was a big
revolving globe and from time to time he looked on it for
some country or other and then wrote hastily in the exercise-
book underneath the film-actors' faces.   The red-haired
girl came in.   Her hair was short and clipped in a fashion
which was popular that year and which was called *à la
fièvre typhoïde*.   But only her hair was fashionable ; her dress,
on the contrary, was wide and ungraceful, with a round
neck to it, and was of an ugly sort of lemon yellow.   The
girl held her usual broom in her hand and she swept the
carpet violently and then said, "Giuma, it's not very
amusing for this little girl.   Leave the film-actors and show
her *The Child's Treasure-House*, or take her into the garden
and play ping-pong with her."

They looked at *The Child's Treasure-House*.   There were
several volumes of it and all sorts of things were to be
seen in it—flowers and birds and machines and cities.   In
front of each picture, Giuma stopped for a moment and
they both looked : then he said, "Finished?" and she
said, "Yes".   "Finished" and "yes" were the only words
they spoke.   Giuma's thin, brown hand turned the pages.
Anna was ashamed of having thought they would become
great friends.   Then all of a sudden a great clamour was
heard all through the house, and she jumped and Giuma
laughed : he had white, sharp teeth like a wolf's.   He said,
"It's the gong.   We must go to lunch."

The old gentleman sat at the head of the table.   He
was deaf, and had a little black box on his chest, with an

electric wire which he kept hooked on to his ear. He had
a white beard which he placed on top of his table-napkin
when he started to eat ; he had a gastric ulcer and could
eat only cooked vegetables and pieces of soaked bread with
oil. Beside him sat the red-haired girl, who was called
Amalia, and it was she who helped him to food and seasoned
it with oil and poured mineral-water into his glass. At the
other end of the table sat his wife, wearing a very hairy
blue woollen jumper and a little pearl necklace ; then
there was a person that you couldn't be quite sure who he
was, he wasn't a guest because he was wearing slippers ;
he had Giuma beside him and Giuma poured water into
his wine out of spite and then laughed with his fist over his
mouth ; the man took no notice of him and talked stocks
and shares with the old gentleman, but he had to yell
because the little box was slightly broken. Then they all
started talking about Amalia's new way of doing her hair,
à la fièvre typhoïde, and the Signora said she wanted to do
hers like that too, because she was a bit tired of her fringe.
Amalia shouted the conversation into the old gentleman's
ear. The little box was called " Papa's apparatus " ; and
even the old gentleman alluded to himself as " Papa ".
He said, " Papa wants to take a long nap after lunch
to-day. Papa is very old ". Then the Signora began to
get angry and to look out of the window because of Emanuele
failing to arrive. Emanuele was the one who was about
the same age as Ippolito, and he arrived almost at the end
of lunch. He was lame, and he arrived all red and sweating
from the fatigue of limping. He looked like Giuma, except
that he hadn't teeth like a wolf ; he had broad, square
teeth that stuck out over his lips. After lunch they wrapped
the old gentleman up in a rug on the sofa and put a scarf
over his eyes because otherwise he could not sleep, and
then left him there.

Anna and Giuma played ping-pong. She had told him
that she did not know how to play, so certain was she now
that they would not become friends, so that it did not

matter to her what he might think. He said he would
teach her how to play, it was easy. While they were playing
the man in the slippers came and watched. He was called
Franz. He was small, with light eyes and a face which
was sunburnt and all furrowed. He and Giuma began
punching each other and chasing each other round the
garden. Anna sat and looked at them, playing idly with
the ping-pong ball. The dog was not there because it had
been sent to some friends of theirs in order to be mated.
When it grew dark, Signora Maria called to Anna from
the window and she went home.

Her father's funeral took place soon afterwards. Anna
had imagined a real funeral with priests and white lilies
and a cross. But she had forgotten that her father disliked
priests. So there were no priests and no lilies. There were
some of Concettina's *fiancés*, in fact the most important of
them : Danilo and two or three others. Then there was
the music-master who still wanted to know in what way
he had offended the old man, and he asked Concettina's
fiancés and Signora Maria's nephew if they knew. While
the old man was ill he had written him letters in which he
said he was consumed with regret at having offended him
without knowing why, and he asked for his forgiveness
whatever the reason might be. But the old man had not
read any of the letters, because he was too ill.

They buried the old man beside his wife in the cemetery
and Concettina started sobbing violently. Then the people
who had come said farewell, with the usual mysterious,
ceremonious air, to the relations of the dead, and the latter
went back home, and at home they sat down to dinner
and there was macaroni and vegetables as on any other,
ordinary day.

Signora Maria made her nephew come to the house to
take a bath, because he had no conveniences in the room
where he lodged and the public baths were so crowded ;
and Concettina was annoyed and said to Ippolito that that
nephew of Signora Maria's would always be getting in their

way now. Ippolito no longer had to do typewriting and
read aloud, and now he was studying for his solicitor's
exams, walking up and down the terrace with a book in
his hand ; each of them knew that he could do what he
liked now ; Giustino brought home four white mice in a
cage that he had bought out of his savings and said he
would tame them ; and Signora Maria complained that
they stank horribly. Anna believed that in a house where
someone had died no one ought to laugh for a very long
time : instead of which, a few days after the funeral,
Concettina was laughing like a madwoman with her and
Giustino, because she had made herself a false bosom with
wool out of a mattress.

There was a great freedom in the house. But it was a
freedom that was a little alarming. There was no longer
anyone to give orders. Every now and then Ippolito made
a kind of attempt to give orders, but nobody paid any
attention to him, and he would shrug his shoulders and go
back and walk up and down the terrace again. He and
Signora Maria quarrelled over money. Signora Maria said
Ippolito was mean, and also that he was suspicious and did
not trust her. There were now the mourning clothes to be
thought of. But Ippolito did not want to give her the
money because he said there was very little of it : he said
she must arrange for the mourning to be made at home,
as so many people did. Signora Maria went to the chemist
and bought some packets of black powder and put the
clothes to soak in a big pot : there was a kind of broth in
it that looked like lentil soup. But when the clothes were
dried and ironed Concettina was not satisfied because they
had not come out a fine, deep black ; it was a black that
had a brownish tinge in it. Concettina was sulky with
Ippolito for several days over this matter of the clothes,
because she said she could easily have bought a little cheap
material : and she did not come and sit at table but took
her meals up to her own room.

Anna did not expect to go and play again at the house

opposite. However Giuma went on inviting her. They formed the habit of playing together and not a day passed but he invited her. Anna did not enjoy herself very much with him. She far preferred to play in the street with her own school-friends. But when Giuma invited her she had not the courage to refuse. She did not know why, but she had not the courage. She rather hoped he would lend her *The Child's Treasure-House* some time : but she did not dare to ask him. And she felt rather proud that he should invite her. They scarcely ever played ping-pong ; Giuma liked the game of re-enacting films that he had seen. He would tie her to a tree with a rope and dance round her with a burning piece of paper and her arms were sore because he tied her so tightly. If they stopped playing this game, then he would begin to talk. That first day he had hardly talked at all but now he talked, he talked so much that he even became a bore. He told her stories of things that had happened to him, but to her it seemed that almost the whole thing was an invention. He told her of prizes he had won in rugby matches and boat races—gold and silver cups ; but it was never possible to see these prizes, he had given them away or his mother had put them in a place where they could not be got at. Sometimes Emanuele and Amalia, Giuma's brother and sister, would come out on the balcony and start listening, and would laugh loudly. " Buffoon ", Emanuele would say to him. Then Giuma would fly into a rage and run away upstairs to his room. He would come back after a short time with his eyes red and his hair untidy. For a little he would sit silent on the grass, but then he would find the rope and start the rope-and-tree game again. Anna would go home in the evening with her head full of Giuma's stories, and of the stories of the friends who took part with him in his rugby matches and boat races : Cingalesi, Pucci Donadio, Priscilla and Toni. They had strange names and you could never make out whether they were boys or girls. Nor was it possible to make out why he never got them to come and play in the garden with him, and preferred to play alone with a little girl who had never taken part in a boat race in her life.   Perhaps it was that with those other friends his inventions and boastings were not so successful. He would walk up and down on the lawn trailing the rope behind him, boasting and inventing.   Anna sat on the grass and her neck ached from so much nodding and her lips ached too, from pretending to smile.   From time to time she asked him a question or two.   They were prudent questions and she pondered them silently for a little while.   She asked, " Is rugby a good game ? "—or again, " Was Cingalesi there that day ? "   Of Toni she preferred not to speak because she had never understood whether Toni was a girl or a boy.

Then Giuma began to talk about when he would be going away.   He was going to spend the winter at Mentone where they had a villa.   Giuma did not go to school, he was given lessons by professors, and later perhaps he would go to college in Switzerland and there he would play rugby all day long.   And Anna had a feeling of great repose at the thought of his going away.   She would return to playing in the street with her own girl friends : there were boys too, and they hit her sometimes.   But they did not tie her to trees.   Once when Giuma had tied her to the tree it was almost dark already, and he told her he was going to the kitchen to fetch a knife so that he could cut her throat and eat her.   So she was left alone in the almost dark garden, and tied up too, and suddenly she was frightened and started shouting, " Giuma, Giuma ! "—and it was getting darker and darker and her arms were hurting her. Then Emanuele came out and cut the knot with his penknife, and took her into the bathroom and put Vaseline on her arms where the skin was grazed and purple.   " That brute of a brother of mine," he said.

In the house carpets were being rolled up and trunks and suitcases had appeared.   Emanuele was the only one who was not going away, because he had to attend lectures

at the university. In truth Amalia did not want to go
either, and her stepmother said that if she really did not
like the idea of a change she might just as well be left at
home ; but the old gentleman said that Amalia was run
down and was in need of some sea air. Amalia could be
heard weeping because she did not want to go away. So
then the old gentleman said to the man called Franz that
he must try to persuade her and Franz went and spoke to
her and came back after a little to say that he had persuaded
her and that she would go.

And so, one morning, they could all be seen getting into
the car, Giuma with the dog under his arm and Amalia
and the man called Franz who was to drive, and Mammina,
as they called her, and the old gentleman. Mammina was
wearing a very ample tweed cape and dark glasses : and
Amalia had also put on a tweed cape which seemed to be
more or less copied from the other, but Concettina who
was watching from her window said that she looked as if
she was everyone else's servant. The old gentleman made
them bring him a quantity of newspapers and fixed them
in layers underneath his waterproof, because he said there
was nothing like newspapers for protecting one's stomach
from the cold. Emanuele was left alone on the pavement
waving his handkerchief : and he saw Anna at the window
and told her she could come whenever she liked and read
Giuma's books and, if she had to learn geography, she could
look at the globe too. He did not look in the least sad
at being left alone, and went back into the house limping
and skipping and rubbing his hands briskly together.

3

Anna tried two or three times to play in the street with
some of the other girls from her school, but they no longer
found these games very amusing and got into the habit of

walking along the road beside the river, chatting and strol-
ling arm in arm.   There were many things to talk about,
and games were less enjoyable now.   Giustino, too, used to
walk along by the river with his friends ; Giustino had
become a big boy now, he wore Ippolito's cast-off clothes
and plastered his hair down.   At carnival-time he went to
the fairground and afterwards told Anna how he had played,
a game of *briscola* with the man who played cards with his
feet.   He was always wanting money and he sold his white
mice to a friend ; by now he was bored with his white mice
and never remembered to give them anything to eat.   .Some-
times he was very nice to Anna but then she would discover
that he was needing something—to borrow ten lire or the
grey pullover that belonged to Anna but which he liked
wearing.   He had worn it so much that he had completely
spoilt its shape.   He was bad at his lessons and Ippolito
used to coach him in Greek in the evenings, and every now
and then he would lose patience with him and hit him with
his fist, and Giustino would jump down from the balcony
and run away.   Ippolito would shrug his shoulders and say
that after all he really didn't care.   One evening Giustino
stayed out all night long, and in the morning Signora Maria
was on the point of telephoning to the police-station.   But
Giustino came back.   He did not say a word to anyone and
went into the kitchen to find something to eat.   His trousers
were covered with mud and his hands all scratched.   He
went the whole day without speaking and then he said to
Signora Maria that he had come home, yes, he had come
home but he didn't want Ippolito to give him any more
coaching, otherwise he would run away again, and for good.
And Ippolito said that in that case Giustino could make
his own arrangements about learning Greek, and he himself
didn't care in the least, no, not in the very least.

And then all of a sudden it came about that Emanuele
and Ippolito made friends.   It was strange because Ippolito
had never been friends with anybody, he had never been
heard to speak of any friend that he had.   Emanuele and

he started talking to each other over the gate, and they lent each other books, and one day Anna when she came back from school found Emanuele sitting at dinner with the others, eating vegetable soup. He gave her a wink and said, " We're old friends, you and I,"—and after dinner he made her pull up the sleeves of her jersey to see whether she still had the marks of the rope on her arms.

Anna thought Emanuele would become one of Concettina's usual *fiancés*, one of those who wrote her letters and gave her flowers and took her to the cinema and fell in love with her. But not at all. Emanuele was not much interested in Concettina. He was quite nice to her, he brought her fashion-plates he had found in Mammina's or Amalia's room. He was quite nice but he was always telling her all the things that were wrong with her : her way of dressing and her way of walking and her way of putting on rouge. When Ippolito was not there he stayed chatting with her in the sitting-room and they turned over the fashion-plates together, and he explained to her how she ought to dress. Concettina said she had not the money to dress well. But he was of the opinion that money had nothing to do with it, you had only to look at Amalia to see that money had nothing to do with it ; she bought her clothes from a big dressmaker in Turin and yet she was always got up like a servant-girl. Every time he talked about Amalia he sighed and scratched his head. Now she had had her hair cut *à la fièvre typhoïde* and she looked like a monster. She had fallen in love with that Franz. He, Emanuele, had been aware of this for some time, but no one else in the house had realized it. Franz was a person whom Mammina had unearthed at Monte Carlo and had trailed behind her all the way home. He had told her he was the son of a German baron and had escaped from Germany because of the Nazis, because his father had been a great general under the Kaiser and he still believed in the monarchy. Mammina was ingenuous and always believed everything, and Papa was deaf and easy-going and accepted anything that

Mammina put in front of him, just as he accepted the sops of bread that they put in front of him at meals. But he, Emanuele, had from the very first moment distrusted this Franz, and from the very first moment had felt there was something suspicious about his story. And that Amalia should have fallen in love with this fellow was a disaster. To Emanuele he seemed a person who would not think twice about marrying for money. " It's better not to have any money ", said Emanuele to Concettina, and he gave her a little tap on the cheek. But if Ippolito arrived, Emanuele immediately insisted on Concettina leaving the room, and she would go off in a huff with the bundle of fashion-plates.

Emanuele and Ippolito had great discussions, but no one quite knew what they were about, because if anyone else was present they started talking in German. Concettina said they were obviously telling dirty stories, for otherwise they would not have found it necessary to use a language that nobody else knew, or else to be all alone in the sitting-room. Sometimes Emanuele stayed on late into the evening, and the sound of a discussion and of someone walking up and down the sitting-room could be heard, and then all of a sudden bursts of laughter could be heard from Emanuele: he had a way of laughing that sounded like the cooing of a pigeon. And then Emanuele would go away and Ippolito would stay up reading for his exams, for he never had any need of sleep and had accustomed himself to staying up all night, ever since the time of the book of memoirs. But now he no longer looked the same young man as had given his father injections and read Goethe to him, the young man with the subdued, weary look who had been bullied by his father over the tobacco and the dog. Now, ever since he had become friends with Emanuele, he had a shining, restless look in his eyes which seemed always to be looking for something, and his step, when he went to meet Emanuele at the gate, had become vigorous and elastic. Sometimes he stayed all alone for hours in the sitting-room, stroking his face and smiling and muttering to himself. Anna asked him whether he wasn't going to Le Visciole to fetch the dog ; she had imagined that after their father's death he would rush off at once and bring it back. But he assumed a strange expression when he heard the dog spoken of. He twisted his mouth in a strange, bitter way, perhaps because he suddenly remembered the bitter, unkind things his father always said to him, at the time when he did not know he was dying and was always talking about his own death, and about the day when Ippolito would go for walks in the town with the dog. In the meantime the dog remained at Le Visciole eating the rotten food the *contadino* gave it, but in any case it had been eating this rotten food for so many years that by now it must have grown accustomed to it.

One evening as they were just finishing supper Emanuele arrived with Danilo. It was the first time Danilo had set foot in the house, and Concettina went very red, with red patches even on her neck. Concettina was peeling an orange and pretended to be deeply absorbed in peeling it, and she did not look at Danilo, and Danilo threw her one quick, knowing glance and went on talking to Ippolito who was saying that he had been expecting him for some time. Signora Maria was very frightened, because Danilo had always frightened her, with his mania for standing quite still in front of their gate. Danilo and Concettina had met at a dance, and after that they had sometimes gone for a walk together, but Concettina said he had made a vulgar remark to her, a very vulgar remark ; Signora Maria asked what it was but Concettina would not repeat it. He came of quite a high-class family but they had become impoverished and his mother was reduced to working as cashier in a cake-shop. And there was a sister who was by no means a steady character. Concettina had given him to understand that she did not wish to see him any more. But he remained unconvinced and was always standing in front of the gate, and when Concettina went out he always walked behind her, without speaking but with a threatening look on his face,

Concettina said. And now Emanuele had brought him into the house and Ippolito had said that he had been expecting him for quite a long time, and there he was, sitting quietly at the table, peeling an orange that Ippolito had given him. But when he had eaten the orange Ippolito told him to go up with him into the sitting-room ; Emanuele, on the other hand, stayed to try and convince Signora Maria that Danilo was a charming young man, the best in the world, and that it was quite impossible that he should have made a vulgar remark to Concettina, probably there had been a misunderstanding. And it was not true that his sister was not a steady character ; he, Emanuele, had seen the sister and she had seemed to him a very steady character ·ndeed ; in any case he had a whole pack of sisters, from sixteen years old to three months. But Concettina said there had been no misunderstanding at all, it had really been a very vulgar remark ; she did not want Danilo in the house and she was very angry, she rushed out of the room, banging the door. Emanuele and Ippolito stayed talking to Danilo in the sitting-room until late, and Signora Maria had left her work there and wanted to go and fetch it, but Giustino told her she must leave it and that it was impossible to disturb them. And after that evening Danilo took to arriving at any moment with Emanuele, and Ippolito would shut himself up with them in the sitting-room. And Ippolito told Concettina that he would receive anyone in the house that he wanted to, and Concettina started sobbing loudly, and then Emanuele in order to comfort her took her to the cinema to see *Anna Karenina* with Greta Garbo, and when they came back Concettina was comforted ; she always liked so much to see Greta Garbo, and imagined that she was just a little like her, because Greta Garbo too had no bosom. " This Danilo has got a real crush on Concettina ", said Anna to Giustino. She had learned from her school-friends to say " a crush ", and now she was pleased when she had an opportunity of using the word. But then Giustino said that Danilo didn't care twopence about Concettina, and that when he stood in front of the gate he did it to annoy her. Danilo had quite other ideas in his head. Anna asked what ideas Danilo had. Giustino wrinkled up his nose and his lips and brought his face close to hers with a more and more ugly grimace upon it. " Politics ", he whispered into her ear, and ran away.

" Politics ", thought Anna. She walked about the garden, amongst Signora Maria's rose-trees, and repeated the word to herself. She was a plump girl, pale and indolent, dressed in a pleated skirt and a faded blue pullover, and not very tall for her fourteen years. " Politics ", she repeated slowly, and now all at once she seemed to understand : this was why Danilo had taken to coming so often to the house— because he was talking politics with Ippolito and Emanuele. She seemed to understand about the sitting-room, and the sentences in German, and Ippolito stroking his face, and his restless eyes that were always looking for something. They were talking politics in the sitting-room, they were once again doing a dangerous, secret thing, as the book of memoirs had been. They wanted to overthrow the Fascists, to begin a revolution. Her father had always said that the Fascists must be overthrown, that he himself would be the first to mount the barricades, on the day of revolution. He used to say that it would be the finest day of his life. And then his whole life had gone past without that day happening. Anna now pictured herself upon the barricades, with Ippolito and Danilo, firing off a rifle and singing. She went very quietly up to the sitting-room and slowly pushed the door open. They were all three sitting on the carpet, with a big bundle of newspapers in front of them, and they got a great fright when they saw her coming in. Emanuele threw Danilo's coat over the newspapers and shouted at her to go away and as she was going she heard Danilo say to Ippolito that he was a fool not to have locked the door.

She wanted to tell Giustino that she had seen the newspapers. Giustino started waving his arms about as though he had been scalded, and then he pinched his lips together

with four fingers so that they stuck out and looked like the
lips of a negro, and at the same time he made whispering
and squealing noises.   He pinched *her* lips together, too, with
his four fingers—so hard that he hurt her.   In the end they
came to blows.   Signora Maria clapped her hands in the
next room, because it was their bedtime.   Giustino blew
contemptuously in the direction of this hand-clapping.
" Newspapers that come from France ", he chanted under
his breath, putting his books back in his satchel.   He turned
towards her, and again pinched her lips together.   " Mum's
the word ! " he said.

And soon Concettina, too, began to understand.   Danilo
came to the house at all hours, till late at night there was a
light burning in the sitting-room and Ippolito thumped on
the typewriter, as in the days of the book of memoirs.   Concettina and Danilo would sometimes meet on the stairs and
greet each other distantly, she always rather red and frowning, he with his usual impertinent, sly smile.   Concettina
used to go and sit in the dining-room with stockings to mend,
and there was the sound of footsteps and chairs being moved
in the sitting-room above, and of Ippolito thumping on
the typewriter : and, from time to time, that laugh of
Emanuele's that sounded like the cooing of a pigeon.
Signora Maria complained that one could no longer be in
the sitting-room, it was the warmest and most comfortable
room in the house, and the piano was there too and Concettina might feel inclined to play a little.   Signora Maria
considered that Ippolito had become altogether too arrogant,
he who had seemed so subdued when his father was alive
and who had now suddenly taken to lording it over everybody.   He could surely have seen his friends somewhere
else ; they even had the unpleasant habit of rummaging
about in the kitchen, late at night they would start rummaging in the kitchen, and eating bread and cheese ; for
obviously that young man Danilo did not get enough to eat
at home, and so he came to their house to satisfy his hunger.
Concettina went on mending her stockings without replying ;

and every time the bell rang at the gate she would give a
start and run over to the window to see who it was.   Signora
Maria told her she had been very nervous now for some
time, and what she needed was to go and take a good cure at
Chianciano, for nervousness depends entirely on the liver ;
but Ippolito was too mean to think of sending her to Chianciano, the only thing he was not mean about was cheese,
which he gave to his friends even at night.   Signora Maria
had not understood anything, and still believed that Danilo
came to the house in order to pester Concettina and eat
cheese ; and when Emanuele and Ippolito started talking
German, she was offended and said it was not at all polite
to talk a language she did not know in her presence.   In
any case she had rather forgotten about the Fascists, since
the time when the old man had been there, talking about
them all the time : and if she recollected them for a moment,
it seemed to her that the old man had gone much too far in
his anger against the Fascists, because in the end they had
taken Africa, where later on they meant to grow coffee.
She still brought her nephew to the house to have baths, and
then made him stay and keep warm beside the stove in the
dining-room, because he had had pleurisy as a little boy ;
and she used to bring him Ippolito's books to read, so that he
could learn something.   And Ippolito was much annoyed
when he saw Signora Maria standing on a chair, looking in
his shelf for some book for her nephew.

4

" Papa and Mammina are coming back ", said Emanuele.
There was in fact a great beating of carpets in the house
opposite, and they had put all the chairs out in the garden,
and the windows were wide open all over the house and you
could hear the hum of the vacuum cleaner.   Papa and

Mammina came back, but Giuma did not.   Giuma was at school in Switzerland.

Nor did Amalia come back, for she had gone to Florence to a nurses' training-college.   Emanuele said it was difficult to understand just what had happened, Franz had suddenly left Mentone, and there had been no sign of him and no one knew anything about him ; and then Amalia had produced this idea of the nurses' college, she wanted to be a Red Cross nurse, she wanted to nurse the wounded if war came ; she was disgusted with Mentone, she was disgusted with the idea of coming home, she just wanted sick people to look after, nothing else.   Of course she could have had sick people to look after at home, said Emanuele, for Papa suffered a great deal with his gastric ulcer, and Mammina had a kind of nervous exhaustion : she lay all day on the bed in her room, with her eyes closed, and the shutters closed, and refused to see anyone.

Emanuele had also been at school in Switzerland for two years, like Giuma, at the same school where Giuma now was. He had not liked it very much, and was always begging Mammina to take him away : he had never managed to be left alone for a minute, and when he had started reading in his room they used to come and call him to go out on one of those silly lakes.   Giuma, on the other hand, would be very happy in Switzerland, said Emanuele, because Giuma was a brute and brutes are happy anywhere.

Emanuele was rather annoyed at his parents' return, because Papa always sat up waiting for him at night, he waited for him at the top of the stairs and asked him where he had been till such a late hour.   Emanuele would answer that he was preparing for his exams with some friends of his, but he had to shout, because Papa was getting more and more deaf and his apparatus never worked very well ; and then Mammina would wake up too, and would ask from her room in a feeble voice what had happened ; and Papa would become very angry because they had woken up Mammina in that way ; so every night there was trouble.

Emanuele said he had no more patience with Papa and
Mammina, they had really worn him out and he was
finished with them. Danilo had now taken to saying
" Mammina " when he mentioned his own mother, in order
to tease Emanuele ; he would say " Mammina " and make
a kind of mewing noise. Danilo's little *mammina*, the cashier
at the cake-shop, was a great big woman who sat perpetually knitting at the cash-desk, with round, bulging eyes
and a big bush of white hair. Danilo used to say that his
mammina had brought him up by slapping his face, with the
idea that slaps are good for strengthening the facial muscles.
But after he had reached the age of fourteen she had left him
alone, in fact she had declared that she had had enough of
bringing him up, and that now he must see to bringing himself up. His father, on the other hand, had never tried to
bring him up at all ; he was a type of person who counted
for little in his own home, he had changed his job very many
times and now was travelling all over Italy selling post-cards.
When Danilo came home late at night, his mother was
always up and about still, washing and ironing, but she
never said a word to him and all she did was to take out of
the drawer two or three *Tre Stelle* cigarettes which she had
saved for him. As for our parents, Danilo used to say, as
soon as they have finished bringing *us* up we have to begin
bringing *them* up, because it is quite impossible to leave them
as they are.

Then, all of a sudden, Danilo vanished. A whole week
passed without Danilo's face being seen, and Signora Maria
was very pleased, and she asked Emanuele whether at last
he had broken off relations with that odious Danilo. But
Emanuele at once disillusioned her : Danilo had gone to
Turin on business and would be back soon.

One morning, while Anna was dressing to go to school,
there was a loud ring at the gate. She went to answer it :
Signora Maria was out doing the shopping and Concettina
was still asleep. She found herself face to face with one of
Danilo's sisters, the sixteen-year-old one, the one whom

Concettina believed to be not a steady character. She asked
for Ippolito, but Ippolito had gone out. Then she asked for
Concettina. Anna went upstairs to call Concettina. Concettina was fast asleep, with her untidy fringe sticking out
above the bedclothes. It was not at all easy to wake her
up ; for some time she went on groaning and turning over
on her other side. At last she woke up. When she heard
that Danilo's sister was there she was seized with anxiety,
she thrust her trembling feet into her slippers and went
downstairs tying the girdle of her dressing-gown.

Danilo's sister was sitting waiting in the sitting-room.
She had a quantity of little comma-shaped curls on her forehead and temples, and she was wearing a beret stuck on all
crooked, with a long silk tassel that hung right down to her
shoulder. She had come to say that Danilo had been
arrested in the station at Turin. And Danilo, before he left
for Turin, had told her that if by any chance anything bad
happened to him, Ippolito must be the first to be informed.
She spoke very slowly and quite calmly, and as she spoke
she smoothed down her comma-curls and shook her tassel up
and down. Concettina turned so pale that she seemed on
the point of fainting, and she clasped her dressing-gown
round her with trembling hands.

When Danilo's sister had gone away, with the tassel
dancing up and down on her back, Concettina told Anna
that she must give up going to school and must run and
fetch Emanuele and Ippolito, both of them.

Anna went out into the street and called Emanuele to the
window, and he came and looked out. He did not know
where Ippolito was, he had only just got up. The best thing
would be to go and look for him at the library, where he
always went in the mornings. Anna told him to go at once
to Concettina who wanted to speak to him. Then she ran
off through the town, her heart beating fast with terror and
with joy, because Danilo had been arrested, and because
she had to find Ippolito and for the first time she found herself mixed up in an important, secret, dangerous affair, she

had been really needed and Concettina had not allowed her
to go to school. She found Ippolito on the stairs at the
library. In a whisper she told him about Danilo, and for a
moment he stood quite still with his hand on the banisters,
fluttering his eyelids very quickly and pressing his lips
together. He started off homewards, so rapidly that Anna
had difficulty in keeping up with him.

Emanuele said they must hold a council of war. He
limped up and down the sitting-room and told Concettina
and Anna that there was no further need now to make a
mystery about it, since they already knew so much, and
briefly the matter was like this : Danilo had been arrested,
and in a short time the police would come and arrest them
too, and there was stuff that had to be burnt and they must
act quickly. Ippolito had opened the stove and was throwing newspapers into it, as his father had done with the book
of memoirs. But the newspapers were so many that they
seemed to go on for ever. And when it seemed that the
newspapers were finished, Ippolito pushed the piano aside
and pulled out from behind it a whole heap of little pink and
green books. Outside it had begun to snow and the stove
smoked when it snowed. Concettina and Anna were helping to put the papers into the stove, and making sure that
they got burnt. Emanuele limped up and down the room,
wiping his red, sweating face and explaining what Concettina and Anna were to say when the police arrived : they
were to say that Danilo came to the house because he was
so much in love with Concettina, poor chap, and that was
all they knew, they must try to seem as silly as possible, they
must seem to be silly girls who were interested in nothing
but dancing and fripperies. As he said " dancing and fripperies" he twirled his fingers in the air, as if he were
imitating the fluttering of butterflies. Ippolito paid no
attention to him, but, in his shirtsleeves and with his eyes
full of tears from the smoke stood dumbly looking at the
flames leaping up from the stove ; and upon his face you
could not detect any thought or any surprise, but only the

calm, weary expression he had worn on the day the book of
memoirs had been burned.

When Signora Maria came back from her shopping, there
was nothing left to be burned and she noticed nothing.
Concettina told her she had not allowed Anna to go to school
because she thought she had a slight cold : and Anna made
an effort to sniffle and cough, and anyhow she had no difficulty in this, with all the smoke she had swallowed. Giustino came back from school and Anna ran to tell him about
Danilo, but Giustino already knew he had been arrested,
because people were by now talking of it in the town : in
any case it was never possible to tell Giustino anything new,
because he was always informed about everything, nobody
knew how.

They waited for the police. They waited all that day and
again the next day, sitting in the sitting-room. Ippolito
told Emanuele it would have been better for him to stay in
his own house instead of being always with them, for when
the police came it was not a very good thing that they should
be found together. But Emanuele answered that, in the
nervous state he was in, he did not feel like staying in his own
house, and he begged Ippolito to let him remain with him :
when the police came he could always tell them that he too
was desperately in love with Concettina, or even, as far as
that went, with Anna, because the police like love stories.
Anna stayed at the window watching the snow, it seemed to
go on snowing for ever and the street was silent in the snow
and empty, and no policeman appeared. In the ante-room
lay Danilo's gloves ; the last time he had been to see them
he had left them there. As she passed through the room
Anna glanced at them and had a strange feeling, and Danilo
seemed very far off, it seemed like a dream that it had once
been possible to look at him and touch him. He seemed
very far off like the dead, and as with the dead it seemed
that never again would it be possible to hear from him about
the new things he was seeing and thinking.

Anna asked whether it would not be a good thing to burn

the gloves as well. But Emanuele burst into loud laughter; after all Danilo's gloves were not marked with his name. Giustino liked these gloves very much ; they were fine gloves made of sham pigskin and he wanted to take them for himself. But Emanuele forbade him to touch them. They must be given back to Danilo's mother, the bush of hair at the cash-desk. Emanuele went and waited for her one evening outside the cake-shop. He gave her the gloves and also some money to send to Danilo, because in prison one needs money, otherwise they give you nothing but tasteless soup, a little bread and nothing else. Danilo was in the New Prison at Turin, he was well and quite calm. His mother also was quite calm and Emanuele was astonished ; the day they arrested *him* Mammina would certainly have a fit, with screams reaching to heaven.

They waited for the police. But no policeman was to be seen and they were somewhat dumbfounded. Emanuele said that obviously the police were letting himself and Ippolito go free in order to spy upon them. They would have to be very careful. They decided that Ippolito should go to Le Visciole for a month and that Emanuele should go and see Amalia, to see whether she had learned to be a nurse and whether she had forgotten Franz.

5

Ippolito came back from Le Visciole with the dog. He made a kennel for it in the garden, out of old boxes. He spent a day sawing and nailing the wood, and when the kennel was ready he painted it green. But the dog quite refused to go into it. Perhaps it was the smell of the paint that it did not like. It sniffed round about it for a little and went away. It still ate the armchairs and was always dirty, even though Ippolito gave it a bath every Friday.

The dog at the house opposite, on the other hand, was no longer there ; they had given it away, because it barked at night and kept Mammina awake.   No one now played ping-pong at the house opposite, and the table stood forgotten with the net torn, and the only person to be seen in the garden was the old gentleman in a deck-chair basking in the sun, his stomach well stuffed out with newspapers, so that when he got up he made a great rustling noise.   One day Franz reappeared.   He was dressed in white because the hot weather had now started, with a dark blue jersey of the kind then in fashion, and he was carrying a large suitcase and some tennis racquets.   Surprised exclamations were heard from the old gentleman, and Franz's voice shouting into his ear that he had come from a tennis tournament.

So Emanuele, on his return, found himself face to face with Franz, in fact he was the first person he saw coming towards him, and afterwards he told Concettina that he had felt like getting back into the train and going away again, because he really could not bear the face of this man Franz and he had an idea he was a spy, paid by the Fascists to spy upon him and Ippolito, and in any case it was hard to understand where he got his money from, because he did nothing and was always so well dressed.   Emanuele had been to Florence to see Amalia and had then gone to Rome and Naples with her, because he had found her very thin and wasted and had suggested that she should give up the nursing college and go on a journey with him.   He scratched his head violently when he recalled this journey, it had not been at all a cheerful affair, he had dragged Amalia through the Vatican Museum, had shown her the Raphael frescoes and she had wept, then they had gone to have something to eat and she had ordered a boiled egg and had wept into it.   She was weeping for this man Franz.   Emanuele made great efforts to explain to her that she meant nothing at all to Franz.   But Amalia said that, on the other hand, she did mean something to him, she had understood that she did mean something to him, but there was a thing she could not say, a horrible thing, and she covered her face with her hands and started to sob. Emanuele said he was not in the least curious to know what this thing was, this thing that Amalia had discovered one evening at Mentone, and Franz had left next day : Emanuele shrugged his shoulders and snorted and went red. And then it had come out that Amalia did not in the least want to be a nurse, she wanted to give that up, and she herself did not know what to do. She wanted to study the history of art. And yet she had been all over the Vatican Museum without looking at anything, Emanuele said, there were the Raphael frescoes and she had wept. He had left her in a boarding-house in Rome, she did not want to come home, and in any case, now that Franz was there again, it was better that she should not come. Emanuele was very depressed, what with Danilo in prison, his sister not knowing what she wanted and his father with a gastric ulcer, and so many exams to pass and no politics, no politics at all, no hope of ever being able to do anything serious again, with that man Franz paid to spy upon him. But Ippolito shook his head and said that probably Franz was not a spy, he was just a poor fool and nothing more, no use for anything except winning tennis tournaments.

Emanuele went to his own home merely for eating and sleeping, and passed the days with Ippolito on the terrace, with the books that he ought to have been studying, but he had no inclination for work and Ippolito got on his nerves because he, on the other hand, worked hard, stopping only in order to prepare the dog's food. He said Ippolito was like an old lady when he took the dog out for a walk and gave it its food, he said that all of a sudden his soul had turned into that of an old lady.

From time to time Danilo's sister came to give them news. She no longer had a tassel but a hat with a crown, with bunches of cloth flowers on it, standing straight up on her head. She no longer had a tassel and perhaps she missed having something to swing, for she swung her head and her shoulders, this way and that. Danilo was well and was quite calm, they had not found anything against him. He had been arrested only because of the people he had visited in Turin during those few days, a small group of three or four who were now all in prison, and would be tried by the Special Tribunal. Danilo, on the other hand, would almost certainly not be brought to trial ; they would give him his release earlier. The only trouble was that he would find himself behindhand with his studies, after an interruption of so many months. Danilo was studying book-keeping and accountancy, but he always said he did not like these things and that he would like to do something else, goodness knows what he wanted to do. In prison he had taken to studying German, and he wrote to his mother that he hoped they would not release him before he had learned to write and speak German well ; he wrote dull letters and his mother was angry. When Danilo's sister came Ippolito stayed working on the terrace, as though he were not in the least interested in hearing news of Danilo, and left Danilo's sister to be received by Emanuele and Concettina. And then, when Emanuele and Concettina came back to the terrace and gave him the news, he scarcely seemed to listen. And then Emanuele would exclaim that he had gone as cold as a fish, a thing that makes you cold even to look at it. Ippolito would just give a little crooked smile and go on walking up and down with his book in his hand. Emanuele said that Ippolito got seriously on his nerves, but Concettina did not get on his nerves, Concettina was so charming, and he took her hand and kissed it on the palm. And he told her she had grown thinner and also more beautiful, with those eyes with dark circles round them because she too had been sitting up at night working for her exams. Concettina had discarded all her *fiancés*, and was thinking only of her studies, and perhaps she was thinking of something else too, Emanuele said, perhaps she had taken to thinking of Danilo who was in prison, and had fallen in love with him a little. Then Concettina was angry and snatched away her hand from Emanuele's hands and ran away from the terrace. Emanuele laughed and said there was no doubt about it, Concettina was sorry now for her rude behaviour towards Danilo and for the long hours she had left him in the cold outside the gate. " We have to go to prison to make women love us," Emanuele said, " otherwise we get nothing."

It was very hot and Mammina went with Franz to bathe in a lake near the town, for she had now recovered from her nervous exhaustion, she was very well and had a great number of flowered dresses and a very large straw hat. She and Franz would get up early in the morning, take the car and go swimming in the lake, and not come home until three in the afternoon. Emanuele was always much worried until they came back, because Franz drove the car like a madman, he always said that unless he drove fast he had no enjoyment in driving. In the meantime the whole town was whispering about Mammina and Franz, but Emanuele did not know this, or did not show that he knew. On the other hand Signora Maria knew of it, and when Emanuele was not there she would start talking about those two who were always together and had no shame, and would look out of the window at the old gentleman sitting in the garden and be sorry for him for being made to wear horns like that, poor old gentleman. But the old gentleman sat in his deckchair nursing his stomach which was all stuffed up with newspapers even in full summer, because he was always afraid of a possible draught, and he would wave good-bye to Mammina and Franz as they went off together ; it did not look as if his horns worried him very much, perhaps because he had gradually become accustomed to them and was resigned to wearing them, poor old gentleman. But his ulcer *did* worry him and people in the town said perhaps he was dying, and he did die, and Emanuele rushed off to call Mammina who was swimming in the lake with Franz.

The old gentleman's funeral was a big funeral with a very long procession, a snake that curled itself all through the town. There were a great many large wreaths, and the driver of the hearse wore a white wig and a tall hat, and the horses had black hoods. In the first row could be seen Mammina with a black veil, leaning on Emanuele's arm, and Amalia and Giuma who had been summoned by telegram, and Franz with a grey overcoat and grey gloves and a sad, severe expression. Behind came all the people from the soap factory, and among them was to be seen Danilo's mother with a big tortoiseshell comb planted in her bush of hair, for she had been dismissed from the cake-shop, perhaps because of the affair of Danilo, and Emanuele had had her taken on at the soap factory. At the cemetery a long speech was made about the old gentleman, about the soap factory which previously had been nothing at all and he, gradually, had succeeded in making it big and important, and Anna and Concettina were very much bored and the heat was terrible. Anna looked at Giuma who was there right in front of her. He had long trousers now and the face almost of a grown-up man, big and hard, but he brushed the hair away from his eyes with the same gesture as before. Anna only saw him that day at the funeral and they did not say anything to each other, and a little time after the funeral Giuma went back to school.

Immediately after the opening of the will Amalia departed too, as though the ground were scorching her feet. She was going back to the nurses' college to finish her course, so Emanuele said, but goodness knows whether he was telling the truth and goodness knows where she was really going. She and Mammina had scarcely spoken to one another and Amalia had stayed almost all the time in her own room, as indeed Mammina had too, and Franz roamed the house with an unhappy expression, and tried to talk to Emanuele who barely answered him. The reading of the will was a very long and tedious ceremony, everyone sitting round the table with the uncle who was a colonel and the lawyer ; the uncle who was a colonel was the old gentleman's brother and the old gentleman in his will had appointed him to be the guardian of Giuma who was a minor. In the meantime Franz who had nothing to do with the reading of the will waited in the next room, and from time to time he put his head in at the door to make some foolish remark, to announce the arrival of the upholsterer or the dyer or to say that lunch was ready, and the uncle who was a colonel would give him a look of annoyance. According to the will Mammina had the usufruct of the inherited property, and the shares in the soap factory were to be divided equally between Amalia, Emanuele and Giuma. Mammina went very red and asked what a usufruct was, but the uncle who was a colonel told her to be quiet and that he would explain it to her afterwards.

A few days after Amalia had gone Franz said that he must go away too on stockbroking business. So Emanuele and Mammina were left alone, at lunch and at dinner the two of them were alone at that long table, and when they had finished Mammina would lie down on the sofa and take off her shoes, and say how unkind Amalia had been to her, she had done her no harm at all, she could not understand what Amalia had against her. Then she asked what usufruct was and whether it was much or little, and whether she would still be able to have a dress or two made for herself now and then, and Emanuele kissed her and told her she could have all the dresses made that she wanted. And Mammina said that Emanuele had always been so good to her, and this consoled her for Amalia's bad behaviour and for Giuma's air of indifference, Giuma had become so cold and arrogant with her. Emanuele suggested that they should go out for a little, and they took the car and went out of the town, but as they were passing along the lake Mammina said she did not wish to see the lake, and never again would she swim in it, because the lake reminded her of the day Papa died, while she was enjoying herself swimming. Emanuele accelerated and Mammina kept her eyes shut, until he told her that the lake was no longer to be seen. Mammina said she really could not have imagined that Papa was going to die just that morning, she had gone to the lake because it had not seemed to her that Papa was so very ill, he was quiet and as rosy as a baby. And then she said they must have a fine bronze

statue made of Papa by some good sculptor, to put in the
courtyard of the soap factory.

When he was able to leave Mammina Emanuele went
back to his studies on the terrace with Ippolito, and Ippolito
told him he was now the head of a business and despised his
poor penniless friends, and the soap factory belonged to him,
the soap factory was his very own, and from the terrace he
pointed towards it with his outstretched arm, but Emanuele
covered his eyes with his hands and would not look.   He
would go and work in the factory, he said, after he had got
his degree, because he had promised his father he would do
so, but he had no desire to work there, God knows what he
would have given to work somewhere else.   He was not in
the least interested in soap and would like to bash in the face
of anyone who dared to show him even the tiniest little bit
of it.

The exams went well for everyone except Giustino, who
as usual was told he must take them again in October.   And
after the exams Ippolito began asking what they were waiting
for, why didn't they go to Le Visciole, and no one had any
desire for Le Visciole and they suggested he should go there
by himself, but he could not make up his mind to go all by
himself.   Signora Maria was hoping for an invitation from
her sister at Genoa, and Anna and Giustino were hoping
that the usual invitation would come from Cenzo Rena to
that castle of his with the small towers, and perhaps it would
be possible to accept, now that the old man was no longer
there to forbid it : but Cenzo Rena was in Holland and
wrote from there.   No invitation arrived for anyone and
they left for Le Visciole, otherwise Ippolito would have given
them no peace ; but Concettina was obstinately determined
to stay in the town, because she had to prepare her thesis
and to consult books in the library.   She was preparing a
thesis on Racine, but so far she had written only three pages
of it and Ippolito had read them and considered them to be
idiotic.   Emanuele had to accompany Mammina to Mentone but promised that as soon as he had established Mam-

mina there he would come himself to Le Visciole, and Signora Maria said wasn't it too stupid, to have a villa at Mentone and come to Le Visciole, where there wasn't even running water and to get a bucket of water you had to pump for an hour in the courtyard.

6

Emanuele arrived at Le Visciole at the beginning of July. So now Ippolito was no longer alone in his wanderings round the countryside, but Emanuele limped quickly along beside him up and down the paths, red from the sun and heated with discussion. Giustino spent his time in the village square, in company with the sons and daughters of the Humbugs, and in the evenings went and danced on the open-air platform, with its paper lanterns swaying amongst the foliage. They did a great many things now which their father had not allowed them to do, and Anna swam in the river at a place where there was a quiet pool, and Signora Maria sat in the sun on the bank, where the wives of the Humbugs went with their babies, their work and their picnic lunches, and at last Signora Maria was able to speak to them.

One evening, while they were having supper under the pergola, a motor-car stopped at their gate. They heard the door of the car bang and the creaking of the gate as it opened, and did not understand who it could be at that hour, and they saw at the bottom of the drive a man in a long white waterproof and a hat all out of shape. Emanuele rose and started limping nervously round the table. But it was not a policeman. It was Cenzo Rena and he began embracing them all.

And so at last they saw him, this Cenzo Rena who sent chocolates and post-cards from every part of the world.

They had always imagined him as being very old, as old as their father, and yet he did not look so very old, he had just a few grey streaks in his hair and moustache. Signora Maria had always said he was very rich, and now again she was saying so and boasting of it while she prepared him a little supper, and at the same time she was cursing the idea that they all had of coming to Le Visciole, from Mentone, from Holland, they all came and planted themselves in this miserable hole where she already had so much to do.

Cenzo Rena did not appear very rich, just to look at him. He had on this very long waterproof which looked like a nightshirt, and underneath it he had on a thick sweater, all discoloured and dirty, which hung in folds over his stomach. He had enormous suitcases tied up with cords ; he ran off and pulled them out of the car and started furiously untying the knots, and then pulling out socks and drawers, all higgledy-piggledy. Anna and Giustino stood watching, expecting a present of some kind, but, instead of that, Cenzo Rena dug out from under the socks merely a few photographs of Holland which he had taken ; he seemed very proud of these photographs, but in reality they were not very clear, all you saw was a sort of blur, and Cenzo Rena explained that he had taken them in the rain. Then all at once he tapped himself on the forehead and apologized for having forgotten to bring any presents, he had intended to bring all sorts of things for everybody and had forgotten. From underneath the socks he pulled out also a tin of tunny-fish in oil, and they all sampled it and stayed till late under the pergola, because Cenzo Rena was eating and drinking and smoking and did not seem ever to want to go to bed.

When they went into the house, Cenzo Rena suddenly stopped at the foot of the stairs with his eyes full of tears, and said that he seemed to see the old man coming down those same stairs with his eyeglass and his white flannel trousers, and that he seemed to hear his snappish tone of voice when he said, " Make yourself useful, seeing that you're not ornamental ". Cenzo Rena started stroking Ippolito's head, untidying his hair a little, and said that Ippolito was the very image of his father as a young man : but Ippolito remained stiff and motionless, with downcast eyes and frowning brows, as he always did when someone behaved with tenderness towards him.

Cenzo Rena stayed for several days at Le Visciole. In the morning he wanted to have a bath, he was dirty but he always had a bath, and he said he remembered that there was no bathroom at Le Visciole and so he had brought expressly a rubber bath. So Signora Maria had to go and pump water in the courtyard, and run up and down the stairs with buckets, and it was no use because he came out more shaggy and untidy than before, after splashing water all over the room. Cenzo Rena was tall and big, and his face was all hair and eyebrows and moustaches, and he wore glasses too, glasses with tortoiseshell rims. He did not choose to dress like other men, with a tie and a jacket, but always wore blouses and sweaters and strange things, and he wore strange things on his feet too, slippers or galoshes or sandals, never real shoes. He had brought with him a great many bottles of brandy and a great many tins of tunnyfish in oil, and at the end of lunch, as soon as he had finished his fruit, he opened one of these tins of tunny and started swallowing it in spoonfuls, and Signora Maria was offended and went over the lunch in her mind, to see if it had been good and plentiful enough. In the morning as soon as he woke up he at once started smoking, drinking and eating the tunnyfish in oil, and writing quantities of letters in a tearing hurry, and he upset a bottle of ink on a carpet in his room, and Signora Maria took the greatest trouble rubbing the stain with milk and breadcrumbs but it did not come out, a beautiful carpet ruined for ever. And Cenzo Rena stood watching her as she rubbed, he said it was Lady Macbeth's spot, which all the perfumes of Arabia could not remove. But Ippolito, too, was annoyed about the carpet, he said nothing but you could see he was annoyed. And at table Cenzo Rena from time to time slapped Ippolito hard on the

shoulder, hard enough to make him jump, and set to work
to try and comfort him about the carpet and promised to
send him a very beautiful new carpet, a carpet from Smyrna.
But then he shook his head and said that certainly Ippolito
resembled his father physically, but was very different from
him in spirit, for his father, at Ippolito's age, was ready to
set all the carpets in his house on fire and the chairs too.

Cenzo Rena often went for country walks with Ippolito
and Emanuele, and went out shooting with them, but he
said that Ippolito had no idea at all of how to take up the
right position nor of how to take aim, and indeed he hardly
ever hit anything, and in any case it was impossible to go
out shooting with that dog. When he came home Cenzo
Rena was tired and out of temper, he threw himself into a
chair under the pergola and shook his head, for a long time
he shook his head and he said to Ippolito and Emanuele
that the two of them were full of nothing but smoke and
fog, they thought themselves goodness knows what and yet
they didn't even know how to shoot little birds. Two little
provincial intellectuals, that was what they were, and that
is the dreariest and oddest thing that can exist on earth.
They had never seen anything ; he, Cenzo Rena, had been
in America, in Constantinople and in London, and he knew
what Italy was when looked at from Mexico or from London,
Italy was just a flea, and Mussolini a flea's droppings. But
Emanuele and Ippolito did not even know Italy, they had
never seen anything except their own little town, and they
imagined the whole of Italy to be like their own little town,
an Italy of teachers and accountants with a few workmen
thrown in, but even the workmen and the accountants
became rather like teachers in their imagination. And they
had forgotten that in Italy there were peasants and priests
as well, in fact if you came to think of it there was really
nothing else, because teachers and workmen were, fundamentally, nothing but priests or peasants. And in Italy
there was the South, cried Cenzo Rena, and he jumped up
from his chair when he said the South, and banged his hand

on the table and threw out his arms. They didn't know what the South was, or what the peasants of the South were, with nothing but a few beans to eat. Emanuele limped up and down the lawn and wiped the sweat from his face, and from time to time he turned his head quickly and drew in his breath as if he wanted to answer, but he did not answer. And Ippolito did not answer either, but sat sideways on his chair with the dog between his knees, and gave a little crooked smile as he stroked the dog's ears. On the other hand this was all vain chatter, went on Cenzo Rena, because in a short time there would be war, a war with poison gases and cholera germs rained down from aeroplanes. And so there would be nobody left on the earth.

Then all at once Cenzo Rena discovered the *contadino*. He was not a *contadino* of the South, but he liked him all the same. He was not a *contadino* who ate beans, he was a *contadino* who ate chickens and rabbits, and big bowls of soup flavoured with bacon, far better than the thin, pallid soups made by Signora Maria. Anyhow he was a *contadino* and Cenzo Rena liked him, and he gave him cigarettes and the *contadino* gave him bread and sausage. They spent hours sitting together in the courtyard, and the *contadino* began talking about Ippolito being always so suspicious and arrogant. The *contadino* had known him since he was born and had taken him for rides in his cart when he was a little boy, and now it pained him to find himself so unkindly treated. He was never satisfied with the harvest, it always seemed to him too little, he knew nothing about country matters and tried to pretend that he did know. Cenzo Rena listened and looked as though he immensely enjoyed hearing Ippolito spoken ill of, and when Ippolito and Emanuele came back from shooting he rushed to tell them that he found it far more enjoyable to converse with the *contadino* than with them, because the *contadino* had not so much fog in his head as they. And he explained to Ippolito that, seriously, it was not at all clever to put a *contadino* against him in this way. He stole, yes, of course he stole, but why in the world shouldn't he keep a little of the corn after he had spent the whole of his time upon it, while Ippolito stayed in the town thinking of an Italy in which *contadini* did not exist? Besides, he stole because he knew the world was badly arranged and people lived by stealing, by tearing the shirts off each other's backs, and of course some day or other this thing would have to stop, but it was not at all simple and why should Ippolito's *contadino* have to be the one to begin? Emanuele muttered that these were commonplaces. Commonplaces, cried Cenzo Rena, of course they were commonplaces, but why not repeat commonplaces if they were true, and this was just what had happened to them, for fear and shame of commonplaces they had lost themselves in vain and complicated fancies, they had lost themselves in fog and smoke. And gradually they had become like a couple of old children, a couple of very old, wise children. They had created around themselves, as children do, a complete dream-world, but it was a dream without joy and without hope, the arid dream of a pedant. And they did not look at women, they never looked at women, they passed numbers of women on their country walks and did not look at them, lost as they were in their pedantic dream-world. Cenzo Rena called Giustino, slapped him on the shoulder and rumpled up his hair, and started praising Giustino for being healthy and sensible. And he begged Giustino to take him to dance on the platform with the daughters of the Humbugs, for he found them very charming.

And so Ippolito had found someone else who took pleasure in tormenting him, and it seemed to be his fate that people should torment him. Cenzo Rena told him he was very handsome, but even this was said in order to provoke him. He said, " A pity, such a handsome young man, look how handsome he is, he might make plenty of women fall in love with him and instead of that he takes no interest in women. He takes an interest in carpets, in corn, in his own foggy, smoky ideas, but as for women, he doesn't wish to look at them and when they go past he turns the other way."

Giustino and Anna looked at Ippolito, for the first time they came to know that he was handsome. He was lying back in an armchair under the pergola with his shabby fustian jacket thrown carelessly over his shoulders, his worn shooting-boots on his feet, his long, delicate hands stroking the dog's ears, his hair streaked with gold and curly at the back of his head, his mouth twisted in the bitter smile that he wore when people tormented him. It was thus that Anna and Giustino were to remember him always, as they had seen him that summer at Le Visciole, when he had been discovered to be handsome because Cenzo Rena had said so.

Cenzo Rena made a long stay at Le Visciole because he enjoyed it. He liked the daughters of the Humbugs and took them out for rides in his car. He liked swimming in the river with Anna and Giustino, and then lying in the sun on the bank while they fanned him with a branch. He liked the dog, and used to whistle to it and take it down to the river with him, partly in order to provoke Ippolito who was then unable to go out shooting, and in any case, Cenzo Rena said, the dog suffered when it was taken out shooting, because it had never been a sporting dog and the noise of firing frightened it, and also it was hot and it was good for it to plunge into the river. After bathing he would drag off Anna and Giustino to drink grenadine in the village square, and then they would wander round the shops, and Cenzo Rena would buy everything that could be bought in a small village like that, corkscrews and cheese and straw hats, and many yards of unbleached calico to make himself drawers. And the village seemed transformed since he had been there to wander round it. It no longer seemed a tedious village of flies and dust, but it seemed all at once to have turned into an amusing, strange place where there was something strange and amusing to be bought in every shop. Every now and then Giustino would say feebly that perhaps he ought to go back home and get on with his work. But Cenzo Rena told him not to do any work, that it was useless, that the schools in Italy were badly organized and that they

made boys study a lot of things that served no purpose in
life.   He himself had never had any desire to study, and
yet now he was quite satisfied with the way in which he had
spent his life.   All they had taught him at school he had
forgotten, the ablative absolute, if he thought about the
ablative absolute he found nothing but a black hole and he
was frightened of it.   And nobody had ever asked him about
the ablative absolute when he went to Constantinople or
London to arrange sales of shipping.   He had found a job
which allowed him to make long journeys, and then he
would return to his own home, in a small village in the
South, and there he could spend his time with the *contadini*
and listen to them, for there was no one who was so well
worth listening to as *contadini*.   Giustino and Anna would
have to come and visit him in his house for a little, it was a
house and not a castle, and there were no towers, goodness
only knows how those towers had arisen out of the old man's
head.   In the village they called it the castle because they
had called it so for years and years.   It was the home of his
family, an extremely old house, and all he had done was to
rearrange it a little.   There were no towers, there was just
a kind of terrace on the roof, which from a distance might
possibly look like a tower, but it was just a terrace and he had
put a telescope up there to look at the stars.   For a long
time he would be travelling, and then he would go back
home and he was always pleased to see his own house again,
high up on the hill, with the pine wood behind it and below
it a tumbled mass of rocks.   It was a house without any
carpets, he could not be bothered with carpets, and he liked
to hear his footsteps echoing through the big rooms.   Certainly he had made money from his job as well, but that was
not important.   It was not important because he could lose
the whole of that money at one stroke without blinking an
eyelid.   He had no special needs.   He needed only a little
brandy and a few cigarettes, and he begged Anna and
Giustino never to let him want for them, even if he suddenly
became very poor and ended up in rags on a bench in a

public garden. Perhaps they would then be rich and important and would come to his bench in a motor-car with a few bottles of brandy.

One evening when Cenzo Rena had gone with Giustino to dance on the platform they came home very late and they were both drunk, they both felt ill and Signora Maria had to get up and make coffee and lemonade for them. Next day Cenzo Rena stayed in bed, he was gloomy and green in the face and complaining. The doctor with the chicken-feather hair came to see him, and there was nothing wrong with him, it was just that the wine had made him ill. But the doctor with the chicken-feather hair told Ippolito that there was a scandal in the village, because Cenzo Rena when he was drunk during the dance had started annoying a girl, the daughter of the Superintendent of Police, and the Superintendent had been on the point of striking him and they had been separated only with difficulty, and the women had been frightened. Giustino would not say anything about what had happened, and he too was gloomy and green in the face and did not leave his room. Then Signora Maria, with her parasol and her shoes with bows on them, went and called upon the Superintendent's wife and explained that they must be patient with Cenzo Rena, because he was not quite right in the head, and in any case he would be gone in a short time. And she also found a way of mentioning that he was very rich, for to wealth all things are forgiven.

They had had enough of Cenzo Rena by now, and he too, all of a sudden, had had enough of them, all of a sudden he started to hate the village with its Humbugs and Humbugs' daughters, and he said that it was only in Italy that certain things are still to be met with, idiotic superintendents of police who strike you with their fists and idiotic girls. The middle-class girls in Italy, he said, go mad if they see a man, and at once they get it into their heads to try and get themselves wooed and married, they don't know how to have healthy relations with men. How disgusting they are, the

middle-class girls in Italy, he said, and at the same time he
started packing his bags to go away, and he thrust shirts and
socks into them higgledy-piggledy, together with the straw
hats he had bought. The new drawers that he had had
made for him by the *contadino's* wife, out of the unbleached
calico he had bought in the village, were rough and scratched
his behind, and Signora Maria suggested washing them in
order to soften them, but he was unwilling to wait for them
to be washed and dried. He did not wish to stay even one
hour longer in this dreary village, he wanted to breathe free
air, without any superintendents and girls.

He left and all was quiet again at Le Visciole and in the
village, and nothing remained of him but a pair of worn-out
slippers on the rubbish-heap behind the courtyard, and the
dog went and fetched them and chewed them, and snarled
if anyone took them away. Cenzo Rena sent post-cards
from London, to them and to the *contadino*, but to the little
chicken-feather-haired doctor, on the other hand, he wrote
a long letter, to tell him that when he had gone into the
chemist's shop in the village he had discovered that it was
entirely lacking in serum against snake-bite, and it was a
piece of gross stupidity in a neighbourhood where there
were so many snakes, and so he had better give up being a
doctor, because he did not even know what there ought to
be inside a chemist's shop. The doctor came to Le Visciole
and read the letter, half amused and half mortified, and he
explained that he had ordered the serum and it was not his
fault if they had not yet sent it. Emanuele burst into a great
fit of laughter, one of the long, deep fits of laughter that were
characteristic of him. These long fits of laughter, like the
cooing of a pigeon, were now coming to be heard again, but
all the time Cenzo Rena had been there Emanuele had
roamed round the house mortified and frowning, and he
said he almost wanted to go back to Mammina at Mentone,
because it was not very nice of him to leave her alone the
whole summer. However, immediately after Cenzo Rena's
departure he became cheerful again, and in fact he said that,

at bottom, Cenzo Rena was a fine fellow, and he mimicked him when he shook himself because his drawers were scratching him, and when he rose to his feet to shout out about the *contadini*.

But one day Emanuele had a letter from Amalia, in which she informed him that she had married Franz. After that his long, deep fits of laughter ceased again, even though he said that, when all was said and done, he did not care in the least.

7

When they went back to the town they found Concettina in tears, because her thesis had been rejected. It was twenty-five pages long, and Danilo's sister had typed it for her and bound it up in a big album tied with red tapes. But the professor had said that it would not do. Concettina had slept in all the rooms, one after another, because, what with her violent exertions and her discouragement, she had never been able to induce herself to make her bed, and in the kitchen there was a great confusion of eggshells and opened tins, and Signora Maria took three days to clean the house and she said the house looked as if it had been lived in not by one single girl but by a regiment of *bersaglieri*. But Concettina was in such a state of despair that even Ippolito did not have the heart to be angry with her, even though black-beetles had appeared in the kitchen through its being left so dirty. Concettina said she had no desire to go to the library again to look for more books on Racine, in any case she had come to hate Racine and wanted to try somebody else, but she did not know who. Emanuele tried to comfort her : surely she would not need to submit a thesis at all, since within a year she would be married. But Signora Maria said that within a year was too soon, because

Concettina must first learn how to keep a house clean. Emanuele said, " If you don't find anyone to marry you, Concettina, I'll marry you myself. It doesn't matter to me whether the house is very clean or not, and I don't very much mind blackbeetles. I should be making rather a sacrifice in marrying you because I don't much like women without bosoms. But if you really don't find anyone else I'll take you on. Or perhaps you might marry Cenzo Rena, who is very rich and would take you to see Constantinople and explain to you all about *contadini*." And in order to cheer up Concettina Emanuele started to tell stories about Cenzo Rena and to imitate him when his drawers were scratching him. But Concettina said she did not want any joking because she had too many troubles. So Emanuele asked, hadn't he his own troubles too ? Hadn't his sister got married to that fellow Franz ? And Mammina was on the point of coming back from her holiday and still knew nothing about it and he would have to break the news of it to her gradually. And there had been the treaty of agreement between Germany and Russia and now it was impossible to understand anything, it was impossible to understand what might happen, everything was confusion. Cenzo Rena had said that perhaps Germany and Russia were coming to an agreement together, and Emanuele had not believed it, and now it had really happened. Emanuele suggested to Concettina that she should put on a nice dress and a nice hat and come out for a walk with him ; they would have ices at a café in the Corso and then they would go to the cinema without troubling about anything. But Concettina was now going every evening to study shorthand with Danilo's sister. And as soon as she had gone out Emanuele said how ingenuous Concettina was to think that her plans would remain a secret. It was clear that she was studying shorthand with Danilo's sister so that Danilo on his return should think well of her, for being such a brave and simple girl and studying shorthand with his own sister. And he limped about the room, delighted with the idea of

Danilo and Concettina married and with a heap of babies. But the recollection of the Russo-German treaty came back to him, who would ever have thought it, and now goodness knows what might not happen. Meanwhile Signora Maria was complaining that Concettina never paid any attention to her, she had begged her so often not to go and see Danilo's sister because she was certainly not a steady character, and as for Danilo, they had put him in prison. Of course the political affair was just a story, they must have put him in prison for swindling or smuggling. For smuggling watches, perhaps. And she herself would never consent to a marriage between Concettina and Danilo, Emanuele's ideas were quite nonsensical. Nor did she like Concettina's studying shorthand, what on earth was the use of shorthand to her, her father hadn't sent her to the university for her to finish up in some little office as a shorthand-typist.

Mammina came back on the very day that Germany invaded the Polish Corridor. England and France declared war on Germany and everybody believed that Italy would now enter the war too, no one in the town spoke of anything else. Mammina was seized with panic and made Emanuele telegraph to Giuma to come back home at once. She was so terrified that Emanuele did not dare say anything to her about Amalia and Franz. Mammina went down into the cellar to see if they could take refuge there in case of air raids. She sent for one of the Civil Engineer Corps whom she knew, to see if the cellar was safe. The Civil Engineer went round tapping all the walls with a small hammer and said the cellar was perfectly safe, the whole house might fall in but the cellar would not. Mammina had armchairs, blankets and a bottle of brandy taken down to the cellar. Meanwhile she was also trying to find out what could be done about gas-masks, where they could be bought, and she wanted Emanuele to go to Turin to get information. Everyone was talking about these masks but no one had ever seen them, and in any case it was not certain that they could be used against every type of gas. Mammina was always sniffing the air and thinking she smelt a strange smell, an asphyxiating smell. And still Giuma did not arrive, perhaps they had already closed the frontiers, perhaps Giuma had been overwhelmed in a horde of refugees.

Giuma, however, took it easy and did not arrive for a fortnight, and he said that at his school the rugby matches were going on and he had wanted to stay because he felt sure his side would win, and indeed it had won. He was very handsome, healthy and fresh and sunburnt, and Mammina was happy to see him because she had imagined him dead or overwhelmed, and then at last Emanuele told her that Amalia and Franz were married. Mammina said she knew already, she said this in a very faint, rather harsh voice, and then immediately went on talking about the cellar and about asphyxiating gases, and about all the stores that must be laid in, about sugar and oil, because in a short time everything would disappear. Signora Maria, also, was scouring the town in search of oil and sugar, but Ippolito would not give her the money and all she managed to buy was a few pounds of sugar; in reality the shops were full of stuff, but everyone was buying and prices were going up. Signora Maria, too, was thinking about air raids and she hoped to be able to go and take shelter in the cellar of the house opposite, because the cellar of their own house did not seem to her at all safe. She had suddenly started being very nice to Emanuele, and she begged him to persuade his mother to allow them to come to that fine cellar of hers if air raids were suddenly to begin.

Emanuele left his radio only in order to run over and tell Ippolito the news. But the war was still a long way off, in Poland, Italy had made no move and Emanuele did not know what to think; he said that if Italy did not enter the war there would never be an end of Fascism. But Ippolito said to him that it no longer mattered to know whether there would be an end of Fascism or not. Because in Poland people were dying, every day people were dying on one side or the other, while he and Emanuele were sitting talking on the terrace and Signora Maria was searching the town for sugar. Emanuele blushed and limped up and down. Cenzo Rena was right, said Ippolito, Fascism was nothing but flea's droppings. Emanuele went back home and explained to Mammina that the question of Italy was not important, because in Poland bombs were falling while she was sitting drinking tea, in Poland houses were falling down and when there were houses falling down it was of no importance whether they were falling in one place in the world or in another.

One day Emanuele had a letter from Franz, brought by hand by a girl friend of Amalia's who had seen them. They were living in a *pension* in Rome. In the letter Franz told Emanuele that he was not a German, and he was not a baron, he had been lying all the time. He had grown up at Freiburg, where his father at one time sold waterproofs. But his father and mother were Polish, and now they lived in Warsaw. And his mother was of Jewish origin and the Germans would kill her. He himself was listening to the radio all day long and weeping. If Italy came into the war there was no knowing what would become of him, seeing that he had a Polish passport in his pocket. If Italy came into the war on the side of Germany, it was all up with him. Some people were saying that perhaps Italy might still ally herself with England and France. He begged Emanuele to let him know whether there was a possibility of this happening. But it would be too good, it could not happen. He asked forgiveness for having lied all the time, he had not lied out of malice, but only like a child telling a fairy story. He begged Emanuele to take care of Amalia if anything should happen to him. He begged him to send some money because they had almost nothing left. Emanuele shrugged his shoulders, he was vaguely moved but he could not also help laughing a little, owing to the waterproofs making their appearance like that all of a sudden. Goodness knows why anyone should be ashamed of being Polish and of having sold waterproofs, and should then

confess to it all of a sudden amidst sobs.   He sent a cheque
made out to Amalia ; only afterwards did he realize that he
had not made it out to Franz, and reflected that he must
therefore still be mistrustful of him.   He made Mammina
read the letter, Mammina cast a glance at it and at once
thrust it away from her, she said she had known all about
these things for some time, and she spoke in that same very
faint voice.

At the end of September they began to think that Italy
would not now do anything, that she would allow the others
to destroy themselves while she herself sat looking on, so as
to throw herself in at the last moment on the winning side.
Only Mammina continued to be frightened, she would not
allow Giuma to go back to Switzerland, because she would
never be able to sleep if she knew he was far away, with the
danger of war hanging over them.   Giuma was now going
to the local high school and was in Giustino's class, and
Giustino described how he gave himself all sorts of airs with
his rugby and his Switzerland, and everyone in the class had
begun to hate him.   Emanuele started work at the soap
factory.   He had a room all to himself, with a big armchair
and a long desk and a quantity of magazines, and on the
walls he had hung reproductions of pictures he liked, Piero
della Francesca and Botticelli.   And when he could he went
downstairs and talked with the workmen.   He had all sorts
of reforms in mind, a big nursery and crèche for the workers'
children and a canteen where you could eat for a mere song ;
the workmen now had to bring their food with them from
home.   He sat at his desk writing out long menus of unusual
and excellent meals for each day of the week, and thinking
of these meals made him so hungry that he had to ring the
bell and send out an office-boy to fetch him sandwiches from
the bar on the other side of the street.   But when he spoke
of these plans to the managing director, the managing director shook his head and told him he was too young.   Ippolito also was working now, he had been taken on at a lawyer's
office, and he and Emanuele could no longer spend their

days together, but in the evening after dinner Emanuele
would run straight over to Ippolito and relieve his feelings
about the managing director, he hated him and he said what
he would like to do to him, shake him hard from head to
foot, take his two cheeks between his fingers and pinch them
hard, take down his hat from the peg and trample it on the
floor. And so he would do as soon as he had managed to
get a little authority in the factory, he was nothing now, he
was just the boss's son who had come to learn the job. He
would not sack the managing director, he would not do anything to him, he would just throw his hat on the floor and
trample on it a bit.

8

One day, at two in the afternoon, when they were all
together in the dining-room eating a creamy cake that
Emanuele had brought from his own home, suddenly
Danilo appeared in the doorway. Concettina had opened
the gate to him, and was now beside Danilo in the doorway,
pale, rather breathless, with frightened, sparkling eyes.
Emanuele ran to embrace Danilo, and gave him two smack-
ing kisses on the cheeks. Danilo looked surprised, and
raised his eyebrows a little. Emanuele was immediately
ashamed of the two kisses, he went red and threw open
the door of the sideboard to look for a knife and a plate ;
Danilo must at once have some of the cake, Giustino must
go and buy a bottle of champagne and have it put down to
his account, Signora Maria must wash the glasses. But
Signora Maria told him that she was not his servant and
was not taking any orders, and she wanted to rest now
because she had a headache. You could see she was in a
state of fury and of terror too because of Danilo, she looked
and looked at him with an expression of horror, and finally

left the room muttering to herself. It was Concettina who
went to wash the glasses. But Danilo did not turn to look
at Concettina as she went out with the tray. Danilo was
much changed, indeed he was hardly recognizable. He was
dressed in new clothes, with a bowler hat and an overcoat
of a heavy kind of cloth, and in his hand he actually held
an umbrella because it was raining that day. He had a
precise, prudent look about him, almost like a policeman.
He sat on the edge of his chair with his umbrella, his hat
on his knee, and a crumb of cake fell on his sleeve and he
flicked it away with his finger-nail and looked very carefully
to see whether it had left a mark. Emanuele told him how
smart he had become, exclaiming at great length about
his overcoat and his hat, with deep, echoing bursts of
laughter. Danilo explained that he had stopped a few
days in Turin to furbish up his wardrobe, his mother was
now making good money, and he gravely thanked Emanuele
for having taken her on at the soap factory. Emanuele
began to relate how he had quarrelled and intrigued in
order to convince the managing director, he began to talk
about the managing director and about all the things he
intended to do some time or other. But Danilo did not
laugh. They noticed that his face was yellow and as though
slightly swollen, and he no longer seemed capable of laughing, he did not laugh at all. The only time he laughed a
little was when he got up to shut the door, he said it pleased
him so much to be able to open and shut doors again, oh
how lovely it was. Emanuele wanted to know a thousand
things all at the same time, whether there were bugs in
prison, whether they let you read novels, whether he had
learned German. Giustino came back with the champagne
and Concettina came back with the glasses. Concettina
was looking very pretty, with her fringe thrown back so
as to leave her forehead uncovered, a look of astonishment
in her eyes and her lips pale and trembling. Emanuele
asked Danilo if he knew that Concettina was now going
to his sister for lessons in shorthand. Danilo answered yes,

he knew, and he took his glass from Concettina's hands but his face did not light up as he looked at her, the old sly expression seemed to have vanished from his face.   They drank the champagne without any gaiety, Ippolito refused to drink and said that champagne gave him a burning in the stomach, so Emanuele got angry with him, was it possible he should think so much about his stomach, he seemed like a real old lady.   It was by no means an every-day happening that a friend should come out of prison. Danilo announced all at once that he was getting married in a short time.   At Turin, during the days before they arrested him, he had met a girl, a girl of the working class, and when he came out of prison he had seen her again and they had decided to get married.   In prison he had thought about many and various things, he said, and it had seemed to him that he had always lived like a fool, that he had lost a great deal of time.   In prison you grow up, he said, and you get so that you can't stand any kind of affectation or pose.   In prison he had made a critical examination of the whole of his past life, he said, and had realized that there had been nothing good about it, it was only the hours he had spent with this girl that had not seemed to him so wasted and useless.   She was a very simple, serious girl, and he could marry her with confidence because she would not be frightened on the day when they put him in prison again, she would just go on with her work and she was prepared for this idea, she was a very " prepared " kind of girl.   Emanuele asked if she was pretty and Danilo answered that he did not know, he had never asked himself that question, in any case he did not need a great beauty, he needed a quiet girl who was prepared for anything.   For the present they expected to live with Danilo's mother, all that was needed was one more bed, and Marisa—the girl was called Marisa—would look for a job here in the town, possibly even Emanuele would manage to get her taken on at the soap factory, as well.   Ippolito got up and said he ought to have been back at his office long before this, and Danilo said he was going out too because he had to go to the joiner to order the bed for his wife. So Emanuele and Concettina were left alone in front of the table covered with plates and glasses. Emanuele said he had no desire to go to the factory that day, he was sleepy and he felt sad, that champagne was not very good, it had been a mistake to send Giustino out because champagne unless it is very good does you harm. Concettina all at once laid her head down on the table and began to sob. Emanuele jumped up in a fright and started to comfort her, he asked if it had really been such a serious thing, if she was really rather in love. Concettina shook her head violently, she was not in love, she herself did not know why she was crying like that. Emanuele said that he felt very sad too and did not quite know why. He too had been distressed at seeing Danilo so changed, with his bowler hat and his prudent look, it had been much better when he wore a beret and spent hours outside the gate. But there was no reason for crying, Concettina would find plenty more men to fall in love with her, she would forget Danilo, she had got ideas into her head and dreamed about Danilo in prison, suddenly she had seen him as a hero, a very natural thing and not in the least tragic. Poor Concettina, who had even gone so far as to start taking lessons in shorthand. At the mention of shorthand Concettina sobbed more violently, she had come to hate shorthand and didn't want anything more to do with it, she didn't want to go on going to Danilo's sister in the evenings, and now what was she to do about Danilo's sister who would expect her? But surely she could sent a note, said Emanuele, laughing, any excuse would do, it wasn't a problem. Emanuele stayed till the evening comforting Concettina, caressing her and holding her hands in his.

Danilo and the prepared girl were married a few days later. Everyone had pictured this prepared girl as being rather ugly, but she was not ugly at all, in fact she would have been rather pretty if she had not had such a worn-

looking face and hair all scorched with peroxide. Her hair
was terrible, said Emanuele to Ippolito and Giustino as
they walked back from the wedding, he himself would never
have taken a wife with such scorched-looking hair, with
curls that were rough and dead and of a yellow colour
that was almost green. He could never stroke hair like that.
Her face was pretty but very much the worse for wear,
her complexion already faded, her skin rough and dead.
Giustino, however, had liked Marisa, he said Emanuele
understood nothing at all about girls, goodness knows what
scarecrow of a wife he would marry, some snobbish old
bird planted on him by his mother. They were coming
back from the wedding party at Danilo's, Concettina had
been asked too but she had not come. Danilo's mother
had started talking to Emanuele in a corner, she was asking
whether it was possible to get Marisa taken on at the soap
factory too, she was asking whether it had been sensible
for them to get married, with Danilo who hadn't yet got
his accountant's diploma, and the girl wasn't up to much
anyhow, at twenty her complexion was already so much
the worse for wear. Emanuele complained that now he
would have to quarrel and intrigue all over again, to get
Marisa taken on at the factory. However it was not necessary, for Marisa at once found work at the foundry. She
got up early in the morning and before going to work she
cleaned Danilo's shoes and brushed his suit, and she brushed
his bowler hat long and carefully, and it became more and
more stiff and lustrous. And then she cleaned the room
and Danilo's room was now no longer recognizable, with
the floor polished and the curtains ironed, and a little set
of bottles and glasses on the chest-of-drawers. But Danilo's
mother, when she saw Emanuele coming out of the factory,
complained always about the girl, who perhaps was not
actually bad but who never seemed content with anything,
she went back and washed the salad again after they had
washed it ever so many times, and she sniffed the butter
and the meat, she sniffed everything. And she was sure

that Danilo had not married for love but as a matter of reason, and things which are done as a matter of reason never turn out well.

Danilo resumed his habit of coming to see Ippolito all the time, and Signora Maria had to resign herself to seeing him arrive at the end of dinner, even though it dismayed her each time to reflect that he had been in prison and that he had married a working girl, one who worked all day long at the foundry in a black apron. Danilo always came alone, because his wife was tired in the evenings and went to bed immediately after supper. Signora Maria ran away as soon as she saw him coming, but Concettina did not run away, in fact she would start making jokes with Emanuele and uttering shrill shrieks of laughter, but as soon as she stopped laughing her face would suddenly become all wrinkled and tired. She would disappear and reappear immediately with her hat on and pulling on her gloves, and would open the window and talk to someone waiting underneath, then she would run downstairs and her shrill shrieks of laughter would still be heard, and the sound of a car driving away. She had unearthed her old *fiancés*, and had resumed her visits to the library and had taken up with Racine again, and the young man with the car waited for her at the door of the library, smoking one cigarette after another.

Emanuele related the news he had heard on the radio, but there was never much news. The Germans and the others were carrying on the cold war, on the Maginot Line and on the Siegfried Line, no one was winning or losing, just a few shots in the air from time to time. Emanuele said they had now invented the cold war to make him die of boredom, no one would ever win or lose, the cold war would go on for ever. But Ippolito only asked himself what was happening in Poland, what it could be like there in the winter with the houses fallen down and with the Germans, with the Germans taking people away to die in the concentration camps, and he said his will to live left him at the thought of those camps, where the Germans put their cigarettes out against the prisoners' foreheads. Then Emanuele, too, began to wonder what had become of Franz's parents. But Danilo said that for people who were dying in the camps there was nothing to be done; on the other hand something could be done for his friends who were still in prison, they had taken them to Rome in a prison van and now they had to stand their trial by the Special Tribunal, and did Emanuele and Ippolito know what a journey in a prison van was like, a journey that went on for ever, all chained together? Did they know what prison was like? They didn't put their cigarettes out against your forehead, but it was not comfortable, and people became consumptive if they ate nothing but the soup they gave them, unless they had money to buy themselves something else. And they needed money also to pay the lawyer at the trial, and money to help their families. To raise money, that was the important thing, not to sit by the radio and be bored because the war was a cold war. Emanuele went red and said that perhaps he could give them just a little money, not much because he could not touch his capital, his uncle who was a colonel would know if he did, he always started to stammer a little when he spoke of his capital. But he could save a little on his cash expenses. Danilo shrugged his shoulders, more was needed than Emanuele's small savings, which he put aside a little each day as a good child does. A good big sum was needed and it must be raised at all costs.

Anna was always hoping they would start on their politics again, with their newspapers and pamphlets, but Giustino told her they would not start again, all they thought of was finding the money for Danilo's friends in prison, in any case that was politics too, finding the money was called Red assistance and it was very dangerous. But nobody now shut themselves up in the sitting-room and the sitting-room was always deserted, with the shutters closed and a cold fit to kill you, because Ippolito said they must economize with wood, and there was no need to light the stove in that room as well. Signora Maria complained that Concettina could no longer play the piano, but Concettina said she did not care in the least about the piano and in fact she had decided to sell it, the piano belonged to her and she could do what she liked with it, it had been her grandmother's and her grandmother before she died had said she was leaving it to her. Every day at table she talked about selling the piano, and she asked Emanuele what had to be done to put an insertion into the paper, how much it cost and where you had to go. She said she had decided to sell it because she wanted to make herself a trousseau, she couldn't possibly go naked to get married. So Ippolito said that when she had somebody to marry she could then think whether or not to sell the piano, at present she had no one but those *fiancés* of hers, she had had them for years and years and not one of them was any good to marry. And Concettina said there was one who was extremely good to marry, the one who always came to take her out in his car, and she was marrying him at once, at the end of the month. And he was a young man who was extremely good to marry, he was far better than Ippolito and Emanuele and the usual run of their friends, he was a young man who was fond of her and he had been waiting for her for a great many years. And in any case she had no need to give explanations to anyone and was acting according to her own ideas. She went out banging the door and they were all left looking at each other in bewilderment, and then suddenly they heard the sound of Concettina's violent sobs coming from her room, and Emanuele wanted to go to her, but Ippolito restrained him. Giustino said he knew the young man with the car perfectly well, he was a Fascist and he went round in a black shirt in processions. Emanuele knew him too and said what his name was, he was called Emilio Sbrancagna, Concettina would be Signora Sbrancagna, a fine name too. Emanuele wanted Ippolito to go at once to Concettina and persuade her to give up this fellow ; couldn't they hear how she was crying, she was marrying him because she was desperate and discouraged and goodness knows what ideas she had got into her head, perhaps she had got it into her head that if she didn't get married now she would never get married at all. But Signora Maria said that she had looked at this young man from the window and he was tall and distinguished-looking, and she had also sought a little information about his family, because she always thought of everything. It was an extremely good family and in good circumstances, they lived in a villa a little way out of the town, the father owned a chemical works and the son worked there too. At this moment Danilo appeared, and asked what they were doing sitting round the table with that troubled look on their faces. So Emanuele explained to him that Concettina wanted to marry Signor Sbrancagna, a Fascist. Danilo asked what was so tragic about that, the Fascist would help them when they got into trouble. Then he at once started talking about something else, as though Concettina had been any ordinary person and he had never waited for her for whole afternoons at the gate.

Next day Signora Maria started cleaning the house, because Concettina had told her that Emilio Sbrancagna was bringing his parents to see her. The sitting-room windows were thrown open and Signora Maria climbed up on a ladder to clean the panes. Anna in the meantime had to dust the piano and the furniture, and she tried to move the piano to see if there were still any pink and green pamphlets hidden behind it. There was nothing, only a few flakes of dust on the floor. Concettina did not help with the cleaning, Concettina stayed lying on the bed in her room, stifling a sob in her handkerchief from time to time. Signora Maria thought she was weeping because of the trousseau, and said Ippolito ought not to allow her to sell anything, he ought to go and draw the money out of the bank, she was convinced there was a heap of money in

the bank and that Ippolito was unwilling to touch it.
Every now and then she came down from the ladder and
went to comfort Concettina, she told her that as a matter
of fact not much was needed for a trousseau, just a few
practical, washable things, no artificial silk because it was
vulgar, just linen or batiste.   By eight o'clock in the evening
the sitting-room was ready, with the stove lit and the tea-
cups ready on the piano, and Signora Maria had put on
her black dress with the lace *jabot* and had suddenly started
ordering everyone about, Giustino was to warn Danilo that
he was not to appear, Concettina was to wash her eyes
with boracic lotion and smooth back her fringe, Emanuele
was to appear for a moment, say how d'you do and go
away at once.

Emanuele, however, refused utterly to go into the sitting-
room, he crept away into the kitchen with Anna and together
they watched the Sbrancagnas getting out of their car, the
father a tiny little man and slightly deformed, with long
hay-coloured moustaches, the mother tall and white-haired,
the young man with his hair cut *en brosse*, a black feather-
brush above a brow high and narrow as a tower.   Emanuele
kept on saying, " Poor Concettina, what a terrible business,
what a terrible business," and cursed Ippolito for not doing
anything to stop the marriage ; he just let things slide,
he always let everything slide, in reality nothing and nobody
mattered to him, in reality he was a cynic.   Concettina,
who had helped to burn the newspapers, was fated to finish
her career amongst the Sbrancagnas, she was fated to end
up in a family of Fascists, with a portrait of Mussolini at
the head of the bed, she, the daughter of her father, a man
who had died in sorrow at not seeing the revolution.
Concettina, out of melancholy, out of spite, goodness knows
why, was fated to end like that.   And apart from everything
else there was also the danger that one of these days she
would tell her husband about the time when they had
burnt the newspapers, and he could already see Emilio
Sbrancagna rushing to report it to the police, and then

what a fine to-do there would be. Emanuele limped about
the kitchen and kicked out at the legs of the table, and said
poor Italy that had to depend on types like Ippolito for
the revolution; Anna nibbled biscuits, until Concettina
came running in and took the silver dish away from her.
Emanuele followed her into the passage and made her swear
on the memory of her father never to say anything about
the day when they burnt the newspapers. Concettina
swore, but a great fury against Emanuele suddenly came
over her, she gnashed her teeth and pulled his ear violently,
then she broke away from him and went back into the
sitting-room with the silver dish. Emanuele returned to the
kitchen to kick at the table-legs, rubbing his ear which was
hurting him.

In the sitting-room Signora Sbrancagna was sitting with
Signora Maria on the sofa, Signora Maria sat with two
fingers pointed on her knee and talked about her travels,
about the time when Concettina's grandmother's fur coat
had been stolen at the Grand Hotel in Cannes, a fur coat
made of " skuntz ". She talked and talked and all of a
sudden was seized with nervousness, she looked at the
biscuits and they seemed very few, she looked at the door
in anguish lest she should see Danilo coming in. Ippolito
was silent, stroking his face, Concettina was crumpling a
handkerchief in her sweating hands, and to Signora Maria
it seemed that Concettina was looking ugly that evening;
with her fringe smoothed back and the blue dress she had
put on she no longer looked like a *cocotte*, but on the other
hand she looked like a schoolmistress. Signor Sbrancagna
ate the biscuits and got his moustaches all full of crumbs,
and tried to make conversation with Ippolito, but it was
not easy to force a word out of Ippolito when he started
gazing into the void and stroking his face. But young
Emilio Sbrancagna appeared to be quite indifferent to conversation and to everything, and lay back in his armchair
with his fingers intertwined and his feather-brush standing
up straight on his forehead, and he looked at Concettina

with a very gay and knowing smile, and he sat in the arm-chair as though he had always been there, rocking his long, loose-limbed body backwards and forwards in it, then suddenly he jumped up and played a few chords on the piano, and Signora Maria, on the sofa, gave a start and looked at the piano, thinking that now it could never be sold, now that they had all seen it. Signora Sbrancagna wanted to know about Cannes, she had never been there, her husband had refused to take her there because he had heard that the women went on the beach stark naked. She herself had once been robbed of a brooch in an hotel at Vicenza, a brooch of great value, but her husband told her not to talk nonsense, no one had ever robbed her of anything, she had lost the brooch because it was not properly fastened, in any case it was an ugly brooch and worth only a few pence. Signora Sbrancagna whispered to Signora Maria that her husband always behaved like that, he took great pleasure in mortifying her in front of other people. All of a sudden, when no one was expecting it, Signor Sbrancagna started saying that there was no reason for keeping silence about the thing that lay so near all their hearts, his son and Concettina wanted to get married, well then let them get married, he would have preferred a girl with a certain amount of dowry, but if there was no dowry never mind. Signora Maria said that Concettina, after all, had something, a share of Le Visciole was hers ; Signor Sbrancagna said he knew this but that that little piece of land, which had to be shared between four, could not be called a dowry. However he intended to pass over the question of a dowry. There remained the question of politics, which was a more thorny one, he wanted to be sincere and he knew that Concettina's father had been a revolutionary, and he himself had always had a great fear of revolutionaries, and he rose to his feet and fixed Ippolito with two staring eyes. However he knew that he had also been a fine person, he knew that even amongst revolutionaries there were fine people, it seemed strange but there were fine people to be found

everywhere. He said this in a very low voice but his wife
was at once frightened, she looked all round and asked if
the maid slept in the room next door, with maids you
could never be quite sure, and a person could find himself
in trouble over a misunderstood word. Then he grew
angry with his wife, he had not said anything wrong, what
he had said could perfectly well be shouted aloud in the
piazza, that there were fine people even amongst revolutionaries. Then Signora Maria said that Concettina's father
had been far more than a fine person, he had been a very
superior man, he had spent his whole life in love for his
children, and also, as well, in writing a book of memoirs,
but in the end he had burned the book, goodness knows
why. Young Emilio Sbrancagna all of a sudden burst out
laughing, he rocked backwards and forwards in his armchair and laughed, pulling up his knees and shaking his
feet. Everyone looked at him in astonishment and his
mother asked him severely why he was laughing like that.
He said he couldn't help laughing at the idea of his father
shouting aloud in the piazza in defence of revolutionaries.
And after this burst of laughter they all felt light-hearted,
and Concettina, too, seemed to be soothed and serene, and
Signor Sbrancagna as he went out shook Ippolito's hand
warmly and said he hoped to be able to have more conversation with him, for the moment he looked into his
eyes he had felt a great liking for him, and he hoped he
was not a revolutionary but, when all was said and done,
never mind even if he was, and his wife was thumping
him in the back all the time, and she explained to Signora
Maria that in her house it was always like this, her husband
and her son said things they ought not to say. Finally the
Sbrancagnas went away, and the others found Emanuele
still in the kitchen, sleeping with his head on the table, so
they woke him up and sent him off to bed.

Next day Signora Maria took the grandmother's jewels
to the pawnshop, to be redeemed later with the money
from the next harvest. Then she searched the whole town

for some pure linen, she had a horror of mixed materials, she stopped for an hour in each shop and ran up ladders to ransack the shelves. Finally she came home with yards and yards of linen and started cutting out and stitching up undervests and nightdresses, until late she was stitching and embroidering and could talk of nothing but buttonholing and hem-stitching. Concettina wanted to make herself a close-fitting black *redingote*, exactly like Mammina's, and she took up her position at the window to watch Mammina when she went out wearing the *redingote*, but she never managed to see properly and questioned Emanuele at great length about the buttons and the pockets, Emanuele promised to go at night on tiptoe and look at the *redingote* in the wardrobe and get the whole matter fixed in his head. Emanuele however did not stop tormenting Concettina about politics, as a bride she would be sleeping with Mussolini's portrait over the head of the bed. Concettina blushed and said that even the Fascists had done some good things, the bridges and the roads for instance, and it was very strange to hear her talk like that about bridges and roads, she who had never bothered about a road or a bridge in her life, had never asked herself whether there were enough of them in Italy. Emanuele covered his face with his hands and groaned, my God, how little had been needed to make Concettina go all to pieces, all that was now left of Concettina was a handful of crumbs to throw to the birds. He never wanted to see Emilio Sbrancagna, and he begged them to put a black handkerchief tied to a stick in the window if Emilio Sbrancagna was in the house, and, if he wasn't there, a white handkerchief, and then he would come. Danilo on the other hand said that he wanted to meet this Emilio Sbrancagna, because one ought to discuss things with Fascists, to understand what they have in their heads. But Ippolito said that Emilio Sbrancagna had very little Fascism in his head at all, he put on a black shirt as he would have put on any other, and all the rhetorical side of Fascism had passed over him without defiling him, he was as fresh and healthy as a young calf in a meadow. And Danilo said that the Fascist party had in it plenty of these young calves, it was by no means entirely composed of wolves and eagles, there were the calves as well and to-morrow they would be going off to be killed in the war, exactly like calves going to the slaughter-house. And it was an important thing to talk to these young calves in the meadows, it was an important thing to talk to anything that was still alive in Italy.

Only once did Giustino remember to hang up the black handkerchief on the stick, so that Emanuele should know that Emilio Sbrancagna was there, but this handkerchief was Signora Maria's scarf, and she went and took it in for fear that it might be spoilt. After that there were no more handkerchiefs, and Emilio and Emanuele began to meet on the stairs and to greet each other, but Emilio at first scowled because he imagined that everyone who came to the house was in love with Concettina, until Signora Maria explained to him that to Emanuele Concettina was like a sister. And gradually Emanuele stopped grinding his teeth as he said the word " Sbrancagna ". And then one day there was the meeting between Emilio and Danilo, and Danilo started questioning him with the policeman-like air that he had acquired in prison, and Emilio fidgeted anxiously in his armchair, with a great longing to escape to Concettina who was sitting in the sun on the terrace. Danilo asked him a number of questions, whether he had read this and that and whether he was frightened about the war, Emilio shook his black feather-brush of hair and turned from side to side in his armchair, he had no desire at all to go to the war, in any case who in Italy now thought about the war ? He told Danilo and Ippolito that he felt himself too stupid to talk to them, they talked to him as though he were very intelligent but really he was stupid, he had never read either Spinoza or Kant, he had tried but had quickly stopped because he did not understand. He wanted to marry Concettina and that was all, he did not look

forward into the years to come, every day that came was
beautiful. He knew that Danilo had been in prison, he
felt a great respect for those who went to prison but he
himself would never have the courage to go there, he put
on a black shirt and marched in processions. In any case
it seemed to him that the Fascists had done a few good
things, for example they had taken Africa and Albania,
perhaps it did not mean a great deal to have taken them
but nevertheless taken them they had. The only thing
he did not like was the Rome–Berlin Axis, he could not
bear the Germans, his father had fought in the war against
the Germans and he himself was small then but he had not
forgotten it. He did not like the Rome–Berlin Axis but
in point of fact Mussolini was not now waging war side
by side with the Germans, perhaps *he* couldn't bear them
either and the Rome–Berlin Axis had been all a joke. On
the whole it seemed to him that things in Italy were really
not going so badly, perhaps they might be even better but
he himself was satisfied, Danilo and Ippolito were too
intelligent to be satisfied and they imagined other kinds of
governments, but he himself was stupid, he was easy to
please and was quite satisfied. At last they let him alone
and he made his escape, and he really did seem like a young
calf or a colt that had been let loose to graze at ease, and
Danilo stayed in the sitting-room arguing on the subject
of calves, there were so many of them in Italy and they
were all like that.

On the night before the wedding Concettina sat up
weeping, but it was a weeping that had no sorrow in it
now ; she sat on the bed with her hands clasped behind
her head and bright, quiet tears ran down her face, and
Signora Maria dozed at the foot of the bed, and from
time to time gave a start and got up with her hair all undone,
with one cheek red and the other pale, and went down to
heat up the camomile. These tears left no mark upon
Concettina's face, in the morning it was a pure, fresh face,
with no swelling or redness, a beautiful face washed clean

by tears, luminous and mild. Refreshments had been prepared in the sitting-room, and Signora Maria had wondered if they ought to invite Mammina, but Emanuele said it was no use, Mammina certainly would not come. On the contrary, Mammina was offended at not being invited, and said to Emanuele that she knew perfectly well that Concettina had copied her *redingote* and that *that* was why she had not wanted to invite her, it did not matter in the least to her that she had copied it but all the same she must not think it suited her, she was too big in the legs and hips to wear a close-fitting *redingote*, and she would have done better to copy her loose sack coat, for a woman with Concettina's figure it would have been much more suitable. Emanuele ran across to say that they ought to invite Mammina, but by now it was too late, Mammina was offended and did not come, she sent some flowers instead. Emanuele and Giuma came; Emanuele said that Giuma looked well at a wedding, he was very smart and made a good appearance. Danilo and his wife also came; Signora Maria did not want them at any price, she was in despair, what on earth would the Sbrancagnas think when they found themselves in company with Danilo and his wife? But Ippolito said it was he who was master of the house, and he had purposely fixed the wedding to be on a Sunday, so that Danilo's wife would be able to come too. Signora Maria said he remembered to be master of the house only when it was convenient to him, usually he was indifferent to everything, and it had been necessary for her to humiliate herself by taking the jewels to the pawnshop in order to provide a trousseau for Concettina. Emanuele was laughing all the time at the thought of the face Signor Sbrancagna would make when he found himself in the company of Danilo, because everyone in the town knew he had been in prison. But Signor Sbrancagna and his wife lived a detached sort of life in their villa outside the town, and he knew nothing about Danilo, and asked Ippolito who the young man was who looked so very intelligent and distinguished. During the whole time of the ceremony in church and again later while they were taking refreshments at the house Signor Sbrancagna stayed beside Ippolito, because he had taken a great liking to Ippolito, and he started telling him all about himself, how he had come to marry his wife and how he had set up his chemical works, and he asked in a low voice whether Italy would come into the war on the side of the Germans, as for the Germans, he could not bear them, he had fought against them and once a man has fought against a country he never forgets it, how can he then make friends, the human heart is after all the human heart and remains deaf to political expediencies. And then the Russians were now allied with the Germans, what a mix-up it was. As for the cold war, it was impossible to believe in it, goodness knows how many dead there had been already, there was little movement because the winter was coming on, but in the spring there would be a disastrous explosion. And Ippolito said he thought so too.

Anna stood in one corner of the room in a dress of yellow velvet which Signora Maria had cut out of a curtain for her, she was thinking that she was sick of being dressed in curtains, no one could fail to notice that what she was wearing was a curtain, it still even had its tassels at the bottom, because Signora Maria had said that they made a fine trimming and that it would be a shame to take them away. She looked at Giustino who was behaving in a rather silly fashion with Danilo's wife, he was sitting on the arm of her chair and telling her that in the winter he would take her out ski-ing, he would teach her to come down like a snow-plough, it was easy. Danilo's wife had a flame-red blouse which went badly with the colour of her hair, but at least it was a blouse and not a curtain, Anna wondered why she should be the only one who had to be dressed in a curtain. She would have liked Giustino to have taken her out ski-ing too, but he certainly wouldn't, he would go alone with Danilo's wife so as to behave in a silly fashion with her, as though Danilo's wife really wanted to pay any attention to him. Danilo's wife was listening to him absent-mindedly with her tired, worn expression, and from time to time she broke into a laugh which sounded like a cough. Giuma was there beside them, his lips curved in a contemptuous smile, evidently Giustino's boastings about the snow-plough seemed to him very foolish, no doubt he was very good at ski-ing and the snow-plough must seem to him just a piece of nonsense.

Giuma saw Anna looking at him and came over to her. "We two used to play together when we were small," he said. He said it as though he were speaking of a very distant and far-off time ; since then he had been in Switzerland, had won goodness knows how many rugby matches, his cheeks had become hard and bristly, his shoulders square and strong. He had become very tall and elegant, he had a silk shirt with his initials on it, he had a watch in a kind of black shell hanging at his belt. He stood in front of her and fiddled with the chain of this watch, his hair still fell over his eyes and he threw it back, curving his lips as he did so. "We used to read *The Child's Treasure-House*," she said. "*The Child's Treasure-House !* yes, yes . . ." Giuma started laughing a great deal at the recollection of *The Child's Treasure-House*, he threw back his head and laughed, and she saw again his small teeth like a wolf's. She would have been amused to read *The Child's Treasure-House* again, several times she had asked Emanuele what had become of all those volumes bound in blue, Emanuele knew nothing about them, perhaps Mammina had had them taken up to the attic. "You used to tie me to trees with a rope," she said. "Really ? I'm sorry. I hope I didn't hurt you too much." He had become. very charming, when his contemptuous smile vanished he seemed even a little shy, it seemed to her that he remained beside her out of shyness, because he did not know anyone else in the room. But she felt a great boredom, a great fatigue at being with him, the same boredom and the same fatigue that she had felt in the days when they had played together. To her those days did not seem so far off, it seemed to her that so few things had happened, they had burned the newspapers and they had expected the police and then no one had come at all. Giuma asked her in a low voice who was the monster in the red blouse, she told him it was Danilo's wife but he did not know who Danilo was, certainly he did not know anything about the time when they burned the newspapers, Emanuele had told them all that his brother was an impossible person. Giuma said he did not know any of Emanuele's friends, in any case he and Emanuele did not see each other often, just for a moment in the morning at the bathroom door, at table rather seldom because they ate at different times, and he himself often had to accompany Mammina out to lunch and to play bridge. He pressed the spring of the black shell and looked at the time, Mammina was expecting him even on *that* day, he said that Emanuele had been clever enough not to learn bridge, so did not have to accompany Mammina to various boring drawing-rooms. He asked Anna if she would be free next day to go to the cinema with him after school, he would wait for her in the avenue, they had played so much together as children and now there was no reason why they should not see each other. And so he would have an excuse for not making a fourth at bridge. Anna said yes, she was free, and thought with a feeling of fatigue and fear of the afternoon they would spend together, perhaps from now onwards Giuma would want to be often with her, she was proud of it and at the same time fatigued and frightened and she felt for him a kind of distress and did not know why.

When the guests had gone Concettina's suitcases, full of the trousseau all made of pure linen, had hurriedly to be closed, and Concettina and Emilio went off by car for their honeymoon.

9

When Anna came out of school next day she found Giuma waiting for her in the avenue, and they went to the cinema to see *The Mark of Zorro*. Giuma paid for her. All that day she had been wondering whether the money she had would be enough for the ticket, if they went to a cinema in the centre of the town it certainly would not. She talked about it at school to her desk-neighbour, she was her dearest friend and they told each other everything. Her friend started laughing, she often went to the cinema with boys and knew that they always paid. She told her that Giuma would certainly kiss her, boys took girls to the cinema simply in order to kiss them. Giuma however did not seem to be thinking of kissing her, he sat beside her in the almost empty, dark theatre and stamped and champed, you just couldn't go to the cinema nowadays, there was never any possibility of seeing a decent film. Only at the end did he stop fuming, there was a duel on the balustrade of a terrace and even he was left breathless. But when they came out he spoke scornfully even of the duel, he started telling her about a long film of duels that he had seen at Geneva, Anna couldn't understand what he was talking about because it was a very tangled story. They walked towards home and on the road beside the river they met Emanuele and Ippolito, Emanuele raised his eyebrows and opened his eyes wide when he saw them together. At the gate Giuma told her he would wait for her in the avenue again next day, it would be nice to be together even if they didn't go to the cinema.

They got into the habit of meeting in the avenue every day. Anna would rather have gone to see her girl friend or come straight home to do her homework. As it was she had to stay up after supper to do her lessons. But she

was too proud of Giuma wanting to be with her. Giuma
was a boy. Concettina had told her again and again that
at her age she had had plenty of boys to go out with.
Concettina had scolded her because she came straight
home from school to do her homework. Now she was
impatient for Concettina to come back from her honeymoon, so that she might be seen with Giuma on the road
by the river. Signora Maria, however, was not altogether pleased at her going about with Giuma, she did
not know Giuma, she did not know what type of boy he
was. Emanuele told her he was an impossible type, pre-
sumptuous and fatuous, but in the matter of upbringing
there was nothing to be said against him, he was well
brought up from head to foot and you could safely give
him five hundred girls to take out. But 'Signora Maria
asked why he had not made friends with Giustino who was
in the same class, why with Anna ? Then Giustino said
that Giuma had tried to make friends with him too, but
he had not paid any attention to him and so he had
immediately stopped.

Of Giustino and of the other boys at school Giuma always
spoke with great contempt. They did not read books, they
did not wash properly, they did not go in for any kind
of sport : they gave themselves grand sporting airs but
when it came to the point they could do nothing seriously.
Anna asked him if he was still friends with Cingalesi and
Pucci Donadio : she had always remembered these names
which at one time he had so constantly repeated to her.
Giuma frowned. Pucci Donadio he remembered, he had
never been really a friend of his, he was the son of a friend
of Mammina's, he was much smaller than himself and they
used to take him to play on the beach at Mentone and
he had to make sand-castles for him. As for Cingalesi,
he didn't know who he was. Then he thought hard and
recalled Cingalesi, a boy who used to sell oranges on the
beach. No, he had other friends now. He pulled a bundle
of letters out of his pocket ; he showed her the stamps on

the envelopes, his friends wrote to him from every part of the world, from America, from Denmark, at the school in Switzerland he had got to know people from everywhere. Some of them were still at the school and were waiting for him to come back, they were putting aside bottles of brandy and gin to celebrate his return, he felt he really wanted some gin, perhaps Mammina would let him go back again soon.

He often took her to the cinema, for he always had money to spend. Or they would wander about the town, they would go into bookshops and look at the magazines and the art books, Giuma went into ecstasies over reproductions of pictures in which there was nothing but triangles and small circles. Sometimes they bought roast chestnuts and sat and ate them on a seat in the public gardens. Giuma would pull out the poems of Montale and start reading them aloud. He had explained to her who Montale was, he had explained who the other poets were who were of any importance. Anna sat silent without listening to him, she was quite unable to fix her attention upon his words. She looked at his wide, light-coloured overcoat, at his scarf, at the locks of hair falling over his forehead, at his small teeth like a wolf's. Gradually she had ceased to be bored in his company, she did not listen to what he said but she looked at him, and she was infinitely proud to sit with Giuma on a seat in the public gardens, and it seemed to her that Giuma's light-coloured overcoat and his scarf and his watch in its black shell all belonged partly to her, and it seemed to her that none of her school-friends had anything like this, a boy to go about with like this, her school-friends went out with giggling, tiresome boys who did not read Montale and knew nothing about the painters who made small circles. She sat silent with her hands in her lap, the shells of the chestnuts entangled in the wool of her coat. She could not have said one single word about Montale and she had not understood much of his poetry. Yet she had taken a fancy to certain lines, from having heard them spoken by Giuma : " Un'ora e mi riporta Cumerlotti—Lakmé nell'aria delle campanelle—o vero c'era il falòtico—mutarsi della mia vita—quando udii sugli scogli crepitare—la bomba ballerina." She went home with the *bomba ballerina* and the *falòtico*, for some time the *bomba ballerina* went dancing in front of her. She did not ask Giuma who Cumerlotti was, she did not ask him about the *falòtico*, she was afraid he might get angry, and she was afraid the *falòtico* might turn into something dull and valueless if one discovered what it was.

In the morning at school her friend always asked her whether Giuma had kissed her and she said no. Her friend was much surprised and not altogether pleased and said that never had such a thing happened to her, boys always kissed her. In the end she imagined that they had kissed each other and that Anna wouldn't tell her. Gradually they became a little less friendly. Anna did not tell her anything about the *falòtico*, this friend of hers now seemed to her silly, and also it seemed to her that her neck was a little dirty, she like Giuma had now begun to look whether people washed themselves properly. So that when Giuma really did kiss her she said nothing to her friend. No one knew about it.

Giuma kissed her one day when he was feeling sad. He had got only three marks in Greek, Mammina was angry with him, and then he had said he had got only three marks on purpose, because he wanted to go back to Switzerland, he did not like this nasty school and did not want to stay there any longer. All of a sudden Emanuele had begun shouting at him too. And then he had said it didn't really matter to him so much about the school, but he didn't like staying at home and he preferred to go to a boarding-school, he didn't like taking Mammina about when she went to see those awful women who played bridge. Emanuele had shouted that he must not be lacking in respect towards Mammina, he had gone for him and they had hit each other, Mammina, trying to separate

them, had sprained her wrist, and then the whole day had
been spent in putting vegeto-mineral water compresses on
it. They were not letting him go back to Switzerland,
there was no hope of that. And he was fed up with everything. Only with Anna was he happy, she was the only
person who was kind to him. They sat in silence, Giuma
looked down on the ground, frowning, and made marks in
the dust with his foot. Suddenly he put his arm round
her waist and pressed himself slightly against her. There
was a terrible silence between them, they looked at each
other in a fright, the fright and the silence lasted a long
time. And then Giuma kissed her and they sighed and
smiled at each other peacefully.

Anna knew from Giustino that at school they detested
him, they turned their backs at once if he came up to
speak to them. At first he had bored them to tears with
his rugby matches and his letters from all parts of the world,
he irritated everyone with his letters, he insisted on trans-
lating parts of them which seemed to him immensely funny,
he explained how funny they were and told long tales about
drinks and football matches, laughing on his own account.
Now, on the other hand, he could talk of nothing but the
poems of Montale, he was as vehement about Montale's
poems as if he had written them himself, he dragged in
Montale every time the teacher asked him a question. He
suggested meeting once a week to read and discuss Montale.
And probably he didn't understand anything at all about
Montale. Emanuele asked Giustino why they did not
punch his head, perhaps it would have done him a great
deal of good. But Giustino said they hadn't even any desire
to punch him, nor even to make fun of him, he was too
tiresome, they preferred just to turn their backs when he
came up to them. Nobody except Anna could manage to
endure him, and they went about together because Anna
was silly and ingenuous and took all the nonsense he told
her seriously. Anna was listening, and she tried to curl
her lips in scorn as Giuma did. But she felt mortified, she

thought of how he went up to speak to them and of how they turned their backs, and she felt deeply mortified, just as though they had turned their backs on *her*. And at times she was seized by a suspicion that in reality Giuma knew no more about the *falòtico* or about Cumerlotti than she did, that he had to pretend he knew in order to feel powerful and proud, in order to curl his lips in scorn and walk proudly about the town, without looking too closely at his own intimate self, which was perhaps mortified and suffering and lonely. After a long time perhaps it would be discovered that he knew absolutely nothing about the *falòtico*. Once upon a time he had boasted perpetually about Cingalesi, bringing him into every conversation, and she had thought of Cingalesi as of some terrible, disdainful force. Then the old Cingalesi had gone up in smoke and all that was left in his place was a harmless orange-seller.

His face, when he kissed her, always lost all sign of scorn and of arrogance. His face became gentle, tender, brotherly, as he started removing, one by one, the chestnut-shells from her coat. Then they would laugh about these shells, and it seemed there were so many things they could laugh about together, it seemed they could laugh together even about the *falòtico*, that they could say to each other that they did not quite know what it was. But they did not say this, they never got as far as saying it, it was only for one moment that Giuma continued to be so tender and gentle, the next moment he curled his lips and looked round him in disgust, how squalid these public gardens were, how squalid the town was, you ought to see what the public gardens in Geneva and Lausanne were like. Then he pressed the spring of the black shell and buttoned up his overcoat, Mammina was expecting him as usual to make a fourth at bridge.

In the end Anna told him about the time when they burned the newspapers, herself and Concettina and Ippolito and Emanuele. Giuma did not show much surprise, he said he had suspected for some time that Emanuele was

getting mixed up in politics, he was really an idiot. He
didn't like Fascism himself, but it was better to put up
with it and it wasn't worth the trouble of running risks,
besides Emanuele ought to think of Mammina, if they put
him in prison Mammina would go mad. He didn't hold
with Fascism himself, above all it was a provincial thing,
it made Italy provincial, it prevented people from arranging
exhibitions with fine pictures from abroad. Fascism was
certainly an ugly, provincial, ignorant thing. But it wasn't
worth the trouble of getting oneself put in prison for such
an ugly, clumsy thing, getting oneself put in prison was
taking it too seriously. But there must be a revolution,
Anna said. He started to laugh a great deal, he bent back
and laughed, displaying all his wolf-like teeth. A revolution, he said, Anna wanted to start a revolution. No, he
said, there was no need for that, because Fascism would
gradually fizzle out by itself, like those rubber balloons
that deflate themselves with a whistling noise. No, there
was no revolution to be started and in any case even if a
revolution did have to be started Emanuele and Anna
would not be the people to do it. " And not Danilo
either ? " asked Anna. Not Danilo either, Giuma answered,
not Danilo either, because he had married a wife who was
too twisted and pinched.

10

Concettina came back from her honeymoon, and went to
live with her parents-in-law in their villa outside the town.
Concettina was going to have a baby and all she could
do was vomit and spit. She did not come to the house.
Anna and Giustino went to see her a few days after she had
arrived, she was lying in a big double bed, wearing a yellow
embroidered bed-jacket and spitting into a chamber-pot

of flower-patterned china.　Her mother-in-law was fussing round her, and also a number of grandmothers and old aunts and servant-maids, one of them bringing her soup and another lemons to suck and another putting a hot-water bottle at her feet.　Concettina spoke very slowly, with her teeth clenched to prevent her from vomiting.　She had been to Naples and to Capri, and had bathed in the sea before the time when she started vomiting.　At Capri she had bought a box all made of shells and some shoes of plaited straw.　There were old men there dressed as fisher-men who were really marquises or princes, there were women who looked like men and men who looked like women. There was a lady sitting in a café with a parrot on her shoulder and three cats on a lead.　Then when she had shown them the shoes and the box they found nothing more to say to each other, Anna and Giustino were standing waiting for the moment to go away, there was nothing more to say to this new Concettina who was going to have a baby, in this house full of grandmothers and servants. Old Signora Sbrancagna told them they must not tire Concettina.　So they went away, they had a long way to go to get home, it took at least an hour to walk the distance between them and Concettina.　The house in which Con-cettina lived was right out in the country, and it had round it a small damp garden, surrounded by a wall with pieces of glass stuck on top of it.　" Che ha in cima cocci aguzzi di bottiglia ", said Anna.　But Giustino told her to stop quoting Montale at once, he knew that Giuma read her Montale's poems and goodness knows what they thought about them, he himself had read Montale too and had not understood much of it, he was a poet who wasn't very easy to understand.　The poem about the pieces of broken bottle was the only one that could be understood a little. He told her to be careful with Giuma, perhaps he wanted to kiss her and she must take care not to let herself be kissed, she must not let herself become like Concettina, who before she got married had allowed herself to be kissed by almost

everybody. Concettina had got married all the same
because she was rather attractive, *she* wasn't in the least
attractive and she would never get married if she went
about too much with boys and let herself be kissed. They
were both in a bad temper and they quarrelled all the
way home, Giustino said she was treading on his toes,
couldn't she keep a little to one side? He didn't at all
care about her being seen every day with Giuma, goodness
knows how many times she had let him kiss her, and this
Giuma was an impossible kind of person, at school they
turned their backs on him if he came up to speak to them.
Anna told him that the girl she had seen him with was
an impossible kind of person, that very tall, thin girl who
went out for walks with him in the evening. In any case
he liked pinched-looking women, he liked Danilo's wife
who was so terribly pinched-looking, he liked women who
were all twisted and dried up. Giustino said that the girl
whom he took out for walks in the evening meant nothing
to him, she was not his girl, she was a girl who was useful
to him because she was very good at doing Italian exercises,
whenever he had a difficult exercise he went to this girl
and got her to do it for him. and then as a reward he took
her out for a walk. They got back home and Emanuele
hurried to meet them in order to ask if there was a portrait
of Mussolini in Concettina's bedroom, they answered that
there wasn't and Emanuele was displeased, he said that
perhaps Concettina had taken it down in a great hurry
when she heard them arrive. Signora Maria began implor-
ing them for goodness' sake to leave Concettina out of
their politics, she was not feeling well because she was
expecting a baby. Emanuele said that Concettina would
have a dozen babies all for love of the Duce, so as to provide soldiers for Italy as the Duce wished. Anna and
Giustino felt rather sad, it seemed strange but they felt
lost without Concettina in the house, it seemed strange
because she had never taken any notice of anyone and
always stayed shut up in her room mending her stockings

or filing her nails or nibbling her pencil while she thought about Racine. And now it seemed as if Concettina no longer existed in any part of the world ; this woman who was going to have a baby, this woman who spat into a flowered chamber-pot did not seem to be the real Concettina at all. Concettina had now got rid of Racine for ever, but, to make up for it, she suffered from nausea and would have to bring into the world a dozen babies, all of them tiresome to wash and to put to sleep.

Giuma told Anna that he and Danilo had been to a café together. He was all excited but did not want to show it. They had met on the road beside the river, and Danilo had come up and started talking to him. Anna had known for some time that this was bound to happen, because Danilo had told Emanuele several times that he wanted to get to know his brother and find out what he was like. Emanuele begged him not to bother about it, his brother was an impossible kind of person, an impossible person and that was that. But Danilo replied that it was a good thing to find out even what impossible people were like. Giuma told Anna that he and Danilo had talked and talked, and in the end they had gone to a little café on the outskirts of the town, where there was a gramophone with a horn which played old songs. He and Danilo had talked about all sorts of things, it had got dark and they didn't notice it. They had even talked about Montale, Danilo had wanted to know all about Montale and Giuma had explained to him. On the way home they had also discussed politics a little : Giuma had spoken of his ideas, saying that Fascism would gradually fizzle out of its own accord. Danilo had invited him to come and see him one evening, seeing that they had had such an interesting conversation. Anna was sad, she wanted to tell him about her visit to Concettina and about the things Giustino had said to her on the way home, she wanted to ask if it was true that she was not at all attractive and that she would never get married. But it was impossible for her to say anything, Giuma went on and on talking about Danilo and Danilo and Danilo, he did not even think of kissing her.

Giuma wenь to see Danilo every evening for a week. During that week he did nothing but talk of Danilo and Danilo and Danilo, even Danilo's wife no longer seemed to him so pinched-looking, her hair had got into that state because she went to cheap hairdressers, if she had had the money to put herself in order and to dress herself she would have been rather attractive. During that time they kissed very seldom, Giuma had too much to say, he was continually pressing the spring of the black shell to see if it was getting near the time to go to Danilo's, he had given Mammina to understand that he was going to a friend's house to study. Danilo and his wife were of the opinion that he read poetry very well. Then things between him and Danilo began to go not so well, Anna was immediately aware of it, he began saying that there was a bad smell in Danilo's room, and then, that set of bottles and glasses displayed on the chest-of-drawers, that set of bottles and glasses was a wonder, it was the most provincial thing you could imagine. Danilo wanted to draw him into politics but he wasn't having any, he wasn't a clumsy fool like Emanuele, he didn't want to run idiotic risks. At first they had read Montale but then Danilo had asked him whether he knew about Karl Marx's *Das Kapital*, yes, he knew about it, but he had told Danilo clearly that he didn't want to hear any mention of things like that. Later on he would have to be a director of the soap factory, and Emanuele also would have to be a director, and so they could not possibly be on the side of Karl Marx, they were the owners of a factory and they could not be on the side of those who wished to hand over the factories to the workers. It was perfectly clear and if Emanuele did not understand it he was a complete idiot, if he let his head be turned by Danilo and read Karl Marx. Anna said that perhaps it was not right that they two should possess a soap factory and other people nothing, not even enough to clothe and feed themselves. Giuma got very angry and

said it was perfectly right, it was right because his father
had built up the soap factory out of nothing at all, before
that it had been just a ridiculous kind of shanty and his
father had worked all his life to turn it into something big
and important. In any case justice is not of this earth,
said Giuma, justice is of the kingdom of heaven. And he
said that he as a child had believed in the kingdom of
heaven, but now he had ceased to believe in it, now it
was a thing that only babies believed in. Then Anna
asked where justice could be found, if the kingdom of
heaven, where it could have been found, did not exist.
Giuma said it certainly was a pity not to be able to find
it anywhere. However he did not believe in the justice
of Karl Marx. And he did not want to go to Danilo's
again, he did not want ever to smell the smell of that room
again, he smelt it upon himself, in his clothes, he had them
kept out in the air all night long but the smell did not go
away. Anna suddenly remembered what Cenzo Rena had
said about the peasants in the South, that they ate nothing
but beans, and she said that all the same something ought
to be done about the peasants in the South. But Giuma
told her not to think now about the peasants in the South,
he drew her into a quiet corner of the public gardens and
they stayed there kissing for a while. Then Giuma wanted
to go back to the café where he had been with Danilo, a
café on the other side of the river, smoky and dark, Giuma
said it was like certain cafés in Paris, if you hid yourself
away in there with that old gramophone with a horn and
those old prints on the walls you could really believe you
were in a café on the Seine.

At home Anna found Danilo. He was telling how he
had lost patience, the evening before, with Giuma, because
of all the nonsense he talked about justice and about Marx.
Danilo had been partly laughing and partly angry, and
finally he had lost patience and sent him away. For several
evenings he had been patient, out of kindness he had tried
to make him talk about one thing and another and gradually

Giuma had thawed, he read Montale's poems and they never managed to send him to sleep. But the nonsense he had talked about Marx ! Danilo had been unable to keep calm, all of a sudden he had thrown his hat and coat at him and had told him never to show his face there again if he was going to talk like that. Emanuele was rather mortified, he told Danilo he had warned him that it was useless to waste his time with Giuma, everyone knew what sort of a person Giuma was, after all he was only seventeen and Mammina had spoilt him terribly, and then he had been at that school in Switzerland, a school for rich, spoilt little boys, in any case Switzerland was a country that ought to be consigned to the flames. What a mania Danilo had for wasting his time with everybody, what a mania he had for knowing what everybody was like inside. And Danilo said that this was politics too, to try and find out what people were like inside, to find out the thoughts and reasonings of a boy of about seventeen, coming of a bourgeois family, spoilt, educated in Switzerland. But Ippolito then said that Danilo was not acting rightly, because he set himself the abstract proposition of finding out what people were like inside, and in each one he saw a political problem, and he had an inquisitorial, offensive way of asking questions. And perhaps without meaning to he had done Giuma harm, perhaps he had wounded him deeply, inviting him to his house in a way that was perhaps human and friendly and then suddenly starting to question him in that inquisitorial, offensive way, that cruel way, Danilo did not know it but at times he could be very cruel. Danilo asked him why he himself did not try and discuss things with Giuma, it was an interesting experiment. Ippolito answered that he did not make experiments, he despised everything that was in the nature of mere experiment, all of a sudden he seemed very angry, he had become pale and breathless. He did not make experiments, he left people alone and was indifferent to them, but Danilo who loved to have disciples must learn to control his temper, you

don't invite a boy to your house to have confidential talks
and discussions and then laugh in his face and throw him
out.   Danilo compressed his lips and tapped gently with a
pencil on the table, from time to time he raised his eyes and
fixed Ippolito with a cold, attentive stare, Emanuele limped
restlessly up and down.   But in the meantime Giustino had
come in and was asking why they never tried to study *him*
to find out what he was like, he also was seventeen and came
of a bourgeois family and why didn't anyone ever think of
studying *him* ?   Then they all burst out laughing together
and Danilo put the pencil in his pocket and said he was
going home to bed, there had been so many evenings when
he and his wife had sat up till the small hours reading
Montale with Giuma.

I I

Anna told Giuma nothing of what she had heard.   She
was careful to say nothing to him that might displease or
provoke him.   She pretended to believe all he said to her,
she pretended to believe it was because of the smell that he
had given up going to see Danilo.   She pretended to believe
that he did not like the company of his school-fellows because
they did not wash properly and were silly, she pretended not
to know that they turned their backs on him when he ap-
proached.   She felt cowardly in relation to Giuma, she had
a great fear that he might suddenly get tired of being with
her and of kissing her, if she contradicted him over something
and they started quarrelling.   So she tried never to contradict him and never to quarrel.   They no longer talked
about justice, they no longer talked about the revolution.
But Anna still thought about the revolution when she was
alone in her room, she saw a Giuma who had suddenly
become different, who mounted the barricades with her and

fired shots and sang.   These were thoughts that she allowed
to grow in secret within her, every day she added a new
adventure, the flight of herself and Giuma with guns over
the roofs, Fascists whom Danilo and Ippolito had not succeeded in capturing and whom she and Giuma led in chains
in front of the people's tribunal.   And she and Giuma, after
the barricades, would get married, and they would give the
soap factory to the poor.   While she was with Giuma these
thoughts would dissolve in smoke, she would be deeply
ashamed of them and it would seem to her that she would
never think them again, but she always thought them again
when she got back home and shut herself up in her room, as
soon as she sat down at the little table in her room these
thoughts blossomed joyous and arrogant inside her.

The snow had come and they were cold walking about the
avenues, they went every day now to the café that seemed
like Paris.   They were together every day but not on Sundays, on Sundays Giuma went off ski-ing, sometimes he
had to take Mammina with him who did not ski but sat, all
dressed up in furs, in the hall of the hotel and played bridge.
Giustino also went off ski-ing if he could manage to scrape
together a little money by selling some old books or passing
on his mathematical exercises to his school friends, because
Giustino was good at mathematics.   He used to pass on
his mathematical exercises to Giuma too, he said he made
Giuma pay double rates, because he could not stand him
and because he knew he was always full of money.   When
he had scraped together the money he went up into the attic
and started hammering, his skis were never in good order,
they were old skis with the fastenings all coming to pieces.
Then he put on Ippolito's army trousers with a big patch
in the seat, and a waterproof of Concettina's which Signora
Maria had cut down as a jacket for him.   Giuma told Anna
later that he had seen Giustino on the ski slopes, it was
enough to make you die of laughter, Giustino in a woman's
blue jacket giving great shouts and whistles and rolling down
like a sack, he was covered with snow from head to foot.   On

Sundays Anna stayed at home, she sat at the table in her room and did her homework for the whole week, and every now and then she put down her pen and thought about the revolution.

Gradually these Sundays became very gloomy for her. She had her usual thoughts, gunshots and flights over the roofs, but at the back of these thoughts was the face of the real Giuma, laughing with his wolf-like teeth, and it became more and more difficult for her to pluck out this real face from her heart. At the back of these thoughts there was the figure of the real Giuma who did not make his escape over the roofs but went out to the ski slopes or had tea in the hotel with Mammina all dressed up in furs, so very remote from the revolution and from her. She knew from Giustino that he had taken to ski-ing always with a girl, a girl with white velvet trousers, they held each other round the waist as they ski-ed, and Giustino admitted that she was rather an attractive girl. Anna begged Giustino to take her out ski-ing just once. But Giustino said that she had neither the skis nor the costume, she couldn't possibly go ski-ing in a skirt and ordinary shoes, besides she didn't know how to ski and he certainly had no intention of sticking behind her all the time. Anna said that Giuma would teach her. But Giustino shrugged his shoulders and laughed, just imagine the great Giuma bothering himself about her on the ski slopes, the great Giuma had the girl with the white velvet trousers. In the end Giuma himself also spoke to her about this girl, she was called Fiammetta, she was not stupid and she ski-ed well. Anna asked him if he was in love with this girl. Giuma said no, he had never been in love, if by any chance he fell in love perhaps he might fall in love with this girl but for the moment he was not in love, he liked her just to go ski-ing with. Anna on the other hand he liked for talking to and also for kissing. For kissing there was no need to be in love, it can easily happen that a boy and a girl when they are great friends can give each other a few kisses now and then. Anna asked him whether he had kissed the girl

Fiammetta. He said no, he hadn't kissed her, at least not for the moment. All of a sudden Anna started to cry, they were sitting in the Paris café and outside the windows you could see the river going away into the mist, between telegraph-poles and banks patched with snow. It seemed to Anna that there was nothing in the world so horrible as that river, those telegraph-poles and that café, and that snow, those patches of snow, suddenly she was seized with longing for a scorching summer that would make all traces of snow vanish from the whole earth. Giuma frowned at her tears, he ran quickly over to the cash-desk to pay and told her to come away, she couldn't possibly start sobbing there in the café. They walked along together in the evening light, Giuma kept his hands in his pockets and his face hidden in his coat-collar, she was sobbing and giving little sudden starts, and nibbling her thumbs inside her gloves. All of a sudden, with a weary, resolute air, he drew her behind the bushes on the river bank, they kissed and he begged her not to get such silly ideas into her head, he showed her that she had made a hole in her gloves by her nibbling. They had to make their way through clumps of bushes to get back to the bridge, he pulled off the brambles that had got entangled in her coat as he had done before with the chestnut-shells, there were no chestnuts now, the time of the chestnuts was over. Their shoes were muddy and they cleaned them with a newspaper before they came back into the town.

Giuma told her that Mammina was feeling ill because Franz and Amalia were on the point of arriving. He knew how matters stood, Mammina had been very much in love with Franz before Franz and Amalia got married, and now she did not know what attitude to take on finding herself face to face with him again. So she lay in bed in the dark and would not allow anyone into her room, she would not allow anyone to see her while she was thinking of what attitude she should take. He, Giuma, was not a puritan and it did not matter to him if his mother had had a love affair with Franz, poor Mammina, so much the better if she had

had some days of happiness, so much the better for men
and women if they could enjoy themselves together.   Emanuele, on the other hand, was a puritan and would have
found it scandalous to think of Mammina having a love
affair with Franz, perhaps it had occurred to him but he had
buried the thought in his mind, he was good at burying in
his mind all thoughts that he did not like, burying them so
deeply that he forgot they had ever existed.   After Papa's
death Franz for a moment had been undecided whether to
marry Amalia or Mammina, but he had decided on Amalia
because Mammina had only the usufruct whereas Amalia
had the shares.   And so poor Mammina had been left with
nothing but her bridge.

Later, Mammina put on a resolute, imperious expression
as she waited at the garden gate with her fox fur thrown
over her shoulders and her lorgnette ; Emanuele had gone
in the car to the station, Giuma had stayed with Mammina
by the gate.   The car came back and they saw Amalia and
Franz get out, Mammina kissed Amalia on the brow, to
Franz she put out a long, limp hand without turning her
head.

Emanuele went across to tell Ippolito how transformed
Amalia was since her marriage, she had taken to giving
orders and making decisions for everyone, for herself and
Franz she wanted the red room, not the green room which
Mammina had had prepared for them, which was so far
from the bathroom and so sunless.   And Franz was to start
work at once at the soap factory.   And poor Franz was subdued and sad, he whispered to Emanuele that he would have
preferred the green room because at least you couldn't see
the soap factory from its windows, it distressed him deeply to
think of the soap factory and he would have preferred not to
go and work there at once, he felt rather shaken in health,
he had heard nothing at all about his parents and every night
he had horrible dreams, he woke up all panting and sweating
and Amalia gave him camphor injections, the course she had
taken as a student-nurse had left her with a mania for giving

injections, Franz's behind was as full of holes as a nutmeg-
grater.   It was by no means certain that the camphor was
good for him and he would have liked to consult a doctor,
but Amalia maintained that camphor was what he needed.
He realized that he had to work at the soap factory, he realized that he had to work and could not always remain in
idleness, his life had been full of errors, it had been a long
chain of idle hours and acts of cowardice and lies, he told
Emanuele that some day perhaps he would tell him the
whole story of his life.   He had made up his mind to turn
over a new leaf but not at present, at present everything
frightened him, he could not help thinking all the time about
the Germans and the concentration camps and at night he
saw his parents in those ditches in which they burned the
dead.   But it was Amalia who gave orders and a few days
after their arrival Franz was working in the soap factory,
sitting at a desk with an unhappy expression, and in the evening Franz and Emanuele came home together, and now it
was Franz who complained about the managing director,
and Emanuele contradicted him, saying the managing director was really a fine fellow.   Emanuele was sorry for Franz
and at the same time irritated with him, and was always
wanting to contradict him, and his voice was always a little
harsh when he spoke to him.

12

    Emanuele came to wake Ippolito one morning at seven
o'clock.   The Germans had landed in Norway.   He had
heard this news on the radio, there were not many details.
It was the beginning of April and there had been long days
of rain, but now the sun was shining on the mud in the
town ; Anna thought that the snow up in the mountains
would certainly have melted and now Giuma would stay

with her on Sundays, and the Germans had landed in Norway and they would be thrown back into the sea and scattered, the long winter with the cold war was over.   Ippolito
went to his office but Emanuele stayed with them, limping
round after Signora Maria as she swept ; that morning he
had no desire to go to the factory and at his own home there
were Mammina and Amalia who were quarrelling over the
red room and the green room.

They spent a few happy days hearing of all the German
ships that were going to the bottom.   By now the German
navy was lying at the bottom of the sea, and the landing in
Norway had not been a success for Germany, in a short time
Norway would shake off the Germans and throw them to the
bottom of the sea where the cruisers and other ships already
were, all that was needed was just a little shake, Norway was
in no hurry.   For Germany there was no longer any hope
of winning, now that her navy was at the bottom of the sea.
Emanuele had brought over the radio from his own house
and put it in the sitting-room, and again Emanuele and
Ippolito and Danilo were together in the sitting-room,
gathered close round the radio to pick up the thin thread of
a voice from the forbidden stations.   Ippolito again had the
anxious, feverish look of the time when they were traffick-
ing in pamphlets and newspapers, perhaps he was thinking
of the revolution, perhaps he was thinking that as soon as
the Germans were beaten it would at once be possible to
start the revolution in Italy.   Danilo said they must not be
too optimistic, it was quite possible that the affair would go
on for a long time yet, he was not too pleased about the
landing in Norway.   But certainly it was no joke for Germany
that her entire fleet should have perished like this, at a single
stroke.

Giuma said to Anna that he didn't care in the least about
Norway, or about Germany and the fleet.   Only he had
been annoyed when Emanuele took away the radio, he had
taken it away as though it had been his own property, the
other radio was in Mammina's bedroom and now it was no

longer possible to hear a bit of music if Mammina happened to be resting. Anna said that when he wanted to listen to music he could come over to the sitting-room in their house. But Giuma said he had no wish to find himself in the company of " those people ". " Those people " were Emanuele, Ippolito and Danilo. He was irritated by the air of mystery they assumed when they were all three together, an air of mystery and of triumph, as though it were they who had sunk the fleet. Sometimes Anna and Giuma met Danilo and his wife in the street, Danilo used to go and fetch his wife from the gate of the foundry and they went for a little walk. Giuma would greet them with a little bow and go very red in the face, perhaps he was recalling the time Danilo had thrown his hat and coat at him and turned him out of the house. And as soon as Danilo had turned the corner Giuma would burst out laughing, Danilo walked through the town like a great victorious general, like Nelson after he had won the Battle of Trafalgar. Giuma had left school because the marks he was getting were altogether too bad, he told Anna he had been getting these bad marks on purpose, so that Mammina should make up her mind to let him leave school. At last Mammina did make up her mind, Amalia however did not agree, Amalia and Mammina quarrelled over Giuma's education and over a thousand other things and there was never a moment's peace in the house. But Franz left them to quarrel and roamed about the house, he too with the air of a great victorious general, he too like Nelson, Giuma told Anna that those four German ships that had been sunk had gone to Franz's head too. Giuma was very pleased not to be going to school any more and in the mornings he took his books into the garden and did his work there, he worked very well on his own like that, at school they made you waste such a heap of time. Giuma no longer went ski-ing now but still he was not free on Sundays, he had to go with Mammina to visit her friends or he went to play tennis, Anna saw him from the window going out with his racquet and his white trousers. Anna asked him whether the girl Fiammetta played tennis with him. Giuma said yes, sometimes ; whenever they talked about the girl Fiammetta he used to blush and speak in a thin little voice. And so Anna had nothing to do on Sundays, after her homework she would go into the sitting-room and sit with the others beside the radio, the Germans had started advancing in Holland and Belgium. There was nothing strange about that because in the other war they had advanced at the beginning too, then they had gone back again, but in the meantime it was painful to hear that they were advancing. Holland and Belgium fell in a few days, the Germans crossed the French frontier, and there was no need to worry *there*, said Emanuele, the Maginot Line was impenetrable. Danilo said that it was indeed impenetrable but they were in the act of penetrating it.

Giuma told Anna how Franz had all of a sudden lost his Nelson airs, and in the evening waited for Emanuele's return in order to know whether the Germans had come to a halt, to know also what Danilo had said, for he too had come to believe in Danilo as a kind of prophet. Giuma said he was pleased if the Germans were advancing a little, so that he might enjoy the faces of Emanuele and the others, Emanuele came home in the evenings more and more mortified and from his way of going upstairs you could tell that the Germans had advanced still further. Only he was annoyed that Franz refused flatly to play tennis nowadays. Anna said there was always the girl Fiammetta for him to play with. But Giuma said that the girl Fiammetta was not free always, he said it in a thin little voice. Anna asked him why he did not teach *her* to play tennis, but Giuma said he hadn't the patience to teach anyone anything. But he had taught her to play ping-pong, Anna said. But they were children then, said Giuma, as a child he had done a great many things that he had left off doing later, for instance he had played ping-pong which was a very boring game, he remembered how he had tormented his father to play ping-pong with him, his father did not know how to play and he wanted to teach him. But now he wouldn't have the patience to teach any-one anything. It was hot and when they went to the Paris café they sat outside under the big pergola, at the iron tables, and ate ice cream in big wine-glasses. It was hot and the countryside was all green and humming, with a smell of damp, tender grass amongst loosened earth, with high, white, swelling clouds in the sky. Giuma said that now it was no longer like being in Paris at that café, now that they were sitting outside under the big pergola, with the peasants' carts and the flocks of sheep passing close by, and the town in the distance no longer hidden in mist and darkness, the town with the iron roofs of the soap factory. Giuma sat facing her and sometimes his face was neither proud nor tender, it was perhaps as it was when he was alone in his room, the lips soft and surly and the eyes sleepy and wandering. He seemed suddenly to wake up when they brought the ice cream, he ate his ice greedily as if it was for that alone that he had come to the café, he licked his spoon greedily, sticking out his red wolf-like tongue. Anna felt that something had got lost between them, something that had been there when they were eating chestnuts in the public gardens, it was perhaps still there in the first days at the Paris café, but since then little by little it had got lost, goodness knows why or how. They went away and he drew her down amongst the bushes on the river bank, and they lay a long time kissing in the grass, and he kissed her harder and harder, he held her tighter and tighter and kissed her harder. At home she told herself that nothing had got lost, because Giuma kissed her harder and harder. And so one day they started making love, they lay clinging together in the grass and the world round them was green and humming between the warm puffs of air from the grass and the high clouds in the sky, and Giuma's expression was one of absorption and fury and secrecy, and his eyelids were tight closed over his eyes and his breathing was quick. At home she sat down bewildered at the little table in her room, and with a stab of pain at her heart saw again that expression on Giuma's face, that expression that seemed as it were plunged in a furious, secret sleep, that expression that had lost all trace both of words and of thoughts for her. And afterwards Giuma had stayed a long time lying beside her in the grass, and from time to time he gave her a look and winked his eye at her, but without either gaiety or slyness, the faint wink appeared and disappeared like a shadow on the face that was so remote from her. They had walked home in silence. Anna had sat down at the table in her room and had taken up her pen to do her homework, but she could not manage to write, her hands were trembling violently. She would have liked someone to come and scold her for not doing her homework, to come and tell her never to go again with Giuma amongst the bushes on the river bank. But no one came to say anything to her, no one even came to see if she had come home, Ippolito was thinking of nothing but the Germans advancing in France, Signora Maria spent her days at Concettina's making clothes for the baby that was to be born, Giustino was working for his exams with the tall, thin girl. She was alone, she was alone and no one said anything to her, she was alone in her room with her grass-stained, crumpled dress and her violently trembling hands. She was alone with Giuma's face that gave her a stab of pain at her heart, and every day she would be going back with Giuma amongst the bushes on the river bank, every day she would see again that face with the rumpled forelock and the tightly closed eyelids, that face that had lost all trace both of words and of thoughts for her.

Signora Maria related what she had heard in the shops and from the music-master, whom she still met sometimes on the road by the river. The Germans were sprinkling a kind of powder that made people stupid, the Allies were breathing in this powder and were fighting half asleep. And the French generals were accepting gold coins from the Germans to make wrong moves. And the Germans were dressing up as French peasants and fishermen and were cutting the telegraph wires and poisoning the rivers. And

the roads of France were full of refugees, women running
away with their children, and the children got lost and the
Germans caught them and sent them off to their laboratories,
where they used them for scientific experiments like frogs or
rabbits.   Emanuele put his hands over his ears and besought
them for goodness' sake to make her stop talking ; his nerves
were all to pieces and he couldn't control himself, one day
perhaps he would strangle Signora Maria.   Emanuele disliked the Belgians, the French, the English, the Russians who
had allied themselves with the Germans, he limped up and
down the room and kicked at the furniture.   He disliked
Signora Maria who was spreading panic.   In his own home
he also had Franz spreading panic, he wandered about like a
ghost and said that the Germans by advancing in France
would overflow into Italy.   Emanuele told him he was
behaving as though the Germans were already in Italy ; but
perhaps Mussolini was not sticking by the Germans.   Franz
said he was not afraid of Mussolini, he was only afraid of the
Germans, if he found himself face to face with German soldiers he would go mad.   At night he came to Emanuele's
room and sat on his bed, and made him repeat that the
Maginot Line was impenetrable.   But the Germans went on
penetrating it.   One night he woke Emanuele to tell him
that not only was his mother Jewish but his father too, he
was completely Jewish and it was well known what the
Germans were doing to the Jews, if the Germans came down
into Italy the only thing for him to do would be to put a
bullet through his head.   So many times he had been on the
point of going to America but he liked Italy too much, in
Italy he felt he was safe even though for some time now there
had been laws against the Jews, all you did was to pay a
little and the police left you alone.   But now he felt the
Germans altogether too near, there they were in France
behind the mountains and all they had to do was cross the
mountains to get to where he was.

The newspapers were full of these German victories, there
were little maps and the part taken by the Germans was

black, the other part white, and every day the black part
got steadily bigger. That time when the German fleet
went to the bottom seemed very far away, it was less than
two months ago and already it seemed like many years.
They had been happy at that time but now it seemed foolish
to have been so happy, what was the use of a fleet to Germany
anyhow ? German tanks were filling the roads of France,
women and children in flight were scattered and overwhelmed. Emanuele, too, now began telling stories of gold
coins and poison in the rivers, the same things that sent him
into a rage when Signora Maria said them. Sometimes
Emilio and Concettina came to hear from Ippolito what he
thought about this advance. Emilio asked if Italy would
want to go into the war now in order to snatch a little piece
of France for herself, he asked whether war would break out
at once in Italy, Concettina would be having her baby in a
short time now. Ippolito did not answer, he glanced for a
moment at Concettina and at her big, swollen body, her
drawn, frightened face. Signor Sbrancagna also came and
asked Ippolito what he thought. But Ippolito did not look
as if he thought anything, he sat huddled deep in his armchair
and gave him the same little twisted smile that he gave
when people tormented him. Signor Sbrancagna asked him
whether they ought to take Concettina away to have her
baby in some quiet country place, which the war could never
reach. Ippolito shrugged his shoulders slightly, he looked
at the window and the mountains, they all looked at the
mountains and thought of what was going on behind them,
women and children running away, tanks advancing and
taking the whole of France. It was Danilo who answered
Signor Sbrancagna, saying that in a short time there would
not be a single quiet place on earth in which to have babies,
unless you went to Madagascar. Probably the Germans
did not calculate on getting to Madagascar. Then Signora
Maria cried that this was not a moment for joking, it had
got to be decided where Concettina could go to have her
baby, Ippolito must decide, he was the head of the family

and he was responsible for Concettina and for the others. Ippolito sat there a little longer with the twisted smile on his face, and then suddenly he got up and they saw him go out of the gate and walk away with the dog on a lead, a cigarette between his lips and his small head bent sideways on to his shoulder.

13

Mammina decided all of a sudden that she would take a villa on Lake Maggiore, she was sure that they would be quiet there, whatever Emanuele might say about the possibility of being quiet only perhaps in Madagascar. Mammina this time refused to be frightened, she wrote letters and looked at photographs of villas, and every now and then she went down into the cellar to see if everything there was in order in case war broke out before their departure ; but she was calm and she said that in any case even if war broke out in Italy it would be a matter only of a few days, the Germans were so strong and they would take the whole of Europe in no time. She tapped here and there on the cellar walls to see if they were still firm, and she looked at the cases of soap she had had transported down there, the soap they were putting out now was horrible stuff, big, sticky, greenish cubes that melted into pulp in the water. Mammina had cases and cases of good soap in the cellar, and sacks of sugar and huge flasks of oil, and she walked all round the cellar and considered what ought to be taken to Lake Maggiore and what ought to be left there for when they came back. She was sure it would be a *blitzkrieg* and that she would spend next winter at Mentone, she was anxious to see what had happened to the villa at Mentone, if soldiers or refugees had slept there it would have to be disinfected. And now she was anxious to get to Lake Maggiore and she went off by herself to see villas, it was impossible to understand from photographs. Emanuele took her to the station, Mammina kept on saying she did not know how they could get on without her, it was she who took the initiative and made decisions for everybody. Franz wandered round like a ghost, spreading panic, Amalia thought of nothing except sticking her nose into the kitchen and giving senseless orders, Emanuele spent his days with his friends at the house opposite. Emanuele told her that Franz had good reasons for being frightened, he was a Jew and it was well known what the Germans were doing to the Jews. Mammina said that Franz always told so many lies, she knew him very well, probably he hadn't a single drop of Jewish blood in him and he had invented it in order to make people sorry for him and to make himself interesting. In any case she was sure that the Germans, as soon as the war was won, would be so pleased that they would no longer think of behaving tiresomely to anybody.

Anna and Giuma were now unable to go to the Paris café, because it was being done up and under the pergola there was nothing but ladders, builders and heaps of lime. Amongst the bushes on the river bank they heard the cries and hammerings of the builders, and Giuma was surprised that they should have chosen that particular summer for doing up the little Paris café, just that particular summer when war was expected in Italy at any moment. In any case it would be a war lasting only a few days, said Giuma and he repeated Mammina's words, the Germans would take the whole of Europe in no time. In the meantime for France it was all over, Emanuele kept on saying that the Germans would stop at the gates of Paris but Giuma did not believe it, by now they had broken through and how very little had been needed to make France crumble, by now nothing was left of France but a handful of crumbs to throw to the birds. Giuma remembered Paris, he had been there once with Mammina, and he certainly did not like to think that it would become a German province. He did not like it but it was not a disaster, it was not worth breaking your heart over it, Emanuele and the others were breaking their hearts because they had imagined all kinds of things, they had imagined themselves starting the revolution and becoming deputies or ministers, so filled with presumption were they. Giuma talked for a little before making love, but afterwards he was silent, lying beside her in the grass, the sounds of hammering and the voices and cries of the builders at work on the Paris café echoed loudly over the countryside. Twilight came and the Paris café was left alone, deserted amidst the girders and the heaps of lime, with its little windows blocked up. Anna plunged her head into the sweet-smelling, moist grass, and fear and silence increased within her. She had made love with Giuma and she knew that he did not love her, she knew that he felt rather sad and humiliated after they had made love together, and she would have liked to go back to the times when they used to read Montale's poems and eat chestnuts, and the war was still a cold, distant war, the Germans hadn't won yet. But now the Germans had won and there wouldn't be a revolution after all, there would be a war lasting a few days and then Germans and more Germans, German tanks on the roads of the whole earth. And upon this earth that was full of German tanks the story of herself and Giuma had no importance, it was nothing, it was nothing and it was very sad.

Concettina's baby was born a month before its time, before they could find a quiet country place which the war could never reach. Concettina lay silent in the big double bed, with the window open on to the garden, and Signora Maria sat at the foot of the bed and finished the cross-stitch embroidery on the coverlet for the cradle. Signora Maria had forgotten the war, all she could think of now was of hastily finishing the coverlet for the cradle, with mushrooms and little flowers and little houses worked in cross-stitch. In a big cradle draped in blue taffeta beside Concettina's bed, the baby's long, narrow head, with a feather-brush of black hair on it, stuck out on the pillow, and Signora Maria every now and then would put down her work and start talking to the feather-brush. But Concettina had not forgotten the war, and she looked incredulously at the cradle and the coverlet with the mushrooms on it that Signora Maria was embroidering, and she wondered how much longer the baby would sleep in that big cradle of blue taffeta, she already saw herself running away with the baby in her arms amongst tanks and the whistling of sirens, and she hated Signora Maria with her mushrooms and her futile chatter. And from time to time the grandmothers and the old servants would come and gaze at the baby and express astonishment at his black feather-brush and chatter to him. Towards evening Anna also came sometimes, she would sit for a moment beside the cradle and look at the black feather-brush, she would look without chattering, she looked at it as though she had known it for a very long time, and a humiliated, weary expression came on to her face as she looked. Then Concettina was hurt, she did not like this humiliated way of sitting beside the cradle, without either astonishment or chatter. For a moment she wondered what was wrong with Anna, why she had had this weary, humiliated expression on her face for some time. But her thoughts at once broke loose, her thoughts were running away with the baby through the streets amongst tanks and Germans, she had no time now to wonder anything about anybody, she had the baby now and she had to run away with the baby to protect him from the war. She fell into a dark, troubled sleep, she woke up and found herself alone, Signora Maria and Anna had gone away. She remembered how once upon a time she had believed that having a baby was a thing that made you feel very calm, a thing that made you love everybody and made you feel at peace. But instead of that, ever since she had had the baby all she could think of was running away so as to protect him from the war, she no longer loved anybody, she was alone on earth with her baby and she was running away. She had travelled thousands and thousands of miles lying still in that

bed, every time she fell asleep she took the baby in her arms
and ran away.

Anna now knew that she too was going to have a baby.
She went home with Signora Maria, she walked along in
silence with Signora Maria who trailed behind her the bag
with her work in it and went on expressing astonishment
over Concettina's baby and chattering about his black
feather-brush and his little hands. She had forgotten the
war. Anna had not forgotten the war, she hoped that the
war would come and kill her with the secret child inside
her body, she hoped to hear suddenly an enormous crash
which would tear the earth asunder. She walked with her
heart in expectation of this enormous crash. Signora Maria
trotted along swinging her bag and chattering, and from
time to time she stopped chattering and flew into a rage
with Anna because she was walking too fast. Anna believed
that by walking fast she would get rid of the baby. She had
heard it said that it was not difficult to get rid of a baby,
she had heard it said that all you had to do was to walk
fast, to go for very long walks in the heat, walking fast. She
would go with Giuma to swim in the lake, at the place where
Mammina and Franz had so often gone to swim. Perhaps
going for a long swim might help, too. One day she suggested to Giuma that they might go to the lake but Giuma
said it wasn't a lake, it was a tepid, dirty pool that was full
of fat women in the summer. Besides they would have a
heat-stroke if they walked as far as that. Giuma knew
nothing of the child that was inside her. They lay down
and made love in the bushes by the river, and then they
were silent with their faces in the grass and Anna hunted
for words in which to tell him of the child that was inside
her. But she looked at Giuma's face in the grass and
allowed all the words to escape from her. It seemed to her
that she had become grown-up since the moment when she
realized she was to have a baby, and it seemed to her that
he, on the contrary, was still a little boy, with his heat-
flushed face and his rumpled hair. He started to complain

of how Emanuele would never let him touch the car, he would begin shrieking every time he saw him go near the garage.   If they had had the car perhaps they might have been able to go and swim in the lake, it was a tepid, dirty pool but perhaps it wouldn't have been so bad to take a dive into it once in a way.   But they couldn't go there on foot.   He himself, in any case, would be leaving in a short time, Mammina had arranged for the villa up above Stresa and in a short time would be coming back to fetch him, she had also arranged for a tutor to give him lessons, in October he was to take his final exams.

14

    Emanuele did not come so often now to see Ippolito, he would appear now and then towards evening and say he had spent the day sleeping, whenever he had serious troubles he comforted himself by sleeping.   Danilo also would appear and they would turn on the radio for a moment but turn it off again at once, they would flee from the sitting-room and start walking idly about the town.   They walked side by side but it was as though they were not walking together, it looked as though they had nothing more to say to one another and were no longer very friendly, they would sit down for a moment in a café but get up again immediately, as soon as the radio in the café started shouting.   Danilo would leave them to go and study book-keeping, he said he wanted to take his accountant's diploma, seeing that now there was nothing better to do.   Emanuele and Ippolito strolled along the river for a little and sat down on a bench in the public gardens, Emanuele teased the dog, he pretended to throw a stone so that the dog should make great efforts to hunt for it, Ippolito told him to leave his dog alone.   Emanuele said they had fallen very low, sitting there like a couple of old men on a seat in the public gardens. When they came home they saw Anna and Giuma saying good-bye at the gate, Emanuele said they were seeing altogether too much of each other, those two, they were always, always together, he told Ippolito that he ought to keep a better watch over his sister, after all Ippolito was the head of the household and was responsible for everybody. Ippolito did not answer, he smiled his usual twisted smile, and then Emanuele tried to imitate the smile, he went off with his face all screwed up. Ippolito shouted to him to come over and see them after supper, but Emanuele made signs of refusal from a distance, he now went to bed immediately after supper and slept like a log till eleven o'clock next morning, he had discovered that sleep is the one joy of man. Ippolito, on the other hand, could not sleep, Anna had the room next to his and heard him walking and fidgeting about the room all night long, opening and closing the shutters, opening and closing the drawers of the writing-table. Anna lay still in her bed and she too did not sleep, she had an obscure feeling of fear at what Ippolito might be doing in his room, at all his walking about and fidgeting. For a moment she felt sorry for Ippolito, she thought of his expression in the morning after these sleepless nights, she thought of how he looked in the morning drinking his coffee in the kitchen, sitting at the table slowly stroking his thin, stubbly cheeks, it was very rarely that he shaved since the Germans had been in France. Then he would get up suddenly and go off to his office, carrying out into the morning air his small head with its streaky fair hair and his usual twisted smile. She was sorry for him but her pity was mingled with rage, she detested that twisted smile and that tall, disgusted-looking body, what sort of ideas had he got into his head to have acquired that disgusted, goggle-eyed look, had he really imagined that he was going to start a revolution with Emanuele and Danilo, in Italy, in Germany, goodness knows what kind of great revolution they had imagined they were going to start. She too had thought

about the revolution but now she knew quite well how
stupid it had been to think about it, she had thought about
the revolution and had imagined herself escaping with
Giuma over the rooftops, those thoughts now seemed to her
very distant indeed, lost in a remote and ancient time, only
a few months had passed and they seemed like so many
years. Now she had the baby to get rid of. She did not
think about it all the time. She did the things she had
always done, she went to school and sat on the ink-stained,
penknife-scratched bench beside the girl who had been her
dearest friend, but now they hardly spoke to each other.
She came home again and threw her satchel down on the
round table in the anteroom, she went up to her bedroom
and looked at herself in the looking-glass, she was the plump
girl she had always been, and suddenly she would remember
the baby, with a little plunge into darkness she would
remember the baby. These were the last days of term and
she had much work to do. Sometimes when she was sitting
working at her little table she would suddenly start thinking
about a real baby, how it would come into the world and
how it would play in the garden of the house opposite, with
Mammina grown all at once very old and kind. But she
went to the window and looked at the ivy-covered walls of
the house opposite, and heard the furious voices of Emanuele
and Giuma quarrelling. And the real baby disappeared
with a plunge into the darkness, and nothing but fear and
silence was left inside her, the baby was again nothing but
darkness inside her. With her handkerchief she wiped her
sweating, trembling hands, and hunted for words with which
to ask someone what she must do. She went to Signora
Maria's room. Signora Maria was packing her suitcase,
she was leaving for Le Visciole with Concettina and her
baby, Anna and Giustino and Ippolito were to join them
there in ten days' time. Signora Maria was happy, she was
always happy when she had a suitcase to pack, and now she
was happy at going there with Concettina's baby, she grew
tender at the thought of the baby and chattered about his

black feather-brush as she put her shoes in their little cloth
bags into her suitcase.   Anna saw that she would never be
able to say anything to Signora Maria, she had thought of it
for a moment but how foolish it had been to think of it, she
stayed there for a little looking at Signora Maria as she went
backwards and forwards in her old lilac dressing-gown,
completely absorbed in her little cloth bags.   Anna wandered vaguely about the house and waited for the war to
come and tear the town and the house asunder with a great
crash.

   She heard voices in the garden opposite and went over to
the window, she saw that Mammina had come back,
Emanuele was running limping to meet her and Mammina
was much irritated because no one had come to fetch her
from the station, she had had to come home from the station
in a cab.   She refused to embrace Emanuele, she was much
irritated, she had suffered from the heat on her journey and
said she was sick of always having to think of everything.
And now the trunks had to be packed and they had to go
away again, she swore she would not touch the trunks, she
would not pack even so much as a handkerchief.   The
trunks must be taken charge of by Amalia.   Anna listened,
hiding behind the half-closed shutters, and it seemed to her
that Mammina was irritated not with Emanuele or Amalia
but with her.   She stood there behind the shutters and
thought that she must speak to Giuma before he went away,
they must think together at once what to do to stop the
baby.   It seemed to her that she could endure that baby
inside her no longer, not even for a moment.   She left the
window and sat in the half-darkness, and suddenly she began
to imagine that Giuma would decide not to go away and
that he would stay and marry her.   In a determined, quiet
voice Giuma was explaining to her that nothing must be
done to stop a baby.   So she answered him that they
couldn't get married and have a baby together, he had the
girl Fiammetta to get married to, and she was rich and
Mammina would be pleased.   But he said he didn't care in

the least about Mammina and the girl Fiammetta. At that moment Emanuele came to take away the radio, Mammina wanted to get it packed at once and sent to the villa up above Stresa which she had taken. They were leaving in two or three days, just as soon as the packing was done. Emanuele called Giustino to help him carry the radio downstairs, they must be quick about it, Mammina was in a fierce mood. At the bottom of the stairs he sat down for a moment to wipe the sweat from his face, he said he himself was leaving with the others, Mammina was frightened at night in that isolated villa, with Franz having nightmares and waking up in the night shouting. So he was going, he had no wish to go but he was going, because he did not want any discussions with Mammina and because in any case one place or another was all the same to him, since he spent his days sleeping and no longer thought about anything. And he said that truly he was quite pleased to go and not to see Ippolito's face any more, that death-like face that he had assumed ever since the Germans had begun to take France.

Anna saw Giuma next morning in front of the school, the lists of examination results were hung up outside, and he told her that as he was passing he had stopped to look at his fellow-pupils' marks, beside his own name there was nothing but a small red cross because he had left the school. He had the same jeering, arrogant expression on his face that he had always worn amongst his schoolfellows. Giustino had got his remove, but Anna had to take her mathematical exam again in October. Giustino was there with the tall, thin girl who was crying, she had got her remove but not with the marks she had hoped for. Giustino was comforting her. To Anna on the other hand he said that it served her right that she had to take the exam in October, she had been terribly slack recently, every time he came into her room he found her staring into vacancy. It served her right that she had to take the exam in October, it was always he, Giustino, who had to do these October exams, and now for once in a while he would be free for the whole summer. Anna and

Giuma went off together. Giuma was laughing at the tall, thin girl, God what an idiot she was to cry like that over a few marks. Anna started crying too. Giuma told her to stop crying at once, he couldn't bear girls who cried about things to do with school, after all an exam in October wasn't a world catastrophe. They sat down on a seat in the public gardens, Anna went on crying, and then he said he must go home quickly to do his packing, Amalia had told him he must do all his packing himself. Besides, it was no fun being with a girl who was crying. He asked her if she was crying about the exam or about his going away. Anna said, " I'm going to have a baby." Giuma turned towards her in a flash ; his forelock fluttered and fell back in a shower over his eyes. They sat dumbly looking at each other, and Giuma's face became gradually covered with a hot redness. Anna understood then that what had happened was a terrible thing for them, never when she had thought about it alone had she felt so great a horror inside her. The garden was blazing and deserted in the midday sun, the seats abandoned and scorching and the fountain dry, with the big stone fish on top of it opening its empty mouth to the sky. It seemed they would never be able to rise from the seat, they sat there leaning against the back and she was slowly weeping, he had lit a cigarette and was smoking it as it were in little sips, combing his forelock with trembling fingers. She asked if they could not tell Emanuele about it, so that he might explain what ought to be done. Then Giuma was seized with rage, what nonsense she was talking, never must she dare to let drop even one word either to Emanuele or to anyone else, she had thought of telling Emanuele, had she, Emanuele indeed! She asked if going for long walks might perhaps get rid of it. Giuma shook his head, he didn't believe in long walks, he had been told that sometimes quinine served the purpose, you could go on taking it until you heard a noise like thunder in your ears. But as soon as there was that noise like thunder you had to stop at once. She said, " Why can't we get married ? "—

and he shrugged one shoulder and said, " Yes, I know "
Then suddenly she wondered what it was that made it impossible for them to marry, what obscure reasons forbade it,
in reality it would be so simple, she would live in the house
opposite, from its windows she would see her own house with
the dried-up wistaria on the terrace, Signora Maria shaking
out her duster, Giustino in bathing-drawers doing exercises
with a dumb-bell, the long wires with Signora Maria's black
underclothes hanging on them. But it seemed to her that
she would not much like living in the house opposite. She
said, " We can't get married because we don't love each
other so very much. That's why——". Giuma said, "It's
not a question of very much or not very much. We can't
get married, we're too young, and besides there'll be
the war, too." She had almost forgotten the war. She
said, " I should like the war to come quickly, and to be
killed."

They went home in silence. At the gate they decided to
meet that afternoon, he would bring her the quinine, Mammina had plenty of it in her medicine cupboard. Now that
Signora Maria had gone, she had to get lunch ready. But
when she arrived Giustino and Ippolito had already started
eating, Giustino had cooked the lunch, with tomatoes and
eggs and ham all fried together. At the last moment he
had added half a glass of milk, he was very pleased with this
half glass of milk, he said that great cooks always add half
a glass of milk at a certain point. He was proud of his dish
and ate more of it than anyone. Ippolito went off immediately after lunch, they saw him cross the garden and disappear with the dog on the lead. Anna asked if he now
took the dog to his office. But Giustino said that for some
days Ippolito had not been going to his office, he wandered
goggle-eyed about the town with the dog on the lead, he sat
down on a seat in the public gardens and watched the dog
chasing lizards in the dust. Giustino said he did not like
the look on Ippolito's face, he had never seen him so goggle-
eyed, and at night he never slept and stood at the window

smoking and walked about the room and fumbled in the drawers, goodness knows what he was fumbling for. He, Giustino, had thought for a moment that he had been having trouble with some girl, but Ippolito never went in for girls, if he had had a girl he would have known. It was entirely about France that he was upset, the happenings in France had fallen upon him and crushed him, it had seemed to him the end of everything. And one day he had told Danilo that if the war came to Italy and he was called into it he would not shoot, rather than shoot in a war he would prefer to let himself be killed. And Danilo had said that he, on the other hand, would shoot calmly, so as to keep himself alive for the day of the revolution. But Ippolito had said that there would never be a revolution now, just Germans and Germans all one's life and even after that, Germans and Germans through the centuries, Germans with tanks and aeroplanes, masters of the whole earth. Anna was washing the dishes and Giustino was wiping them. Giustino said that for some time he hadn't liked the look on *her* face either, even before the news of the October exam. He said, " If you've got any troubles you'd better say so at once." She was washing the dishes in the bowl, passing the dishcloth slowly over them. She said to him, " I haven't any troubles. What troubles should I have ? " " I don't know," said Giustino.

Giuma was waiting for her at the bridge. They went amongst the bushes on the river bank, and he at once brought out the quinine, but after two or three tablets she already thought she heard the noise like thunder in her ears. " I'm afraid," she said, " I don't want to die ". " But this morning you *did* want to die," he said, " you've forgotten all about it." He was no longer very much frightened, he said that perhaps she had dreamed about the baby. He told her to take some more quinine in the evening before she went to bed, he left her the phial. Then all of a sudden he pulled a thousand-lire note out of his pocket, these were his savings, for some time he had been putting aside money to buy himself a motor-boat. He was giving up the idea of the boat now, if she was really going to have a baby and did not succeed in doing anything with the quinine, she could go to a midwife, a thousand lire would be enough. She asked him where there was a midwife, he said there were midwives everywhere, you saw midwives' door-plates all over the town. They needed a little persuasion but then they would help. Anna took the thousand lire together with the quinine, she was thinking of how she would look for a midwife and would try and persuade her, she was thinking of the words she would say to the midwife to try and persuade her. She felt so strange with the thousand lire clutched in her hand, it was the first time in her life she had held a thousand lire in her hand, and it seemed to her that she had gone right outside her life, far, far away from home, with a thousand lire in her hand, along unknown roads where there were midwives whom she had to try and persuade. She said, " You don't want to marry me because you don't love me. You love that girl Fiammetta and you want to marry her." Giuma said, " What's all this about getting married ? I don't want to marry anybody, the only thing I want is a motor-boat but for the time being I must give up that idea." They remained silent. They did not make love, they would never again make love, thought Anna, never again. Never again would she see the expression on his face when he made love, the furious, secret expression, with the eyelids tight closed over his eyes and the quick, deep breathing. To-morrow he would be gone. And she would go and look at the midwives' door-plates in the town.

They said good-bye at the gate. He gave her his thin, sunburnt hand, there was no need to say great farewells because in a short time he would be back again, if the war came of course it would only last a few days, in October they would be back at school again, he to take his final exams, she that other exam. Amalia appeared at the window and called him and he disappeared into the house.

Anna went up to her room, she hid the thousand lire and the quinine in a drawer in the desk.

Next morning she looked out of the window to see them go. They had loaded a quantity of stuff on to the car and they were laughing at how heavily loaded it was, you could hear Emanuele's laughter that sounded like the cooing of a pigeon. Inside the car were Mammina and Amalia buried amongst a mass of hat-boxes and suitcases, they had sent Franz on by train with the servants. Emanuele limped round the car which had its hood down and poured water into the bonnet, and he was cursing Giuma all the time for not helping him to load the baggage. Finally Giuma himself came out, with his waterproof over his arm and his tennis-racquets. He saw Anna at the window and gave her a slight wink, he shook his tennis-racquet gently in the air and got into the car. They were on the point of leaving when Ippolito looked out. Emanuele leant out of the car to say good-bye to him, his deep, prolonged laughter could be heard, Ippolito answered with a wave of his hand. Mammina was getting impatient, Emanuele hurriedly closed the window and they started.

And now the house opposite was closed, completely closed in its fur-coat of ivy, with some cherry-stones placed in a line on Giuma's window-sill and dried up by the sun, sometimes he used to look out of his window and eat cherries and place the stones in a line on the window-sill. Anna saw him again looking out and eating cherries, sometimes she had looked out at the same time but they never spoke to each other from the windows, he had the idea that talking to people out of windows was only a thing for servant-girls. Anna tried to take some more quinine, Giustino came in and asked her what she was sucking, she gulped down the tablet hurriedly ; Giustino brought a letter from Signora Maria who said she was expecting them at Le Visciole and sent a long list of the things they must put into their suitcases. Giustino told Anna to hurry up and pack, if she was waiting for Ippolito to do it she would be disappointed. Ippolito had gone out with the dog. He, Giustino, did not in the least want to go to Le Visciole but seeing that they were expecting them they must go, besides, the air at Le Visciole might perhaps do Ippolito some good, and going out shooting and forgetting about France. They waited for Ippolito for lunch but he did not come in. Anna pulled out the suitcases from under the wardrobe. From time to time she remembered the thousand lire and the quinine, she went to look if they were still there, she thought she would go on taking quinine at Le Visciole and at a certain moment the baby would go away. Then she would send back the thousand lire to Giuma in a letter, and he would be able to buy himself the boat. She was content now to go to Le Visciole, so as not to have to look at the house opposite all closed up like that, with no one ever looking out of the windows.

She and Giustino spent the afternoon packing the suitcases, and suddenly Danilo appeared and asked for Ippolito, and told them that Italy was going into the war on the side of Germany. They went out into the street with Danilo, the radio was shouting from the open windows of the houses, people were standing in groups under the windows and round the cafés. The town was full of that yelling voice, and the people stood silently in groups, and then someone said they must think about the black-out, they must put black curtains in the windows so that not even a thread of light should filter through. Then everyone went in search of black material, Anna and Giustino too, and Danilo who had found his wife. They bought yards and yards of black material. Danilo told his wife that he himself almost certainly would not be sent to the war, he had been a political prisoner and people like him were not sent to the front for fear they should go over to the other side. Probably a person like him would be put in prison again.

Anna and Giustino went home with the big parcel of black material, and in the kitchen they found Ippolito giving the dog its dinner, and they asked him if he had heard about the war. Ippolito said yes. His shoes were dusty and he had a very tired look on his face, he must have been walking all day long, goodness knows where. He was preparing the dog's dinner, mixing together some remains of macaroni and crusts of bread and old cheese-rinds. Giustino asked him whether they would go next day to Le Visciole, Ippolito thought for a moment and said yes. Giustino said they would have to get up very early to catch the train, that local train would be very crowded since everyone was leaving the town, because there was a war on now and everyone was afraid that they would begin bombing immediately. Ippolito said they would not bomb their little town immediately. He spoke a great many words, for days and days they had not heard him speak so many words. He seemed pleased that war had finally come. He looked at the black material they had bought and laughed a little, he asked them whether they wanted to dress up the whole town in mourning. Giustino measured the windows and Anna cut out big black curtains and they got up on the ladder and fixed them to the window-frames with small nails. Then they made themselves something to eat, tomatoes and eggs fried with half a glass of milk, and Ippolito said it was a very good dish. After supper they went on sitting, all three of them, round the table, and Ippolito said that if he went to the war they would have to take care of his dog. He advised them to send it to the dog show, he had heard that there would be a dog show in the town before very long. Giustino remarked that it would be difficult for them to hold a dog show, with the war going on. But Ippolito said that war was not as they imagined it, things were going on as usual except for black curtains at the windows, cinemas were going on, and theatres and dog shows. Except for black curtains at the windows. Giustino asked him if he wasn't going to go and say good-bye to Danilo, Danilo would probably be put straight back into prison to-morrow, because people like Danilo were not wanted at the front. Ippolito said that indeed it would probably be like that. He himself, on the other hand, was not so lucky, in a short time he would be sent to the war and would have to shoot, and there was nothing he disliked so much as shooting, he liked shooting at birds but not at people.   He said he wouldn't go and say good-bye to Danilo, he was too tired, he wanted to go straight to bed, seeing that they had to get up early next morning and go away.   All of a sudden he bent down and kissed Anna, he gave her arm a little squeeze, then he went up to Giustino, gave his usual twisted smile and kissed him too.   They heard his footsteps on the stairs and finally the thump of his shoes on the floor, and the creaking of the bed as he lay down.   They were left looking at each other in bewilderment, he had kissed them, it did not often happen that he kissed anybody.   He had kissed them, therefore he must be thinking that he would be sent at once to the war, and perhaps he thought he would die there at once, he would throw his rifle on the ground refusing to shoot, and then they would kill him at once, perhaps that was what he was thinking.   But Giustino was sure that in war even Ippolito would shoot, everybody shot.   How strange he had been all the evening, said Giustino, and then when he had started talking about the dog show, perhaps he might really have gone off his head, wanting to send that extremely ugly dog to the dog show.

Anna slept soundly all night, because she was tired and because she had partly forgotten the baby.   During the night she heard the dog barking down in the garden, then she heard the gate creak, she wanted to look out of the window but fell asleep at once.   In her sleep the dog was barking, she dreamed that Ippolito was putting on soldier's uniform and going off to the war, Giuma too was going off to the war with a tennis-racquet, the war was in the meadows beyond the river and it was just a wooden enclosure full of dogs.   Giustino came to awaken her, it was six o'clock in the morning and they had to go, but Ippolito was not in his room, there were just his pyjamas on the unmade bed, he had looked for him all over the house and had not found

him. Anna dressed hurriedly and they went out into the
cool morning, in the garden the dog was barking, it was
scratching the ground and worrying at the gate and barking.
Goodness knows where Ippolito had gone, he was really off
his head. They walked along the road by the river, they
went as far as Danilo's house but everyone there appeared
to be asleep, all the shutters were still closed. They waited
for a little outside the door and then Danilo's wife came out,
going to the foundry, no, Ippolito had not been with them.
They walked a little way with Danilo's wife. Danilo's wife
advised them to go to the public gardens, Ippolito had
acquired a habit of going there to sit on a seat and smoke
early in the morning, she saw him when she passed that
way to do her shopping in the market, certainly he had been
behaving very strangely for some time now. They left
Danilo's wife at the main gate of the foundry, that day was
not a market day, she would have liked to go with them but
she was already late. The road by the river was now
beginning to be crowded, the air was becoming dusty and
hot, and thick white smoke was rising from the chimneys of
the soap factory. Their train had left some time ago, they
had heard it going off with its shrill whistle into the country.
As they went into the public gardens they saw, standing
round a seat, a little group of people and two policemen, so
they started running. On the seat was sitting Ippolito,
dead, and beside him on the ground was their father's
revolver.

It was an old revolver with an ivory handle, it was the one
that their father used to keep on his table when Danilo was
standing waiting for Concettina at the gate. There was not
much blood to be seen, just a line along his cheek, and a
little on his shirt-collar and on the worn collar of his coat.
The small head with its streaky fair hair had fallen back on
the back of the seat, and you could see the fine white teeth
between the parted lips, and the thin line of blood on the
stubbly cheek, how rarely he had shaved since France had
been defeated. And his hand hung down white and empty,

the hand that had fired the shot and then dropped their father's revolver on the ground.

A doctor in a white overall looked at the wound, he unbuttoned the shirt over Ippolito's chest and bent down holding a black trumpet to his ear. And then two men took up the long, inert body from the seat and carried it home. All at once the house was full of people, there were Danilo's sisters and Signora Maria's nephew and the music-master, and later Danilo's mother came rushing in, her bosom heaving and her comb stuck crookedly into her cloud of hair. They had laid Ippolito on the bed in his own room, they had lit wax candles round him and had tied up his face tightly with a handkerchief, Anna had had a long search for the handkerchiefs in the suitcases. In the garden the dog went on barking and scratching, it had dug a hole in front of the gate and was sniffing round inside it and barking. Danilo and his wife appeared. But upon Danilo's face there was no surprise, there was hardly even any sadness, it was as though something had happened that he had been expecting for a very long time. He sat on the edge of an armchair in the sitting-room as if he were paying a visit, with the same precise, prudent look as he had worn on the day he came back from prison. His wife was weeping, every now and then she burst into a sob which sounded like a cough. Later Signor Sbrancagna also arrived, and sat down in an armchair with his hands crossed on the handle of his stick, and he asked Danilo whether Ippolito had said anything to him. No, said Danilo, Ippolito had not said anything to him. And Signor Sbrancagna said that he had at once taken a great liking to Ippolito, from the very first day he had seen him, and also he had had a suspicion that he might have some secret trouble, a woman perhaps, who knows? He was such a silent boy, he had no words of friendship or pity for anyone and yet one felt the better just for being with him, as though a great power of friendship and pity proceeded from him. Perhaps few people had understood him. He himself had understood him, he had always sat beside Ippolito with great

pleasure and had told him all about himself.   Perhaps Ippolito had never got over the death of his father.   Then the
music-master started to speak of Ippolito's self-sacrifice in
looking after his father, in giving him his injections and reading aloud to him.   Giustino suddenly asked whether there
was no way of keeping the dog quiet.   But then he remembered that Ippolito had asked him to take care of the dog,
and he went into the kitchen to get its dinner ready.   At the
windows the black curtains were fluttering in the sunshine,
and Signor Sbrancagna asked Danilo what he thought about
the war.

Towards evening Signora Maria arrived, they had said
nothing to Concettina, Emilio had remained at Le Visciole
to break it to Concettina gradually.   When Signora Maria
arrived she looked very, very small, if ever a misfortune
occurred she had a way of contracting herself and growing
smaller, and this was a misfortune that she could not manage
to understand, there she was with her hat all crooked and a
little twitch in her shoulder.   She wanted to know who the
girl was who had refused to marry Ippolito, she asked her
nephew, Signor Sbrancagna and the music-master.   Danilo
she did not ask because she had never been able to endure
Danilo, she was sure it was Danilo's fault that Ippolito was
dead, she did not know how but she was sure it was his fault.
There must surely be a letter somewhere, surely Ippolito
must have left a letter, they had not looked properly.   She
was sure it would not have happened if she had stayed in
town, she would have understood from Ippolito's face that
he was in some sort of trouble, she would have made him
speak and she would have gone to the girl and put things
right.   She told Signor Sbrancagna that Ippolito had so
much confidence in her.   But Giustino said that there was
no girl, no letter, nothing.   Signora Maria wrung her hands
and lamented that she had gone away, something in her
heart had told her she ought not to go, why, oh why had she
not listened.   She knelt down and prayed at the foot of
Ippolito's bed, she would have liked Anna and Giustino to

kneel down too and pray with her, she considered it had been a mistake on the part of their father not to allow his children to kneel down and pray sometimes. Their father said one should not go down on one's knees in front of anyone, not even in front of God, and one did not know whether God existed or did not exist but if He did exist He liked to see people standing and with their heads held high. Signora Maria thought now that the old man had said many foolish things, perhaps Ippolito would not be dead if as a child he had been taught to pray.

15

All the portraits of Ippolito were taken out and framed and arranged on the piano in the sitting-room. The house was searched for yet more portraits, was it possible that there could be so few, why had nobody thought of having more photographs taken of him? Memories, also, were searched for words that he had spoken. But he had spoken so few words. It seemed impossible now that nobody should have asked him for a few more words, it seemed impossible that nobody should have asked him whether perhaps he needed help, that nobody should have followed him when he went out for walks alone, or sat down with him when he was smoking on the seat in the public gardens. After the funeral the drawers of his desk were tidied up, the few letters collected and tied together, there was nothing except a few letters from his father and a few picture post-cards, there were no letters from girls. And Anna and Signora Maria spent a day polishing the floor of his room with wax, tidying up the books and the shelves and cleaning the windows. Anna had forgotten her baby, if she thought of it she said to herself that by now it must certainly be dead, she had sobbed so much and the baby must have been killed by

her sobs.   Then the room was shut up, the mattresses rolled
and covered over.   Two days after the funeral Emanuele
arrived.   He thought he would still be in time for the
funeral, he had driven his car like a man in desperation
but he was too late for the funeral.   He fell into an armchair in the sitting-room and burst into sobs.   Anna and
Giustino stood in front of him in silence, they had already
sobbed a great deal and now they had no more tears left,
they had nothing left inside them but amazement and
silence.   Emanuele could not forgive himself for having
said good-bye so casually to Ippolito on the morning he
went away, just a wave from the window, the figure of
Ippolito at the window would stick in his memory for ever,
and that little wave of his hand.   And he could not forgive
himself for having gone away, he was sure that if he had
stayed Ippolito would not be dead, he would not have
allowed him to think of dying, he would have told him
that it wasn't all over.   He took up the portraits of Ippolito
one by one from the piano, looked at them and began
sobbing again.   He had known about it through a letter
from Danilo, a very short, cold letter, which did not even
mention the day of the funeral.   He asked Giustino to go
and look for Danilo, but Danilo was no longer there, he
had been summoned to the police station and sent away
to an island, and there he would have to stay until the
end of the war.   His mother said there was always typhus
on that island, and perhaps typhus was worse than war.
His wife had not been able to follow him, she could not
lose her job at the foundry.   For a short time people in
the town had talked of Ippolito, in whispers and in secret
because he was a suicide, the Fascists did not like suicides
mentioned, in the newspaper the news had been given that
a young man had been killed in the public gardens while
cleaning his revolver.   But soon everyone had forgotten
Ippolito and started thinking about the war again.   Italian
soldiers had begun firing up in the mountains, the Germans
were entering Paris.   Emanuele said he himself did not

feel it was all over. He asked Signora Maria whether she would let him sleep in the sitting-room, he did not want to sleep all alone in his own house. He limped up and down the sitting-room till late talking of Ippolito, never again would he have a friend like Ippolito, never again. No one had known him, he alone could say that he had known him well. And if he had stayed in town he would not have let him die, he would have followed him everywhere and would have snatched the revolver out of his hands, he would have explained to him that the Germans might take Paris and London too, into the bargain, and yet it would not be all over. He went away again next day. He put another case of soap into the car, Mammina always had a horror of being left without soap, of having to wash with those greenish cubes that were being turned out now. Anna and Giustino helped him to load the case on to the car, and stood on the pavement waving their hands until the car disappeared.

They left for Le Visciole, Signora Maria said that Concettina could not stay there all by herself, with that baby that frightened her because it was the first baby she had ever seen, and with her grief for Ippolito and her fear that her husband would be called to the war. In the train everyone was talking of the bombing of Turin, some of them had been there at the time, the sirens had sounded when the aeroplanes were already streaming over the town. There were fourteen dead, said the newspapers, but goodness knows how many there had really been, you had to multiply what the papers said by ten if it was bad, muttered someone, divide it by ten if it was good. It was an old pedlar who spoke, with a drawer full of laces and buttons tied round his neck, he was a little drunk and kept on talking about multiplying and dividing, he counted on his fingers and got all muddled up. He also told a story of a young man who had shot himself through the head in the public gardens, because he did not want to go to the war. His neighbours made him keep quiet. The pedlar had seen

Giustino looking at him, and tried to insist on selling him a few pairs of shoe-laces.

Concettina was sitting under the pergola suckling her baby. When she saw them arriving she immediately started crying, but the *contadino's* wife ran over to tell her that she must not cry when she was suckling the baby or else her milk would be salted with tears. The *contadino's* wife was now also weeping for Ippolito, and so was the *contadino*, and they remembered how they had given him rides on the cart when he was a little boy. But the dog was running after the hens and the *contadino's* wife said that hell had begun again for her with that dog.

Emilio came back late in the afternoon and went off early in the morning : on Sundays he stayed all day. He was no longer so calm and fresh as he had once been, he no longer seemed so like a grazing calf. He had taken to thinking all the time about Ippolito, he too was always searching his memory for words that Ippolito had spoken to him. When he went through the public gardens he seemed to see Ippolito sitting dead on the seat. He said that he, Emilio, had never suffered much, even when he wanted to marry Concettina and she refused he did not suffer very badly, he had an obscure feeling that they would get married some day. But now it had occurred to him that perhaps there were a great many things that had to be suffered, and that the reason he himself did not suffer was merely because he was incapable of thinking about these things, when he wanted to start thinking about something very important or very remote his breath failed him and he became as it were giddy, and it had occurred to him that perhaps this was not at all a good thing. Ippolito had thought about everything, he had died thinking about everything. But he himself, if he was called to the war and if it happened that he was killed, would be dying so very poor in thoughts, so very poor in sorrow, he would be dying without having thought about all there was to think about. He did not feel at all ready to die, if God

existed what would he be bringing to this God, God would
ask him what he was bringing and he would not know
what to answer, he had worked a little in industry with
his father, he knew a little about monosulphides and
hydrates, he had got his hands a bit stained with acids, he
had put on a black shirt and had marched in processions.
Concettina started crying, she asked why he too had to
die, Ippolito was dead already, why did she have to lose
everyone she had ?   And then Emilio told her for goodness'
sake not to cry, perhaps the *contadino's* wife was right,
perhaps if she cried her milk would be spoiled in some
way or other.   Together they went to look at the baby.
He had lost his black feather-brush, his head was now all
covered with a fine down which glistened in the sun.   The
baby started yelling and immediately Concettina was
frightened, perhaps her milk was not so very good now, she
touched her breast to feel if there was still milk there.
Concettina said how silly she had been as a girl, she had
tortured herself so much on account of her breast, she had
been distressed at having so little of it, now all she wanted
to know was whether what breast she had was suitable for
suckling the baby.   Emilio left her alone and went off to
roam about the countryside like Ippolito, with Concettina
it was now quite impossible to hold a sensible conversation,
all she could talk about now was milk and babies.   He
wandered for a long time among the vineyards and the
oak-trees, in the places where he knew Ippolito had been
in the habit of walking with the dog ; and whenever he
knocked his foot against a stone he wondered whether
Ippolito had also knocked against it, with those feet that
now were dead ; and wherever he rested his eyes on the
countryside he reflected that Ippolito too had looked at
that spot, and he thought how strange it was that the eyes
of men should pass across things without leaving any trace,
thousands and thousands of dead men's eyes had rested
upon that green and humming countryside.

Anna did not roam about the countryside, she lay on

the bed in her room with the curtains drawn, she did not want to look at the countryside, she did not want to look at the brow of the hill where once upon a time Ippolito could be seen passing and repassing with his gun and his dog. The days flowed past, and she knew now that her baby was still there, she had finished all the quinine, she kept the thousand lire in an envelope pinned to her under-clothes, she thought that one day she would go into the town in the little train and look for a midwife, she would tell Signora Maria that she had left one of her mathematical books behind. She pictured the midwife as looking rather like Danilo's mother. Gradually she came to picture her as being more and more kind-hearted and motherly, she did not even want the thousand lire and did everything for nothing, so sorry was she for her. But on the other hand there were times when she imagined that she would let this baby come into the world, and that she would go and live with it in some distant town, and work hard to support it, and all of a sudden Giuma would appear by chance in this distant town, he would have left the girl Fiammetta for good because he had realized that she was an impossible kind of person. And Giuma wanted to marry her but now she no longer wanted it, she ran away with the baby to some even more distant town, she worked even harder, she sat at an office desk and handled business affairs, she handled them with vertiginous speed and the manager came and told her that no one could handle affairs so speedily as she. And the Germans were there but all the same it suddenly became possible to start a revolution. She and the manager were running over the roof-tops, placing secret papers in safety. But the baby had to be placed in safety too, the house in which the baby was had caught fire, she and the manager threw themselves into the flames in order to save the baby.

Giustino came and sat down in her room. He looked at her a moment and said she had got very fat, if she went on like that she would become like a barrel. So then she thought that she must go to the midwife as soon as she possibly could, before everyone noticed the baby inside her. Giustino was smoking, smoking had now become disgusting to her, she tried not to breathe so as not to smell the smell. Giustino asked her whether she and Giuma wrote to each other, she said no, Giustino said that of course the great Giuma would not condescend to write to her. Giustino on the other hand was always getting letters, the tall, thin girl wrote to him on stiff blue paper with her initials printed on it, Giustino when he received these stiff blue letters would go and hide in the woods in order to read them. Anna asked him to let her see them, he said no, it would not be behaving correctly towards the tall, thin girl, but he assured her that they were very fine letters, she was a girl who was able to write very well. Answering her was rather an effort, sometimes he got a headache trying to find things to say to her, he waited for rainy days to answer her letters, days when the daughters of the Humbugs did not come to the village square. For some time now coffee was not to be had, and Giustino and the Humbugs' daughters drank substitute coffee in the little bar in the square. The Humbugs' daughters were waiting for zero hour, the hour when the Germans would land in England. Then the war would be over and Germany and Italy would divide the English colonies between them, and from the English colonies would come coffee and other things, the English were the people who ate five meals a day because they had all those colonies. The newspapers could talk of nothing but zero hour. One day there was a rumour that the Germans had already crossed the Channel in barges, ships like small sailing rafts that moved very fast, the sea round the coasts of England was quite black with men. The Humbugs' daughters were very pleased and so were the Humbugs, everyone in the village square was talking about these little rafts, they were very very light and they had reached the coasts of England by night, swift and silent as arrows. But the newspapers said nothing about it, and gradually people

were forced to conclude that it was not true, goodness knows
how the news got started, the Humbugs began playing
bowls again, zero hour had not yet struck.

Giustino told Anna that none of the Humbugs' daughters
meant anything at all to him, nor did the tall, thin girl
mean anything to him, never yet had he fallen in love,
zero hour had not struck for him either. He did not write
love letters to the tall, thin girl, in fact he said to her in
every letter what a beautiful thing friendship between a
man and a woman was, the tall, thin girl asked if such a
thing could exist and he swore it could. He had found a
stanza of a French poem which said : " Si tu savais quel
baume apporte—au cœur la présence d'un cœur—tu t'as-
séyerais sous ma porte—comme une sœur." He had copied
out this stanza for the tall, thin girl, and so she knew that
she had to sit at his door and that was all, nothing more.
With the Humbugs' daughters it was different, he teased
them and flirted with them a little. He was not like
Ippolito, who walked along a street without ever looking
at a woman. Then Anna and Giustino were silent, both
of them thinking of Ippolito, how they had found him that
morning in the public gardens. And then Giustino said he
was going to look for the Humbugs' daughters, they were
so silly that they kept him cheerful.

16

Anna left the house to go to the butcher's shop one day
when it was raining very hard. Signora Maria had told
her that she must have the meat, she had given her the
basket and told her to be as quick as possible, Giustino
had locked himself in his room and had shouted that they
could go to the devil with their meat. Obviously he was
writing to the tall, thin girl. As she walked Anna was

thinking of the tall, thin girl, who had to sit at Giustino's door " *comme une sœur* ". And yet she was lucky, that tall, thin girl, to get a few letters from Giustino, even if he wrote to her only on rainy days. Giuma had never written to *her*, there had arrived simply a visiting card of Mammina's with condolences. All at once it seemed dreadful to Anna that Giuma had never written to her, that he had not even troubled to find out whether the business with the midwife was over. The rain came hissing down over the countryside, the paths were muddy rivulets and the ears of corn were bent down to the ground, whipped by wind and water. She ran floundering through the mud and thought how nobody loved her, they sent her out in the rain for a little bit of meat. She thought how she had neither father nor mother, and how she had found her brother dead on a seat and how she had a baby inside her. But she had not the courage to tell anybody about the baby, nor had she the courage to go and look for a midwife in the town. It seemed to her that she would have courage only for starting a revolution. She ran in despair through the rain. There was a car standing in the village square, a man was just coming out of the tobacconist's and trying to light a cigarette in the rain. He was wearing a long white waterproof which looked like a nightshirt, and a hat which was all out of shape and dripping. For a moment they looked each other in the face and she discovered all of a sudden that that was the only face in the world that she wanted to see. Then she ran across to him with a cry and started to weep on the shoulder of his waterproof. Cenzo Rena pulled out a big coloured handkerchief to wipe her eyes.

He took her to the car and they sat talking for a little shut up inside it under the hissing rain, underneath the big stone young man with the badge and the fez. She told him how it had been with Ippolito, how they had found him that morning in the public gardens. Cenzo Rena knew all about it already, he had had a letter from Giustino.

He sighed and rubbed his hands all over his face while she was telling him.   They went out of the village and the car started floundering slowly through the countryside. Really there was no need to go home at once, he said.   He drove with one arm round her shoulders, she was crying and talking, she had no need to hunt for words, she told him everything little by little and her heart grew light, she wondered suddenly whether they were really such great friends, she and Cenzo Rena, she had not thought about him very often but she had felt a great joy at seeing him, as though she had been waiting for him for a very long time. She told him how Ippolito had been while the Germans were invading France, how he used to walk up and down in his room and fumble in the drawers at night.   But it had not been on account of a girl, it had been simply on account of the Germans and France and the war, and perhaps a great many other things too which nobody knew much about, very distant things, possibly.   She felt that at last there was someone who was listening to her, when she talked to Giustino or Giuma there was always a kind of doubt in her mind as to whether they were really listening. She had no need to hunt for words, little by little she told him about the baby she was going to have, she looked at him and on his face she saw neither fear nor horror, his face was looking back at her attentively and was sorry for her.   She pulled out the envelope that she kept pinned to her underclothes to show him the thousand lire, she said to him that he must come with her one day to look for a midwife in the town, perhaps it might be necessary to hunt round all over the town, it would be so much easier with the car.   Then he asked her whose the baby was.   She said it was Giuma's, she did not find it very easy to talk about Giuma.   This was what Giuma was like, she said, he had blue eyes, he was always pushing back his hair from his forehead and he had small, sharp teeth, a little bit like a wolf's.   He asked her whether they loved each other.   And she said that perhaps they did not love each other so very much, Giuma had the girl Fiammetta as well, who went ski-ing in white velvet trousers. He asked her why they had made love if they did not love each other so very much, he asked her whether she wanted to spend her life making love here and there with anybody. She said she had not yet thought of how she wanted to spend her life. He asked her how old she was and she said she was sixteen. He said that at sixteen a person ought to begin to know how he wanted to spend his life. She said she wanted to spend her life making a revolution. Then he started laughing heartily, he had small teeth but not like a wolf's, he had separate, gay little teeth like so many grains of rice. He told her that there was no question of a revolution now.

She started talking again about the girl Fiammetta, and about Montale and the café which was like Paris. How was it like Paris, asked Cenzo Rena? It *was* like Paris, she said, Giuma thought it was really very like Paris. But later on it stopped being like Paris and they had gone more often amongst the bushes on the river bank. And perhaps they did not love each other so very much, she used to feel humiliated and unhappy when she got home. She had realized she did not love him so very much when Giuma gave her the thousand lire, she had found herself with a thousand lire in her hand and had realized that the affair between the two of them was over, and had also realized that it had been a very stupid, poor sort of affair, with Giuma having to give up the idea of buying himself a boat. Before that, she had perhaps almost believed that they would get married. But instead, he had given her a thousand lire so that she might go by herself and look for a midwife in the town. And she did not know where midwives were to be found, there was Concettina's midwife but she had not the face to go to her. She had not told Concettina, she had not told anyone. He, Cenzo Rena, was the only person she had told, and she didn't know why it should have been him, particularly. She asked him if it meant that they were great friends, because the moment she saw him she had been able to tell him the things she had been keeping from everybody for such a long time. She said she had not even thought about him very often. And Cenzo Rena said he had not thought about *her* very often, either. He had thought more about Giustino, it had happened more often in the case of Giustino than with her. But he was glad she had told him so many things. He told her not to go on thinking so much about the mid-wives and the thousand lire, he would take her into the town next day to get this problem solved. For a long time they went on floundering very slowly about the countryside. From time to time she cried but she felt quiet and serene, as though she were washed clean by her tears, as though the fear and the silence had suddenly been discharged from her heart.

It was late when they reached home, and Signora Maria came forward to meet Cenzo Rena with outstretched hands and half-closed eyes and breathing heavily, so as to join with him in remembrance of Ippolito. But Cenzo Rena's face was amused and happy and high-coloured from the open air, and he waved his dripping hat at Signora Maria and started taking out his suitcases. Signora Maria asked Anna where she had put the meat, Anna clapped her hand to her forehead, she had not remembered the meat. Cenzo Rena said it did not matter, he had plenty of tins of tunny-fish in oil and some beer too, and they could have a splendid dinner, a wedding feast. Signora Maria said afterwards to Concettina that one did not arrive with such a happy face to visit a family which had had a great misfortune. But Cenzo Rena had always been a little mad, and in reality she was pleased that he had come because he would talk to the *contadino* about the harvest, he was mad but he knew how to deal with *contadini*. This time, however, Cenzo Rena did not make himself agreeable either to the dog or to the *contadino*, he wandered round the rooms with an amused expression, his hands in his pockets.

They sat down to table, and Cenzo Rena ate spoonfuls of tunnyfish in oil and talked about the war. Anna, now that she saw him amongst the others, was ashamed of all that she had said to him. Cenzo Rena seemed to have forgotten her. But suddenly he raised his eyes to her face and gazed at her with a steady, calm, profound look. Then he started talking about the war again. He did not believe that the Germans had now won, this was a war in which no one would win or lose, in the end it would be seen that everyone had more or less lost. Certainly it would last many years and it would not be at all cheerful. For now there were so many different ways of driving people mad, there were machine-gunnings, carpet bombings, incendiary bombs, all sorts of bombs. And the Germans killing just in order to kill, allies or non-allies, just like that. Concettina sat listening with her baby at her shoulder, and her eyes had dark circles round them and she asked all of a sudden why it was, then, that she had brought this baby into the world. Cenzo Rena told her not to ask silly questions. She had brought this baby into the world in order to love him and give him milk. Babies were not brought into the world in order that they should be comfortable, with plenty to eat and warm feet, they were brought into the world so that they should live the life they had to live, even if it was carpet bombings and want and hunger. But later he told her that if carpet bombings started, she and the baby could come and take refuge with him in his village. Perhaps the war would not reach that black village of his, hidden amongst its hills. Talking of carpets, he said, he was sorry he had forgotten to send Ippolito the Smyrna carpet he had promised him. He spoke of Ippolito without lowering either his eyes or his voice, he spoke as though Ippolito were alive and in the next room. Only just for a moment did he take off his glasses and rub his open hand over his eyelids and his face. Then his face reappeared, redder than before and as it were sleepy-looking. He was sorry now that he had made ink-stains on the carpet Ippolito was fond of, he was sorry he had taken the dog away from him when he wanted to go out shooting. And he was also sorry that he had said some unkind words to him. He wished he could be there in front of him again so that he could say some quite different words to him. He would never forgive himself for the unkind words he had said to him. He had said unkind words to him because he had imagined that by doing so he could help him to become a free being. But on the contrary, he had not helped him, he had merely humiliated him, he could still see that twisted smile of his. Emilio then said that Ippolito had been a free being, he had himself chosen the day of his own death. But Cenzo Rena said that a man had not the right to choose the day of his own death. And in any case Ippolito had not made any choice at all, he had allowed himself to get all tied up by his own thoughts, so that he had been killed by them. He died strangled by his own thoughts, he was dead even before he sat down that morning in the public gardens. Emilio then asked whether a man who did not think was a free being. And Cenzo Rena told him not to ask silly questions. The man who accepted the life he had to live was free. The man who made health and wealth out of his own thoughts was free, not the man who made them into a noose to strangle himself with. Then he began to yawn and stretch himself, waving his long arms, and he said he was going to bed. Emilio asked Concettina whether this fellow would be staying long at Le Visciole, he did not care for him very much, he knew quite well that he was silly but he didn't much like being told so to his face. And Concettina told Giustino to do what Cenzo Rena did when his drawers were scratching him. But Giustino said he did not know how to do it, it was Emanuele who knew how to do it. Besides, he didn't think it was right to laugh at a person the moment he had left the room.

Next morning Giustino went to look for worms, because he hoped to go fishing with Cenzo Rena in the afternoon.

He collected a quantity of fine long worms, but in the afternoon Cenzo Rena said he was going with Anna into the town to buy her a watch, he wanted to give her a present and had noticed that she hadn't a watch. Signora Maria was very pleased, she thought of a little gold watch, of a good make, which Anna would wear on her wrist all her life. But Giustino was disappointed and went fishing by himself, and he did not catch anything and in the end he threw away the worms and started eating big rolls of bread, as he always did when he felt sad. It seemed to him that Cenzo Rena had nodded to him absent-mindedly, it seemed to him that they were no longer such friends, yet it was he who had written begging him to come, and he had been so pleased the evening before when he had seen his car down at the gate. As he passed he saw the Humbugs' daughters in the square but he had no wish for Humbugs' daughters that day, fishing with Cenzo Rena was the only thing he would have liked, or again choosing a watch for Anna with the two of them in the town. But Cenzo Rena had not told him to get into the car with them, he had just nodded to him in an absent-minded way.

Anna and Cenzo Rena drove towards the town, the sun was shining and the road was dry but not yet dusty, the car swayed in the deep ruts caused by the rain. Cenzo Rena said he had once had a friend who was a doctor in the town, but he did not know if he was still alive and if he still lived at the same address. He said it was better to keep away from midwives, midwives might even kill you, so many poor girls had come to a bad end like that. Anna had been thinking all night of a midwife with the face of Danilo's mother. All at once she was frightened, she asked what they would do to her, whether it was easy to face death. Cenzo Rena said no, what was needed was to go to a doctor, midwives sometimes did not wash their hands properly. If they could not find that friend of his they could perhaps fall back upon the little doctor with the hair like chickens' feathers. But Anna said she would be too much ashamed to go to that little doctor, she wanted a face she had never seen before and that she would never see again. Cenzo Rena suddenly stopped the car, he asked her if she really wanted to get rid of the baby. Anna asked what else she could do, Giuma would never marry her and possibly she herself would not have at all liked marrying him, she had made a mess of everything and so what would that baby have if it came into the world, nothing but a mother who had made a mess of everything and had no courage. Cenzo Rena said that no one found himself with courage ready-made, you had to acquire courage little by little, it was a long story and it went on almost all your life. They had stopped at the gates of the town, the tin roofs of the soap factory could be seen. He told her that up till that day she had lived like an insect. An insect that knows nothing beyond the leaf upon which it hangs.

He asked her if she would marry him. In that way she would not have to get rid of the baby. The streets were full of babies and certainly they grew up into men with scowling, nasty faces, and yet it seemed to him sad that one of them should be got rid of. He himself would not remember often that this baby was not his own child, in any case all those stories about the voice of the blood were very silly, *his* blood had no voice. He had never dreamed of wanting a child, but seeing that there was one to be had he would take it. Perhaps he was very old to marry her but all the years he had behind him did not weigh much, he had galloped through them so fast, never had he looked back to count the things he had lost. And what made people grow old was to keep looking back in order to count, counting made you grow very old all at once, with a sharp nose and gloomy, rapacious eyes. He himself had always galloped on. Then she looked at him in bewilderment and wondered how old Cenzo Rena could be, fifty, sixty, goodness knows. There was no further need to look for a doctor who would do something or other to her body to make the baby disappear. She would marry Cenzo Rena, and so her life would be over, nothing unexpected or strange would ever happen to her again, it would be Cenzo Rena and Cenzo Rena for ever.

She said yes, she would marry him. But she told him she felt a little cold at the thought of having decided something for the whole of her life. Cenzo Rena said he himself felt very cold too, he felt long, cold shudders down his back, but anyone who was afraid of a cold shudder did not deserve to live, he deserved to hang on a leaf all his life. And she, now, had got to come away from her leaf, only insects remained on leaves, with their little staring, sad eyes, and their little motionless feet, and their short, sad little breathing. In order to get married it was necessary to know whether you felt free and happy together, with cold shudders down your back because even joy has its cold shudders, and with a great fear of making a mistake and a real desire to go forward. And he himself had never felt so free and happy as he had the day before when he had begun to think he might marry her, for he had thought of it at once and had been awake all night thinking about it, and he had had such long, cold shudders that he had got up and drunk some brandy and put on his sweater over his pyjamas.

They turned back, and stopped at an inn on the road. Cenzo Rena ordered wine, *salame* sausage and figs. The figs were in a basket covered with moist leaves, the *salame* was cut in slices and was full of little white eyes and grains of pepper. Anna asked if she would still have to take her mathematical exam in October, Cenzo Rena said no, they drank a toast to the mathematical exam that had rolled away like a cloud. Cenzo Rena told her they would get married at once, in a few days' time, and then they would leave at once for his own village, he pulled out a map of Italy and showed her where his village was, far away where the South began. There the baby would be born and no one would ever know that the father of the baby was not

himself, Cenzo Rena, but a boy with teeth like a wolf.
There they would stay until the end of the war, afterwards
he would start travelling again if there was an afterwards,
at present it was not worth thinking about. She could
burn all her school books in the stove, she would be learning
other things now, perhaps she would learn from La Maschiona how to make an omelette with onions. He drew
a picture of La Maschiona on the edge of a newspaper,
La Maschiona had been his servant for almost twenty
years. He drew a triangular face underneath a kind of
black cloud and two big feet coming out of the ears. La
Maschiona was like that, he said, all feet and hair. He
immediately wrote her a post-card to say he was arriving
in a few days with a wife and she must wash the stairs.

Then they went into a barber's shop because Cenzo Rena
needed a shave and it worried him. In the barber's shop
they stood looking at themselves in the mirror and the
barber waited. They laughed a great deal at seeing themselves like that in the mirror, he with his long waterproof
all muddy and crumpled and she dishevelled and bewildered
in a dress that had once been a curtain. They did not
look at all as if they were just going to undergo a wedding
ceremony, he said. They did not look at all exultant and
triumphant. They looked like two people who had been
flung against each other by chance in a sinking ship. For
them there had been no fanfare of trumpets, he said. And
that was a good thing, because when fate announced itself
with a loud fanfare of trumpets you always had to be a little
on your guard. Fanfares of trumpets usually announced
only small, futile things, it was a way fate had of teasing
people. You felt a great exaltation and heard a loud fanfare of trumpets in the sky. But the serious things of life,
on the contrary, took you by surprise, they spurted up all
of a sudden like water. She had not quite understood what
it was, this fanfare of trumpets, she asked him as he was
sitting in the revolving chair with his face all covered with
soap. A fanfare of trumpets, he said, a fanfare of trumpets.

The way fate had of teasing people. Some people waited all their lives for some little fanfare or other, and their lives passed without any fanfares and they felt defrauded and unhappy. And others heard nothing but fanfares and ran about hither and thither, and then they were very tired and thirsty and there was no water left to drink. There was nothing left but dust and fanfares. As they went out of the shop they took another look in the mirror, she told him that at all events she never again wished to wear dresses made out of curtains. Cenzo Rena said she was wrong, dresses made out of curtains suited her very well. When they were inside the car he bent down and kissed her, and then she saw very closely the grey streaks in his hair and moustache and his tortoiseshell spectacles and all the grains of rice.

It was dark when they arrived back at Le Visciole, and Signora Maria was waiting at the gate. She said that ever since the affair of Ippolito she was always expecting misfortunes, she was not as brave as she had once been, as soon as it became dark she was worried if they were not all in the house. She wanted to see the watch at once, she took hold of Anna's wrist so as to look at it. Cenzo Rena clapped his hand to his forehead, he had quite forgotten about it but there was still time to buy watches, there was plenty and plenty of time. Signora Maria was disappointed and much astonished, what had they been doing then for so many hours in the town? Cenzo Rena said they had not been in the town. He stopped to pat the dog and play with it, he asked its pardon for not having greeted it properly on his arrival the evening before. They went into the dining-room, Concettina was there putting the baby to sleep, Emilio and Giustino were playing chess. Cenzo Rena said that he and Anna were getting married at once, as soon as the papers were ready, in fact someone must speak to that same superintendent of police who had once tried to hit him, and must promise him a present if he would hurry up and get the papers together quickly,

Signora Maria must speak to him because he himself did not wish to see that policeman's face. He said this and they all sat still and in silence, and they looked now at Cenzo Rena and now at Anna, and Concettina all of a sudden gave the baby to Signora Maria and came forward to Cenzo Rena and said that so long as she was alive this dirty thing should not happen. She told him to look at himself in the looking-glass, perhaps he had not noticed that he was an ugly old gentleman. He had money and so he believed he could buy anything, but they were not to be bought, their father had not brought them up so that when the moment came someone might be able to buy them. Cenzo Rena said he no longer had so very much money, though he still had a little. He often looked at himself in the looking-glass and he had known for some time that he was an ugly old gentleman. But perhaps something worse might happen to a girl than to marry him. All at once he flew into a terrible rage, he upset the chess table with his knee, something worse, he shouted, something worse. Giustino bent down to pick up the chessmen from the carpet. What did they know about Anna, shouted Cenzo Rena and walked up and down the room, what did they know about each other, they had let Ippolito die on a seat. Then Concettina started to cry, it was not her fault that Ippolito was dead, she had never imagined that he wanted to die. She sobbed with her face between her hands and the baby screamed, Signora Maria rocked it gently on her knee and looked round with troubled eyes, Cenzo Rena was mad, he was mad and it might easily happen now that he would wreck the whole house. The chess table was lying on the floor with a broken leg. But Cenzo Rena calmed down suddenly, he asked Concettina's pardon for having made her cry, he helped Giustino to collect the chessmen and looked at the table with the broken leg, it could perfectly well be mended, it was easy. Concettina said they must never speak to her about that seat, never never, she was always carefully trying not to think

about that seat, she was trying to tear it away from in front
of her eyes. She asked Cenzo Rena's pardon for having
said that he was an ugly old gentleman. Cenzo Rena told
her she had spoken quite truly, he was an ugly *rather* old
gentleman, he was almost forty-eight. But he was not
thinking of buying anybody and he did not want to do
anything dirty, he wanted to do good and not ill. They
were all very quiet and sad now, they were gathered round
the baby cracking their fingers to make him stop screaming,
Concettina was still sobbing gently and they gave her a
glass of water to sip. Then they remembered Anna and
gave her some water too, because she was looking very tired
and pale. And Cenzo Rena told Concettina that he wished
to speak to her alone for a moment and he went upstairs
with her. Giustino went to fetch the glue and he and
Emilio tried to mend the leg of the table.

When she came back to the dining-room Concettina was
very cold and severe. She sat down in an armchair and
lit a cigarette, Signora Maria told her that smoking was
not good for her milk but she took no notice. She smoked
and looked sideways now at Signora Maria and now at
Anna. She said that Signora Maria must go to the superintendent of police at once next morning, they wanted the
papers for the marriage at once. She told Anna to go to
bed and Giustino to stop messing with the glue and go up
to his room. And so they were left alone, Emilio, Concettina
and Signora Maria. Signora Maria said she felt her head
going round, was it really going to happen that Cenzo Rena
and Anna were getting married, were they giving Anna in
marriage to a madman, to a madman like that? And
they had not even asked Anna whether she liked marrying
this madman, but in any case even if she liked marrying
him it made no difference, goodness knows what sort of
stories this madman had been telling her, goodness knows
how he had made her fall in love with him. Her head
was going round violently, she closed her eyes and dug her
fingers into the arms of her chair, but Concettina said she

did not believe in these fainting fits of hers, in difficult
moments she always imagined she was going to faint but
she never did.   Cenzo Rena was not in the least mad, said
Concettina.   Nor had she herself any wish to give a lot of
explanations, they were getting married and that was
enough.   She smoked and smoothed down her dress over
her knees.   Cenzo Rena had persuaded her, after all he
wasn't so very old, he wasn't even forty-eight and there
were plenty of marriages that went well in spite of that,
very old men and very young women, or the other way
round, it didn't matter in the least.   And now she wanted
to be left in peace, she didn't want any questions.   Signora
Maria tried to say that there was also the question of the
drinking.   But Concettina said that Signora Maria had a
fixed idea on the question of the drinking, after all Cenzo
Rena didn't drink so very much.   On the contrary Signora
Maria ought to be pleased with Cenzo Rena who had
money, she had always so much liked people who had
money, she never stopped moaning about the money the
old lady had had almost a century before.   And furthermore
they would have to pay more attention to Anna, no one
had ever bothered to find out anything about Anna, what
her life was like and what she thought.   Goodness knows
what Signora Maria did all day long, messing about making
dresses out of old curtains.   Signora Maria gazed at Concettina with troubled eyes, she could not understand why
all at once Concettina had become so unkind to her.   She
said Anna was a quiet girl, there was no need to pay so
very much attention to her, she was not like Concettina
who as a girl had always had so many *fiancés*, she used to
change them every week, and Danilo always standing at
the gate.   Anna had no *fiancés*, she just went out occasionally
with Giuma, who was a well-brought-up boy of good family
and they had known each other ever since they were
children.   Concettina moved her chin to signify agreement,
very hurriedly and frowning at the same time.   And that
day she had allowed her to go out with Cenzo Rena so

that he might buy her a watch, said Signora Maria, and he had not bought the watch and perhaps he had made her fall in love with him in some unaccountable way, he was a man in whom there was nothing to fall in love with, she had not believed any harm could come of it, she begged Concettina to tell her if there had been any harm in it. No, said Concettina, no. She had finished smoking and she stubbed out her cigarette-end furiously in the ash-tray, and then begged Emilio to stop trying to mend the table, they were full of little tables at Le Visciole and that one could well be thrown into the fire.

Anna and Cenzo Rena were married two weeks later, Signora Maria asked how she could possibly get married like that without any trousseau but Cenzo Rena said they would buy the trousseau on the way home, a little bit here and a little bit there. Signora Maria was in despair at the thought of what they would buy, and besides, she said they were in mourning and they ought to have waited at least a year before they got married, but nobody paid any attention to her. Cenzo Rena and Anna were married in the little village church early one morning, and the witnesses were Emilio and the doctor with the hair like chickens' feathers, it was early but all the Humbugs' daughters had come to the church to watch. And then Cenzo Rena and Anna got into the car and left for that famous village of Cenzo Rena's, but at the last moment Cenzo Rena decided to take the dog with him, because it seemed to him that it looked very unhappy when he said good-bye to it. Anna turned her head to take one last look at Le Visciole, and at Concettina and Signora Maria and Giustino at the gate, and then everything disappeared in a cloud of dust, and the three who were standing at the gate could no longer see the little grey car darting away in the dust, they could only hear the barking of the dog in the distance, perhaps it would bark like that during the whole of the journey, because it did not like going in a car and was frightened. Giustino was disappointed that they had taken away the dog, he had grown used to preparing its dinner every day and taking it down to splash about in the river, and he was offended with Cenzo Rena for having taken away the dog without even asking his leave, and he was annoyed with Cenzo Rena and Anna for getting married, it was a thing that could not be understood, a thing without any sense in it. He had expected Cenzo Rena to explain to him why he was getting married, but Cenzo Rena had almost forgotten to speak to him, and yet once they had been friends, they used to go together and dance with the Humbugs' daughters, and besides, Giustino had written him a great many letters, in which he told him a great many things about himself. He did not at all like to think of Cenzo Rena and Anna being married, of their living together far away in that famous village, Cenzo Rena had said to him that he must come and see them some time or other but maybe he would not go. When the summer was over he would go back to the town and would live alone with Signora Maria, and in the town was Ippolito's seat, and the road by the river and the soap factory. Giustino sometimes thought he would like to go to the war, he would not mind shooting when everyone else was shooting, it would at any rate be better than staying at home with Signora Maria, with the road by the river and the tall, thin girl. He had stopped writing to the tall, thin girl even when it rained, the tall, thin girl was at the seaside and had sent him a photograph of herself in a bathing-costume, he had stopped writing to her because he thought she was too thin.

PART TWO

CENZO RENA's village was called Borgo San Costanzo. Once there had been a train to it, but not since the beginning of the war. Now the rails lay rusting in the lush, thick grass along the river, and the house which had been the station-master's house had for some months been turned into a dance-hall, but then had come an order forbidding dancing because of the war. Now the station-master's house was nothing at all, its windows were smashed and its doors broken down and old men who had nowhere to sleep came and slept there, and they hung up their ragged trousers on the wooden fence, amongst dried and fallen sunflowers. The grass was lush and thick only along the banks of the river, as it rose up the slopes of the hills it became shaggy and scorched, and the hills on the west side had on them neither houses nor trees, on those to the east, on the other hand, could be seen wind-lashed vineyards amongst sandy paths and rocks, and higher up there were small, rugged pines, and where the pines began was Cenzo Rena's house, hanging over a tumbled mass of rocks.

The village was cut in half by the road, and along the road passed the bus twice a day, swaying beneath a load of people who had climbed on the running-boards and on the roof. The bus stopped for a few minutes in the village square, the mail-bag was flung out of the window, and then the bus went on, swaying along the sandy road. In the square grew four small trees, with clipped, round heads, and there, too, the old Marchesa's carriage always stood, with the coachman on guard chasing away with his whip the boys who tried to climb up into it. From time to time the Marchesa would come down to go for a drive, and then the little carriage with its canvas awning would go bowling up and down the street, with the Marchesa's black feather boa fluttering in the air. The Marchesa's palace was hemmed in amongst narrow lanes and little streams of water, amongst crooked, smoky houses and pigsties, and it had a great doorway with double doors of bronze and blue friezes painted on its façade, and in the courtyard stood an oak-tree full of birds.

Such was Borgo San Costanzo, Cenzo Rena's village, and the day that Anna and Cenzo Rena arrived in the village square all the people had come out to see what sort of a wife Cenzo Rena had taken to himself, and they were disappointed with this little wife with her dishevelled hair, wearing Cenzo Rena's waterproof that came down to her ankles. They decided that she looked like the daughters of the draper, but worse, and they considered that there was no need to go a long way away to find a wife like that. The old Marchesa, too, was peering out of her carriage, with her plump, powdered face and blue paint on her eyelids and all round her eyes, and to Anna they all appeared to be *contadini* of the South, including the old Marchesa and the draper, who was standing in the doorway of his shop with his fingers thrust into his waistcoat. And after a minute she had a terrible longing to be back again in her own home, at Le Visciole or at the house in their own little town, with Giustino and Signora Maria and without any *contadini* of the South, and as soon as she found herself in the village square even Cenzo Rena seemed like a stranger, even he seemed something like a *contadino* of the South, and all of a sudden he appeared to have forgotten her and he had started talking very earnestly to a man on a donkey, they were very friendly and goodness knows what they were planning together, something to do with Government land. They laughed loudly and slapped each other on the back, and there was she, standing waiting amongst those four trees, and beside her she had La Maschiona with her big bare feet in the dust, and she hunted for a few words to say to La Maschiona but could not find any words at all, and La Maschiona was looking at her in a fright, and every now and then would heave a sigh and rub her big brown nose with the palm of her hand. The dog, on the other hand, was very pleased to be out of the car, and was running about the square barking in the midst of a heap of children, and rolling in the yellow, sandy dust, and then it went and scratched in the rubbish heap behind the draper's shop.

Cenzo Rena at once had a collar made for the dog with iron spikes on it, because sometimes in the winter at Borgo San Costanzo the wolves came down, they came down from the pine woods and all the dogs had collars of this kind so as to be able to defend themselves. On account of the wolves La Maschiona had never consented to sleep in that house at the edge of the pine wood, and in the evening she would take her bucket with the offscourings of the plates and run off to sleep at her own home down below, amongst a heap of nephews and nieces and sisters, for even in summer she thought she could hear a howling of wolves in the pine wood at night. The offscourings of the plates were for the pigs, her own pig and Cenzo Rena's, which were brought up together in her mother's pigsty. She came back early in the morning, climbing with her big bare feet up the tumbled mass of rocks, and circled about the rooms with a flask, sprinkling water over the brick floors.

Cenzo Rena's house consisted of large, almost empty rooms, with black cupboards that looked like coffins against the white walls, and with canvas deck-chairs, Cenzo Rena could not bear any other kind of armchair but these. All round were to be seen the useless and not beautiful objects that he bought when he went on his travels, tobacco-pouches embroidered in silver and long pipes with carved bowls and Tartar cloaks and fur caps, but nothing succeeded in filling those big rooms, with their cold deck-chairs.

Sometimes *contadini* would come to Cenzo Rena's house.
They would come even from distant villages, to ask his
advice and get him to write letters for them, they asked
his advice about everything, about illnesses and marriages
and the buying and selling of farms and about questions
of Government land and about how not to go to the war.
Sometimes they had nothing much to ask him, but they
enjoyed sitting on those strange canvas chairs and seeing
whether La Maschiona would bring *grappa* or wine.   Cenzo
Rena called them all by name and laughed loudly with
them, and Anna did not like the way he laughed with them
and slapped them on the back and talked the local dialect
with them.   It seemed to her that he enjoyed acting as
the protector of the *contadini*.   When no *contadini* came,
Cenzo Rena was very gloomy.   He wandered idly about
the rooms, he touched the Tartar cloaks and the pipes and
said he was dying to go on his travels again, to get into a
train and be carried far away, to get out at a strange station
and fill his pockets with strange newspapers and sit down
in a bar and order something green to drink.   He cursed
the war for not allowing him to travel, and he cursed the
smell of the mutton that La Maschiona was cooking for
supper, black, old mutton was all you could get to eat at
Borgo San Costanzo since the war had started, and all
desire to eat was taken away by the memory of the big
wethers coming back from pasture with their old paunches
encrusted with mud.   Then he would take the car and go
off with Anna beyond the village along the sandy road,
in search of other villages scattered amongst the hills and
other *contadini*, there was always someone who welcomed
him and offered him wine and talked to him about the
Government land.   And so Cenzo Rena would be happy
again.   Anna would sit in a corner and sip her wine slowly,
and she had a terrible longing to be somewhere else, in
some place without *contadini*.

Cenzo Rena explained to Anna that these were not among
the most wretched of the villages, the truly wretched villages

were still further south, villages of utterly poor *contadini*, without either schools or chemists' shops or doctors. At Borgo San Costanzo there was a doctor and a school, but the doctor took no interest in illness and the schoolmistress took no interest in teaching, with the years they became more and more depressed and more and more cynical, allowing their work to crumble away in their hands. And so even that was a fairly wretched village, and after the war there would have to be a revolution. Anna, at the mention of revolution, woke up and asked if he would allow her to take part in the revolution with him. But starting a revolution meant, to Cenzo Rena, going to the municipal offices and pulling out all the old deeds crumbling in the drawers, and making the Marchesa disgorge money for improving the drainage and setting up a dispensary, with an active doctor who would not let himself crumble away. All these were things that at present seemed like a dream, because Fascism was in power and Fascism wanted people to let themselves crumble away. This kind of revolution did not please Anna, revolution to her meant shooting and escaping over the roof-tops, and she felt sad at the thought of Cenzo Rena's dull revolution, just a few deeds thrown away and a quarrel with the old Marchesa.

One day they came to Cenzo Rena to tell him that some Jews were on the point of arriving at Borgo San Costanzo. The police authorities were distributing Jews here and there in small villages, for fear that if they remained in the towns they would harm the war in some way. There were some already at Masuri, at Scoturno, only San Costanzo seemed to have been forgotten. But now they were on the point of arriving. For a short time the people of San Costanzo had hopes of the Jews, at Masuri and the other villages very rich Jews had arrived, who spent a great deal of money. They waited for the Jews in the village square. But the Jews who arrived at San Costanzo were poor Jews, three ragged little old women from Livorno with a canary in a cage, and a Turk who was trembling with cold in a light-coloured overcoat. The little old women from Livorno at once started showing the kind of shoes they were wearing, with soles worn right through to their stockings. The Secretary of the Commune took the Turk to the inn which was close by, in the village square, on the floor above the wine-shop, and the old women were taken in by the tailor, in a kind of barn that he owned. The little old women's canary died at once, La Maschiona had predicted that it would, this was no village for canaries.

Gradually the Turk and the little old women became village faces, everyone had grown accustomed to seeing them and had found out all about them, and now everyone said that Jews were just the same as other people, and why in the world did the police authorities not want them in the towns, what sort of harm could they possibly do ? And these Jews were poor, too, and they had to be helped, anyone who could gave them a little bread or some beans, the little old women went round asking and came back with their aprons full. In exchange they mended clothes, they did it so well that there was nothing to be seen, they mended not with thread but with their own hair, it was a custom of the Jews. They often came up to Cenzo Rena's house and La Maschiona would make them sit down in the kitchen and would give them coffee and milk, they were old and she thought of her own mother, supposing she had had to go round begging. Only she was disgusted at the idea of the mending they did with their own hair. The little old women were three sisters, one very tall and two very short and just alike, it made a curious impression to see those two little old twin sisters that you could not tell one from the other. The Turk sat all the time in the village square, like an old monkey sick with cold, and he wore a woollen jacket with red and yellow checks which had belonged to Cenzo Rena, and he was always waiting for Cenzo Rena to come down into the square to talk Turkish with him. Winter had come all of a sudden to San Costanzo, after a long autumn, dusty and hot as summer.

Winter at San Costanzo brought snow and wind and sun, a dry wind that bit at your throat and flung a cold, fine dust in your face, and whistled in the loose tiles of the roofs and shook the smoke-yellowed panes of the little windows. The paths were paved with ice and big fringes of ice hung from the fountains, and the people of San Costanzo were stupefied by all this cold, every year they were stupefied by it and complained as though they were seeing winter for the first time, and the women groaned and shivered as if taken by surprise, with bare, purple arms and fluttering little scarves round their necks. La Maschiona, too, was still wearing her torn blue summer dress, but now she wore thick black woollen stockings and men's boots, and a black scarf round her neck. Cenzo Rena had several years before given her a coat with a fur collar, but La Maschiona kept it in a cupboard and had not the courage to put it on, she went sometimes and stroked the collar and rubbed her cheeks against the sleeves and was filled with pleasure, she did not put it on because she was afraid people would laugh at her, coats were not worn in San Costanzo.

Many men from the village had gone off to the war, they had done all they could to stay at home and those who owned pigs had given the police-sergeant presents of sausages and hams, the women had gone by night to the police-station with the sausages hidden in their shawls. And some had succeeded in staying at home because of the sausages but they were few, or the amount of sausages had been small and even the police-sergeant had not been able to do anything about it. And now in almost every house there was someone who had gone to the war and a family waiting for the post. At one o'clock you could hear the radio news bulletin in the village square, but no one listened to it except the Turk, Cenzo Rena and the draper, the others did not come and listen because they could not make out from these news bulletins what was happening to the Italians, whether they were winning or losing, and they preferred to have it all explained to them by Cenzo Rena, who explained it on the map.

The Turk was very pleased that the war was not going well, in Africa the Italians were running away over the desert, in Greece there was slush and snow and mud and the Italians were unable to advance. But Cenzo Rena told him in Turkish not to delude himself too much, the war would go on for a very long time yet, the Italians were not fighting well because they had no boots and because they did not like the war, but the Germans had boots and everything, and they liked the war very much because they liked killing. The Turk trembled and grew pale at the mention of the Germans, if the Germans won the war what would happen to him, a Turkish Jew, he would never go back home again. With the Italians he had no great quarrel, all they had done to him was to send him to San Costanzo, they had spotted him in Rome selling carpets in the street and had put him in prison for a little and then had sent him here. He was getting on all right but he was very cold, even with Cenzo Rena's sweater and the coat with red and yellow checks, all they put in his room at the inn was a bowl with charcoal embers in it, which was barely enough to warm his hands. You could see he had sold carpets because he always kept his shoulders bent, as though beneath a heavy weight of carpets, you could easily picture him walking with long carpets hanging down from his shoulders.

2

In December thick, heavy snow began falling, the whole countryside was covered with it, the sun disappeared, swallowed up in grey snow-clouds, and La Maschiona called Anna to come and listen to the wolves howling in the pine wood ; Anna listened carefully but she heard nothing. La Maschiona, by this time, was no longer at all frightened of her, she kept calling her every minute to the window to show her something, the dog which was eating the snow, or her old seducer driving past in his cart ; this was a thing that had happened many, many years ago and the baby had died after only a few hours, La Maschiona thought it was on this account that she had never found a husband, for she had not been by any means ugly once upon a time. She rubbed the window-pane with her shawl so as to have a good sight of her seducer as he drove away bumping up and down in his cart, she was pleased that he should still be a handsome man with big moustaches that were still quite black, she bore no resentment towards him after all those years, he had afterwards married a woman from Masuri who owned a great deal of land, they were full of children and one of them was now fighting in Greece. La Maschiona was pleased that her baby long ago had died after only a few hours, because now he might have found himself fighting in Greece in all that snow and slush, and she might have been waiting and waiting for a letter. But as it was, she was not waiting for anything, either for good or for bad. But Anna's baby that was soon going to be born would never fight in any war, said La Maschiona, because Cenzo Rena knew so many dodges to save people from going to war, and he was so rich that he would find a way to prevent his going. La Maschiona was delighted at the idea of the baby that was going to be born, and she was knitting some little woollen socks, and Anna felt ashamed at the sight of these little socks, and at the thought that the baby that was going to be born in the house was not the child of Cenzo Rena but of a far-away boy with teeth like a wolf's. She herself knew it, and Cenzo Rena and Concettina, and that was all, Cenzo Rena had made Concettina swear never to say a word about it to anybody. And there was no knowing what Giuma knew, or where he was, she had sent back the thousand lire to him at Stresa in a registered envelope. She kept saying Giuma's name to herself; how strange it was that a boy called Giuma should ever have existed, a boy who read Montale and ate ice cream at the Paris café. All of a sudden she found herself back again in the hot summer, with France having lost the war and Ippolito on the seat. But she did not want to think about Ippolito, she thrust away that seat from in front of her eyes, she was afraid that the baby would suffer if she started sobbing.

She had become very big and heavy, and she spent the days sitting with her hands in her lap, letting the baby grow inside her. She sat at the fireside and rummaged in the fire with the tongs, she thought about the baby and saw him with blue eyes and sharp teeth, it seemed to her that as soon as he was born he would have a whole lot of wolf-like teeth in his mouth. She felt no rancour against Giuma, just as La Maschiona felt no rancour against the man who went past in the cart, to her too it seemed that many years had gone by, she felt now quite a different person from the one who had been with Giuma amongst the bushes on the river bank. Now, when she thought of " the river " she saw only the San Costanzo river, the narrow, clear river amongst the grass along the rusty railway lines, a river that wasn't even on the map. The fire was kept burning all day and from time to time La Maschiona would come in and throw on a log and a few dry pine-cones and blow on it. It was warm only within a few feet of the fire and the rest of the room was icy; Cenzo Rena said that after the war he would have a central heating plant put in, if there was an after, but there was no knowing whether there would be an after, perhaps there would not. He wore two sweaters and a jacket lined with sheepskin, and he sat at the table reading, he had made up his mind to become cultured seeing that he was not travelling. The horn of the bus would be heard and La Maschiona would look out of the window to watch the bus starting off, heavily laden and swaying back and forth in the snow. Anna

sometimes imagined to herself that Giuma had all of a
sudden arrived at Borgo San Costanzo, for instance with
Franz who was a Jew and had been sent there just as the
Turk and the three old women had been sent ; all of a
sudden Giuma and Mammina and Amalia and Franz all
got out of the bus. They took rooms at the inn, and she
could not help laughing at the thought of Mammina at
the inn in company with the Turk, eating tough stewed
mutton. But when she had finished thinking of Giuma's
arrival there was nothing more left to think about him,
what could she and Giuma have had to say to each other
now, he had vanished out of her life for ever. Cenzo Rena
took up his book and came and sat by the fire opposite
her, he had now discovered a man called Ricardo, Ricardo
with only one *c*, he was a great economist and he had fore-
told almost everything. He read aloud from the pages of
this man Ricardo, and every now and then he stopped and
asked if it wasn't splendid. But she was not listening to
Ricardo, just as she had not listened to Montale when
Giuma was reading, and now instead of thinking about
Ricardo she was thinking about Montale, and she was
thinking that she would like to have the poems of Montale
with her. But the poems of Montale were not amongst
Cenzo Rena's books. Cenzo Rena was her husband, she
reflected, but she still had not persuaded herself that he was
her husband, sometimes she still, to herself, called him
Cenzo Rena. Sometimes in the morning when she awoke
she did not at once turn round, so as not at once to see that
strange grey head beside her. In the morning when she
awoke that head was unknown to her, as though in sleep
all the days they had spent together had been lost, and the
consciousness of being husband and wife. Then she would
begin to reflect that Cenzo Rena had indeed always been
in her life, he had been a friend of her father's, he had sent
post-cards and chocolates from all parts of the world, the
post-cards that Signora Maria slipped into the looking-glass
of her dressing table. That grey head beside her had

known Ippolito, Giustino and Signora Maria. And yet she found it strange to turn towards that head on the pillow. She turned round and the day began, with the fire on the hearth and La Maschiona and the thoughts that she was gradually disentangling, once again immersed in her insect-like silence. How difficult it was to be husband and wife, it wasn't enough to sleep together and make love and wake up with the head close by, that wasn't enough for being husband and wife. Being husband and wife meant turning thoughts into words, continually turning thoughts into words, and then you would be able to find that a head beside yours on the pillow was no longer strange, provided there was a free flow of words that was born again fresh every morning. She remembered the days at Le Visciole when she had talked so much with him, but now she found it difficult to talk, now again she had gone into her insect-like silence. Cenzo Rena told her not to make that insect-like face. She shook herself and rubbed her eyes, and tried to blow away the silence from her heart. She told him she had not understood very much of Ricardo, he said he knew that quite well but it did not matter, above all she must remember that Ricardo was spelt with only one *c*, not two. He asked her if she would like to go for a walk in the pine wood, they went out taking with them a long stick with iron spikes because of the wolves, they walked in the soft, deep snow amongst the pine-trees, they saw imprints in the snow and Cenzo Rena said they were the imprints of wolves, until he discovered that they were merely the imprints of the dog which had run on in front. Cenzo Rena, as he walked, beat his stick against the trunks of the pine-trees to make the snow drop down, he told her not to worry if she did not understand Ricardo, there were other things that she must understand first, now in a short time there would be the baby to understand. They went home again and in the dining-room they found the *con-tadini*. Anna went back and sat in her place by the fire, and she took up the tongs again and rummaged amongst the embers. The *contadini* had a look at her and were of the opinion that Cenzo Rena had not found anything special in the way of a wife even though he had roamed over so many countries ; she was a wife who did not even make you feel shy, so plain and so young was she, without anything of a lady about her. The *contadini* had hats on their heads and scarves round their necks, they sat round the table and swallowed their wine, they had come in just for a moment to ask about the war, but it was not going at all so well and people were losing patience ; if only it would finish soon. Then they described how the Marchesa was writing anonymous letters against Cenzo Rena to the police in the neighbouring town, every week she wrote one, but at the police-station they perhaps already knew her handwriting and put them in the waste-paper basket without opening them. The Marchesa wrote that Cenzo Rena kept his servant called La Maschiona chained up and whipped her till she bled, or else she wrote that Cenzo Rena was a Communist because he spent all his time with *contadini*, or else she wrote that he had several hundredweight of coffee in his cellar. The *contadini* called to La Maschiona to show them the marks of the chains, and they had a good laugh, bending forward with their hands on their knees, and then they swallowed down some more wine, and one of them described how the Marchesa shaved every morning, lathering her face in the proper way with a brush. And Cenzo Rena laughed too and drank and slapped everyone heartily on the back. But as soon as the. *contadini* had gone away, he turned to Anna and asked her why she put on that insect face while the *contadini* were there.

And Anna told him one evening that she put on her insect face not because she did not like the *contadini*, but because she did not like him, Cenzo, when he was with the *contadini*, the way he slapped them on the back and talked dialect with them, as though he enjoyed pretending to be the *contadini's* protector. Cenzo Rena remained silent a moment, and then all of a sudden he went very red and the veins in his neck swelled, he did not pretend to be the *contadini's* protector, he *was* the *contadini's* protector, he was the friend and spokesman of the *contadini*, the only thing the *contadini* had in that dismal country, where everything was gradually rotting to pieces. The *contadini* went to the municipal office and waited for hours and hours sitting on the floor in the entrance-hall and on the staircase, until they were called into the room where the local secretary and the mayor were sitting at a table, and the secretary sat listening to them cutting his nails with a pair of curved scissors, then he would write something in the register and nod to them to leave the room. And they would shrug their shoulders and sigh and go out, and they knew that nothing more would happen, everything they asked for at the municipal office dropped into the register like a stone into a well. And even the mayor who seemed to be one of themselves when they saw him milking his cows in his stable and selling the milk, even the mayor, behind that table, was transformed into the municipal office, into a well that swallowed up the poor little stories of the *contadini*, swallowed them up and made them disappear for ever as though they had never existed. But when *he* arrived at the municipal office the mayor took fright and became a little *contadino* again, he apologized for his shaky handwriting, he had spent his whole life digging the ground. And the secretary took fright as well and put down his scissors and started fumbling amongst archives and registers. In this way he, Cenzo Rena, had obtained relief for poor people, by digging out old crumbling records from the bottoms of drawers, and each month he went to the municipal office to see whether they had distributed the relief, and he went to the chemist's shop too to see if they had any serum against snake-bites, he went round all the time making himself a nuisance to everybody, to the doctor and the vet and the schoolmistress, yes, he even went to the schoolmistress to see what she was teaching the children, and in fact he had had the annoyance of a schoolmistress who had once fallen in love with him

and had hoped to get him to marry her. And he had a
great many plans for after the war, if Fascism collapsed and
if there *was* an after, if there was an after he had a whole
heap of charming little plans that would be a nuisance to
everybody. He walked up and down the room and talked
as though to himself. But all of a sudden he remembered
her and told her to go to bed, the fire had gone out and she
might catch cold. He was still, perhaps, rather angry, and
he merely waved his hand as she went out.

3

There came a letter from Signora Maria saying that she
and Giustino were coming to San Costanzo about Christmas-
time. Anna was very pleased, never had she thought she
could be so pleased at the idea of seeing Signora Maria.
Together with La Maschiona she started cleaning the rooms,
and in the meantime she told her about Signora Maria
who always wore little shoes with bows on them, goodness
knows how she would ever manage to climb up those rocks
with shoes like that, and goodness knows whether she would
ever eat that tough old mutton, she was always so tiresome
about meat and about the smell that it had. La Maschiona
told her not to think about the mutton, at Christmas-time
there would be some veal. The whole village knew at
once when the butcher was going to kill some veal, and
some people ran off secretly to the butcher, even the day
before, to take him presents so that he should put aside a
piece of meat for them, and at night, at the door of the
butcher's shop, there were two policemen and a queue of
women, who waited for hours and hours and grew gradually
fiercer and fiercer and began to throw insults at each other,
and La Maschiona, planted in front of the door to protect
her place, was the fiercest of all. On veal nights there

was a great clamour of voices to be heard in the square
in front of the butcher's shop, and then suddenly the door
would be heard opening and there would be loud shouts
and a rush into the shop and the policemen would be
stormed and thrust aside. Cenzo Rena looked out of the
window and called Anna to come and see and said that
that was the South, poor people ready to get themselves
trampled upon for a little piece of meat, and very often,
after all those hours of standing and after this great battle,
all they took away was a piece of lung, because the money
they had was not enough to buy anything else. But they
even enjoyed the battle, and La Maschiona, when she
heard about the veal, became cheerful and fierce, at the
thought of how she would wait and shout at the door of
the butcher's shop at night.

It was a veal night and Anna could not sleep, partly
because of the noise in the square and partly because
Giustino and Signora Maria were to arrive in the morning.
She turned over and over in bed with her heart beating
very fast, and then at last it was morning and La Maschiona
came in to display the big piece of veal she had captured,
and the bruises on her arms from the pinching and punching. Anna and Cenzo Rena waited in the village square,
they waited for a long time and then at last they saw the
bus a long way off, swaying from side to side and heavily
laden, and then Signora Maria slipped out from inside the
bus with a heap of bundles and boxes and a wine-flask of
coffee and milk, and Giustino came down from the roof
and a little later Emanuele also, he had been in Rome
on some kind of soap-factory business and he too had wanted
to have a look at San Costanzo. Emanuele and Cenzo Rena
greeted each other very warmly, it looked as if they had
forgotten that time at Le Visciole when they had not been
such great friends, now they clapped each other on the
shoulders and shook each other violently, and resounding
peals of laughter, as usual like the cooing of a pigeon, came
from Emanuele. Anna, hearing these peals of laughter,

gradually recalled everything, the garden and the ivy-covered walls of the house opposite, and Ippolito and the radio and France and at the same time Giuma and the bushes on the river bank, it all came back to her heart in a strong, deep rush. The dog had dashed forward and was barking round Giustino and Giustino bent down to pat it and speak into its ear, Signora Maria told him he took more notice of the dog than of his sister. Signora Maria was dressed as for the North Pole, in a big, hairy grey cloak that she had had made when she went to St. Moritz with Anna's grandmother, and she was not wearing her shoes with bows on them but high, laced-up boots. She had her hands full of bags and boxes, La Maschiona wanted to take them from her but she would not hand them over.

Emanuele was very pleased because the war was going really badly, the Italians were getting into trouble all over the place and in the meantime the Germans had not succeeded in landing in England, England was still there in the middle of its own sea and no one talked now about zero hour. It was not like the time of the fall of France, he said, when he used to spend his days sleeping so as not to hear any more about it, and tears came into his eyes when he remembered Ippolito, he could not forgive him for having wanted to die, he might have been with them now to see the fine new things that were happening every day. The story of France now seemed only a small episode, at the time it had looked as though it was all over and yet fine things could still be seen happening. He had begun to feel himself reviving when he had heard that the English had retaken Sidi-el-Barrani, he had lain awake all night and had kept on repeating ; " They've retaken Sidi-el-Barrani ", and now the name of Sidi-el-Barrani still made his heart beat, he wanted to go and see Sidi-el-Barrani as soon as the war was over. But now Cenzo Rena began to get angry, what were all these fine things that were happening every day, poor innocent people dying in Africa and in Greece, so many poor young fellows. They were passing

through the narrow lanes of the village and Cenzo Rena
pointed out the houses where there was someone away at
the war, and already news of dead and missing had arrived,
faces he still seemed to see about in those lanes ; they
had taken sausages by night to the police-sergeant so as
to stay at home, but they were small black sausages and
the police-sergeant had not been willing to take any trouble.
Emanuele immediately went red and apologized for saying
the wrong thing, he himself also suffered at the thought of
the people away at the war, if he had not had that lame
leg he would be away at the war too.   But it was not his
fault that he had a lame leg.   Limping and panting he
climbed up through the snow and the rocks, and he wiped
the sweat from his brow and looked at the houses and the
hills, and he said to Cenzo Rena that San Costanzo was
just as he had imagined it to be from what he had heard
about it.   He told Anna that she had not changed much
during those months, she had not taken to looking very
much like a married woman, apart from her big belly
she had remained the same.   He said it made a great
impression on him to see her with that big belly, he still
remembered her when she went to school with her satchel
and when she went out for walks with Giuma and Giuma
recited Montale to her, of course she had forgotten Giuma
by now, Giuma who had once upon a time been her admirer.
Even infants now thought about getting married, even
Giuma had suddenly declared that he wanted to get married
to a girl called Fiammetta, he kept a photograph of the
girl Fiammetta on his desk and acted as if he was engaged
to her.   But he had failed in his exams, failed with unheard-
of ignominy, and now he had started going to school again
and was silent and gloomy, and had more or less given up
reading Montale and instead had all the books of Kierkegaard on his desk.   They had given up the villa above
Stresa, Mammina had wanted to come back to the town
in the autumn and she was not giving much thought to
the war, she said it was a small war that was not causing

much trouble. And poor Franz had been sent away by
the police to a village rather like San Costanzo but even
further south, together with other foreign and Italian Jews,
and Amalia had gone there too and they had rented a kind
of ducal palace in which they were quite comfortable but
Franz was dying with fright all the time and drew breath
again only when the English seized a piece of Africa, all
day he sat with his atlas and his radio, but at night the
amount that the English had seized seemed to him very
small, he would waken Amalia to tell her how small it
was and then she would give him a camphor injection.
In their own little town everything was as usual, but he,
Emanuele, was all alone, and when he went through the
public gardens and saw Ippolito's seat he could not bear
the thought that he had wanted to die, he could not forgive
him for that, he turned away his eyes so as not to look at
that seat on which people came and sat, it seemed to him
cruel that people should sit there. And Danilo too was far
away and so he had no friends left, he shut himself up and
worked in his office at the factory, but even there he was
in a state of despair because of the disgusting soap that
was now produced. He saw Danilo's wife sometimes, he
went and fetched her at the foundry with Giustino and
they spent the evening with her, to keep her company and
to comfort her for the rude behaviour of her sisters-in-law
and her mother-in-law, since Danilo had gone away they
treated her very badly.

At table they were all astonished at the veal and the white
bread, in the town meat was rationed and they gave you
two or three little slices once a week, of course anyone who
could bought in the black market but prices were always
going up. And the bread in town was rationed and was
a kind of soft, grey dough that you couldn't ever digest,
the bread was like the soap and the soap was like the
bread, both washing and eating had become very difficult.
And Mammina was getting meaner and meaner about her
supplies in the cellar, previously Emanuele had managed

to steal a few little pieces of soap or a little sugar for Danilo's wife or for Signora Maria, but now there was no longer any possibility of Mammina parting with the cellar keys for one minute, and she was constantly in the cellar walking up and down with her eyeglasses amongst the sacks and the boxes and the demijohns. La Maschiona brought a piece of soap to show them the kind that she made in the house with fat that was left over, Emanuele took it and started sniffing at it to make it clear that he understood such things and cried that it was marvellous, and they all passed round from hand to hand the big piece of soap which still had incrusted in it clots of fried bacon and hunks of rind. Cenzo Rena said that La Maschiona also made the bread at home, she used to make it even before the war and La Maschiona's bread was famous at Borgo San Costanzo. Then Signora Maria said that she too had started to make the bread at home with the flour they brought her from Le Visciole, but there was not much of this flour and the *contadino* talked about the bad harvest and about the number of hundredweight that had to be given to the Government pool, there was this Government pool now to upset things still further. But Giustino said he still preferred the soft, grey rationed bread to the white bread, as hard as marble, that Signora Maria made at home. Signora Maria said that of course her bread was hard because it was unleavened bread, in any case she did not make it for Giustino but for Concettina who had to suckle her baby, and Concettina soaked it in her broth and found it very wholesome and light. Concettina's baby was becoming more and more beautiful, said Signora Maria, and at once she started to tell them about Concettina's baby's nose and mouth and eyes, and she started whispering to the baby just as if she had had it there beside her. Giustino gave a heavy sigh, both at lunch and at supper Signora Maria never failed to entertain him with this subject of Concettina's baby's nose and mouth and eyes. When Signora Maria had gone off to rest on her bed, Giustino said he was sick and tired of living alone with Signora Maria, she had become terribly tiresome and would give him no peace, she came running after him in the street with an umbrella and a scarf and treated him like a small child, and then every evening she asked that nephew of hers to come in and was deeply offended if he did not stay in the sitting-room and make conversation. He said he was really sick and tired of it and wanted to get a divorce from Signora Maria. He said that as soon as he had passed his final exams he would go to the war as a volunteer. Emanuele told him that by the time he passed his final exams the war would be finished three times over. Cenzo Rena said no, he would be wanted before the war was over. And he said it was a fine reason for going to the war as a volunteer, that Signora Maria was so tiresome and asked her nephew to come in in the evenings ; in any case it would not be long before the nephew was called up, gradually they would be calling up everyone, perhaps even himself, Cenzo Rena, though he was old, and Emanuele, though he had a leg like that. Giustino said that at any rate he was sick and tired of it and he was going. He was fed up, and he wanted to see what war was like, but above all he was fed up. Emanuele put his arm round his neck but Giustino threw off his arm and retired into a corner. Then Cenzo Rena asked Giustino whether he would not like to go out for a little in the pine wood so that they could have a talk by themselves.

In the pine wood it came out what was wrong with Giustino, he had fallen in love with Danilo's wife and was suffering and wanted to forget her, because she was the wife of a friend of his and this friend was in banishment. Giustino told Cenzo Rena what an extraordinary woman she was, she endured all the unkindnesses of her sisters-in-law and her mother-in-law and had never a bitter word, and she ate nothing so as to send money to Danilo, Emanuele sent him money too but it was never enough because Danilo had fallen ill away there on the island and had to have expensive treatment. Emanuele used to invite her to lunch

at a restaurant so as to make her eat. She was an extraordinary woman, said Giustino, and he would never be
able to fall in love with anyone else, and every day he made
up his mind not to see her again, however he always went
with Emanuele to fetch her at the foundry, and he knew
he would go on seeing her until he succeeded in going to
the war as a volunteer. Cenzo Rena and Giustino walked
for a very long time in the pine wood, and Giustino thought,
as he had thought once upon a time, that Cenzo Rena
was his dearest friend, the friend to whom one could say
anything, but when they came back to the house Giustino
was irritated by the sight of Anna and by the recollection
that she was Cenzo Rena's wife and was even going to
have a baby, it seemed to him an uncomfortable and depressing thought that Cenzo Rena and Anna slept together.

Cenzo Rena looked out of the window to see if the
contadini were coming, he had so often said that the *contadini*
came all the time and now he was upset that just that day
nobody should come. But at last two or three *contadini*
did arrive. Signora Maria had made tea, she had gone
into the kitchen with La Maschiona and had shown her
how to arrange the cups on the tray, with slices of lemon
cut thin and toothpicks stuck into them and little napkins,
she had brought some lemons with her from home because
she had an idea that lemons were not to be found at San
Costanzo, and indeed they were not to be found there in
the winter and Signora Maria said how strange it was to
have to bring lemons with you when you were coming to
the South, and how strange it was, too, to come to the
South and find such a cold winter, and to have to dress
as you did at St. Moritz. La Maschiona did not know
what St. Moritz was and she stood and looked at Signora
Maria getting the tray ready, Signora Maria wanted her
to put on a white apron to serve the tea but La Maschiona
was unwilling because the *contadini* were there, seeing her
with a white apron they would not have been able to keep
from laughing. So she went into the dining-room in her

torn blue dress with her scarf over her mouth and banged
down the tray on the table and Signora Maria said to Anna
that this woman çalled La Maschiona had a great deal to
learn.   The *contadini* drank their tea in silence, they felt
rather shy at all these new faces, but the word had already
gone round the village that there were new faces at Cenzo
Rena's and that tea was being drunk, and more *contadini*
arrived.   Emanuele, too, was shy and happy at seeing all
these *contadini*, all these *contadini* of the South, he sat there
very serious and red in the face and hazarded a few questions about grain and wine and pigs and Government land,
speaking in a hesitating, thin voice and in great fear of
asking the wrong questions.   And Giustino in a whisper
asked Anna whether he did not look like a provincial snob
finding himself for the first time in a drawing-room full
of duchesses.   Anna said yes and they burst out laughing,
and then Cenzo Rena came over to them and asked them
what they were laughing at, and they told him and he
laughed loudly too and Emanuele looked towards them
suspiciously but immediately went on again asking his
questions about matters suitable to *contadini*.

Next day Emanuele had been into the kitchens of all
the *contadini*, his long, deep peals of laughter resounded all
over the village, he limped excitedly about the lanes and
called the *contadini* by name and shouted out words in the
San Costanzo dialect, and behaved as though he had been
there at San Costanzo for many years, he slapped people
on the shoulder and talked flirtatiously to the *contadini*, and
before he left he had a photograph taken of himself with
some of them in the village square.   Giustino unexpectedly
decided to leave with Emanuele, he ran off and hastily
packed his bag and climbed on to the bus just as it was
starting, and Signora Maria was bewildered because he
had said before that he would stay at least a week, until
the end of the holidays.   Emanuele leant out of the window
with a red and radiant face to say good-bye, and shouted
words in the San Costanzo dialect and waved his arms to

bid farewell to the *contadini*, it was clear that he was going to plague Giustino with grain and Government land during the whole journey.   Signora Maria complained at Giustino's going away again, he had only just arrived and now he had gone away again, how little affection he had for his sister and what on earth could he have to do in the town that was so urgent, for some time now he had been very reserved and strange, and he had become quite unmanageable too, what an unpleasant character he had developed.   After the bus had gone Cenzo Rena found the Turk standing close to him, he was very saddened and severe because he had not been introduced to the relations who had come from outside, all the *contadini* had been invited to drink tea and they had not remembered him.   Now he wanted to be presented at least to Signora Maria.   He bowed before Signora Maria with a cold obeisance.

They took the Turk back to the house and offered him tea, and all at once the Turk and Signora Maria struck up a great friendship, they started talking about carpets and Signora Maria had a great knowledge of carpets and was happy to be able to talk about them.   Anna went and shut herself up in her room to think over all she had heard, Giuma wanting to get married to the girl Fiammetta and keeping her photograph on his desk, and no longer reading Montale but Kierkegaard instead, and Mammina with her eyeglasses amongst the sacks in the cellar, and Amalia and Franz in a ducal palace in a village like San Costanzo. All the new things she had heard were beating violently in her heart.   Giuma was marrying the girl Fiammetta, the girl Fiammetta, suddenly Giuma was close to her again, he was reading Kierkegaard, no longer Montale but Kierke-gaard instead, there were no books by Kierkegaard amongst Cenzo Rena's books.   And Giustino had fallen in love with Danilo's wife, Cenzo Rena had told her about it the evening before while they were undressing.   She felt mortified at all the things that were going on so far away from her. And now, for goodness knows how long, she would not hear any more news, outside the snow was falling and you could see the little village with its down-at-heel, crooked houses beneath the violent blasts of snow and wind, and the long snow-covered street with deep ruts made by the bus, and the house which had been the station-master's house and the river which was so narrow and green and the low hills.   And there she was, sitting at the window in a deck chair, and she was knitting a garment for Giuma's baby, a baby who would never know anything about Giuma nor Giuma about him, Giuma goodness knows where, with the girl Fiammetta and Kierkegaard, the baby there at San Costanzo where the first things he would see would be the black houses whipped by the wind and the low hills.

Signora Maria said she would stay until the baby's birth. Cenzo Rena said to Anna that this was a calamity, they would tell her that the baby was being born prematurely but Signora Maria was certainly able to distinguish premature babies from those that were not.   Cenzo Rena said it was the fault of the Turk, if it had not been for the Turk Signora Maria would have gone away again, if it had not been for the Turk coming to see her and the pair of them drinking tea together.   But it was not only on account of the Turk that Signora Maria was staying, she had also taken it into her head to teach La Maschiona a whole quantity of things, she wanted her to wash the dishes with soda and La Maschiona tried to explain to her that if she washed the dishes with soda she would no longer be able to give the pigs the lovely greasy water from the plates, and Signora Maria did not understand and kept on pouring soda into the tub, and La Maschiona became desperate because of all the washing-up water that had to be thrown away.   In the end Cenzo Rena forbade Signora Maria to poke her nose into the washing-up.   Signora Maria also took to going round the kitchens of the *contadini*, and she looked at the children and came home in a state of indignation, saying that all the children had scabs on their heads and lice.   Cenzo Rena said that the lice on their heads

were the least part of the trouble, a great number of them
also had those white lice on their backs and chests, the
kind of lice that lived in the warmth of people's underclothes.   Signora Maria asked him what then he was doing
at San Costanzo, what did he tell the *contadini* if he did not
even tell them that they ought to get rid of lice.   Cenzo
Rena asked her whether it was an easy matter to delouse
an entire village.   And lice were the least part of their
troubles, he said, lice did not cause people to die, but there
were other things of which people died, pneumonia and
dysentery.   Dysentery was the worst of all, each summer
numbers of children fell ill with it, and he went into the
houses to explain about diet and made the doctor come
with him, and even left money for them to buy rice.   But
the *contadini* did not buy the rice and sewed up the money in
their mattresses, and the children trailed about the lanes
and sucked cabbage-stalks and fig-skins, and they cried and
then their mothers took them on their backs and carried
them down to the shop and for a few lire bought them
pieces of almond paste, and the children still cried and
then one night they died, and they carried them off to
the cemetery in little boxes.   It was a village that knew
nothing beyond its own misery, and the *contadini* who came
to see him, Cenzo Rena, and listened to him and understood him and liked him, even they, in their homes, had
money sewn into their mattresses which they were incapable
of spending on medicines or rice, even they had children
in the lanes sucking cabbage-stalks and pieces of almond
paste, with bare bellies and lice and dysentery.   And the
misery was just as contagious as the dysentery, because even
the rich ones lived in the same way as the poor ones, with
all their money sewn up in their mattresses and nothing to
cover themselves with in winter and dysentery in summer,
and that same diet of almond paste and cabbage-stalks,
and always lice.   But afterwards Cenzo Rena thought about
lice all night long, and next day he called the schoolmistress
and told her to get the hair cropped of all the children

who came to school, in fact he was angry with her for not
having thought of it before.

In the village, at present, the whole talk was of pigs,
the ones of the year before that had to be killed and the
little ones that had to be bought, and the village square
was full of little pigs squealing in carts and in wooden
cages, and people came to buy them and dragged them
away on the end of a rope. La Maschiona was continually
running off to her own home to see to the preparation of
sausages and hams, and hurrying away to Masuri and
Scoturno to buy salt, because there was little of it to be
had in that year of war and you had to go searching for
it from one village to another, and Signora Maria was
continually calling La Maschiona and La Maschiona wasn't
there, the fire was going out and Signora Maria had to
throw logs on it and blow, and when she blew a long time
she felt herself getting giddy. La Maschiona would come
back in the evening and display the sausages to show how
fine they were, but Signora Maria was not moved by the
sausages because she feared they would be harmful to her
liver. Signora Maria drank tea with the Turk and relieved
her feelings to him on the subject of La Maschiona and
all the rest, for Anna paid no attention to her and it seemed
that in marrying Cenzo Rena she had married the whole
of this village of San Costanzo, including La Maschiona
and the lice and the pigs.

Signora Maria did not stay until the birth of the baby,
because a letter arrived from Concettina to say that her
husband had been summoned to the district recruiting-
office and would certainly be sent off to the war, but they
did not know where. Concettina was in despair and Signora
Maria decided to leave at once, she was reconciled with
La Maschiona by the time she left because La Maschiona
made a big buckwheat cake for Concettina, and she was also
reconciled, at the last moment, with Cenzo Rena, because
he told her not to worry about money but to spend calmly
what was left in the bank and he would be responsible

for sending her more money if they were left without. Signora Maria told Anna that she had always been wrong about Cenzo, he was not in the least mad when you came to know him well, and besides, there was also the advantage that they could not call him up into the army because he was no longer so very young. She got into the bus with all her parcels and boxes and with her wine-flask of coffee for the journey, Cenzo Rena had offered her a Thermos but she did not believe in Thermos flasks, she had never believed in them. She said she would come back to see the baby. Signora Maria, however, never came back to San Costanzo.

4

The baby was a girl and was born at the beginning of March. Cenzo Rena intended to go in his car to fetch a doctor from the town, because he had not much confidence in the San Costanzo doctor, but he left it too late and the baby was born under the charge of La Maschiona and the midwife. The San Costanzo doctor, a man who was always very lazy and gloomy, was there too, that day he was even gloomier than usual because he had discovered, no one knew how, that Cenzo Rena wanted another doctor and had no confidence in him. They gave the baby the name of Silvana because Cenzo Rena said it was the name of his first love. He went and looked for the picture of his first love so as to show it to Anna : she was a lady with a long skirt right down to her feet and very tight, it had been many, many years ago. At the christening the baby was held by La Maschiona and by the gloomy doctor, Cenzo Rena said they must do something to comfort him for having thought they had no confidence in him. The baby was fair and thin and bore no resemblance to anybody.

Spring came on muddy and rainy, in the village people walked about in mud and water rushed in torrents from the gutters, and the Turk complained because the rain came through into his room at the inn, he had to sleep with his umbrella up. Cenzo Rena invited him to sleep at their house but the Turk did not accept, in the evenings he listened to the radio with the landlord of the inn, they were even able to get foreign stations. Cenzo Rena was suddenly astonished that he did not possess a radio, he rushed off at once to the town to buy one. The Turk came and slept at the house one night, but the police-sergeant sent for him in the morning and told him he would not allow him to sleep at Cenzo Rena's because Cenzo Rena's house was too far away from the police station, the Turk must never go far away from the police station. Then it came to be known that the police-sergeant was angry with Cenzo Rena because he had given orders to the school-mistress to have the schoolchildren's heads cropped, amongst these children was the police-sergeant's son who had beauti-ful fair curls, his mother put his hair in curl-papers every evening. The police-sergeant had not allowed them to crop his son's head. The police-sergeant was now going about the village saying that this man Cenzo Rena was passing all bounds, who was he that he should give orders to crop the children's heads, who was he that he should lord it over everybody in the village? But he was frightened of Cenzo Rena because Cenzo Rena had lent him money when he had had to buy the furniture for his house, he had paid him back some of the money but very little, he had made him promise not to tell anyone about it and what a figure he would cut if Cenzo Rena started telling people in the village that he had lent him the money to buy his furniture. So he always greeted him with a low bow when he met him, and his only way of unburdening himself was by writing long anonymous letters attacking him, the con-tadini used to come to see Cenzo Rena and tell him about these anonymous letters that the police-sergeant, as well

as the Marchesa, was now sending to the police in the
town, letters in which he accused Cenzo Rena of favouring
the internees, as the Turk and the three old women were
officially called.   The Turk had been very much frightened
by the police-sergeant's reproof and now no longer dared
go up to Cenzo Rena's house, he no longer dared to go
even a hundred yards from the police station, and when he
met Cenzo Rena in the village square he said to him in a
low voice what a lovely night he had spent at his house,
with fresh, clean sheets and a soft mattress, at the inn he
had a thin mattress and could feel all the springs of the bed
through it.   In a low voice he complained about the war,
the Germans had come to the help of the Italians in Greece
and in the end the Italians had won, and Jugoslavia too
was now held by the Germans and the Italians, and the
English had allowed a big piece of Africa to be taken back
from them, it was a story that seemed to be going on for
ever.   A family of Belgrade Jews had arrived at Scoturno.
Cenzo Rena wanted to go and see them, he was always
anxious to see new faces.   He and Anna sat down at the
inn in Scoturno to wait for these Jews to go past, at last
they saw a lady with a white parasol and a gentleman with
a walking-stick stopping at a vegetable-garden to buy some
onions.   They were unable to explain themselves properly
in Italian and Cenzo Rena went over to help them, they
wanted some lettuce too and Cenzo Rena went with them
to choose some small, tender lettuces.   They thanked him
very warmly, they had had a long journey and had also
been in prison and now the one thing they wanted was a dish
of salad with onions.

All at once the mud came to an end and it was summer,
the sun rose sudden and scorching and the mud turned
into the fine, sandy dust of summer, and along the edge
of the road which was all white with this fine dust the tall
poppies were already faded, and the hills were already
thorny and burnt-up and the river flowed quiet and dark
amongst clouds of mosquitoes.   Anna went with the baby

down to the river to watch La Maschiona digging her field,
Cenzo Rena came too and they sat down on the ground and
Cenzo Rena took a leafy bough to drive away the mosquitoes
from the baby's face. La Maschiona shouted to them not
to hold the baby with her face to the sun and she tore off
the sweaty handkerchief from her head so that they might
use it to shelter her, but Cenzo Rena said that the sun had
never done anybody any harm, he and La Maschiona
quarrelled and threw the handkerchief backwards and forwards to each other. People passed and said to the baby,
" sleep peacefully ", and to Cenzo Rena they said, " when
will it end ? "—meaning the war.

Concettina's husband had been sent to Greece, then from
Greece to Jugoslavia, and Signora Maria wrote that she
could not come, because Concettina was sad and needed
her. Signora Maria also was very sad, because her nephew
had been sent to the war as well, and Giustino was working
for his final exams and was very nervy and was treating
her badly. Cenzo Rena, now that he had a radio, spent
the evenings trying to pick up foreign stations, he clung on
to those tenuous voices and afterwards told the news to
the *contadini* and the Turk, the Turk was now too much
afraid of the police-sergeant and did not dare listen in to
foreign stations with the landlord of the inn.

One evening Anna was in bed and was feeding the baby
and suddenly Cenzo Rena came in and told her that Germany was going to war against Russia. There he was,
with a flask of wine in his hand, in the evenings when he
was listening to the radio he always kept a flask of wine by
him. He was happy because Germany at last had a very
big, strong country as an enemy. He was very happy and
wanted to go and wake up the *contadini* and tell them, but
he was afraid that if he went out he might meet the police-
sergeant and be seen by him with an altogether too happy
expression on his face. He walked up and down the room
with the flask of wine, and said that the war was now
becoming rather interesting. He said that Russia was so

very strong and that it might even come about that in two or three months' time it would all be over. At San Costanzo, perhaps, after the war was over and the Fascists had gone up in smoke, they might want to make him mayor, but he would not accept. A *contadino* friend of his called Giuseppe would do very well as mayor ; to the devil with the police-sergeant, he said, and out he went with the wine-flask to go and wake Giuseppe and tell him to get ready to be mayor and to drink with him to Russia which was now fighting against Germany.

Cenzo Rena decided next day that they would go to the seaside for a month with the baby, in that way he would not be seen by the police-sergeant with too happy an expression on his face. La Maschiona was very pleased to see them go because now she could work all day long in her field, Cenzo Rena told her the only thing she must do was to look after the dog, she must take it with her when she went to her field because if she left it alone it would become savage and melancholy. They went in the bus to the town and there they got into the train, if they had gone by car they would have needed too much petrol and petrol was now to be found only on the black market and was extremely expensive. Between the bus and the train Cenzo Rena rushed off to the town market to buy bathing costumes, he seized two costumes at random off the counter from amongst corsets and garters and ran off with them, offending the woman who wanted to wrap them up in a parcel for him. This woman came from Masuri and he knew her, and afterwards he wrote her a post-card to explain that his train was just leaving and that was why he had offended her.

The costumes were of poor quality and when they were wet they hung down in all directions. While Anna went to bathe Cenzo Rena stayed with the baby in the shade in the garden of the hotel, even there there were mosquitoes and he drove them off with a bough. Anna came back with her bathing-costume all slack and shapeless and he

laughed as he looked at her, it was certainly the ugliest
costume on the whole of the beach. Anna combed her
hair and squeezed the water out of it and out of the edges
of her costume. He told her that she had not had quite
so much of an insect face recently, perhaps it was since the
baby had been born, they looked together at the baby and
he said to her that this was the baby she had once wanted
to get rid of. He said he hardly ever remembered that
this baby was not his own daughter, in any case why
remember it, it was he who chased away the mosquitoes
and even sometimes walked the baby up and down when
she cried, and in the meantime no one knew what on earth
the baby's real father was doing, perhaps he was sitting for
his exams and being ploughed once again. They were
there at the seaside when they had a letter from Giustino,
he had sat for his exams and had passed and now he was
asking to go to the war. Anna cried all day, she was sure
Giustino would be killed in the war, she still seemed to see
him going off in the bus with that reserved, gloomy expression that had come to him in the last few months, ever
since he had been living alone with Signora Maria. But
Cenzo Rena told her that Giustino would never be in
time to go, the war would last only another month or two.
Cenzo Rena rowed and swam and had scorched the whole
of his back, at night he had to sleep on his stomach. He
was still very happy about Russia but gradually he began
to be a little less happy, the Germans were taking pieces
of Russia. There at the seaside there was no means of
listening to the foreign broadcasts and you had to be content
with the Italian communiqué put up in the hall of the
hotel, Cenzo Rena came to hate that hall because he always
heard bad news there.

All of a sudden they both realized that they were homesick for San Costanzo, Cenzo Rena was certain that the
baby too, when she cried, cried because she wanted them
to take her back home. Cenzo Rena said he was homesick
for the *contadini* and even for a sight of the police-sergeant's

cloak, and he said that perhaps he had gradually become accustomed to being a kind of person whom everybody knew well, here at the seaside no one knew him and he did not like it that no one should know him. Once upon a time, when he was on his travels, he had been happy to be knocking about all alone in hotels and trains and towns, without even a dog knowing who he was, but now perhaps he was beginning to grow old, and all he wanted was his *contadini* and the police-sergeant's cloak, he wanted to have the same things always in front of his eyes. And Anna wanted to be at home, with La Maschiona spirting water from a wine-flask on to the floor in the morning. At the seaside she had realized all at once that that house had become her home, that house with the pine wood at the back and a tumbled mass of rocks down below. At the seaside there were ladies on the beach in black spectacles who asked her questions, and were astonished that she, so young, should already have a baby, and were astonished that Cenzo Rena, so old, should be her husband, they did not exactly say " so old " but they were astonished and they pulled up their black spectacles so as to have a good look, and all of a sudden Anna was ashamed of having an old husband, and was also ashamed of their bathing-costumes that had been bought in the market. But she told Cenzo Rena that she was ashamed and he told her she was an idiot, at San Costanzo the *contadini* did not like her and were astonished by her and *he* was not ashamed.

They went back to San Costanzo and Cenzo Rena immediately started quarrelling with La Maschiona because the dog had become melancholy and savage just as he had thought, of course La Maschiona had left it alone tied up in front of the house, she had gone off to work in her field and had neglected the dog. Cenzo Rena lay on the bed with the dog on top of him making him all dirty with earth, and he talked to the dog and said bad things to it about La Maschiona for having left it alone all the time, he asked

it if it was not true that she left it alone all the time and
had paid no attention to anything except her own field.
Then La Maschiona said that at the seaside they had neglected the baby, they had let her be bitten by mosquitoes
and had allowed her to grow even thinner, a nephew of
hers born a whole month later was three times as fat.
Cenzo Rena shouted at her not to talk about her nephews
because they had dysentery, as he got out of the bus he
had met the doctor and had heard from him that the
village was full of dysentery.   La Maschiona said yes, her
nephews too had a touch of dysentery but it was nothing
much, and Cenzo Rena said that of course she bought
them those pieces of almond paste at the shop, and if he
ever saw her give a piece of almond paste to his own baby
he would turn her out of the house for good and all.   After
being one hour at San Costanzo Cenzo Rena was bored
to death with La Maschiona and with everything else, but
he remembered that at the seaside he had been bored with
the seaside and he thought it must be the fault of the war
that he was bored and did not feel at ease anywhere.   The
very next day he started going round all the houses with
the gloomy doctor, to see the babies with dysentery, and
he quarrelled with the women and with the doctor as well
because he told him he was no use as a doctor with that
disgusted, gloomy appearance.

Anna went up through the pine wood with the baby.
The pine wood was dark and cool, one of the few dark,
cool spots in that country of sun and dust, and Anna sat
down and put the baby on a cushion with her feet wrapped
up in a blanket, the baby threw off the blanket and stuck
her red, thin feet up in the air, Anna covered the thin
feet again and again the baby stuck them up in the air,
then she sucked one of her hands with a prolonged murmur-
ing sound, for some time she made this prolonged mur-
muring sound and sucked at her hand with loud clucking
noises, and Anna sat looking at her and found nothing to
say to her, because she did not know how to chatter to

small babies in the way that Signora Maria chattered to
them.   As soon as the baby had gone to sleep she started
trying to disentangle her endless thoughts, she collected all
the scattered threads of her own life and wove them together,
and she was able to stay for hours in the pine wood beside
the baby without being bored, weaving together and then
separating her endless thoughts, beside the baby who for a
long time had been merely a piece of darkness within her,
and then suddenly had become a real baby in the hands
of La Maschiona, with feet that were thin and red and
long, tender, pale hair, and the name of Cenzo Rena's
first love, she sought Giuma's face in the sleeping face of
the baby but there was no sign of any other face in that
naked sleeping face, with its little lips pursed and pale
and its short breathing.   Cenzo Rena came and brought
the post with him, Giustino had left for Russia, Signora
Maria had gone to stay with Concettina and had let the
house to some relations of Emilio's, Emilio too had been
sent to Russia, Signora Maria could not come to San
Costanzo because she had swollen ankles and would never
be able to manage those rocks, she was sorry not to be
able to come and see the baby, she chattered about Concettina's baby and about Anna's baby, she filled pages and
pages with her chatter.   She was well off with the Sbrancagnas and they were very kind but even with all the maids
that there were in the house she still had a lot of work
to do, perhaps she had come by her swollen ankles by standing too long at her ironing.   There was also a letter from
Emanuele in which he said that Giuma had scraped through
his exam this time but had got it into his head to study
literature and philosophy, Mammina on the other hand
wanted him to study commercial sciences, otherwise he
would not be able to work at the soap factory.   Giuma
was now saying that he did not feel himself to be cut out
for the soap factory.   Emanuele wrote that he felt even
more lonely without Giustino, he saw Concettina every now
and then and certainly Concettina had become rather tire-

some, she always had the baby with her and one could
never manage to have a sensible conversation with her,
absorbed as she always was in combing the baby's hair and
cleaning his hands with a handkerchief and calling him
if he moved even one step away from her, but she was still
Concettina and he was very pleased when he met her with
the baby on the road beside the river, they walked along
together for a moment or sat down in a café and recollected
the same things. But Concettina became very ill-humoured
if Danilo's wife went past and he, Emanuele, called to her
and greeted her, Concettina said it was the fault of that
woman Marisa that Giustino had been so determined to go
away, she had played the coquette with Giustino who was
only a boy until she had made him fall in love with her, and
now Giustino was where he was, when he might have been
still at home studying, instead of which he had gone off
with a tragic air, and she herself had been left with Signora
Maria to look after, and it was very boring to have to spend
the whole day with her. Then Emanuele said that Marisa
had not played the coquette at all, in any case she had
other things to think about than playing the coquette, with
a sick husband to whom she had to send money and with
all the extra hours she was working at the foundry, and he
told her that she, Concettina, ought to have respect for a
woman who worked, she who spent her days without doing
anything, except petting and spoiling her baby. Concettina
was deeply offended, her baby was not in the least spoilt,
and of course everyone nowadays ought to have respect for
all the people at the foundry. But then they made it up
and he went back home and felt sad when he looked out
of the window at seeing the Sbrancagnas' relations in the
house opposite, and no more of Signora Maria's black
underclothes hung up on the line, Mammina on the other
hand was very pleased at not seeing the underclothes any
more and she was also pleased because the Sbrancagnas'
relations did not manure the rose-trees with dung as Signora
Maria did. Anna's heart beat fast as she waited for the

post, but afterwards, as soon as she had read the letters, she always felt slightly mortified, as it were, because of the things that were going on without her.

5

Autumn went by, with the tomatoes laid out in front of the houses to dry, for the making of tomato paste, and then with the maize and the beans laid out to dry, and with people coming down from the pine wood with sacks of pine-cones ; there were even some who broke off entire branches from the pine-trees and the forest guard would arrive with his gun and there would be a great sound of running down through the pine wood and the forest guard shouting and firing into the air. The pine wood was also full of a certain kind of white mushrooms shaped like little ears, they were tough to cook and they tasted like pith, but the whole village feasted off them. There were also some real mushrooms but not very many, all those that there were were found by a little old man who lived down at the old station. He was a little old man with a dirty white jacket and white trousers turned up to the knees, as a young man he had been a servant in the house of a naval officer, and he had had this white uniform given to him as a present. He used to come down from the pine wood in the evening, looking as if he were in his drawers, and carrying, tied to a stick, a little bundle of real mushrooms, and Cenzo Rena, if he happened to be at the door of his house, would buy the whole bundle of mushrooms, and would be very pleased because he knew he was doing something to annoy the Marchesa, who was waiting at her window for the mushrooms, and when the little old man passed under the Marchesa's window without any mushrooms she would call him into the hall and make a

furious scene. The old man would swear he had not found
any mushrooms, and the Marchesa would swear that she
had just seen him selling his mushrooms to Cenzo Rena,
and she would pull out a pair of her coachman's cast-off
shoes and swear to the little old man that she would make
him a present of them if he brought her mushrooms every
evening. But the little old man did not believe that she
would ever make him a present of the shoes, the Marchesa
was miserly and never gave away even so much as a pin.

Autumn went by and winter began and by now Anna
knew well all the people in the village, from the little old
man in white to the man with the corkscrew leg who came
past with his cart full of pots and pans, from La Maschiona's
seducer to the farrier who burnt the hooves of the mules,
in front of his door there were always mules' hairs scattered
about and a smell of scorched skin. La Maschiona's
seducer's family were still waiting for news of the son who
was at the war and had been posted missing, a man from
the village who had come back from Greece told of how
he had left him at a cross-roads and after that had heard
nothing more of him. His mother kept thinking about
that cross-roads, she had been told that in Greece there
were so many cross-roads and it was easy to get lost, she
came to Cenzo Rena to ask if this was true, and she had
letters written through the Red Cross. La Maschiona hid
herself when she came because she did not wish to meet the
wife of her seducer, and she told Anna about this young
man who was missing at the cross-roads, a fine young man
he was, very tall and with black moustaches like his father.
But still, it was better to be missing in Greece than to be
missing in Russia, said La Maschiona, because in Russia
it was so cold that the birds fell down dead out of the sky,
and Russia was very big and just one great expanse of
snow, and anyone who got lost in that snow never found
the road to come back home again. News arrived constantly, sometimes at Masuri and sometimes at San Costanzo, of men who had been killed in Russia or wounded

or missing, all of a sudden as you walked through the lanes
you would hear shrill cries, an official announcement had
been made that someone had been killed. La Maschiona
wanted to put Mussolini in a cage and send him round very
slowly through the lanes of all the villages, so that everyone
could do whatever they liked to him.

In the winter Giustino had a month's leave because he
had been wounded in the shoulder. The wound was not
a serious one and he came to San Costanzo one day towards
Christmas. Men belonging to San Costanzo had also come
home on leave and they stood about in the village square
and told people about Russia, so many men had had their
feet frostbitten because of the boots that the Government
provided, the Germans and the Russians did not get frostbitten feet because they had boots of a different kind. No
one knew very much about who was winning or losing, it
was all a matter of going forwards and then back again.
They had been afraid of the Russians but also of the Germans, they were allies but all the same they made you
afraid of them, they were completely armed from head to
foot and well protected from the cold. Giustino was seen
getting out of the bus one day, he had given them no
notice that he was coming. He was strange in his soldier's
uniform and he had allowed his beard to grow, and it
grew all curly and chestnut-coloured, just a little lighter than
his hair. There he sat in the dining-room and he supported
his shoulder with one hand because it still hurt him a little.
There he sat with a rather crooked smile on his face which
looked just like Ippolito's smile, the curly beard making his
face look thinner and older, with its eyes that had seen the
war.

They asked him many questions but he had no desire
to tell stories. He had not regretted having gone to the
war because he had always had a wish to know what sort
of a thing war was, now he knew it was a bad thing but
he had not regretted going, he wanted to be like other
people, he wanted to be neither better off nor worse off

than others. He said that Emanuele, when he himself was on the point of going off to Russia, had made an angry scene with him, he was too young to be called up and he could have stayed at home, and instead of that he was going as a volunteer to fight in a Fascist war, he was going to help the Fascists not to lose this war of theirs, because he had perhaps taken to loving his country, he had perhaps believed all that rubbish about his country that Fascism taught in the schools. But there wasn't a grain of truth in it, said Giustino, he had never dreamed of loving his country, he never thought about any country whatever when he was at the war, firing at the enemy. Moreover, none of the men that were with him did think about it. Nor did anyone ever remember that it was against the Russians that they were firing. It was just firing, neither for anybody nor against anybody, just firing with your feet like pieces of ice in your boots, and with your eyes dazzled by the snow. When he went away he had simply wanted to know what sort of a thing war was, and then too he was fed up with being at home with Signora Maria, and then there was another story as well that wasn't worth mentioning. But little by little he had realized that he was at the war in order to be like other people, in order to have cold feet too, and to wait for things from home, and to fix on a point in the snow and then fire. He did not believe he was helping the Fascists to win the war, what difference did it make, one person firing more or less, surely the war was already hopelessly lost for the Fascists, they had America against them as well now, obviously America was coming into the war too, in a short time. But Cenzo Rena said the war would go on a long time yet, you couldn't see the end of it yet, when Russia had come in he had thought it would end quickly, and instead of that Germany had taken big pieces of Russia. And he said that Giustino had done well to go to Russia thinking as he did, that he was a person like the others fighting for no particular country but for the innocent people who were there on the spot, and *that*,

in fact, was his country, his country was the poor devils
sent off to Russia from a great many villages like San
Costanzo, poor devils who had cold feet and were firing
neither for nor against anybody. Anna looked and looked
at Giustino and kept on thinking that he would be killed
in the war, she looked at him as he was now with his curly
beard and Ippolito's smile, she looked at him because she
remembered that she had never looked properly at Ippolito
and then all of a sudden he was dead. She was holding
the baby in her lap and Giustino for a moment took the
baby's fingers in the tips of his own fingers, and he said
she was much better than Concettina's baby, which was
petted and spoilt and tiresome, what with Concettina herself
and Signora Maria and all those grandmothers and old
women that were always hovering round for fear it should
come to some harm. Signora Maria and Concettina
quarrelled over the baby and what it should eat, Signora
Maria complained of her ankles and of a backache that
she had because she had tired herself out with working ;
she also complained that the Sbrancagnas' villa was damp,
and that there was very little to eat and that the servants
ate up everything. She said that one of these days she
would come to San Costanzo but Giustino did not believe
she would come, she had grown very old and everything
frightened her.   Giustino had also seen Emanuele and they
had made it up again, Emanuele had asked his forgiveness
for all the unkind things he had said to him when he was
going away to the war. Emanuele was full of troubles
at the soap factory, and besides, he was worried about
Giuma who had been thrown over by that so-called *fiancée*
of his and had taken it in a tragic manner, and he was
always going and sitting on Ippolito's seat and was always
going and looking at a picture of Ippolito on Emanuele's
desk, Emanuele was afraid he was thinking of doing what
Ippolito did, some time or other. He had let himself be
persuaded to study commercial sciences but he never uttered
a syllable now at home, he never went either to ski or to

play bridge and he dressed untidily and behaved like a
poète maudit. Giustino said that in Russia he would have
learned how to ski very well.

When Giustino had gone away again Cenzo Rena clapped
his hand to his forehead, again this time he had forgotten
to introduce the Turk, the Turk who set so much store on
being introduced to people who came from outside. La
Maschiona said how handsome Giustino was now with his
beard, a fine young man he was, what a pity he had to
go back to the war and perhaps be killed. Cenzo Rena
shouted at her to be quiet and not to bring misfortune, he
touched a big horse-shoe that the farrier had given him,
which he kept hung up on the wall in the dining-room.
Once again there was the question of the pigs that had to
be killed and La Maschiona was always running off in
search of salt and of ox-gut to make the cases for the sausages,
then came the things that are eaten as soon as the pig is
killed, black puddings and the little fried curls of fat which
they called *sfrizzoli*, and the sausages that have to be eaten
at once, which they called *salsicce pazze* or " crazy sausages ",
perhaps because they jump about and explode in the pan
while they are frying. But everyone was complaining about
the pigs which it had been impossible to fatten up properly
that year, because neither bran nor vetch could now be
got and they had had to bring them up entirely on grass
and potatoes. But still, anyone who had a pig was lucky,
said La Maschiona, because even with these lean pigs you
had something to eat anyhow till the end of July, and yet
a great number of people in the village had neither pigs
nor anything else and scraped along with nothing but the
rationed stuff, with the grey *pasta* that tasted of mud and
the maize bread that was made at the communal bake-
house, but still they were lucky to have that little bit of
yellow bread because you knew what there was in it, there
was maize flour in it and that was all right, whereas with
the grey bread they had in the town you didn't quite know
what there was in it, they put a bit of everything into it

and possibly even the vetch that ought to have been given
to the pigs.

In the winter the baby began crawling about the house
on all fours, and her knees were always red with rubbing
against the bricks of the floor. Her cheeks were red and
rough from the wind and the snow, because Cenzo Rena
was always taking her off into the pine wood, and La
Maschiona would shout from the kitchen window that there
were wolves in the pine wood, and would ask if they wanted
to make the child die of cold. Cenzo Rena went on up
into the wood with the baby on his shoulder, but when
they were some distance away from La Maschiona he took
off his scarf and wrapped it right round the baby's head,
and he asked Anna whether it was really too cold, after
all what did he know about babies, this was the first baby
he had ever happened to carry on his shoulder. Anna
said she didn't know either, after all when had *she* ever
had to do with a baby ? But Cenzo Rena said there were
certain things that women ought to know, she knew nothing
because she had always lived like an insect. She had
always lived like an insect in a swarm of other insects, said
Cenzo Rena, and Anna unwrapped the scarf a little from
round the baby's face and Cenzo Rena wrapped it round
again, and then all of a sudden he flew into a rage and
handed her the baby and ran on ahead, but he stopped
because he remembered that there were wolves in the pine
wood. Who were all this swarm of insects, Anna asked
him. Concettina, said Cenzo Rena, Concettina and Signora Maria. Only Giustino was not an insect, Giustino
was a real person, just as their father, with all his oddities
and his follies, had been a real person. And Ippolito too,
in his own way, had been a real person, even though he
had come to that insect-like end. Why an insect-like end,
asked Anna and she started crying, he ought not to speak
like that about Ippolito. Why not, said Cenzo Rena, you
ought to talk about the dead as if they were living, you
ought to judge them as you judge the living, he, when he

died, did not wish to be adored on bended knees, he wished
to be judged. The wind was blowing violently and they
went back to the house. Anna sat down with the baby
and gave her something to eat, the baby now ate La
Maschiona's bread soaked in milk from the mayor's cow.
Cenzo Rena watched the baby eating for a bit and said
that the only good thing about the mayor was the milk
from his cows, as a mayor he was worthless. He went
over to the window and waited for the *contadini*. But the
contadini had not been coming so much for some time now,
they came only if they had need of something but not just
for conversation ; Cenzo Rena said they came less because
they were afraid of the police-sergeant, now that the police-
sergeant was hostile to him. It really wasn't worth troubling
yourself about this rotten village, said Cenzo Rena, he now
had only one friend left and that was the *contadino* Giuseppe,
he always came, every evening. The *contadino* Giuseppe
wore a green hat which he never took off, and he always
told the story of how he had been a bricklayer in Rome
and in the cemetery had seen written on someone's tomb :
" Lived and died a Socialist " ; and that was what they
ought to write on *his* tomb when he died. And then he
talked about a book he read at night while his wife was
asleep, Jack London's *The Iron Heel*, Cenzo Rena wanted to
lend him other books but Giuseppe did not believe that
anything could be as fine as *The Iron Heel*. Cenzo Rena
sat with him listening to the radio and drinking wine, and
he explained to him what he would have to do when
Fascism went up in smoke and they made him mayor,
Giuseppe said he was not sure that he would make a very
good mayor, it would be better to make Cenzo Rena mayor,
they discussed which of them ought to be mayor. Anna
had already been asleep for some time when Cenzo Rena
came up to bed, but he woke her up because he was
incapable of undressing in silence, he walked up and down
the room and hurled garments and shoes into the air and
poured water into the jug and flung open the cupboards.

He put on his striped pyjamas and made the whole bed bounce up and down as he slipped between the sheets, and he said what a fine chap the *contadino* Giuseppe was, one of the dearest friends he had ever had. Anna's father had been a very dear friend of his, too, they had quarrelled only because he had given him his book of memoirs to read and Cenzo Rena had been unable to tell a lie, he had said that the book of memoirs was a thing quite without any sense. And so they had quarrelled and had said words to each other that they had never been able to wipe out. To Ippolito, too, he had said words which he would have liked to be able to wipe out, he did not recollect them very well now but he recollected that they had been intended to mortify him, he could still see Ippolito under the pergola at Le Visciole with the dog between his knees, he had mortified him so deeply and now he was dead and he could never ask his forgiveness. Now he wanted to take care never to mortify anyone again, there were times when he wanted to fly into a rage with Giuseppe for his everlasting reading of *The Iron Heel*, never anything but *The Iron Heel*, there were evenings when he longed to tell him that really and truly *The Iron Heel* was not of any importance, and that he was also sick of hearing him always repeat : " Lived and died a Socialist ". However he said nothing. He did not wish ever to mortify anyone again, there was the war going on and the *contadino* Giuseppe might go to it and be killed, and to himself too, to him, Cenzo Rena, it might happen somehow or other that he might be killed in the war, the war would not always be so far off, at any moment, even there where they were, something might come about that would cause people to be killed, revolution or war. He asked Anna whether she still thought all the time about revolution. Anna said she still thought about it when the baby was asleep, however when the baby was awake the only things she could think about were the things that were good for babies, sun and fresh air and milk and bread and butter, and long monotonous days with no one firing.

But as soon as the baby went to sleep she immediately started thinking again about all the things she used to think about before, she herself, Anna, firing on the barricades, she climbed with her rifle on to the barricades as soon as the baby went to sleep. Cenzo Rena asked with whom did she climb on the barricades, she said that she climbed up with him, with the Turk and with the *contadino* Giuseppe. Cenzo Rena laughed a great deal at the thought of the Turk on the barricades, he himself believed that the Turk would shut himself up in the house the moment there was even the smallest revolution. They lay talking in the dark till late, and in the morning when they woke up Anna found that the head beside hers on the pillow no longer seemed so very strange. La Maschiona came in with the baby, since the baby had been born Cenzo Rena had forbidden her to go down and sleep at her mother's. She came in and threw down the baby on their bed, she was always very untidy and fierce-looking in the morning, she was very much annoyed with them because they no longer allowed her to go home to her mother's at night. She banged down the tub with the hot water on the floor and started sweeping out the rooms with a grim look on her face. Cenzo Rena fumed with rage at this grim face, he got into the tub and floundered about in it for a little, and then he went outside in his bath-gown to look at the morning, at the big dark patches of grass that were appearing amongst the snow on the ridges of the hills, at the man with the corkscrew leg who was passing with his cart, at the Turk who was going to ring at the door of the police station, he had to ring every so often to show that he was still there. Cenzo Rena poked about round the house in his bath-gown and breathed in the morning, and he said that he felt happy, bored to death with this village that was always there in front of his eyes, bored to death and happy, he did not understand how one could be so bored and so happy at the same time.

6

During the summer Anna had a letter from Signora
Maria in which she stated, in obscure terms, that she never
wished to see Concettina again, nor Concettina's mother-in-
law either, she had come away from that house for good.
She wrote from Turin, she was in a boarding-house at
Turin and was very ill, she would have come to San Costanzo but she was unable to move. Cenzo Rena said to
Anna that she must go and fetch her, Concettina was really
a monster to let a poor old woman go and die in a boarding-
house at Turin. He himself could not leave San Costanzo
because the dysentery season was just on the point of beginning, and he did not trust either the doctor or the chemist,
he had to stand over them both all the time. And besides,
he had started teaching English in the evenings to the
contadino Giuseppe. He told her to leave the baby and go
off alone and free, it was the first journey she had ever
taken by herself in her whole life and very likely she would
quite enjoy it.

She started off and during the journey her heart beat
fast with the pleasure of travelling alone for the first time.
She rather forgot Signora Maria and listened to the strong
pulsating of the train as it went through fields and towns,
and she was very happy not to have San Costanzo in front
of her any more, but a swift flow of changing things in that
strong pulsating movement. It was a long journey, she
had to pass through a great part of Italy. Before leaving,
Anna had had a dress made for herself by the San Costanzo
dressmaker, a dress which, in the dressmaker's room, she
had thought beautiful but which she now saw was not
beautiful at all, when she looked at the dresses of the ladies
in the train ; it did not resemble any of these dresses but
instead it resembled a curtain. Anna thought that Signora

Maria would think it beautiful because it so closely resembled the dresses she herself used to make for her. Signora Maria, however, did not consider it at all beautiful, she looked at it from every direction and said it was very badly cut, in any case it was crumpled from the train and needed ironing. Signora Maria was living in a boarding-house called the " Pensione Corona ". Anna met her in the street a few steps away from the boarding-house, with a string bag full of small green tomatoes. She was surprised to see her in the street, she thought she was ill in bed. Signora Maria said she had got up only that morning and had continual fits of giddiness, she put two fingers up to her forehead and swayed as though she were on the point of fainting, she had come out simply in order to buy three or four little tomatoes because at the boarding-house there was not enough to eat. They went up to her room and Signora Maria at once started cutting the tomatoes in slices and pouring oil upon them out of a small beer-bottle, but now and then she remembered that she had been ill and swayed slightly. The room was full of folded tablecloths and towels, all the things which Anna's grandmother had left to Signora Maria, and besides that there were Signora Maria's dresses and coats and hats of which she had a very large number, there were some on the bed and on the chairs and even outside on the balcony. She wanted Anna to eat the tomatoes but Anna did not want to, so she started to eat them herself and all the time she talked about Concettina, she could never have believed that Concettina could be so unkind to her, of course she had been egged on by her mother-in-law who was a miserly, suspicious old woman and who always came into the kitchen to see what Signora Maria was cooking, sometimes she was cooking herself an apple to eat in her room before she went to sleep, because she slept better if she had eaten an apple. One day she had taken the baby out and it had started to rain slightly, she had gone with the baby into a doorway and he had hardly got wet at all, and when she came

back home Concettina had started shouting that it was
her fault if the child was always catching sore throats, she
felt the child's feet and said they were soaking wet, so
she told her that she had gone into a doorway, but all of
a sudden Concettina's mother-in-law had come in and they
both of them shouted at her, Concettina and her mother-
in-law, and the mother-in-law said she was always in the
kitchen brewing up mixtures and using up all the sugar,
she had even come close up to her and given her a bit of
a shaking, Signora Maria had said she was not going to
allow anyone to lay hands on her. Signor Sbrancagna
had been the only one to defend her, he had said that the
child was not wet and that in any case it was a warm rain.
But she had packed her bags and left, right up till the last
moment while she was getting ready to go she had thought
that Concettina would come and ask her pardon, but
Concettina had stayed shut up in her room. Signora
Maria recalled all the sacrifices she had made for Concettina, how she had gone to pawn the jewellery for her
trousseau, and how she had made her trousseau for her
all out of real linen, now, with the war on, you couldn't
find the smallest piece of real linen in all Italy. Signora
Maria did not wish ever to see Concettina again, Concettina
might drag herself on her knees to the Pensione Corona
but now she could never forgive her. She was only sorry
on account of the child who had grown so very fond of
her, she chattered for a moment about the child but very
soon stopped again. She said she was not coming to San
Costanzo because she hadn't the strength to walk up over
those rocks, and besides, she didn't want to become fond
of Anna's baby, she did not wish ever to become fond of
anyone again because it only led to trouble. No, the
Pensione Corona was the right thing for her now, it did
not cost much and in any case Cenzo Rena sent her some
money from time to time, he was a man who had understood
her situation. Once upon a time she had made a will in
which she left a great part of what she had to Concettina,

but now she had torn up that will, now she wanted to leave what she had to Anna. She made a sweeping gesture in the direction of the shoes and towels scattered about the room and said, "After my death all this will be yours."

They went down to lunch at the *table d'hôte* and Anna realized that Signora Maria was happy at this Pensione Corona, perhaps it reminded her of the hotels in which she had stayed once upon a time with the old lady, but it was just a dreary boarding-house and the *table d'hôte* was a table in the form of a horseshoe at which a large number of little old ladies like Signora Maria had their meals, each one had her little bottle of oil and they ate bowls of hot water with herbs in it and a couple of anchovies and eight cherries each. Signora Maria was very friendly with these other old ladies, and she introduced Anna as her niece, she explained to her in a low voice in French that it was no use going into a great many details. In the afternoon Anna went out for a walk by herself because Signora Maria was very much taken up with the other old ladies, they invited one another to their rooms and drank substitute coffee. Anna would have liked to go and see Concettina at their own town, but Signora Maria told her that Concettina had gone off to the mountains with the baby and her mother-in-law, Concettina belonged entirely to her mother-in-law nowadays and had no more sisters and brothers, she might as well have a cross put up over her.

Anna went for many walks by herself during those days that she stayed at Turin, because Signora Maria always had engagements with the little old women in the boarding-house and with other acquaintances whom she said she had in Turin, Anna used to see her going out with big parcels under her arm and suspected that she was going off to sell clothes or towels, things that the old lady had left her. But as for clothes and towels and shoes, there was always a heap of them in her room, there were even some

on the desk, between a picture of Ippolito and the plate
of tomatoes.

It was the month of July and the streets of Turin were
hot and deserted, the asphalt was melting and stuck to
your shoes, Anna walked along very slowly on this burning
asphalt with big bags of cherries and ate them as she looked
into the shop windows, there were not many things in the
windows but she enjoyed looking into them all the same
because at San Costanzo there were only two shop windows,
the draper's and the food-shop with the famous almond
paste that sent Cenzo Rena into a rage.   The public gardens
were now to be seen without any railings because the iron
had been requisitioned, and inside the public gardens were
to be seen stone kiosks and arrows pointing to the underground air raid shelters, the air raid warning would sound
and people would go without haste and without any
confidence down those short stairs, they were not much
frightened because there had not been any big raids and
very often the siren would sound and then nothing would
happen, in any case people said that the underground
shelters were not dug deep enough below the ground to
be really safe.   These underground shelters were usually
occupied by couples for the purpose of making love, people
who went down into them when the air raid alarm sounded
used to find quantities of couples kissing and whispering.

One afternoon when Anna was walking along the Corso
all of a sudden she saw Giuma coming towards her.   He
had not recognized her and was walking quietly towards
her, his jacket thrown over his shoulders and the usual
lock of hair over his eyes.   Suddenly they found themselves
face to face and he gave a start, but he recovered himself
and made her a sort of little bow.

They walked along together and exchanged a few first
hesitating words.   He was there studying, he had told
Mammina that he refused to have anything more to do
with their own little town.   He was studying commercial
sciences but he still thought of taking a degree in philosophy

some time or other. He was attending lectures in philosophy all the time as well. He was living in a furnished
room and taking his meals at a students' canteen, very
often in the evenings he cooked something for himself in
his room so as to save money. It was vacation-time now
but all the same he was not going home, at home there
was Mammina whom he could no longer manage to put
up with. He had made a mess of so many of the things
in his life, he said, now he wanted to live in quite a different
way. Anna saw that his shoes were dusty and worn and
that his white trousers were rather dirty, they were his
old tennis trousers but dirty and worn, and he no longer
had the watch in the black shell, he had no watch and he
asked a passer-by what time it was. He invited her to
have some substitute coffee with him. They went into a
café and sat down inside in the half-darkness, all of a sudden
the expression on his face relaxed and he smiled, he seemed
very pleased to be there with her in the café. He asked
her if she still remembered the Paris café. Its owner had
never had the money to finish doing it up and had sold it,
the Paris café had now become a tobacconist's shop.

He asked her for news of Giustino at the war. He said
that he himself would never go to the war, if the war went
on for a long time and they called up his class he would do
anything in the world not to go, perhaps he would manage
to develop some serious illness. Or perhaps he would do
as Ippolito did, on a seat in the public gardens. He
thought a great deal about Ippolito, very often he had a
great desire to do as he did. He was sorry he had not
been a friend of Ippolito's, he understood now what a lot
of things they might have said to each other, very often
nowadays he was alone in his room and he talked to
Ippolito just as though he had him there in front of him.
It had been a beautiful death. It had been a beautiful
death and it had left a full and serene memory to anyone
who could understand it, of course there were vulgar people
who did not understand it, who thought it was cowardly

to choose a seat in the public gardens to die on. But he himself, Giuma, lived by the thought that he could always choose himself a seat in the public gardens some time or other. He had had difficult moments, he said, and he lowered his eyes, clasping and unclasping his hands. Very difficult moments, and he had thought much of seats in public gardens. Anna asked him if it had been because the girl Fiammetta had been unwilling to marry him. That too, he said, that too, and his voice went small and fragile, but in truth that girl had been just a small detail in the whole mass of things. His chief trouble was that he had no one to talk to, and so he took to talking to Ippolito, who was dead. It was not cheerful, talking to the dead. Also he found it very difficult to remember Ippolito's face, he had seen him only a few times and as it were hastily, he used to go into Emanuele's room to look at his portrait. What a beautiful face Ippolito had had, nobody among the people you met had such a beautiful face. But Emanuele had at once been frightened at seeing him looking at the portrait of Ippolito, he had asked him what there was for him to look at, and when he went out he had followed him with a very suspicious air. He had followed him but then they had not known what to say to each other, Giuma when he was with Emanuele felt a tightness in his throat and not a single word would come out. It had been Emanuele who had insisted upon Mammina allowing him to study at Turin. Every now and then he came to see him in Turin and asked him clumsy questions, he wanted to know whether he had any girl friends. No, he had no girl friends now. He had no friends of any kind, he stayed shut up in his room reading the philosophers, he never even went to the cinema and he was careful not to spend money because he had come to hate money, it made him think of the people who were dying of hunger. He asked Anna whether she still remembered their conversations about justice, now all of a sudden he had seen that she had been right about justice, he remembered that he had laughed when they had talked about the revolution. Now all of a sudden he had started to believe in the revolution. He ordered some grey-looking cakes and ate three or four of them hurriedly, he said that was the only dinner he had, he did not have anything else. Anna asked him all at once whether he knew she had had a baby girl. Yes, he said, he had heard about it, and immediately he went red and looked away from her. He started violently stirring his sham coffee. And how was San Costanzo, he asked her, Emanuele had spoken to him about it but in his usual superficial, fatuous way, Emanuele was a good chap but so very superficial. He could not endure Emanuele and Mammina any longer, if he ever went home he felt that he would explode, Mammina still had her provisions, her lady friends and her bridge. He could not understand now how he could have lived so long in that house, dragging round the drawing-rooms with Mammina, expecting to have a job in the soap factory some day. He was studying commercial sciences to please Mammina but he had no intention of ever setting foot in a factory. It was getting late, Anna said she must go, she had to pack her bag because she was leaving next day. He begged her to stay a moment longer, he still wanted to say something to her, Anna waited with her heart beating fast. He pushed back the lock of hair from his forehead and asked her if he had made her suffer a great deal, he himself had suffered too now and he knew what it was, he knew he had been very cruel to her. No, Anna said, no. Then he heaved a long sigh and slipped on his jacket and they went out of the café. And afterwards they could hardly find anything to say to one another, he merely went on and on repeating that he was now going to his room to read and that he had already had his dinner, his whole dinner had consisted of those grey cakes and that sham coffee. He said good-bye to her at the door of the Pensione Corona, he looked for a little at the front of the Pensione Corona and said it was like Paris, poor Paris, he said, poor

France, now there was General Pétain. He walked off with a step which had grown very slow and listless, she stood looking at him from the door, he turned round towards her again for a second and waved his hand, he smiled with his wolf-like teeth. She started going up the stairs of the boarding-house and wondered if it had really been true, if she had really spent that afternoon with Giuma in a café. She left Turin again next morning, on the platform at the station stood Signora Maria waving her handkerchief exactly as she had once been used to shake the dust out of her duster at the window. At the last moment Signora Maria had wanted to make her a present of a cape, she said these were much worn. As soon as the train moved Anna took off the cape, which was a mantle of pale lilac silk.

For the whole of the journey she did nothing but talk to Giuma, telling him all the things she had not been capable of telling him when she had had him in front of her. For the whole of the journey she told him all about the baby that had been born from the two of them. But she remembered how he had looked away when she had started to talk to him about the baby, she saw again his bewildered eyes avoiding hers. She tried to wipe out the memory of those bewildered eyes, perhaps they had not really been avoiding hers, perhaps he was expecting her to talk for some time about the baby and had been surprised at her stopping all of a sudden. She was sorry that he had seen her wearing the ugly dress made by the San Costanzo dressmaker, he had become contemptuous of fine clothes and yet she was sorry that he had seen her like that. She had bought herself rather a fine dress at Turin with Signora Maria's clothing coupons, a dress she had found ready made in one of the big shops. But the day she met Giuma she was not wearing it because Signora Maria had already put it into her suitcase. What a mania Signora Maria had for always packing bags before it was necessary, Anna felt a great rage against Signora Maria, what a pity Giuma had not seen her wearing that dress, it was beautiful and did not look like à curtain. She was seized with rage against the cape, too, and wanted to fling it out of the train, but she thought she might give it to La Maschiona for when she went to Mass on Sundays.

La Maschiona was immensely pleased with the cape, but she shut it up in her cupboard together with her coat and could never make up her mind to wear it. The baby clung to La Maschiona's skirts and had become surly and savage, Cenzo Rena said that La Maschiona made everyone surly and savage that remained in her company. Anna looked out of the window at the village and realized how she had forgotten it during those few days; at Turin, when she had tried to remember it, all she could see was the man with the corkscrew leg and the pieces of mules' hair lying outside the farrier's door. Now, little by little, she found everything again as it was. Then she started unpacking her suitcase and showed Cenzo Rena the dress she had bought in Turin. Cenzo Rena looked at it absentmindedly and said it was not too bad. But when he heard how much it had cost he became gloomy and said it was too much, he hadn't very much money now, they must be economical and limit themselves to what was absolutely necessary. He had had to make another loan to the police-sergeant because his wife had to have an operation for a tumour of the breast, they had taken her off to the town in a motor ambulance. The San Costanzo doctor had not realized it was a tumour, he had kept saying it was nothing at all, doctors from the town had had to be called in for a consultation. Cenzo Rena said this was altogether too much, they must get rid of this doctor as quickly as possible. The police-sergeant and Cenzo Rena had made peace again, the sergeant had confessed with a blush that he had been forced to have his little boy's curls cut, because the mother was in hospital and no one in the house knew how to put in those curling-pins in the evening. Now, without its curls, the face of the police-sergeant's son looked bare and flat like that of the sergeant himself, you could see his big, squashed-looking nose and Cenzo Rena thought that the boy now looked like a little police-sergeant, and he thought that after all they had not been altogether wrong to leave him with curls all that time. The police-sergeant was still suffering at the thought of those shorn curls, he did not know how to tell his wife about it. The sergeant also had a pair of twins of a few months old and as yet they had no curls, in the twins' curls now lay the only hope.

Cenzo Rena was in a very bad humour and he was annoyed also at having made peace with the police-sergeant, because the sergeant now came often to see him, and he had to be comforted and told that his wife would get better. Very often he came in the evenings, too, and found the *contadino* Giuseppe there, and it was no longer possible to listen to the forbidden radio with the police-sergeant sitting there, he sat there in his cloak and on his chest he had a decoration on which was inscribed : " God curse England."

Anna asked Cenzo Rena why he too did not go away on a journey, why he did not go for example to Turin. Why to Turin, asked Cenzo Rena, why should everybody now have to go to Turin, the most boring city in Italy ? No, he did not want to go anywhere, he wanted to stay at San Costanzo and see if he could manage to get another doctor to come to the village. Meanwhile the doctor had come to know that he was not wanted any more, and every day he became more melancholy. He tried to occupy himself to some extent with the dysentery. When he met Cenzo Rena he told him he had not really understood what was wrong with the police-sergeant's wife, it had seemed such a small thing, just a nodule, he had prescribed linseed poultices for her. A nodule, said Cenzo Rena, a nodule. And he started to explain to him that it was useless for him to persist in being a doctor. The doctor asked what else he could do, he had spent his whole life in being a doctor, winter and summer he had been trudging

round those roads. Now he was nearly seventy. As a
young man he had thought it a fine thing to cure people,
but then gradually he had started asking himself what he
was trying to cure them for, they were *contadini* and they
were all the same, they called in the doctor but then took
no notice of what he said, in reality they only believed in
their own pieces of witchcraft. When a child had a con-
vulsive cough they gave it urine to drink, yes, that was
what they did, in any case Cenzo Rena must know that.
He himself had gradually become very melancholy, the
only thing he liked now was good food, lunch-time was
the best moment of his day. Yes, he was sorry about the
police-sergeant's wife, but in truth there was nothing to
be done for a cancer of the breast, she would have died
just the same even if he had diagnosed it before. And
besides, what sort of a life did the police-sergeant's wife
have, very little better than the lives of the *contadini*, between
the washing and the children she wore herself out and they
said that the police-sergeant beat her. And then, those
breasts of hers were nothing but a wreck and a ruin, a
couple of limp bags that it was painful to see, and he himself
tried to look at them as little as possible when he was called
in to visit her.

Cenzo Rena told Anna that he would be sorry for that
melancholy doctor, if it really happened that they found
another one to take his place. But he said that all men
made you sorry for them if you looked at them closely, and
that in fact one ought to guard against that excess of com-
passion which arose suddenly, from looking closely at people.
He was sitting on the bed in their room, he had taken off
his shirt and there he was bare to the waist with his plump
chest all covered with grey hairs, he scratched his back
and he scratched in front among the hairs and uttered great
yawns, Anna told him she had once seen a lion at the zoo
and it was yawning just like him. When had she been to
the zoo, he asked, she had never told him about that.
Anna said that she had been there once in Rome as a

little girl, with Giustino and Signora Maria. In any case there were lots of things she had never had time to tell him, for instance she had not told him all about Turin, because he himself did nothing but talk about the doctor and the police-sergeant's wife. In Turin, she said, she had met Giuma and they had gone together to a café. Cenzo Rena slipped on his pyjamas and lay down on the bed, and suddenly stopped yawning and scratching. He said nothing and looked at the ceiling, he had taken off his glasses and his face always looked very strange without glasses, all goggle-eyed, as it were, and naked. He said nothing and blinked his eyelids and swallowed, and a profound silence fell between them ; Anna was standing near the window, still fully dressed, she was wearing the dress she had bought in Turin. Outside it was night, an August night, you could see the hills in the moonlight, and a strong smell of dust and withered grass came in through the windows. And what was he like now, this Giuma, asked Cenzo Rena at last, what had he turned into now ? But Anna no longer wanted to talk about Giuma, she stood there in the corner of the window and thought how strange the name of Giuma sounded in that room, how strange was Cenzo Rena's voice as he uttered it, Cenzo Rena and Giuma were two things that could not be thought of together. Cenzo Rena told her to take off that ugly dress that she had bought at Turin. What a stupid journey it had been, he said, she had bought that ugly dress and had not succeeded in carrying off Signora Maria from the Pensione Corona, he himself was very glad not to be falling over Signora Maria there in his own house but she couldn't possibly stay for ever at the Pensione Corona, however little you spent in a boarding-house you were still spending something and he could not go on sending her money for ever. Everybody wanted money from him and in a short time he would not have any left. Anna undressed hastily and put out the light, and then suddenly she asked him whether she had done wrong in

going to sit in that café with Giuma.   No, he said, no.
And he turned to her and the whole bed bounced up and
down and he said to her, didn't she know he was very,
very fond of her and was always a little afraid she might
go off with Giuma or someone else and leave him alone ?

7

The police-sergeant's wife was sent home from the hospital
because there was no hope for her, and she died in the
autumn, she died without knowing she was dying, very
happy at not being in hospital any more but lying in her big
mahogany bed that had been bought with Cenzo Rena's
money, and with the window open on to the village square
and the mild autumn days.   Her room was on the top floor
of the police station, and every two or three hours the Turk
could be heard ringing the bell, for he had had orders from
the police-sergeant to ring often, and now the sergeant was
in despair at having given him these orders because these
continual bell-ringings disturbed his wife's rest, he looked
out of the window and shouted to the Turk to ring more
gently.   For the three old women it was enough to ring
just once in the morning, for it was impossible that they,
being so old, should run away ; yet nevertheless they came
to see the police-sergeant at all moments to complain about
something or other, now that someone had not paid them
for their mending, now that they had not closed an eye
because the children of the tailor who gave them their room
screamed all night.   The police-sergeant answered that he
himself never closed an eye all night because the twins cried
and his wife complained.
    The death of the police-sergeant's wife moved the whole
village, they had never been able to endure the police-
sergeant, but now they grew tender over the widower and

his little orphans. The *contadini* had taken to coming to
Cenzo Rena's house again, partly because he had now made
peace with the police-sergeant, partly because they wanted
to talk about the sulphur for the vines which was not to be
got, even sulphur had disappeared owing to the war, and
the few San Costanzo vines, tossed always by the wind on
the ridge of the hill, were devoured by phylloxera. The
contadini hoped that Cenzo Rena would know some trick or
other to get sulphur, but he too had vines and he too could
not get sulphur, he took the *contadini* to look at his few vines
with their sickly leaves, only the mayor had any sulphur and
goodness knows how he managed to get it. The police-
sergeant had no vines, but nevertheless it was unlikely that
he would ever be left without wine, because those who did
not want to go to the war brought flasks of wine to him by
night. People soon stopped feeling any tenderness for the
police-sergeant, because he had taken into his house a young
sister of his wife's and they said he had at once started
making love to her on the big mahogany bed that had been
bought with Cenzo Rena's money. Everyone regretted the
dead woman who had been good and gentle, on the other
hand this younger one, whom the police-sergeant would
certainly end by marrying, was trying to order the whole
village about, she came out on the balcony of the police
station and called to the women to come and wash the
clothes or mind the twins and never dreamt of paying them,
but none of them dared refuse for fear of the police-sergeant.
There was also the midwife who was in love with the police-
sergeant and who had been going about with swollen eyes
and a troubled face ever since that girl with the two pear-
shaped breasts had been at the police station, the midwife
was saying all over the village that those two breasts in the
police station were a scandal. Cenzo Rena was hugely
amused by these stories, of which he came to know from La
Maschiona and the *contadini*, and there were even some who
said that the police-sergeant had deliberately brought about
the death of his wife, perhaps he had not exactly killed her

but he had brought about her death by taking her too late
to the hospital, so as not to have those two diseased breasts
in the house but two pear-shaped breasts instead, and so, if
the police-sergeant's wife was dead, it had not been the
fault of the old doctor but of the police-sergeant himself.
No one thought now of trying to get the doctor sent away,
and even Cenzo Rena had gradually ceased to think of it
and said that everything could now be put off until after the
war if there was ever to be any after, if they called in another
doctor now it might well happen that another useless old
bore might arrive, even worse than the one they had.

All of a sudden came the news of a heavy air raid on
Turin, with thousands and thousands of people killed.
Anna rushed to telephone to the Pensione Corona but it was
not possible to get through, and Cenzo Rena walked up and
down restlessly in front of the post office where the telephone
was, they stayed the whole day in front of the post office
waiting to get through. In the evening Cenzo Rena said
that probably there was now nothing but a hole in the place
of the Pensione Corona. Anna wondered whether perhaps
Giuma was dead too.

Some days later they had a letter from Concettina. She
had been surprised by the arrival of a large parcel of towels,
all scorched, and then had had a letter from the landlady
of the Pensione Corona which said that Signora Maria had
been killed on the staircase of the boarding-house, she had
been swept away in the collapse of the staircase together
with a large suitcase, in which were these towels. All the
inhabitants of the boarding-house had gone down into the
cellar when the siren sounded, but Signora Maria had not
gone down with the others, always, at every air raid warning,
she was the last to come down, because she was busy in her
room putting shoes and clothes and towels into suitcases, and
the landlady had to go up two or three times and knock at
her door at the risk of her own life. And this time, too, the
landlady had knocked at the door and Signora Maria had
abused her, she had shouted that she was old enough to

look after herself. The landlady had gone down into the cellar with the other boarders. And then they had heard an immense crash, and when they came out of the cellar there was nothing left of the Pensione Corona but the walls, and everything else was flames and dust, and they had found Signora Maria in the ruins of the staircase, clinging to her big suitcase.

Concettina said she had written several times to Signora Maria telling her to come away from Turin. But Signora Maria had paid no attention. Signora Maria had been offended with her over some piece of stupidity, in any case it had been entirely the fault of Emilio's mother, some nonsense about an apple, Concettina had now had a deadly quarrel with her mother-in-law and did not intend to stay with them any longer. She was now at Le Visciole with the baby because she was not at all sure that their little town was safe, with that stupid soap factory which someone might take it into his head to bomb. They had started bombing Turin and Milan so violently and it looked as if you could no longer be safe anywhere. Giuma had come back from Turin frightened to death, he had been saved by a miracle and they had seen him arrive with his hair still full of plaster, the cellar in which he was had collapsed on top of him. He had been saved because he had crouched back in a corner, against the main wall of the house which had held. And now he and Mammina had gone off together to Lake Maggiore, Emanuele was the only one who had not moved and he was playing the hero a bit, saying that he could not leave the soap factory. It was now some time since Concettina had had any news of her husband, and Giustino had not written either, there was no knowing whether they were still alive, either of them. Concettina was going to remain at Le Visciole, she remembered how bored she had been at Le Visciole as a girl but now it did not matter in the least whether she was bored, all she minded about was that her baby should not be mixed up in the war. She was filled with remorse on account of Signora Maria but she knew it was foolish to feel so much remorse, because nobody was really to blame that she had been killed like that. Cenzo Rena wrote Concettina a letter in which he said that on the contrary it was quite right that she should feel remorse, because she had behaved like a monster to Signora Maria and had allowed her to go to the Pensione Corona where she had been killed, and he too felt remorse when he thought of her dead on the staircase of that boarding-house with her suitcase. But then he tore up the letter without sending it, recalling that he had made up his mind never to mortify anyone again, and he felt glad that he had never flown into a rage with the *contadino* Giuseppe during all the long hours they had spent together, for now the *contadino* Giuseppe was also away at the war. And he himself would have liked to hear again : " Lived and died a Socialist ", and instead, he had to spend his evenings with the police-sergeant, for it was probably not true that the police-sergeant made love to the pear-shaped breasts, probably he was quite indifferent to these new breasts, seeing that he came to spend his evenings with Cenzo Rena.

Another winter went past, another long winter with people waiting for letters from Russia, but certainly the soldiers there had no time now to sit down and write, because every day they had to run away. The Germans too had now started running away, it seemed impossible that they who had always rushed forward should now be running away, and the police-sergeant sat sadly in his cloak and told Cenzo Rena that he did not like the turn the war had taken. Cenzo Rena said that it was indeed a strange turn, he took great care to mind his words when he spoke of the war to the police-sergeant, and as soon as the sergeant had gone away he would puff and snort, because it had become a torture for him to spend whole evenings with the police-sergeant, who always brought the conversation round to the war and you had to be careful to answer him only in vague words. The police-sergeant was always complaining of the Turk who came every moment to ring his bell, he came even during the early hours of the afternoon when he lay down to sleep, he could not bear this Turk any longer and begged Cenzo Rena to tell him to ring a little less often. Cenzo Rena had tried very often to explain this to him but the Turk was very obstinate, the police-sergeant had given him orders to ring the bell and ring the bell he did, and he had got it into his head that if he rang the bell often and behaved himself well, the authorities would perhaps grant his request to be transferred to somewhere further south, because there he was altogether too cold and the only thing he liked about San Costanzo was talking Turkish sometimes with Cenzo Rena, it was such a rare occurrence to find anybody in Italy who spoke Turkish. He said in a whisper to Cenzo Rena that it looked as though the war might be only a matter of a few days now, with the Germans running away and the Russians entering Germany. He was not very fond of Russia because he did not like Communists, but now whenever he thought of Russia he kissed his fingertips, he would never have believed that so much pleasure could come to him from *that* direction. Once he had been afraid of the Communists but now he was afraid only of the Germans, he thought that even if the Communists took the whole earth they would not trouble a person like him who went round selling carpets, the Communists at least did not do anything to the Jews. He had sciatica and walked always with one hand on his back, and he said that at the inn he had less and less to eat and was colder and colder, and the war must come to an end because he could not bear it any longer. Cenzo Rena invited him to lunch but he refused so as not to go far from the police station, where he had to go and ring the bell every moment.

Cenzo Rena said that perhaps the war would really be over in a short time, and Fascism would go up in smoke both in Italy and in Germany, only perhaps when it went up in smoke it would bring the whole earth to ruin. It seemed to him as though the earth were already starting to go to ruin, with whole cities collapsing all over the place, and people trying to escape all over the place, and those long sealed trains in which the Germans put thousands and thousands of Jews. Cenzo Rena recalled the cheerful trains in which he used to travel once upon a time, and he wondered whether some day a train might become a cheerful thing again, into which people got in order to travel and amuse themselves and arrive. He had heard about these sealed trains from the internees at Scoturno, who knew of their own relations and friends who had been lost on these trains, and he went to Scoturno on purpose to talk about these trains, to the Turk he did not talk about them because the Turk did not know that they existed. But he could not help picturing the Turk on one of these trains whenever he met him, and so he was very kind and patient with the Turk and let him complain about his sciatica and about the landlord of the inn, and talk about the war as a thing that must come to an end at once or else his sciatica would never get better. Soldiers and more soldiers were passing along the San Costanzo road, and they sang *Lili Marlene*, a song which Cenzo Rena had learnt and which seemed to him extremely sad, he said it was the song of the earth going to ruin.

He awoke in the morning and floundered about in the tub for a little, but he floundered without joy, and without joy he went outside in his bath-gown to see what the weather was like. The sky was motionless and pure above the pines and the shaggy hills, spring was beginning and there were a few blossoming boughs to be seen in the gardens sloping down to the river, but in that motionless, pure sky there suddenly became visible a small aeroplane glistening like a silver finger-nail, Cenzo Rena knew it was an Italian reconnaissance plane, yet he felt distress and fear at seeing this far-off finger-nail, with its little streak of white vapour that dissolved very slowly in the sky. He went back into the house and pulled the child in after him, and he asked Anna whether perhaps he was growing very nervous in his old age, never would he have believed that he could have felt uneasy because of a passing aeroplane. For some little time now he had been conscious of a feeling of distress which weighed upon him all the time. And then Anna was conscious of a feeling of distress too, and she thought of the Pensione Corona and of the little glistening aeroplanes which had killed Signora Maria. Cenzo Rena said that to be conscious of a feeling of distress was the least thing that could happen, since possibly in a short time the whole earth would go to ruin in one immense crash.

8

One day Anna saw Franz getting out of the bus. He was all dressed in white, as he used to be when he played in tennis tournaments, and he was carrying a big suitcase and some tennis-racquets in presses, and was looking all round the village square, and Anna went across to meet him and then his face lit up with pleasure. Emanuele had advised him to get himself transferred to San Costanzo, because in the village where he had been before there had been gossip which at the moment he could not explain.

Anna and Cenzo Rena took him to the police station and then to the municipal office, and then went with him round the village looking for a room. But he did not like any of the rooms, he explained that in the village where he had been before he had rented a ducal palace, he asked whether at San Costanzo there wasn't also some kind of empty palace. The police-sergeant sent to the Marchesa to ask whether she would be willing to give up a room to this new internee, but the Marchesa had already heard that he was someone who knew Cenzo Rena and sent a rude answer. Franz said he would be comfortable only in Cenzo Rena's own house, with that big pine wood behind it where he could take the fresh air in the mornings. But Cenzo Rena told him he could not bear anyone in his house, he had a horror of living with anyone and for that reason Communism would never suit him, for he had been told that a large number of people had to live together in the same house. Otherwise he might possibly even have liked Communism. Franz finished up at the inn with the Turk, in the room next to the Turk's, and in the company of the Turk, in the back kitchen, he ate the black stew of tough mutton and the other evil things that they cooked at the inn.

Anna asked him where his wife was. He answered in rather a confused manner, they had had some small disagreements but nothing serious, she had now gone to stay with Mammina for a little on Lake Maggiore, and by living apart for a little they were giving themselves time to collect their thoughts. There had been gossip in the village where they were, a story about a woman chemist, he had not even touched this woman but Amalia was always so very jealous. Now he was quite pleased to be alone, in marriage there should always be short periods of separation from time to time, so that one might pause and collect one's thoughts. He was very pleased at the Germans having started running away, it would last another month, perhaps two, and then the mental suffering of the war would be over for good. He asked if there wasn't a tennis-court at San Costanzo. Cenzo Rena took him to the window and showed him San Costanzo, he asked him whether it looked like a place for tennis-courts.

Franz and the Turk never made friends, in fact they took a violent dislike to each other and did each other little spiteful turns, at table Franz would turn on the radio to a programme of light music and the Turk would turn it off again, Franz would open the window and the Turk would shut it again. Franz came to Cenzo Rena to relieve his feelings about the Turk but Cenzo Rena told him he was wrong, the Turk was really a charming person. Cenzo Rena told Anna that Emanuele had made him a fine present in sending him this silly little man in tennis-shorts, what fine friends Anna had, what fine sort of people they were in that house opposite.

Anna told him he had said he never wanted to mortify anyone again, so he must be kind even to this man Franz, besides he was a Jew and might end up in one of those sealed trains ; then Cenzo Rena remembered about the sealed trains and made a great effort to be kind to Franz, even though it put him in a great rage to see him arrive at their house hopping up over the rocks, with his little muscular legs in their tennis-shorts.

Franz was nevertheless very touching when he played with the little girl. He had great patience with her and spent hours with her, throwing the ball to her or digging in the ground with a spoon, and talking to her in a low voice. The little girl was now two years old, and had lost that tender, delicate hair, she now had untidy locks of hair as tawny and dry as straw, and she had two eyes as green as pools of water, and a big, impudent mouth. These locks of hair were always falling down in a shower over her face, and she would sweep them aside with an impudent, imperious gesture, and Cenzo Rena was always astonished at this gesture, he was always astonished to see such a sombre, impudent air in such a very small child. She was always very dirty because she played all day long on the ground, and she screamed and struggled whenever anyone attempted to wash her. If she could she ran off to play in the lanes with the children of the *contadini*, and Cenzo Rena was afraid she might catch dysentery, and Anna would run after her and bring her back and then she would scream and struggle and hit her mother in the face with her little dirty hands. She would stand and watch Franz digging in the ground with a spoon, she would watch him with quiet indifference, standing in front of him with her hands behind her back, he would talk to her but she never answered, but swept aside her straw-like locks from her impudent face. When she saw Franz coming, she would go quietly to meet him and put into his hand the spoon for him to dig with. Franz told Anna how beautiful and strange the child was, he would have so much liked to have a child like that himself. But he would never have any children, Amalia had a narrow pelvis and could not have any. He was very sad at the thought that he could never have children. Little by little he told Anna and Cenzo Rena the story of what had happened with Amalia at the village where they had been, there had been a woman chemist whom he had rather liked, they had gone for a few walks together on Sundays when the chemist's shop was shut, he had perhaps given her a few half-kisses, a matter of no importance at all. But the whole village had known of it and they had written anonymous letters to Amalia and to the woman chemist's husband, who was not a chemist himself but a registrar. There had been a small scandal, he had had to give money to the registrar to calm him down, and Amalia had had hysterics, she gave great roars of laughter and wept at the same time, and then she had fallen down in a faint and he had been terribly frightened. She lay there pale as death on the floor and he did not know what to do, he wanted to go and fetch something from the chemist's shop but in the chemist's shop there was the woman chemist, in the end he had given her a little eau-de-Cologne to inhale and Amalia had come to herself again. He had asked her forgiveness, he had sworn that he was perfectly indifferent to the woman chemist and in thought had always remained faithful to her. And so it really was, he had rather liked the woman chemist because she was beautiful. And besides, Amalia did not go to bed willingly, she always lay there stock still and every time it was as though one were committing an affront against her, he himself, if she had gone to bed a little more willingly, would perhaps not have looked at other women so much. Cenzo Rena told him to be quiet, because they were not interested in hearing of the manner in which his wife went to bed.

The day after her fainting fit Amalia had gone away. She had not spoken one single further word to him, she had been very sombre and very pale, he had been in despair at the thought of her going that long journey by herself and perhaps even fainting again. She had never written to him, he had heard of her arrival through a letter from Emanuele. He himself had written to Emanuele begging him to go on sending him news. After all she was his wife and he loved her, how could he be left without any news, very often at night his heart ached when he thought of her having left him and of his parents who were certainly dead in Poland, he had never heard anything more of them, very often at night he cried into his pillow like a little boy. He felt himself very unfortunate and very lonely. He smeared the tears all over his face with his fingers, and begged Cenzo Rena and Anna to write to Emanuele and ask him to persuade Amalia to come back to him. It was not his fault if he liked girls, he said, he had liked them always so very much, and in any case who didn't like them, here now at San Costanzo he liked the police-sergeant's sister-in-law. She had two nice pear-shaped breasts and nice curly hair, and a tiny beak-like nose, rather pert and charming. When he rang the bell at the police station he looked up to see whether the pear-shaped breasts were at the window, and certainly the Turk also liked to see them at the window, otherwise why should he have rung the bell so constantly. He did not feel that he was committing any offence against his wife when he looked at those breasts as they bobbed up and down under the blouse. He thought that Amalia would not be unhappy at San Costanzo, there were no ducal palaces but the people were honest and not gossipy, they would leave them in peace as far as anonymous letters were concerned. Cenzo Rena told him he might find himself in trouble, for San Costanzo was the very kingdom of the anonymous letter.

The English were striking hard every day against Sicily, and it was there that the *contadino* Giuseppe was, they had had no further news of him, every day Giuseppe's wife came to see Cenzo Rena and ask him what he thought. He himself thought that Giuseppe was dead, and he made great efforts to say nothing of this to her, but to smile and caress the children that she trailed behind her, he asked her if she was giving the children rice and if she was taking precautions against dysentery. But as soon as she had gone away he would puff and snort and wipe the sweat from his face, because he had always to make efforts to keep his thoughts to himself, when really he was longing to tell everybody that everything was useless, because the earth was on the point of going to ruin. At night he would wake up and start thinking about the *contadino* Giuseppe, he would waken Anna and tell her he was sure he was dead. Then Anna would ask whether Giustino was dead too. Concettina's husband had sent a post-card from a hospital at Ljubljana, he had been wounded but it was only a slight thing, nothing had been heard of Giustino. Cenzo Rena would not say anything on the subject of Giustino, he sighed and twisted himself about in the bed, then Anna started crying and said he must think Giustino was dead already, that was why he would not say anything. No, he said, no, Giustino had perhaps written a number of letters which had never arrived, the post from Russia worked very irregularly. He asked her to forgive him for not knowing how to give her any real comfort, he did not want to have to go on comforting people ; what he wanted, on the contrary, was to find someone who would comfort *him*, for he had such a feeling of emptiness inside him. And there was Giuseppe's wife coming to see him every day and expecting words of hope like water to drink, she was living with an ill-natured sister-in-law who kept repeating every moment that there was no hope for Giuseppe with all that was going on in Sicily, where the English were on the point of landing. She would say this with an air of sorrow, wiping the tears from her eyes, and she would go on to say that they must resign themselves to fate, and that Giuseppe was getting the punishment he deserved because he had always been against the Government, and used to read wicked books at night. Giuseppe's wife was small and pale, with a delicate, wasted face and a mouth entirely empty of teeth, when she laughed it was surprising to see so youthful a mouth quite empty. Cenzo Rena was astonished that she should still have any desire to laugh, what with her husband in Sicily and her ill-natured sister-in-law, and a life that was nothing but overworking herself in the fields, and he was astonished that she should have no feeling of modesty about opening that empty mouth of hers. He told her that a cunning fellow like Giuseppe would certainly manage to survive, he would manage to get himself taken prisoner, and so he would stay quietly in America or in India until the war was over. Giuseppe's wife was very pleased, she ran off with one child on her shoulder and leading another by the hand, she ran off to tell her sister-in-law that if a man was cunning he could manage not to be killed in the war.

There was widespread dysentery in the village but Cenzo Rena had in some measure lost interest in dysentery, he did not now go round so much after the doctor into the houses of the *contadini*, in any case it was useless to tell them to buy rice because rice was not to be had. Even the veal nights now seemed a remote and distant thing, it was some time now since any calves had been killed because the *contadini* preferred to sell them in town on the black market, in the village they did not dare to sell on the black market because they were afraid of anonymous letters. A bull was killed because it was old and it was sold at the slaughter-yard, and it seemed to everyone that they could see it again passing along the road as it returned from the pasture, big and black and very old and tired, the meat was very tough to eat but those who arrived in time to buy some of it did eat it, and La Maschiona, too, managed to buy a big piece of it and Cenzo Rena ate it two days running and said what in the world would happen to him now after eating bull's meat, but he said that after the war he wanted to go and live in a town, because he did not like eating beasts that he had seen walking about alive.

9

Mussolini said in a speech that the English would never succeed in landing in Sicily, but would be stopped at the *bagnasciuga* or water-line. Franz could not stop laughing at this word *bagnasciuga*, what an extraordinary word it was, where in the world had Mussolini dug it up? Cenzo Rena told him not to laugh, it was quite possible that the *contadino* Giuseppe might be on the water-line. There were plenty of other people for that, said Franz offended, not only just his friend the *contadino* Giuseppe. But anyhow, surely one might laugh for a moment at the comic words of Mussolini. No, said Cenzo Rena, Mussolini was no longer comic and no longer made one laugh. He had made people laugh for a very long time, when he wore spats and a top hat, and when he had himself photographed with tiger-cubs in his arms, and when he walked with his hands on his hips amongst sheaves of corn and country housewives. But with every year he had become a more and more joyless thing. His big statue-like face passed through towns in motor-cars, stuck itself out, big and waxy, from balconies, becoming with every year more big and more bare. And gradually everything that was made in Italy came to be made as it were in the image of that statue-like face, sculptors carved their statues with the features of that face, even fountains and stations and post-offices imitated the architecture of that face, and ministers and officials tried to look like it and succeeded, no one knew how but they succeeded, gradually they too developed immense bare, waxy heads that at once made you think of a station or a post-office. And perhaps one might still laugh a little, at all those post-offices sitting round in the Fascist Council. But now the real post-offices had collapsed, entire cities had collapsed and that big waxy head had disappeared, no one knew what had happened to it, whether it had

seemed too frightened or too despairing or too mad, or
whether all of a sudden it had been ashamed of being so big
and so bare.   And then all of a sudden it had reappeared in
order to explain about the *bagnasciuga*.   And it was not a
word to laugh at, it was a word which had a mournful and
indecent sound, just as mournful and indecent as that big,
bare head that had suddenly reappeared.   No, Mussolini
no longer made one laugh, the time was long past when one
could laugh at him, the time of the top hat and the tiger-cubs
was long past.   Mussolini now, with his water-line, aroused
a feeling of horror and also, slightly, of pity.   Not pity, said
Franz, not pity, and he was there digging in the ground
for the little girl and suddenly he threw down the spoon, he
was not giving his pity to Mussolini, he had heard nothing
of his parents but he knew that he would never see them
alive again, and so he kept his pity in reserve for himself and
for others like him, who had lost their families without knowing how or where.   He asked Anna's pardon but said that
he was going away, because he had no wish to stay there
with Cenzo Rena and see him getting emotional over Mussolini.   He started going down over the rocks, he went down
slowly because he perhaps expected that they would call him
back, Anna wanted to call him back but Cenzo Rena said
let him go, he was utterly, utterly sick of the sight of Franz's
silly face.   The little girl stood looking at Franz's back for
a moment as he went away, and then all of a sudden threw
the spoon after him.

Franz sulked for a few days, but then he came back.   He
avoided all mention of the water-line, in any case there was
nothing more to be said about the water-line, the English
had crossed it and in a few days they took the whole of
Sicily.   Giuseppe's wife arrived with her empty mouth wide
open with laughter, Giuseppe had written from Bari where
he had been evacuated with his battalion, he was well and
perhaps in a short time he might be sent home on leave.
Cenzo Rena said that Giuseppe was a disappointment, he
had been only a couple of steps from the English on the

water-line and had not been clever enough to get himself
taken prisoner, he had got himself evacuated to Bari, what
disgusting, depressing words the war produced, he did not
at all like to think of Giuseppe being evacuated. Anna told
him that for some time now he could never be pleased about
anything, he had been so afraid on account of the *contadino*
Giuseppe and now he could not even rejoice that he had been
evacuated. Yes indeed, said Cenzo Rena, he was aware
that he had become very tiresome and ill-natured for some
time now, he had taken a dislike to everyone and wanted to
go round uttering gloomy predictions, and also he did not
feel well and both sleeping and eating disgusted him. It
was La Maschiona's fault for having made him eat that bull's
meat, now he was aware of a taste of bull even in the bread,
even the bread had taken on a taste of bull and onions. But
it was at least a month since they had eaten the bull's meat,
said La Maschiona, and when they had eaten it he had not
said a word about being disgusted by it, he had eaten it two
days running with plenty of bread and plenty of onions, in
any case she had to cook what she could get.

There arrived in San Costanzo a family of refugees from
Naples, women and mattresses and babies were unloaded one
morning from a lorry in the village square, and the police-
sergeant was struggling to find accommodation for them in
the village. Cenzo Rena felt he ought to take at least four
people into his house, he thought of all the rooms in his
house, and on the other hand he could not bear the idea of
taking anyone, he could not bear the idea of living with
anyone, he went round with the police-sergeant looking for
somewhere to accommodate them. That was what he was
like, he said to Anna, all day long he groaned over the
bombed houses and then some refugees came and he was
unwilling to take them in, God how unwilling he was, that
was the disgusting kind of person he was. He was not afraid
of their spoiling the furniture, it was not that, he would willingly have given up the whole house to them if he could
have gone off somewhere else, the thing that was repugnant

to him was living together. He looked out of the window
at the refugees from Naples who were now going hither and
thither about the lanes of the village, carrying mattresses and
babies, he looked and said how sad it was to see all these
mattresses carried about here and there all over Italy, Italy
was now pouring mattresses out of her ravaged houses. And
perhaps they too might soon be forced to run away, with
their mattresses and the little girl and La Maschiona and
the dog and the deck chairs, to run away to goodness knows
where through the burning dust of the roads, and a great
weariness had come upon him and he did not feel like carrying his mattresses anywhere. This family of refugees had
suddenly filled the whole village, you saw them everywhere,
these black, half-naked children, and a youth with his arm
in a black sling, and big women in sandals carrying mattresses and combing their hair in the lanes and washing at
the fountain. Cenzo Rena had given money for the refugees
to the police-sergeant but now he thought he had been an
idiot to give the police-sergeant the money, the police-
sergeant would certainly never dream of giving anything to
the refugees and would keep it all himself. Cenzo Rena
had been ashamed to take the money to those fat women
combing their hair, and yet that was what he ought to have
done, but shame was the thing that spoilt human beings,
probably without shame human beings would have been a
little less nasty. But now there was no time left to argue
about shame, there was no time left to trouble about one's
soul, the houses built for human beings were falling to the
ground and mattresses and babies were pouring out of them
because the earth was going to ruin. And Giustino, said
Anna, Giustino, where in the world was he ? Giustino, said
Cenzo Rena, Giustino, where indeed ?

They had news of Giustino, however, in a letter from Concettina, she had talked to someone who had seen him, he
had been wounded in the retreat from the Don and was now
in hospital at Fiume, still too weak to write but in bed and
alive. Concettina was still at Le Visciole and from there

had seen the bombing of their own town, she had stayed out in the garden all night and had seen in the distance a mass of black smoke all dotted with sparks, and had thought that perhaps the soap factory was on fire. However the soap factory had not been hit, nor had their own house nor yet the house opposite, Emanuele had come next day and told her that everything was still standing in the part of the town along the river, but that a whole quarter of the old town had been wrecked and he had spent the night carrying out the dead. Emanuele came sometimes now to sleep at Le Visciole, in order to have a rest from air raid warnings, but he never felt sleepy and kept her up late talking, and he always told her the story of that night when he had bandaged the wounded and carried out the dead in company with the managing director, he was on very good terms now with the managing director and no longer wished to trample his hat into the ground.

10

Early one morning the Turk and Franz arrived, Cenzo Rena was floundering in his tub and Anna who was at the window told him that Franz and the Turk were just arriving together. Cenzo Rena went out in his bath-gown, something must have happened if those two suddenly came to see him together. Fascism was finished, they shouted to him, Mussolini was finished. The Turk sat down breathless on a rock and fanned himself with his straw hat, Cenzo Rena had to give him a cordial because he was on the point of fainting, he had run all the way, dragged along by Franz. So they had really thrown out Mussolini, said Cenzo Rena thoughtfully, the King had thrown out Mussolini, that was right and proper, but who remembered the King nowadays? He sat down on the rock beside the Turk, and wiped his face with the sleeves of his bath-gown. Franz had fetched a rail-way time-table and was studying it, he wanted to leave San Costanzo at once, he wanted to go to Stresa to join his wife. Now that Mussolini had fallen he was no longer an internee, he was a free citizen in Italy and could go where he liked. The Turk also could go where he liked. But the Turk kept fanning himself with his hat and he shook his head and said that the matter was not so simple after all, they were war internees and the war was still going on, for the present he still did not want to look at the railway time-table.

Then the village people began arriving, the farrier and the dressmaker and the draper and two or three *contadini*, those few who had not gone early in the morning into the fields, the ones in the fields still did not know anything about Mussolini. All of a sudden the police-sergeant also arrived, sweating and troubled, he shut himself up in a room with Cenzo Rena and begged him to testify on his behalf. At the bottom of his heart he had always been against Mussolini, as Cenzo Rena ought to know, Cenzo Rena was a man who understood other people's thoughts without very much being said. He had heard what had happened when he was on the way to Scoturno, where he was going to buy a few cherries for his children, and had turned back so as to speak to Cenzo Rena at once, he had thrown that decoration of his with " God curse England " on it into a ditch, in any case for some time past had been disgusted by the words on the decoration, he was a Christian and did not want God to curse anybody. Cenzo Rena told him there was little he could do to testify on his behalf, for the present no one was asking any questions, he told him to stay quietly where he was and go on acting as police-sergeant. And the internees, asked the police-sergeant, what ought he to do about the internees, if they ran away what ought he to do ? Nothing, Cenzo Rena told him, nothing. How could he do nothing, said the police-sergeant, they were war internees and the war was not over yet. Cenzo Rena told him not to think about it but to come and drink some wine with the others.

The dressmaker told the story of how she had hidden the
red flag in her baby's cradle, a baby who was now twenty
years old and had been taken prisoner in Somaliland, but
perhaps he still remembered the flag stuck into the straw
bed of his cradle one night while the Fascists were shooting
all round the house. And Anna told the story of the day
when they burned the newspapers, she and Ippolito and
Emanuele and Concettina, and the dressmaker said that she
too had burned all kinds of things during those years, she
lived next door to the Marchesa and the Marchesa used to
come in every minute with some excuse or other to spy out
what she was burning. The dressmaker said that now
Fascism had gone up in smoke the Marchesa must be made
to pay dearly for all the anonymous letters she had written to
police headquarters in the town, and for all the overbearing
things she had done in the village, one of her daughters had
been a servant in the Marchesa's house and when they had
fetched her back home again she was spitting blood because
the Marchesa had given her a punch in the chest, the
Marchesa had put it about that she was consumptive but
she was not consumptive, she had had something broken
inside her chest. Then La Maschiona came out and shouted
her plan about the cage, perhaps now they would make that
cage on four wheels to put Mussolini in and send him round
the villages, but they would have to make it very big, so that
there would be room in it for the Marchesa too and for a
good many other people who had done overbearing things,
she had her mouth full of spittle and could hardly wait to
spit. Cenzo Rena was coming and going and pulling corks
out of bottles, he was still in his bath-gown and it did not
occur to him to get dressed, he swallowed a lot of wine and
kept hold of the police-sergeant by his cloak, he did not want
him to go away. He told La Maschiona to stop talking
about her plan for the cage, he had heard it all too often
and he did not like it any more. In any case it was useless
to talk any more about Mussolini, no one was thinking about
Mussolini now. Now there was the King, the collector of

coins, who gradually had pulled himself together and wanted
to try and take command.   The King would dig out goodness knows what old ministers, because Italy had had quite
enough of Fascists with big muscular torsos and of athletic
processions and had a gieat longing for white-haired, mild
old gentlemen with crooked, trembling knees.   In a short
time Italy would certainly be flooded with mild old gentlemen, dressed as generals and ministers and dragging behind
them elderly wives, trembling and white-haired, and Italy
would clap her hands at these elderly wives, sick as she was
of the women that Fascism had brought into fashion, bronze
breasts and thighs crowned with ears of corn on the bridges
and the fountains.   The King would go about Italy sometimes on horseback and Italy would clap her hands at him,
he had never imagined that the King's crooked knees could
be pleasing to Italy and yet now it was just those crooked
knees that Italy was greeting with joy and relief, and the
wizened, disdainful, monkey-like little face under the peaked
cap that was too big for him.   If anyone fired a shot in the
air the little monkey would run off and hide himself in the
place where he had been for so many years, the little monkey
would run off to the cellar where his collection of coins was
kept, but at present Italy was pleased and was not thinking
of firing any shots immediately.   The police-sergeant made
as if to rise, because he could not bear to hear the King
called a little monkey.   His father had received a medal
from the King's own hands.   Cenzo Rena held him firmly
by his cloak and poured him out some more wine, perhaps
later on he and the police-sergeant might become enemies
but not yet, not that day, that day they must drink together
over the downfall of Mussolini.   Later on, after the little
monkey had also been put aside, they would have to begin
to do something really fine, but he did not want to tell the
police-sergeant what, because he did not want to cause him
pain that day.
    In the evening Cenzo Rena felt very ill and collapsed on
his bed, he was all red and his eyes were starting out of his

head and he had a taste of bull's meat in his mouth, and he could not go to the municipal office with the *contadini* to burn the Fascist dossiers, the *contadini* came to call him but he was on the bed in his room in the dark, and he lay there complaining. The doctor came and said it was German measles, but Cenzo Rena told him that as usual he was wrong, he might have German measles too but that was the lesser thing, he felt a severe illness coming on, typhus or cholera. He did not sleep the whole night long and had a high fever, and he could hardly bear to wait for morning to come so that he could let the doctor know ; when had German measles ever caused such a high fever ? And he said that now he understood, for some time he had been very gloomy and had felt disgust for everything and had believed that the earth was going to ruin, but the truth was that it was just he himself, Cenzo Rena, that was going to ruin.

After a week the doctor discovered that Cenzo Rena had typhus, but Cenzo Rena could not crow over him in triumph, because he was unconscious and muttering incoherently, with a little bit of a face sticking out above the sheets, all swollen and bristling with grey beard, and a bag of ice on his forehead. But every now and then he would open his eyes and say that of course the police-sergeant had kept the money he had given him for the refugees from Naples, he was really nothing but a scoundrel, that police-sergeant. And he asked Anna whether Mussolini was still well out of the way. Yes, still, said Anna, and Cenzo Rena said he would have to be shot some time or other, but not at once. And the funny part was that the King would have to be shot too, and what on earth would the police-sergeant look like on the day the King was shot ? There would have to be a little trial and then the shooting. Cenzo Rena closed his eyes again and wrapped the sheet round him and fell asleep.

Franz had not succeeded in getting away, the police-sergeant had told him not to move for the present, just as the Turk and the old women and the internees at Scoturno were not moving ; they were war internees and the war was by no means over yet. The only thing was that they could spare themselves the trouble of ringing the bell. Franz was beside himself with rage at the police-sergeant, there was typhus now at San Costanzo into the bargain, Cenzo Rena had it and there were other cases in the village, probably it had been brought by those refugees from Naples, the youth with the black bandage was dead. Franz said that if he died of typhus it would be the fault of the police-sergeant. He spent all his time in the kitchen at the inn seeing whether the food was boiling, and before sitting down to table he made them boil his spoon and fork, and he kept well away from the Turk because the Turk went to see Cenzo Rena. He himself, Franz, was careful not to go anywhere near Cenzo Rena's house, and when he saw Anna come down into the village to do the shopping, he saluted her with great hand-wavings from a very long way off, and shook his head violently, pointing towards the police station, to explain that he had business with the sergeant. Anna had to come down herself to do the shopping because La Maschiona had taken the little girl up to Scoturno di Sopra, to a cottage in the middle of the fields in which lived her grandmother, an old woman of over ninety. La Maschiona wept all day long at Scoturno di Sopra because she was sure that Cenzo Rena would die, and also because she was sure that she and the little girl had typhus too ; but the little girl went off with a long stick in her hand to where the sheep were pasturing, and she also went with La Maschiona's grandmother to cut grass for the rabbits.

The Turk came every day to see Cenzo Rena, he would sit down at his bedside and fan himself with his hat, and would sit there for hours quite silent, looking at that little bit of a face sticking out above the sheets, and at Anna moving about the room on tiptoe with the ice and the medicines. When the Turk went away Anna would go down with him to the door, she and the Turk had become friends and would talk together for a little at the door, the Turk said every day that Cenzo Rena looked well. The Turk would go away and she would sit down for a moment on the staircase of the big, empty house, and she longed to shout to the Turk to stay a little longer there with her, but the Turk was already some distance away along the sandy path, and she had to go back to Cenzo Rena and look at his swollen, goggle-eyed face sticking out above the sheets, and refill the ice-bag and count out the drops into a glass.

The Turk brought Anna little notes from Franz. They were complaining little notes in which Franz moaned about the typhus and about the police-sergeant, and about Amalia never writing to him ; Mammina had let him know that Amalia's nerves were badly shaken and that it might perhaps be necessary to shut her up in a mental home. Anna thought for a moment about Amalia and Mammina and Giuma, and how strange it was that all those people should still exist ; for herself now there was nothing except the typhus, the big, empty, silent house, and Cenzo Rena's face growing ever redder and more goggle-eyed. She wrote to Concettina to ask whether she could not leave her baby with someone and come and see her. Concettina answered that she was sorry but it wasn't possible, she was expecting her husband from day to day and perhaps Giustino would be coming back too. Concettina enquired anxiously whether they would now do anything to her husband for having worn a black shirt and sometimes marched in processions.

The Turk never stopped saying how disgusting Franz was. He saw typhus germs everywhere, and as for those little notes for Anna, he used to throw them to him across the table, and he kept on saying he was mad to go and see Cenzo Rena, and each time he asked him whether he had at least disinfected his hands. He spent the whole day groaning in the kitchen that he no longer had any money, because the authorities had cut off the small allowance given to the internees and he now received nothing from his wife, and the landlady of the inn was sorry for him and gave him credit, but Franz had a big diamond ring on his finger and why in the world didn't he sell it, rather than allow himself to be kept by the landlady ?   The Turk had been provident and had put a little money aside.   Anna had a letter one day from Emanuele, he was in Rome and was running backwards and forwards all day long from one appointment to another, from time to time he remembered the soap factory but thrust the thought aside, he had no time now for the soap factory.   Danilo also was in Rome, he had escaped from his island on the day of Mussolini's fall, he was in very poor health because he had caught a whole heap of diseases on the island and perhaps he ought to go up into the mountains to get well, but who thought of going to the mountains now, there was now the re-making of Italy to be thought of.   Emanuele had appointments all the time with Danilo and Danilo's friends, the ones who had been in prison for so many years and had come out on the morning of July 25th, with people applauding and clapping their hands.   Emanuele sent Anna a cheque for Franz, he said he was really distressed about Franz but he had no wish to write to him, he had other things to think about now than the troubles of Amalia and Franz.   The Turk brought the cheque to Franz and asked him if he was going to disinfect it.

Cenzo Rena lay stiller and stiller and more and more hidden under the sheet, but one evening, all of a sudden, he threw back the sheet and sat up in bed, and he saw the doctor who was on the point of going away, and Anna putting ice into the bag with a spoon.   Cenzo Rena gave a long, squealing yawn, and they asked him if he felt better and if he would like some broth to drink and he said yes, but he was still going to die, he said, he could not see any more days for him to live, he could only see a big black hole in front of him.   In any case he had no wish to live but he had no wish to die either, he wished merely to be ill in his bed for ever, with the Turk coming to see him and the ice-bag on his head.   Anna brought the broth and Cenzo Rena took some of it, and the doctor said that now he was beginning to get well, but Cenzo Rena told him that he was wrong as usual, he did not feel very ill but he felt death

approaching.   In his back he felt death approaching, there
was a spot in his back that trembled and pulsated, right
down at the bottom of his back where his seat began, a spot
which was quite cold and trembling.   The doctor went
away and Cenzo Rena lay down flat again but went on
talking, he talked like that the whole night and Anna was
very pleased, at last Cenzo Rena was talking and getting
better.   He no longer had that goggle-eyed look but had
eyes that could see, and he stroked Anna with a hand that
had grown whiter and smoother, poor Anna, he said, a fine
disaster it would be if he died.   A disaster because, when
all was said and done, he had never made her turn into a
real person at all, when all was said and done she was still
just an insect, a little lazy, sad insect on a leaf, he himself
had been just a big leaf to her.   And now, if her leaf was
taken away, she would fall down and be lost, with her little
wings that could not fly and her little staring eyes, he had
never been able to give her the power to fly and to breathe,
he had been only a leaf and had given her nothing but a
little rest.   He asked her if she still remembered the day
when together they had looked at themselves in the barber's
looking-glass, on that day they had decided to get married
and they had had cold shudders but they both felt very
strong and aggressive and free : wasn't it true that she too
had felt aggressive and free that day ?   But how far off that
day now seemed, and what had happened, he wondered, to
that barber's looking-glass, perhaps a bomb had fallen on
it, if he did not die he would like to go and see if that looking-
glass was still intact, he would like to look at himself in it
again with her.   They had never again been so strong and
free as they had been that day, they were quite contented
together but only like an insect and a leaf, very quiet and
contented in their home, far removed from both good and
evil.   But what ought they to do, asked Anna, what ought
they to do so as not to be outside both good and evil ?
Then Cenzo Rena told her not to ask foolish questions.   But
he asked forgiveness for carrying on this long conversation,

he had been silent for such a long time with his face
under the sheet, he had lain there with his eyes shut as
though he were asleep but he had been unravelling his
thoughts, and he had known that the Turk came often, the
Turk was a dear good man.   If he was going to die he
would like once more to see the *contadino* Giuseppe, " lived
and died a Socialist ", and explain to him thoroughly once
again all the things he would have to do when he was mayor
of the village.   Poor Anna, he said, a fine disaster it would
be if he died.   But really and truly, why should it be a disaster, he said, she was young and had still so much of her
life to live, and perhaps, with him dead, she would all at
once stop being an insect and would turn into a hard, strong
woman, with clenched teeth and a bold, free step, instead
of those little gentle steps, instead of those little sad, gentle
eyes.   For loneliness and sorrow were the salvation of the
spirit, so at least it said in books and perhaps it was true.
He himself had had a little loneliness and sorrow in his life
but not much, women had let him down and he had felt
mortified and bewildered for a few days, sitting huddled in
the corner of a bar in a foreign town, with a glass in front
of him with something green in it.   Yes, he remembered
moments like that.   A glass with something green in it, and
all round him the unknown town quivering and humming,
and he himself dirty and tired and completely alone.   But
they had been mere moments and any little thing had
sufficed to make him feel the earth under his feet again,
the firm, solid earth to walk upon, and all at once he would
feel fresh and happy again, with a great hunger and thirst
to discover the things of the earth.   He thought now that
perhaps it had been bad for him to be always spared in this
way, never to have fallen to the bottom of one of those cess-
pools into which men stumble ; life had given him a great
deal, but a real cesspool, a really deep one, it had never
given him.   And then he had married Anna, and perhaps
if she had let him down it would have been a real cesspool
for him, because he had become extremely fond of her, he

didn't quite know how, when he had married her he had had no idea that he would be able to grow so fond of her. But she had not let him down, and she had been very good and quiet with him there. One reason why she had been so very good there was that she was very lazy, she was a person who stayed where she was put. Very lazy, he said, and he placed his hand over her mouth because she was protesting. The little girl wasn't an insect, he said, the little girl wasn't a person who stayed where she was put. Poor Anna, he said, that child would give her something to think about. He wanted to drink a little more broth and he said it was very good, he said that even Anna had learned to do something at San Costanzo, for instance she had learned to put on a chicken to boil and make broth. But Anna told him that the farrier's mother had come to put the chicken on to boil, and then Cenzo Rena had a good laugh, he asked if the farrier's mother came every day, and he said that the farrier and his mother were dear good people. He felt very well now he had had the broth, he said, he felt very light and fresh, but he still had that spot in his back which made him feel he was going to die, a small patch of skin which was all contracted and chilled, and he pulled up his pyjamas to show her where it was. And then he asked for a looking-glass because he no longer remembered his own face, he looked for a long time at his cheeks and his lips and all the grains of rice, all a little dimmed by the fever. And then he started looking at his hands and his wrists and a blue vein in his arm, and he wanted to look at his feet too and pulled them out from under the sheet, he was ugly but he had beautiful feet, he said, beautiful long, narrow, aristocratic feet. And no one knew what was in store for the dead, he said, perhaps nothing at all but perhaps, on the other hand, there was something, probably a great boredom, he said, a deathly boredom. There was a possibility that he might be made to meet his mother, perhaps it was thought that it would be a pleasure to him whereas he had not the slightest wish to see his mother again, they had never got on well together, she was a capricious and spiteful old woman and she swore he would die in poverty, because he used to lend money to the *contadini*.   She always used to sit with her feet on a stool and she would give the stool a kick when they began quarrelling.   He always remembered very clearly that thud on the footstool, and during those days when he had lain silent with his face under the sheet he had expected every moment to hear that thud, and it would have meant it was the other life beginning.

Next day Cenzo Rena had a high fever again, and this time he was not red and goggle-eyed but very pale and sweating and panting, and the doctor said it looked to him as if he had pneumonia now as well but he was not sure, and he no longer felt prepared to look after him and they must call doctors from the town into consultation.   The doctors came and said that Cenzo Rena must go into hospital at once, and a motor-ambulance arrived and the whole village came out to watch Cenzo Rena being taken off to hospital in the town ; there was the police-sergeant on the balcony of the police station and the young woman with the pear-shaped breasts and the twins, and the wife of the *contadino* Giuseppe washing the stairs at the police station and weeping, and the farrier and the farrier's fat mother sitting on a straw-bottomed chair amongst the mule-clippings, and all the *contadini*, all silent and sad ; and the motor-ambulance moved off to the sound of a long cry, and inside it were Anna weeping with a suitcase on her knees and Cenzo Rena pale and sweaty and muttering.

I I

The hospital was not far from the market-place, that same market-place in which Cenzo Rena had bought the bathing-costumes when they had gone to the seaside, and

Anna now went down there from time to time in search of lemons for Cenzo Rena, but there hardly ever were any lemons because the roads were being machine-gunned and scarcely anything was being brought to market, the only thing for sale was piles of small green broccoli, which grew only two steps outside the town. The San Costanzo doctor came every two or three days to see Cenzo Rena, he came on a motor-bicycle and on one occasion found himself on the road with machine-gunning going on ; he jumped off his motor-bicycle and threw himself into a ditch, and arrived at the hospital white with fear, he had heard a great noise and felt a great wind and it had seemed to him that the aeroplane was stroking his hair. Cenzo Rena was very disagreeable to the doctor when he saw him, he said it was his fault that they had brought him into this ugly hospital, with dirty nurses and never a lemon to be seen, he had a desire for lemons and there was no possibility of ever finding one, they explained to him about the machine-gunnings but he did not quite understand, he was astonished that the war should still be going on. With a great effort he recalled the war, and his eyes went small and misty as he recalled it. And Mussolini, was he still well out of the way, he asked, and where was the Turk now, still at San Costanzo ringing the bell ? They explained to him that the Turk now no longer rang the bell. And wasn't there also a curfew, he asked, he seemed to have heard the curfew mentioned, a new war word ? Ah, so the war was still going on. To him it seemed that he had been ill for many, many years.

Cenzo Rena began to get better towards the end of September. There had been the armistice but he had not known about it, he was too ill at that time, lying there with dry, white lips and great black circles under his eyes, and Anna on her feet for many days and many nights, her hands clenched and sweaty as she watched one hour after another pass over that prostrate body. To her it seemed that she had grown very, very old and very, very small, with her brain confused and contracted and containing nothing, ever, except Cenzo Rena's illness, which had been first typhus and then pneumonia and was causing him to die ; and by fits and starts she recalled all the things of their life, but with horror, everything was sliding to ruin in that hospital where Cenzo Rena lay dying.

The day after the armistice the Germans had arrived in the town, and had filled the market-place with vehicles, and had taken over the two hotels, and were now sitting about, drinking and smoking, in the cafés ; and Mussolini was no longer out of the way, Mussolini had been set free and carried off by car to some place in the North to start governing again. And when Cenzo Rena began to improve Anna told him about Mussolini, that he was no longer out of the way, and she told him about the Germans being all over the town, but Cenzo Rena was very pleased at feeling himself getting better and said that the Germans being there would certainly be only a matter of a few days and that in a short time the English would be arriving in Italy from somewhere or other. He was very pleased at feeling himself getting better, and again he felt hunger and thirst for the things of the earth, and all of a sudden he liked the hospital and the nurses who were charming in their dirtiness, but he had a longing to go back home and see the little girl and La Maschiona and the dog. He was offended because the San Costanzo doctor had not appeared for some time, why in the world had he stopped coming to see him, did he never stir, then, except for people who were on the point of death ? Anna said that perhaps he was afraid of the Germans and Cenzo Rena said that was a fine thing to be, really people mustn't go too far with their fear of the Germans, in any case a doctor ought to be able to move about everywhere. He started to get up and sit in an armchair near the window, and from there he could see the Germans in the market-place ; ah, those were the Germans, he said, well, well.

Anna and Cenzo Rena went back to San Costanzo in a

cab, which looked rather like the Marchesa's carriage but was bigger, with a canvas awning and fluttering fringed curtains, and Cenzo Rena kept saying all the way how nice it was to ride in a carriage, the Marchesa was not far wrong in having herself driven up and down in a carriage. The motor-bus had been requisitioned by the Germans, and the road was crowded with German and Italian vehicles with the *Wehrmacht* markings going this way and that, with long olive-branches waving on their roofs and, inside, German soldiers in uniforms of dirty yellow.

At San Costanzo, too, the village square was full of German lorries, camouflaged in green and yellow, their big, heavy wheels sunk into the dust. In front of the draper's shop a sentry was walking up and down, and the shop shutter was lowered and Cenzo Rena saw, behind the door, the draper himself, who made him a little sign with his chin and quickly hid himself. Women and children had vanished from the lanes, the village looked like a village of the dead. All of a sudden, however, the *contadino* Giuseppe's wife popped out, saw Cenzo Rena and laughed, opening wide her empty mouth. She waved her hand and went back into the house. Cenzo Rena and Anna went slowly up through the lanes, and Cenzo Rena was hurt and sad, it was all very well the Germans being there but why didn't anyone come and greet him and congratulate him on his return? They were a lot of cowards, he said, the Germans were there and so they wouldn't put their heads out of doors. But there were just a few too many Germans, he said, what were those stupid English waiting for, that they didn't come and take Italy? He climbed slowly up over the rocks, leaning on Anna's arm because he was still very, very feeble. At the house there was La Maschiona sweeping the stairs, and the little girl screaming because she wanted to go back to La Maschiona's grandmother's cottage, she wanted the sheep and the rabbits.

Cenzo Rena threw himself down on the bed with a long sigh. But suddenly the door opened and the *contadino*

Giuseppe appeared, in his tattered black jacket and green hat, and Cenzo Rena started embracing and kissing the *contadino* Giuseppe, and he told him at once that he was a fool not to have managed to get himself taken prisoner by the English in Sicily. Giuseppe had run away from Bari after the armistice, he had thrown away his uniform and had been given some clothes, and he had come back home partly on foot and partly on farm carts, and now he was sitting there with his green hat on, and Cenzo Rena slapped him hard on the knees and on the shoulders, a fine fool he had been, at that moment he might have been a prisoner safe in India, instead of where he was. Then the farrier's mother arrived too, and she was weeping, the Germans were going round all the houses stealing the pigs and the hens, and there was no longer even the police-sergeant to speak up for the *contadini*. The police-sergeant had run away at once, as soon as he saw the Germans arriving, and now he was in hiding at Masuri in the house of some *contadini*, and he was no longer wearing the uniform of a police-sergeant but was in civilian clothes, and the children had been sent away to his parents-in-law, and the Germans had gone into the police station and had broken the sergeant's furniture to pieces, they had fired shots at the pier-glass and dismantled the radio, and the beautiful silk quilt that covered the sergeant's bed had departed on a lorry, as also the mattresses and the dinner-service, and the sergeant knew what had happened to his belongings but he could not do anything, he was in hiding over there at Masuri and in fear of death. But the Turk, asked Cenzo Rena, where was the Turk, he was very nearly forgetting the Turk, his memory had grown feeble. And then the farrier's mother and Giuseppe, both at the same time, told him how one day a German lorry had come to fetch the Turk and the three old women, they had looked for Franz too but Franz had jumped out of the window into the vegetable-garden and had been hidden by some *contadini*, the Turk on the other hand had not had time to escape,

and he had helped the old women to get up into the lorry
and then had put on his hat and got up too. The old
women were weeping and screaming amongst all those
soldiers with rifles, the Turk however remained perfectly
still and composed, and flicked the collar of his coat with a
pair of gloves. And the lorry had driven away and nothing
further had been heard of them.

Then Cenzo Rena jumped up from his bed and started
abusing Giuseppe and the farrier's mother, and La Maschiona who had come in to listen, and the police-sergeant
who was in hiding at Masuri, and the priest of San Costanzo
and also himself. He said they ought to have thought of
concealing the Turk and the old women, they were Jews
and everyone knew what the Germans did to Jews, and there
must have been someone in that rotten village who had
prompted the Germans to come and take away the Turk
and the old women, a rotten village it was, full of spies.
And he put on his waterproof and said he was going to
the other Jews at Scoturno to warn them and to find
somewhere to conceal them, if the Germans had not taken
them away yet. But Giuseppe said that the Scoturno Jews
had already gone off in a farm cart, half buried amongst
bags of apples, and had found a hiding-place in a monastery
in the town. And Franz, asked Cenzo Rena, where was
Franz? They said it was no longer known exactly where
he was, for some days he had stayed in bed in the house of
some *contadini*, and he lay with his head under the blankets
and scarcely breathed for fear of being discovered, the
contadini wanted to give him something to eat but he wouldn't
eat. Then he had heard people talking German at the
door, they were Germans asking for eggs, so he had jumped
out of the window into the meadows and had run down
towards the river, he had spent one night in the station-
master's house along with the little old mushroom man, but
then he had run away from there too.

Cenzo Rena walked up and down the room crumpling
the waterproof he had on in his hands ; they had taken

away the Turk, the Turk who was his best friend. The only hope was that the Turk and the old women were already dead by now, that was the only hope, but perhaps they were still alive and were travelling in one of those sealed trains, those trains one couldn't bear even to think of. That swine of a police-sergeant, he said, that swine of a police-sergeant for not having set the internees free after Fascism collapsed, that damned bloody swine of a police-sergeant. To think that nobody had been capable of warning the Turk about the Germans who were coming to take him away, to think that nobody had been capable of helping him to escape. The farrier's mother had already left but Giuseppe did not dare go away, he stood there deeply humiliated and looked out of the window at the darkness falling, at last he said that there was the curfew and he must go. Cenzo Rena told him to go to hell with his curfew, he took him by the shoulders and pushed him out.

Franz arrived that night at Cenzo Rena's house. He was in tennis-shorts and canvas shoes, and his knees were all scratched and one foot swollen because he had sprained it while running, he had been at Masuri the last few days but he did not feel safe because he had discovered that the police-sergeant was there, so as soon as he had heard of Cenzo Rena's return he had come away. He had come through the pine wood and had lost his way, and then he had crouched down in the empty bed of the stream, and had seen night coming on and heard dogs barking, and had thought the Germans were searching for him with dogs, but then he had realized that it was Anna's and Cenzo Rena's dog barking in front of the house. Franz felt feverish and believed he had the typhus, because he had slept a night at the station-master's house with the little old mushroom man, and the little old mushroom man had the dirtiest feet he had ever seen. Cenzo Rena put the thermometer in Franz's mouth and he had no fever, and he told him to stop being frightened now about the typhus, there were the Germans to be frightened of now and you

can't be frightened of too many things all at the same time.
But he was very kind to Franz and sent him off to bed
with a cup of broth, and Franz drank the broth and
trembled and wept and said how lonely he was, Amalia
and Mammina and Emanuele had deserted him, they had
left him without a penny in that village where the Germans
had arrived, no one had given a thought to coming and
helping him.   He went on sobbing gently all night long,
and Cenzo Rena had gone to bed but every now and then
he got up to see how he was, and to put cold water compresses on his foot which was hurting him.   Cenzo Rena
was very pleased at again having someone to hide and to
rescue.

Next day, Cenzo Rena and the *contadino* Giuseppe put
Franz with his bandaged foot on La Maschiona's donkey
and took him up to Scoturno di Sopra to La Maschiona's
grandmother, because Giuseppe said the Germans would
search the houses in the village again for Franz and it
was not wise to keep him there.   At La Maschiona's grandmother's there was no danger of anyone coming to dig
him out, at La Maschiona's grandmother's he could stay
calmly and quietly until the Germans went away.

12

Franz stayed for a month at La Maschiona's grandmother's, but then he came back. He said he could not
bear those long days spent all alone with La Maschiona's
grandmother, in that black, cramped kitchen that filled
with smoke when La Maschiona's grandmother lit her fire
of green boughs under the iron pot. This smoke stuck in
one's throat and then Franz would cough all night. And
La Maschiona's grandmother moved very slowly about
the kitchen, a round back in a black shawl and a pair of

shambling slippers, and Franz would feel he was going mad
at the sight of that round back, he would be sitting there on
a stool in the smoke and feel he was going mad. He had
run off one morning while La Maschiona's grandmother
was out cutting grass for the rabbits, his foot was well
again and he ran off at full speed through the meadows
and the pine wood and arrived once more at Cenzo Rena's
house, Cenzo Rena was sitting reading and saw him appear
in front of him. Franz took a lot of trouble to explain
the matter of the round back, he knew that Cenzo Rena
did not like people living with him but he begged to be
allowed to live there for a few days until the Germans went
away. Cenzo Rena said the question of living with him
no longer applied, in any case the *contadino* Giuseppe was
now living with him, the Germans were now searching not
only for Jews but for soldiers who had run away, and
Giuseppe had come to hide in the house. The house had
the pine wood behind it and was convenient as a hiding-
place, because it was nothing at all to jump from the window
into the pine wood, perhaps the police-sergeant would end
by coming there too. Franz, at the mention of the police-
sergeant, was very frightened indeed and wanted to go back
at once to La Maschiona's grandmother's, but Cenzo Rena
told him that now he had come he had better stop, because
it was dangerous to be running backwards and forwards
from one place to another. Besides, what did he think the
police-sergeant would do to him now, the police-sergeant
was no longer a police-sergeant, he had buried his uniform
and was in shirt-sleeves and braces and was always green
with fear and was in hiding. Cenzo Rena called to La
Maschiona to bring a tub of water for Franz to wash in,
because he looked to him very dirty ; Franz said that at
La Maschiona's grandmother's he had never been able to
wash at all. La Maschiona was much offended with Franz
and looked sulkily at him because he had not wanted to
stay at her grandmother's.

La Maschiona was looking sulkily at the *contadino* Giuseppe

too, because he had come to stay in their house and she
had to make the bed and cook the dinner for a *contadino*,
she was a servant but she was not a servant to *contadini*.
And Giuseppe had put a gun in the cellar among the sacks
of potatoes, La Maschiona had gone to fetch some potatoes
from the cellar and had found herself with a long, cold
gun-barrel in her hand, she had got into a great fright and
had come upstairs again in a rage, did Giuseppe want the
Germans to set fire to the house, as they had set fire to a
mill where hidden arms had been found ? The night they
had burnt down the mill La Maschiona had been at the
window watching the flames far away on the river bank,
how often she had gone to the mill to get her corn ground
for her, the miller was one of her godfathers. All night
long she had knelt on the floor praying for her godfather,
and the day after she had heard that the Germans had had
a grave dug for him along the cemetery wall, and now her
godfather was there along the cemetery wall, La Maschiona
heard him calling when she pushed open the cemetery gate
on Sundays, her godfather wanted to be buried inside the
cemetery and not outside. La Maschiona was again going
down to sleep at her mother's, she did not want to spend
the night in that house where there was a gun, and at night
her godfather talked to her, she was too much afraid unless
she slept close beside her mother. La Maschiona had
always believed that Cenzo Rena was a very strong and
cunning man, the most cunning and the strongest man in
the whole village, but now she was a little disappointed in
him, ever since that night when the mill was burning and
she had rushed to him and begged him to go to the Germans
to speak on her godfather's behalf, to explain that the hidden
arms were not her godfather's ; and Cenzo Rena had looked
at the fire from the window and said that, alas, he could
not do anything for her godfather. Cenzo Rena appeared
not to think much about the Germans, he was always
sitting reading in the dining-room with his head supported
in his hand, and since the typhus he seemed to have become

much older, and quieter and lazier and more kindly, La Maschiona had told him she wanted to go and sleep at her mother's and he had said yes. But he had fetched the Bible and had made her swear on the Bible never to tell anyone, not even her mother, that in that house were hidden a gun and the *contadino* Giuseppe and Franz.

La Maschiona went off before it was dark and Franz helped Anna to peel the potatoes for supper. He was grey in the face because he never went out of the house, the last walk he had taken had been when he had run away from Scoturno di Sopra, and he complained much that he was never able to walk, he who had been so athletic once upon a time. He never even looked out of the window, for fear that the Marchesa might see him from her windows and report him to the Germans, but the Marchesa never looked out either, because she too was very frightened of the Germans. Franz stayed all day long in the kitchen, playing with the little girl and peeling potatoes ; he was wearing Cenzo Rena's clothes and Cenzo Rena's slippers on his feet, his suitcase had been left at the inn and he was always lamenting about his suitcase, La Maschiona had offered to go and fetch it for him but he was frightened, the landlord of the inn and his wife must not discover where he was, the landlord and his wife were certainly spies. Every now and then he would become quite affectionate over La Maschiona and over Cenzo Rena and Anna, how good they were to him, and how good the *contadino* Giuseppe was too, telling him to keep calm at night when he could not sleep and was in despair. He was in despair about the Germans and also because he did not know what had become of Amalia, she was his wife and now he knew nothing about her, but she was certainly very ill in a nursing home, otherwise she would have come to San Costanzo, to hide with him and share his danger. Moreover Emanuele and Mammina had completely deserted him, they knew quite well what danger he was in and they didn't care a damn, Emanuele was there in Rome, no distance away, and he never thought of coming to see whether he was dead or alive. Anna said no one knew whether Emanuele himself was dead or alive, it might well be that the Germans had discovered him at one of his political meetings and had carried him off. Not a bit of it, said Franz, not a bit of it, what would the Germans do with Emanuele, Emanuele was hiding in Rome and eating and drinking.

Franz complained to Anna that Cenzo Rena always sent him into the kitchen to peel potatoes, he would not let him stay in the dining-room where he and Giuseppe were discussing goodness knows what. Then he discovered that they were discussing the new society, they had nothing better than that to discuss with the Germans only a few steps away, they were planning a heap of things to be done in the village as soon as the Germans went away. But goodness knows when they would go, said Franz, and he told Anna to take a look at the Germans on the ridge of the hill, they were up there with big red drums and they were unrolling wire, their voices echoed loudly from one part of the hill to another. God, how close they were to him, said Franz, never had he imagined finding himself in such great danger, and he wasn't even so very much afraid, fundamentally he was hardly afraid at all and he sat there peeling potatoes. At times he applied himself to studying a guidebook to Salerno that Cenzo Rena had given him, if the Germans came he was to say he was a cousin of Cenzo Rena's evacuated from Salerno and that he had lost his papers in the bombings. Cenzo Rena had also told him to let his beard grow so as to have a different face, in case the Germans might have seen some photograph of him at police headquarters, and he had started to let it grow, but as soon as it became fairly long Cenzo Rena told him to cut it off again at once, with a beard he looked so terribly like a Jew. Franz swore it wasn't true, he did not look in the least like a Jew. But he was very pleased to be able to shave off his beard because it made his skin feel so prickly.

But when would the Germans go away, asked Franz, they wouldn't ever go away, those big red drums were for a radio station ; once or twice Anna told Franz that they were rolling up all the wire and Franz thought they were on the point of leaving, but then they started unrolling it again.   Day and night cars and lorries shot along the road, from San Costanzo to the town and from the town to San Costanzo, and from San Costanzo to Masuri where the police-sergeant was hiding, and just think how frightened the police-sergeant must be at hearing German voices in the lanes of Masuri, Franz was delighted to think how frightened the police-sergeant must be.   And he himself, on the other hand, was hardly frightened at all.   But when would they go, he asked, would they never go, when would the English move forward, what had happened that they were standing still, only a few steps from Rome, and never moving forward ?   There were stories that in Rome there was no light or water and nothing left to eat, great carts full of turnips were touring the streets of Rome, and the shop windows were full of a thing that called itself *vegetina*, a green powder that nobody could manage to eat.   And the prisons of Rome were full of people, some of them discovered printing manifestos or making bombs and some of them picked up in the street for no reason at all, and every day lorries were leaving the prison yards for Germany, but Franz was still sure that Emanuele was comfortably hidden and was eating and drinking.   And Giustino, said Anna, what on earth had become of Giustino and Concettina, there were always stories about Rome but about the North no one knew anything, Concettina's last letter, a little before the armistice, had said that Giustino was at Turin, but after that no more letters had come and Cenzo Rena said it was useless to write, Italy was all broken up and a letter took days and days to arrive and when it did arrive what was written in it had ceased to be true.

13

From time to time Fascists in black shirts and yellow fezzes, with big pistols in their belts, came through San Costanzo, but they did not frighten anyone very much because they were well-known faces, faces that everyone had always seen in the bars and under the arcades of the town, and one of them was the son of the San Costanzo chemist and everybody remembered him behind the counter weighing things on a little pair of scales. The Fascists would roam about the lanes for a little, helping themselves to wine and hens, they would roam about the vineyards shooting into the air, and people at their windows told the chemist's son that he would do better to come back behind the counter and weigh things on his little pair of scales again. One day the Fascists went into the forest guard's house and started shooting at the looking-glass in the way the Germans did, and then they took the forest guard's boots, the forest guard himself had for some time been in hiding at a farm-house and there was only his wife in the house, and when she wept and screamed a German came to see what was going on. The German stayed all night with the forest guard's wife, and the Fascists ran off with the boots, and next day the forest guard's wife ate some rat poison, but the doctor came and made her vomit in time. When she was better, the forest guard's wife packed a bag and went off to her parents at Teramo, the German gave her a lift in a lorry.

One day while Anna and Franz were in the kitchen doing the potatoes, Cenzo Rena came in and said that the dog was not to be found. He flew into a rage with Anna because she remained sitting there, so she didn't mind about the dog now, she only minded about the potatoes, what an amount of potatoes she and Franz peeled every day. He went out into the pine wood to call the dog and Anna went after him, Franz was left alone in the kitchen, and all of a sudden there came into the kitchen a German carrying the dog all covered with blood. Franz rose very slowly from his chair, the German shouted to him in Italian that bandages and an antiseptic were needed. He had run over the dog with his motor-bicycle, it was not his fault because the dog had run across the road, he had jammed on his brakes but too late. He had found out in the village whose dog it was, they had pointed out Cenzo Rena's house up above. If they bandaged up the dog at once perhaps they could still save it, there were so many people dying now in the war, dogs at least must be allowed to live. Cenzo Rena came in and stood silent as he looked at the dog jerking and trembling on the floor, he bent down and very gently touched its belly where the grey hairs were all soaked in blood. The German went on explaining how he had jammed on his brakes, he had jammed them on so hard that he had almost fallen off. Cenzo Rena said to him in German that he did not know what that dog meant to them, for them it was like a person, they had known it for so many years. Franz had disappeared, the German asked where the chap with the antiseptic had got to. But Cenzo Rena said that antiseptic was no use now, and it would be better if the dog died at once because it might be that it would go on all night trembling and suffering, he asked the German to shoot it in the ear with his pistol. The German went outside with the dog and they heard the sound of a shot, and Cenzo Rena and Anna dug a hole in front of the house, and in it the dog was buried.

The German stood looking on while they dug the hole, he went on repeating how hard he had jammed on his brakes, his whole back was still hurting him because of the jar that sudden braking had given him. Then he sat down in the kitchen and began playing with the little girl, the child had a little bucket full of horse-chestnuts and he started carving faces on the chestnuts with his penknife. The German was tall and young, with a long, glossy, brown head, and he told them that before the war he had been a waiter in a small restaurant at Freiburg, and after the war he would start being a waiter again if there was still a need for waiters after the war, and he wondered if he would still be able to turn and twist among the little tables with the dishes, it was a job that needed a great deal of patience and he had lost his patience in the war. He had deep white scars on the backs of his hands, Cenzo Rena asked him if they were war scars, but he explained that one day in the kitchen of the restaurant he had upset some boiling soup on his hands out of a tureen. It was the fault of the under-cook, who had knocked into him as he was coming forward with the tureen. The under-cook used to go to bed with him and she made a great lamentation over his hands. But then she had left him, because she couldn't help weeping every time she looked at his hands. Women were like that, he said, they hurt you and then they ran away out of remorse. Men were very often like that too, said Cenzo Rena, but the waiter said no, men were different, for instance he had killed the dog and had not run away. Then Cenzo Rena told him not to talk about the dog any more, he did not know what he had done in killing the dog, he could not possibly know. It was very old and would have died anyhow in a short time, but it might have died in peace on a pillow instead of dying like that. The dog had belonged to a brother of Anna's who was dead. The waiter again asked their forgiveness, now that he had met them he was very sorry indeed about the dog. He asked if Anna's brother had died in the war. Not in the war, said Cenzo Rena, not in the war. The waiter said that never now could he hope for a pillow to die on, for something soft and quiet to die on, he wondered whether it would ever be possible to start dying on something quiet again, and saying good-bye and speaking a lot of kind words. Cenzo Rena told him about how he himself had had the

typhus and had very nearly died. But he had thought
about it too much, and when he thought too much about
a thing it never happened. He had very often thought
of getting married, to a great many different women, and
instead he had got married all of a sudden at a moment
when he wasn't thinking about it. The waiter began to
laugh, he threw back his head and couldn't stop laughing,
and he slapped Cenzo Rena on the shoulder and told him
what a nice person he was, it didn't happen at all often
that you met a person who was so nice to talk to. But
Cenzo Rena said that he had no desire to laugh on the day
that his dog had died.

When the waiter had gone away, Cenzo Rena started
looking for Giuseppe and Franz in the cellar and all over
the house, but not a trace was to be found of Giuseppe or
Franz. Cenzo Rena went out into the pine wood to look
for them, he had spent such a long time that day looking
for the dog and now he had to look for those two idiots
Giuseppe and Franz. He found them in the depths of the
pine wood, Franz was still grasping the little bottle of antiseptic. They had heard the sound of shooting and they
thought the German had killed Anna and Cenzo Rena and
the child. Cenzo Rena brought them back to the house,
he said the dog was the only one who was dead. And he
said the German was just an unfortunate waiter from
Freiburg and had told them a dreary story about a soup-
tureen. From Freiburg, said Franz. He himself had been
to school at Freiburg and the waiter might have met him
goodness knows how many times in the street, perhaps by
now he had already reported him and in a short time they
would come and seize him and carry him off. It was all
the fault of that cursèd dog. Cenzo Rena told him that if
he said ' cursèd dog ' again he would hit him, the dog was
dead, it was cowardly to curse the dead.

That evening Franz did not eat the potatoes he had peeled,
he sat with his head in his hands and from time to time
gave a start and jumped up from his chair as though he

had caught fire, it was from Freiburg that the waiter came, from Freiburg where he himself had sold waterproofs for so many years. Cenzo Rena tried to explain to him that the waiter was quite young, probably he was still a baby in arms when Franz was selling waterproofs. Babies in arms didn't wear waterproofs. But Franz said would he please be quiet, didn't he understand how frightened he was, didn't he understand what it was to be a Jew in a village full of Germans, and how the earth seemed to be burning under one's feet? Cenzo Rena replied that he understood only too well, never for a single minute did he forget the three old women and the Turk on the lorry as the Germans were taking them away. He hadn't seen but it was as though he had seen, always before his eyes he had the sight of the three old women amongst the Germans and the guns, and the Turk flicking his coat with his gloves. In any case, why hadn't Franz stayed up at Scoturno di Sopra with La Maschiona's grandmother, it was impossible for him now to go back to La Maschiona's grandmother, there were German sentries on the road to Scoturno di Sopra, and besides, La Maschiona's grandmother had made it clear that she did not want that difficult little gentleman in her house any more, he was never content either with where he had to sleep or with what he had to eat.

Next day Cenzo Rena hired the famous cab that had brought him home from the hospital after he had recovered from the typhus, and into it he put Franz all wrapped up in blankets and shawls as if he were very ill, and he took him down to the monastery in the town where other Jews were hidden. On the way Cenzo Rena was in a good humour and sang " How nice to ride in a carriage " and Franz was in a good humour too because it seemed to him that there was a great deal of car and lorry traffic, and he thought that perhaps the Germans were at last going away. A little before they reached the town an aeroplane came gliding down almost on to the road, Cenzo Rena and Franz and the driver threw themselves out of the cab and lay down in a ditch. They heard in the distance a sound like the tic-tac of a typewriter but brief and loud, and saw a little plume of smoke rise up behind them on the road. They got into the cab again and the driver said that they must give him a little more money, considering the risk he had run, from time to time he ran these risks with his cab because food was expensive and he had a quantity of children. Franz groaned at the thought of how close to them those Englishmen had been for a minute, so close that they could have picked him up and carried him away to safety, and now there they were again so high up and so far away in the sky.

14

Franz stayed about a month in the monastery, and then he came back. The Germans had come into the monastery at night and had started a careful search of every room, Franz, dressed up as a monk, was shut up in a kind of cupboard, and as it chanced the Germans had not looked inside it. They had seized two Jews as they were running up into the granary, two others had escaped by jumping down from the garden wall. Franz had spent the night in his cupboard, with a big plaster Madonna looking at him. All at once he had started praying to the Madonna, he was a Jew but he had prayed to the Madonna, he asked her to make it happen that the Germans did not search there. Then all at once he had wanted to laugh at the thought that he, Franz, was all dressed up as a monk and was praying to the Madonna. He had wanted so much to laugh that he had had to cover his mouth with both hands in order not to be heard. And then, little by little, his fear had almost left him. And little by little he had started thinking that after all he didn't really mind so very much about going on living ; if he went on living, well and good, but if not, never mind. If not, never mind, he had thought, he had thought this very strongly and had felt very strong and calm, and had remembered the Turk amongst the guns on the lorry. Only a great desire had come upon him to see Cenzo Rena once more, if he had to die. Cenzo Rena had never taken him seriously and had always treated him rather badly. Nevertheless Franz thought that Cenzo Rena was the best person he had ever met. In the morning the monks had come to open the door, he had taken off his monk's habit and had put on his own clothes again, and meanwhile the monks had explained to him that it had been this Madonna in the cupboard that had protected him from the Germans. Why did they keep her in the cupboard, asked Franz ? The monks showed him that she had both feet broken and that was why they kept her there.

Franz had come away from the monastery and had started walking towards San Costanzo. And the town was full of Germans but he had hardly any fear. He had walked for a long way along the frost-hardened road, no snow at all had fallen that winter so far and the morning was cold and clear, with a wind that bit your face. After walking for an hour he had come across the man with the corkscrew leg pushing his little cart full of pots and pans and brooms. The man with the corkscrew leg had stopped his cart and helped him to get into it, and Franz all at once had been seized with fear again and had started begging the man with the corkscrew leg not to report him to the Germans, he had taken the diamond ring off his finger and given it to him. And then he had jumped out of the cart and run to Cenzo Rena's house across the fields.

Cenzo Rena sat listening to this whole story and very slowly shook his head, and finally he asked Franz whether he had not gone a little mad, because he had started doing some very strange things. And he said that Franz was like Pierino's puppet, the puppet which it was no use throwing

over precipices or out of trains or into the sea because
it always reappeared. Franz told him that he had come
back not in order to be safe but to stay with him and the
little girl and Anna, in their house. Because they were the
dearest friends he had ever had, and only with them was
he happy. Cenzo Rena told him to stay as long as he
liked, once upon a time he used to have silly ideas about
people living in the house with him, but no one thought
about such silly ideas now. The police-sergeant was now
living in the house too, he had dropped down upon them
from Masuri one day when he had taken fright. And the
waiter from Freiburg came in every day. But Franz said
he was no longer afraid either of the waiter from Freiburg
or of the police-sergeant. Then Cenzo Rena called to
La Maschiona to bring the tub for Franz to wash in. And
La Maschiona brought the tub and looked very sulky
indeed because she would now have to make Franz's bed
again as well as the others.

The man with the corkscrew leg came next day, hobbling
quickly up over the rocks, he asked to speak to Cenzo
Rena alone and showed him a kind of little white bag
which he had sewed into the inside of his shirt, in it was
the diamond ring that Franz had given him. He asked
whether he could really keep the ring for himself, whether
this man Franz had really made him a present of it, this
man Franz had seemed to him a bit funny in the head.
Certainly his great fear of the Germans had made him a
bit funny in the head. He had never dreamed of reporting
him to the Germans, he also was frightened to death of
the Germans and kept well away from them, and besides,
why should he have reported him, a poor chap who did
no one any harm ? And in any case who in the village
did dream of reporting him, they all knew that he was
at Cenzo Rena's together with the police-sergeant and
Giuseppe but they kept quiet, possibly there had been
someone who had reported the Turk and the old women,
possibly it had been that good-for-nothing son of the

chemist's, but now the chemist's son was away in the North. He touched the little bag under his shirt and asked if it was a ring of much value, after the war he would like to sell it to the jeweller in the town and use the money to have weights put on his bad leg, he had been told that perhaps with weights it might become straighter. The only thing he was afraid of was that these weights might hurt him. He asked Cenzo Rena whether he would do him the kindness of going with him to the jeweller after the war, if he went by himself the jeweller might think he had stolen the ring. Cenzo Rena promised to go with him to the jeweller after the war. The man with the corkscrew leg went away happy, and he went jumping down over the rocks bending right down to the ground on one side, with his trousers rumpling up at every step over his twisted leg.

When the waiter from Freiburg came, the police-sergeant and Franz and Giuseppe ran down the little staircase and hid in the cellar, and Cenzo Rena heaved a long sigh and went to entertain the waiter. In the cellar the police-sergeant and Franz and Giuseppe played cards on the sacks of potatoes, the police-sergeant did not know that Giuseppe's tommy-gun was hidden under the sacks. Franz ate apples, rubbing them hard on his coat to polish them, La Maschiona was very mean over these apples and it was only when he was hiding in the cellar that he was able to eat any. There was nothing much to eat now, it was only of potatoes that you could eat your fill, and Franz was always a little hungry, because potatoes fill you up but do not give enough nourishment. Franz was very fond of the little red apples that La Maschiona kept in the cellar, and ate them hurriedly while La Maschiona was not there to see. They would hear the footsteps of the waiter going away, and Cenzo Rena would open the cellar door and stand for a moment at the top of the little staircase with a lighted lamp. He would be fuming with rage because he did not enjoy talking to the waiter, it was always the same waiters' stories. The *contadino* Giuseppe asked him when he was going to send him packing, this dirty blackguard of a German, Cenzo Rena asked how he could possibly send him packing, he was a German and for the moment he was the master and not a waiter. Giuseppe said that some day he would like to do a German in, any dirty blackguard of a German, yes, even this waiter here. He had heard that in the North people were fighting against the Germans, people were going up into the mountains and shooting, it was only in their own dismal country, where people had no spirit, that nobody had gone up into the mountains. His own tommy-gun was rusting under the potatoes. All day long Giuseppe was thinking of what he could do against the Germans, he wondered whether he could not go out at night and scatter nails on the road to puncture the tyres of their vehicles, or hide in a hedge and shoot with his tommy-gun at every car that passed. Every night he thought of going out but in the end he always stayed in the house, playing cards with the police-sergeant and Franz. He had misgivings at the idea of doing something all on his own like that, in the North there were so many of them, properly organized like an army, so that then you might not even be frightened. He had lost some of his esteem for Cenzo Rena, because Cenzo Rena did not think about organizing anything, but sat in the kitchen and received the waiter, and talked German and sometimes smoked the waiter's cigarettes. Sometimes Giuseppe smoked the waiter's cigarettes too, when the waiter had gone away and there was an almost complete packet left on the table. But he had such a longing to smoke and it did not seem to him that there was any harm in it, because the German was not there to see him smoking, whereas Cenzo Rena accepted cigarettes from the waiter's own hand.

And one day Giuseppe asked Cenzo Rena why they too shouldn't start resistance against the Germans, like the people in the North. He asked why Cenzo Rena did not call together the farrier and the draper and all the *contadini*, and they would arrange, all of them together, to hide

behind hedges and shoot at the Germans at night, or at
least to scatter nails along the road. And Cenzo Rena
said that indeed it would be quite right to do that. But
he himself did not feel any inclination either to shoot or
to scatter nails, he had thought about it sometimes but had
realized that he would be very much afraid, afraid throughout the whole of his body, and he felt his hands all limp
and unwilling to scatter nails or shoot. He asked Giuseppe's
pardon, perhaps he had disappointed him, perhaps now
Giuseppe would no longer have any esteem for him. At
present, when he happened to hear cries and lamentations
from the *contadini* in the lanes, Cenzo Rena would go out
and look, and it would be Germans searching the houses
for young men to put on lorries and send off to work in
Germany, and Cenzo Rena would start talking German and
sometimes he had succeeded in getting the Germans away
from the houses and telling them some kind of tall story to
get them to leave people alone. It wasn't much, Cenzo
Rena said to Giuseppe, it wasn't much but it was all he
was able to do. If he had been given a pistol or a tommy-
gun to fire he would not have shot straight, he would have
shot all crooked into a tree, and in the meantime he would
have started thinking things which it was not right to think.
Giuseppe asked him what he would have started thinking.
And Cenzo Rena said he would have started thinking that
the Germans were all waiters, poor unfortunates with some
sort of a job at the back of them, poor unfortunates whom it
was not really worth while killing. And this was a thought
that in war-time had no sense, it was an idiotic thought
but he himself might happen to have an idiotic thought
of that kind. Perhaps the *contadino* Giuseppe was a man
of war ; if so, let the *contadino* Giuseppe go with his tommy-
gun into the hills. The *contadino* Giuseppe bit his nails and
looked at Cenzo Rena discontentedly, how could he go
with his tommy-gun all by himself into the hills ? But at
least scatter some nails, he said, at least scatter lots of nails
along the road, so that a few tyres might burst from time

to time.   Yes, perhaps scatter nails, said Cenzo Rena, why
not ?   But where were all the nails to scatter, he asked, he
himself had only one nail in his pocket and he pulled it
out, it was a nail that was all rusty and crooked and he
kept it in his pocket to bring him luck.

But Anna, too, was a bit discontented and did not like
the words that Cenzo Rena said to the *contadino* Giuseppe,
and Cenzo Rena was conscious of the doubting and discontented faces round him and he grew sad and withdrawn,
and it seemed as though he were growing older and older
when he started reading with his spectacles rather low on
his nose and his head buried between his shoulders.   There
were not men of war and men of peace, thought Anna, the
war affected everybody and no one had the right to say
that he did not want to take part in the war.   It seemed
to her that it was cowardly to talk like that.   And one day
she said so to Cenzo Rena and Cenzo Rena remained
silent, and he rubbed his hands over his face, and when
his face reappeared, it was redder than before and as it were
sleepy-looking.   And he said that perhaps she did not
believe it but he was not so very cowardly for himself,
the thing that frightened him most of all was the idea of
his village of San Costanzo in flames and the people of
San Costanzo being killed along the cemetery wall.   It was
a little village of no account, a mere flea in the whole
of Italy, but he did not want to see it all in flames, as he
had seen La Maschiona's godfather's mill in flames that
night.   But Anna was still discontented and she thought
of Giustino, who was perhaps at this moment fighting in
the mountains up there in the North, and she wondered
if he was still alive or whether they had not shot him already,
she saw Giustino's face while they were shooting him, a face
with a smile like Ippolito's smile, a little crooked and sad.
Anna would have liked to be with Giustino fighting there
in the North, and to be shot with Giustino beside the wall
of a cemetery, she knew very little of what was going on
up there in the North, but it was known that a great many

people were being shot by the Germans every day, and meanwhile she herself was sitting every day in the kitchen with the waiter and accepting sugar and chocolate from the waiter for the little girl. But when she looked at the waiter she felt she might be able to shoot at all the other Germans but not at the waiter, sitting there as he was in their kitchen with the little girl between his knees, with his long, quiet, solemn head between the child's hands that were busy ruffling his glossy brown hair and pulling hard at his long red ears. La Maschiona was always saying what a fine person the waiter was, he was always bringing sugar and chocolate for the little girl, and he had nothing whatever to do with those other Germans who had killed her godfather, she had told him about her godfather and he had said he was really very sorry indeed about it. La Maschiona considered that it was unnecessary for Franz and the police-sergeant and Giuseppe to run off into the cellar whenever the waiter came, the waiter had nothing whatever to do with the ones who carried people away in lorries, and even if he had known that Franz was a Jew he would not have touched him, he was a German who did not concern himself with Jews. La Maschiona always gave the waiter a great welcome when she saw him arrive, and poured him out a glass of wine—she, who was so mean about the provisions—, and she said how well brought-up the waiter was, he would drink the wine she poured out for him but he never poured out any for himself. La Maschiona now thought again that Cenzo Rena was an immensely clever man, because he had been able to make friends with the waiter with the excuse of the dog, and because he went and talked to the Germans when they were searching the houses, he went and talked and told them some kind of tall story in that clever way of his, and the Germans paid attention to him and left off their searching. La Maschiona now no longer went to sleep at her mother's each night, because she felt quite safe there in Cenzo Rena's house, and she was again very proud of

Cenzo Rena when he went down into the village and she
saw him conversing with the Germans, how clever he was
and what stories he told them.

Franz said to Anna that one must have confidence in
Cenzo Rena, because he was incapable of making mistakes
or of doing things that were wrong, and the day that Cenzo
Rena went to scatter nails along the road he himself would
follow him, because he had no fear now and it hardly
mattered to him whether he died or lived, but as long as
Cenzo Rena did not go it meant that it was right not to
go. And the police-sergeant was very frightened indeed
as soon as he heard any talk of nails, for goodness' sake
let them give up all idea of nails, what was the use of nails
anyhow, a few tyres punctured and nothing more. When
the moment came for shooting they would shoot, at present
the moment had not yet come, he himself, the police-
sergeant, would be the first to shoot as soon as the moment
came. He had buried his gun at Masuri and he would
go and fetch it, he would collect all the guns that there
were at Masuri, at Masuri there were guns for everybody.
But in the meantime they must wait for the English to
advance a little, and as long as there was snow on the
ground they could not advance ; and then the snow began
to melt and the first green patches appeared on the ridges
of the hills. And the news arrived that the English had
made a great bound forward, now the artillery could be
heard thundering behind the hills, the English had taken
San Felice, a village a few kilometres from the town. But
the police-sergeant said it was not yet the right moment
to start shooting, what was the point of hurrying ? The
spring rains began. And the English stopped again and
for many days everything was again quiet in the rushing
rain, the artillery was silent and the Germans were still
there with their big red drums, in long, glossy, black waterproofs and high boots in the rain ; and then suddenly in
the rain the bright, warm sun appeared and changed the
mud into the usual fine, sandy dust, and the apple-trees

rose up in blossom in the gardens and were beaten and despoiled by the wind, and aeroplanes started humming again in the blue sky amongst rags of clouds, and the *contadino* Giuseppe was worried to death because he did not know how his wife would manage the work in the fields all alone, he himself did not move away from Cenzo Rena's house because so many *contadini* had gone to work in the fields and then the Germans had come and loaded them into lorries and taken them away. He had sent the children to Borgoreale to some relations of his wife's. All of a sudden Cenzo Rena decided that Anna ought to leave San Costanzo with the little girl, San Costanzo was on the road and the English as they advanced would be fighting on the road. So one day Cenzo Rena took Anna and the little girl to La Maschiona's grandmother at Scoturno di Sopra.

There were two German sentries on the path leading to Scoturno, but they knew Cenzo Rena and looked for a moment into the hamper and allowed them to pass. Cenzo Rena was carrying the hamper, the hamper was very heavy and he said what a lot of useless things Anna was bringing with her, and yet she had not thought of bringing a Thermos, she was against Thermos flasks like Signora Maria. Why on earth a Thermos, said Anna, what would she do with a Thermos when the weather was so hot? She could put the child's camomile in it at night, said Cenzo Rena, she didn't surely suppose that La Maschiona's grandmother would get up at night and light the fire and make the camomile? The little girl turned round and said that she didn't like camomile.

It was the end of May and the sun was scorching as they went up the path, and the grass was shaggy and burnt; Cenzo Rena swung the hamper as he walked and plunged his feet into the burnt grass, and from high up he looked down at San Costanzo and the village square full of tanks and lorries, then San Costanzo disappeared behind the ridge of the hill. Anna stopped suddenly and asked if it was really necessary for her and the child to go to Scoturno di Sopra, Cenzo Rena told her not to ask silly questions, in a short time San Costanzo would become a field of battle and everyone who had small children was taking them away. Anna thought of long, long days in the kitchen with La Maschiona's grandmother, in the smoke that Franz had told her about.

They found La Maschiona's grandmother lighting the fire under the iron pot, but there was not the slightest wisp of smoke, said Cenzo Rena, it was very comfortable at Scoturno di Sopra and he himself would stay there with the greatest pleasure. Then why didn't he stay, asked Anna, and he said that on the contrary he had to go straight back again, because he had to be at San Costanzo to see what went on all the time. Nothing went on, said Anna, they could manage very well at San Costanzo without him. They quarrelled in low voices while they unpacked the hamper on the bed, what a lot of things Anna had brought, he was saying, she had brought a whole heap of towels, Anna was like Signora Maria. Anna started crying a little at the remembrance of Signora Maria. She sat down on La Maschiona's grandmother's big hard bed and cried, she was thinking of Signora Maria and Ippolito who were dead, and she even thought of Ippolito's dog with its tender, curly muzzle, and she thought of Concettina and Giustino, not knowing whether they were alive or dead, and she looked at Cenzo Rena and was frightened that she would never see him again, in a short time he would go back down the path to San Costanzo and then the English would come fighting all along the road and at San Costanzo goodness knows what would happen. And Cenzo Rena looked at her too and wondered if he would ever see her again, but they were unable to say anything serious to each other, they went on quarrelling about the things that Anna had brought and Cenzo Rena told her she was foolish to cry because she was bored at staying with La Maschiona's grandmother and Anna did not know how to tell him that she was not crying because of that. And Cenzo Rena left her some money and as always when he had to fork out money he complained that in a short time they would be left without any and that it was a fine problem. Then he went away in the hot afternoon and when he came in sight of San Costanzo the sun was setting, reddening the ridges of the hills. He was thinking of Anna and of how he had seen her sitting on the bed crying, and of the little girl who had run off after the sheep with La Maschiona's grandmother and had hardly said good-bye to him, toiling after the sheep with a long stick, her thin bare feet in the dust. Cenzo Rena thought of them and wondered whether this had been the last time he would see them, the war was going on and one always thought that each time was perhaps a last time.

In the meantime the waiter had arrived at the house and as soon as they heard him coming Giuseppe and the police-sergeant and Franz had run off to the cellar, they were not expecting the waiter that day because Cenzo Rena had told him he was going away. In the kitchen La Maschiona was doing some washing at the tub and the waiter sat down and La Maschiona poured him out some wine, and she went on contentedly washing and looking at the waiter as he very slowly drank the wine and rocked himself back and forth on his chair, far away beyond the hills you could hear the thunder of the artillery and the waiter said that in a short time the English would be arriving at San Costanzo and that they themselves would be going away northwards. But he no longer had any desire to fight in the war and he would have liked to stay at San Costanzo and get himself taken prisoner by the English and never fire a gun again. So then La Maschiona asked him why he didn't hide and wait for the English, and he asked her whether she had any place where she could hide him, wasn't there a cellar in the house? Yes, there was, said La Maschiona and laughed, at the moment there were already a certain number of people hiding in the cellar, among them even a Jew. She was telling him this because she knew he was not the kind of German to worry himself about Jews. No, said the waiter, he didn't worry himself about Jews. And was the Jew, for instance, in the cellar now at the moment? Yes, in the cellar, said La Maschiona, in the cellar with the potatoes and the apples, and if he himself wanted to hide there nobody would ever find him out. But all of a sudden she remembered that she had sworn on the Bible never to speak a word about Franz. So she went to fetch the Bible to make the waiter swear he would never tell. But when she came back with the Bible the waiter was at the door of the cellar, pushing against it with his shoulder.

Then La Maschiona started screaming. The cellar door gave way with a thud and the waiter stood at the top of the short staircase looking down by the light of his flash-lamp, the flash-lamp that he wore at his belt, throwing the light now on the pile of logs and now on the potatoes and apples and now on the police-sergeant and now on Franz. And at intervals they could see him too and the waiter's face was quiet and serious, a long horse-like face peering and sniffing, the head of a flattened-out horse in a book, thought Franz. But Giuseppe groped for his tommy-gun amongst the sacks of potatoes and loaded it, and the waiter raised his pistol and had not time to fire because Giuseppe fired first, and the waiter fell down the stairs and La Maschiona screamed.

Cenzo Rena, when he came back from Scoturno di Sopra, found the kitchen deserted with the washtub in the middle of it, and he ran to the cellar and jumped over the broken-down door, and there in the cellar were sitting the police-sergeant and Franz and Giuseppe and La Maschiona sobbing with her fingers in her hair, and only after a moment did Cenzo Rena see the waiter too, his long head dirty with blood amongst the wood-shavings and the potatoes. And Giuseppe asked him if he had done wrong to kill the waiter. No, said Cenzo Rena to him, there was a war on and it was right to shoot. But there was no time now to argue over right and wrong. Cenzo Rena said they must dig a hole in the pine wood and bury the waiter there.

The *contadino* Giuseppe and Cenzo Rena went out to dig the grave. But Giuseppe's hands were trembling violently and he could not manage to dig. And he threw down his spade and said he wanted to run away because he was afraid. But where would he escape to, Cenzo Rena asked him ; and from where they were they could see, through the pine-trees, the Germans in the village square, and it was a miracle that no one should have heard the sound of shots and screams, the Germans were never still and were constantly coming and going through the pine wood, it was a miracle that no one should have passed that way on that day. But the *contadino* Giuseppe said that he wanted to run away, for instance he could try to get through the pine wood to Borgoreale where his wife's relations were. And he started running up through the pine wood and Cenzo Rena saw his tattered green hat disappearing amongst the pine-trees and he gave it a look of farewell and said to himself that perhaps he was seeing that hat for the last time.

Cenzo Rena waited until it was dark and then went and fetched the waiter and laid him down in the hole they had dug in the wood. But it was a small hole, too small for the waiter's big body. And Cenzo Rena felt a weakness in his hands and had no wish to start digging again, and the pine wood seemed to him to be full of the rustling of footsteps. So he took up the waiter in his arms again and it seemed to him that he was carrying a horse in his arms, a very large, sleeping horse. He went as far as the stream and laid the waiter down in the water, he laid him out at full length in the water and reflected that the water was strong and might drag him away. The water of the stream went into the river and once he was in the river no one would ever find him. But he did not stay to see whether the stream dragged the waiter away, he was very tired and wanted to get right away from the waiter and right away from the stream, he was very, very tired and he reflected that he and the *contadino* Giuseppe would never go and scatter nails on the road, goodness knows if the *contadino* Giuseppe would manage to make his escape. All of a sudden he saw Franz looking at him, silently Franz had followed him, and now there he was, leaning against the trunk of a tree and looking at him. Go back home, Cenzo Rena said to him, go back home, you bloody fool. Franz said that the police-sergeant had run off too, he was trembling with fear and he had run off taking some bread and a flask of wine. In the kitchen there was no one but La Maschiona, who was sobbing. It was a miracle that she had not gone to her mother, said Cenzo Rena, woe betide them if La Maschiona went to her mother, she would tell her mother everything and in an hour the whole village would know about it. They went back home and Cenzo Rena dissolved some bromide in a tumbler for La Maschiona, he pulled her head up and told her to drink it, La Maschiona's head was weak and inert, shaken only by that stupid sobbing. Cenzo Rena made La Maschiona lie down on the bed and he poured a bucket of water over the floor of the cellar, there was no blood there but nevertheless he washed the floor very carefully, wiping it over with a rag, and then he poured out a big glass of brandy from a bottle which he kept in reserve in the cellar and he and Franz drank some. And then Cenzo Rena stayed sitting beside La Maschiona's bed because he did not want La Maschiona to run away too. Franz sat down on the floor close by and from time to time he fell asleep.

And then it occurred to Cenzo Rena that if the Germans found the waiter they would take hostages at random all over the village, as they had publicly declared they would do if they found a German dead, for one dead German ten Italians. And he thought he would go to the commandant and tell him it had been he who had killed the waiter. He started to think of the words he ought to say in German.

He poured himself some more brandy and continually changed the sentence that he would say in German, and he felt very well with all that brandy in him, with warm, fresh breaths going all through his body. But down at the bottom of his back he was conscious of that same spot where he had felt he was going to die when he had typhus, a small patch of skin that was all pinched and trembling, a small icy patch in a body on fire with brandy and all quiet and strong. It was only there, down at the bottom of his back, that he had any fear and he touched the spot with his hand, and then he drank some more brandy so that the warm blood in his body might flow to that same spot. And he looked at La Maschiona's black head on the pillow and said good-bye to her, La Maschiona was still half sobbing in her sleep and was pressing a much snivelled-upon handkerchief to her lips. And he looked at Franz's head bowed down between his knees as he slept and he said good-bye to Franz too. And he said good-bye to Anna and to the little girl as he had seen them that day at Scoturno di Sopra, the little girl toiling after the sheep, with her big, bitter mouth and her straw-like hair. And he wanted to find Anna's face again but now he could not find it, sorely he wanted to find it and yet he did not find it. Instead, he had before his eyes the face of La Maschiona's grandmother and it enraged him, an old, wrinkled, grim face under a black handkerchief. Franz woke up and drank some more brandy, and he laughed a little as he remembered how the police-sergeant had run away, whereas he himself was not running away because he had no fear, it no longer mattered to him in the least whether he died or lived, it was very, very strange how it did not matter to him. Recently he had been thinking that he had lived pretty stupidly, what a lot of stupid, useless things he had done in his life, his life was a regular story and he would have liked to tell it to someone. But Cenzo Rena said to him for goodness' sake not to tell him anything because at the present moment he had something else in his head. And Franz grieved that Cenzo Rena would never take him seriously and always treated him so badly. And he bowed his head down on to his knees and went to sleep again.

The morning passed and all of a sudden the church bells started ringing very loudly, La Maschiona pulled herself up dazed from the bed and scratched her head and tried to remember. Cenzo Rena was half asleep on La Maschiona's bed and he was awakened by the farrier's mother shaking him hard and weeping. Cries could be heard in the lanes and the voices of Germans, and the bells ringing, and the farrier's mother was saying that the Germans had seized her son, they had found a German dead down at the river and were seizing people in the houses. They would shoot them if they did not find out who had killed the German. They had seized her son and the man with the corkscrew leg and a brother of La Maschiona's and a number of others, ten men they had seized, and they had put them into the mayor's stable. The farrier's mother told Cenzo Rena that he must go at once to German headquarters and beg them to let them go, he was the only one who knew how to speak German and he was the only one who could save them.

When she heard they had seized her brother La Maschiona started screaming, it was Giuseppe who had killed the German, Cenzo Rena must go to the Germans and say that it was Giuseppe. She wept and screamed and beat her head against the wall and called for her brother and her mother, and she wanted to go to her mother but Cenzo Rena told the farrier's mother to keep her there.

Cenzo Rena poured himself out some more brandy and slipped on his waterproof and went out into the bright morning, with the bells ringing loudly and little shining aeroplanes high up in the sky. He did not know why he had put on his waterproof, he wondered if he was not a little drunk, the waterproof was long and white and it seemed to him that he was wearing a nightshirt. He went jumping down over the rocks, he did not go through the

lanes of the village but by a slope of tall grass, his bare feet
in their heelless slippers rustled in the harsh, tall grass, all
at once he began to run. One slipper slipped off his foot
and he stooped to pick it up and saw Franz running after
him, go back home, said Cenzo Rena, go back home, you
bloody fool. Franz stopped in the grass and Cenzo Rena
went on, but again the slipper slipped off and he stooped
down to put it on again, and Franz was still behind him
with his face all bathed in tears, a face that was happy and
despairing and a little mad, with jaws trembling and hair
falling all over the forehead. Go back home, Cenzo Rena
said to him, go back home, you bloody fool. He put on his
slipper and now they were running together. And all at once
they were both of them very happy as they ran and slid in
the tall grass, and the bells were ringing and the road lay
white and dusty at the bottom of the slope, the road on which
they would never scatter nails because there was no time now.
    There were sentries at the door of the municipal office
and Cenzo Rena asked to speak to the commandant. He
undid his waterproof to show that he was not armed, and
the sentries asked him who Franz was, and Cenzo Rena
said he was a cousin of his from Salerno who had gone a
little mad, poor chap, owing to the war. One of the sentries
and Cenzo Rena went upstairs, the commandant was sitting
where previously the mayor had sat. And Cenzo Rena told
the commandant that he had killed the German with a
tommy-gun that he had, and would they release the hostages
from the mayor's stable.
    Some Fascists came into the room and they were holding
Franz by the arms and one of them was shouting that he
had found him at the door of the municipal office talking
German to the sentries and wanting to come upstairs, and
he shouted that he had recognized him and he was a
German Jew internee, he shouted out Franz's name and
surname. And Cenzo Rena again said that he was a
cousin of his from Salerno and that he had followed behind
him because he followed him everywhere, because he was

mad owing to the war. The commandant tapped his pen slowly on the top of the desk and stared fixedly at Cenzo Rena, at the same time rubbing his chin and pursing up his mouth as if he wanted to whistle.

Cenzo Rena and Franz remained for some hours in the entrance hall, where once upon a time the *contadini* used to sit waiting. All round them were Fascists with pistols and German sentries, and through the half-open door they saw lorries and tanks in the dust of the village square, and boots and more boots of Germans, and Cenzo Rena asked if the hostages had been released and nobody answered him. Cenzo Rena kept touching the spot in his back where he was afraid he was going to die. A patch of skin that was all cold and feeble. The patch had now gradually increased in size, almost the whole of his back was now cold and feeble. But all of a sudden, through the gap left by the half-closed entrance door, he saw the leg of the man with the corkscrew leg running away. And he said good-bye to that happy leg which was running away. And he thought that if there was a God he thanked Him for that happy leg, he did not know if there was one but in any case he thanked Him. He wondered why he so much wanted the man with the corkscrew leg to remain alive, he did not understand why it was. Franz was sitting on the stairs leaning his head against the banisters and he had his eyes shut, and his lip was all bleeding and swollen because the Fascist who had recognized him had struck him on the lip with his pistol. And then Cenzo Rena felt infinitely tired and sad, with the brandy very far away by now and his back all feeble and cold, and his knees trembling and jerking and a cold sweat upon him.

And later they were taken out into the village square and Franz was seized and flung back against the wall and the order was given to fire and Cenzo Rena covered his face with his hands. And he too was flung against the wall and he felt his head bang against the wall and heard bells and voices. And so they died, Cenzo Rena and Franz.

15

When Anna came back to San Costanzo the Germans were no longer there but instead there were the English, and the American and English and Italian flags were fluttering from the balcony of the municipal office. The walls of the village hall and the walls of the police station and of a few other houses along the road were full of round holes from the English shells that had been fired.

The Germans had freed the hostages they had taken that day but then during the night they had come back and taken some more, two sons of the dressmaker's and a sister of La Maschiona's seducer and a shepherd boy of fourteen years old, and they had taken them into the mayor's stable and had poured tins of petrol over the stable and set fire to it. They had searched for the farrier and for La Maschiona's brother too, but they had escaped into the fields.

The mayor's stable was now a heap of ashes, and you still seemed to hear the lowing of the cows and the shrieks of the shepherd boy calling to his mother. No one could understand why the Germans should have burnt down the stable with the cows and the people inside, but perhaps it was only because they had some petrol to throw away. In any case tales were coming in from all directions of the things the Germans had done before they went away, at Masuri they had driven fifteen people into a farmhouse, children and women, and had fired into the windows. The Germans were far away now, beyond Borgoreale, but there were times when the *contadini* were frightened that they would come back. The *contadini* stood looking at the English as they sat smoking on the low garden walls, they stood spell-bound looking at these soldiers dressed like the Germans in yellowish cloth with short trousers and blond, hairy knees. And they asked if the Germans would come back and the

English shook their heads to say no. And the *contadini* were very pleased indeed with these new soldiers who did not kill them, and they were very pleased to eat the insipid bread made of rice flour which they threw away.

The police-sergeant had come to Scoturno di Sopra to give Anna the news of Cenzo Rena and Franz. The police-sergeant, on the night he had escaped with the flask of wine, had later found the *contadino* Giuseppe and together they had gone to Borgoreale and had hidden there. The police-sergeant was again dressed as a police-sergeant now, with his cloak and his sabre, and he came to Scoturno di Sopra with a solemn, funereal air. He wished to break the news deli-cately to Anna and started off on a long, vague speech, say-ing that for instance he too had lost his wife from a tumour of the breast. And the Germans had wrecked his house and had carried off the bed in which his wife had died. Now he lived on for the sake of his little children. At times he had a great longing to throw himself over a precipice but he was a Christian and did not throw himself down, he went on living for the sake of his little children. And in the same way Anna had her little girl. And Anna looked and looked at the police-sergeant's big, flattened nose and all of a sudden she understood that Cenzo Rena was dead.

For a long time she remained lying on La Maschiona's grandmother's bed, the hours went by and the flies buzzed against the white walls. She did not want to see the little girl, all at once she had a horror of the little girl, when the little girl came in she immediately called to La Maschiona's grandmother to take her away. She did not want to look out of the window and she had a horror of the meadow below the house and of the path and of the ridges of the hills.

And then one day she hurried quickly back to San Cos-tanzo because La Maschiona's grandmother told her that La Maschiona was having trouble with the Americans, a *contadino* had told her some story, she hadn't understood it very well. Anna went back to San Costanzo and discovered that she had been lying on the bed for two days only, to her it had seemed such a very long time. Some of the *contadini* had taken La Maschiona into the barber's shop and were shaving her head, because they said it was she who had shown the German where the cellar was. La Maschiona was struggling amongst the *contadini* who had already started shaving her head, they had already shorn off half of her hair. Anna shouted to them to leave her alone.

With great difficulty she succeeded in getting La Maschiona out of the barber's shop, with the *contadini* storming round her and the barber taking La Maschiona's side and trying to sweep La Maschiona's hair out of his shop. La Maschiona was so frightened that she was not even weeping, they had torn the handkerchief off her head and she covered the shorn part of it with her hands. Anna and La Maschiona went up to the house. There the Germans had fired at the looking-glasses and had carried off the mattresses and the radio, they had emptied the wardrobes and wrecked the deck chairs. Anna set about sweeping away the pieces of glass and meanwhile La Maschiona was digging with the spade in front of the house because she had buried her winter coat there, but she did not exactly remember the spot where she had buried it, and besides, she was afraid of the dog coming to light.

La Maschiona went later to Scoturno di Sopra to fetch the little girl, but her grandmother had such a fright at seeing her with her head half shorn that she died after a few days, in any case her time had come to die because she was ninety-three.

The *contadino* Giuseppe was not made mayor. The new mayor was La Maschiona's seducer, who had fine black moustaches and a fine bearing and had inherited a large quantity of land from his sister who had been burnt by the Germans. He had suffered much through the war and the Germans, he had had that sister burnt and a son missing in Greece of whom nothing more had ever been heard. The *contadino* Giuseppe said he was very well pleased not to be mayor, and he went back to work in the fields in his tattered green hat, and sometimes he went to see Anna and spoke very ill of the whole village and of the new mayor, what on earth would Cenzo Rena have said if he could see who had been made mayor, a scoundrel who certainly robbed the community even worse than the previous mayor. They were talking in the village of putting up a stone with an inscription on Cenzo Rena's house but the *contadino* Giuseppe was sure that no one would ever fork out money for the stone, San Costanzo was a filthy village and for this filthy village Cenzo Rena had died.

During the first few days after the arrival of the English a group of *contadini* had decided to go into the Marchesa's house and crop her hair, to pay her out for all the anonymous letters she had sent to police headquarters and for the arrogant way in which she had always behaved. And the Marchesa was there in her big chair, half dead with fright ; while the Germans were still in the village she had become partly paralysed and her face was all twisted. With her was the doctor and they were playing cards, and the *contadini* had taken the cards and sent them flying out of the window. And then they had thrown open the cupboards and had found great numbers of pots of jam, the Marchesa was famous for her jam and they had set about eating the jam with spoons. The doctor had gone down to collect the cards out of the ditches in the lanes, and was cleaning them one by one on his jacket. But all at once the dressmaker arrived and started crying out about her two sons whom the Germans had burnt and about her daughter who had been the Marchesa's maid and had had that blow in the chest and it had broken something inside her and even now she was spitting blood. And she wanted to shave the Marchesa's head and was waving a shaving-brush. And the shouting made her ill and she fell on the floor as pale as death and the *contadini* called to the doctor to stop cleaning the cards and come upstairs. And the doctor had to lay the dressmaker on the Marchesa's bed and rub her temples with vinegar. The Marchesa was groaning and shrieking in her big chair, and in the end the *contadini* had gone away because they had seen that she was nothing but a poor old woman.

And the man with the corkscrew leg circled about all the time among the ruins of the former mayor's stable. On the occasion when the Germans had seized him as a hostage they had torn his shirt and so he had lost the diamond ring that Franz had given him. He looked for it all day long amongst the ashes of the stable and complained that now he would never be able to have those weights put on his leg to make it grow straighter.

Anna one day saw someone come limping up over the rocks and thought it was the man with the corkscrew leg but instead it was Emanuele ; she ran out weeping to meet Emanuele and Emanuele held her in his arms and wept a little too. He had heard about Cenzo Rena and Franz from an Englishman who had come from San Costanzo to Rome. And he and Anna went together to look at the wall of the village hall where Cenzo Rena and Franz had been killed.

Emanuele, during the time when the Germans were in Rome, had been editor of an important secret newspaper and twice the Germans had put him in prison but his friends of the secret newspaper had managed to get him out again. He had slept all over the place, even in a convent, and had eaten almost nothing, for months and months nothing but turnip-tops, because he had no money and the little that he had he gave to the secret newspaper. But he had become very fat. And Giustino was still in the North and he had heard that he was fighting with the Partisans in the mountains and called himself Balestra. And Danilo had been in Rome for a bit and then had gone to the North, he had made a parachute descent from an aeroplane, and Danilo as a Partisan called himself Dan. And Mammina, with Amalia and Giuma, was in Switzerland, and Giuma had got married to an American woman doctor whom he had met at Lausanne. Emanuele had messages from them every now and then through the Red Cross. Of Concettina he knew nothing.

Emanuele stayed only one day at San Costanzo because he was very busy indeed in Rome with this newspaper, now no longer secret, which had to be put together every day.

Winter came and the English went away and La Maschiona sighed over her coat, which had got all spoilt from being under the ground. Her hair had grown again a little but she still trembled at the remembrance of what they had done to her, if Cenzo Rena had been there they would not have acted like that. She and Anna went to the cemetery on Sundays, and La Maschiona prayed on the graves of Cenzo Rena and Franz and her godfather, who had now also been buried within the enclosure of the cemetery and was at peace. La Maschiona knelt and prayed, but Anna did not pray because her father had always told her it was stupid to pray, if God exists there is no need to pray to Him, He is God and He understands what has to be done without being told.

The English went away and some Fascists arrived from Rome, they had been banished there and they had to keep on ringing the bell at the police station. The Fascists lived at the inn and slept in the Turk's room, and they walked up and down the village square just as the Turk had walked up and down, and they complained to the police-sergeant of the cold and of the food at the inn. The police-sergeant had ended by marrying his sister-in-law with the pear-shaped breasts, and now she was pregnant and no longer had pear-shaped breasts, all you could see was a big paunch and no kind of breasts at all, and the twins had no curls because their stepmother said she had no time to stop and put curling-pins on their heads in the evening. The twins had round, cropped heads, and the police-sergeant, to comfort himself, said that Cenzo Rena liked children's heads to be cropped. He had got together a little furniture again with money borrowed from his parents-in-law, but prices had risen and he had not been able to buy himself another pier-glass.

The police-sergeant and the *contadino* Giuseppe remained

friends for a certain length of time, because together they remembered Cenzo Rena, and what sort of a man he was. And together they also remembered the card games on the sacks of potatoes in the cellar and the night they had run away to Borgoreale, creeping through the pine wood and drinking wine out of the flask. But then they began to quarrel over the King. The *contadino* Giuseppe did not want the King and the police-sergeant, on the other hand, did want him, the *contadino* Giuseppe said that the King had betrayed Italy because after the armistice he had run away, and he wanted him to be hanged, in effigy anyhow, but the police-sergeant did not like to hear his King spoken of like that. They went on quarrelling for a little but then they stopped even quarrelling and ceased to greet one another when they met in the street, the police-sergeant told everybody that the *contadino* Giuseppe was a revolutionary and Giuseppe said that the police-sergeant had almost died of fear that night they had escaped to Borgoreale and that he had more or less to carry him in his arms through the woods.

And then the North was liberated and Mussolini was killed and hung up in a square in Milan, and the *contadino* Giuseppe said that the same ought to be done with the King. When people spoke of all that the Partisans in the North had done the *contadino* Giuseppe became bitter and said that in their own country, where people had no spirit, nothing had been done against the Germans, only Cenzo Rena had died for their own miserable country. And if somebody then reminded him that he himself had killed a German, he would blush and turn away his head because it was a story he did not like to remember.

Anna left with the little girl for her own town. She had had a letter from Concettina saying they were all alive and waiting for her, Emanuele would come and meet her with a car at the station in Rome. La Maschiona was to have gone too, and Anna had bought her a pair of shoes with heels, but when the moment came to leave La Maschiona was not to be found and Anna then discovered her in her mother's

kitchen, she was wearing the shoes with the heels and was
weeping and refusing to go.   She was holding tight to her
mother and saying that never would she walk with those
shoes with heels, she liked to see them on her feet but not to
walk in them.   And her hair had not yet grown properly and
what in the world would the people in the train think when
they saw her hair ?

So Anna and the little girl went off alone in an American
lorry, and the whole village was in the square to see them go
and they shouted to them to come back soon because things
might be very bad in the North and there might be hardly
anything to eat.   At San Costanzo the veal nights had begun
again but the mayor had said that in a short time veal would
be sold in the daytime by the light of the sun and there
would be some for everyone.

They travelled first on the lorry and then on a goods train
which stopped every moment.   And at the station in Rome
there was Emanuele waiting for them and they got into the
car and then began the journey through villages with ruined
houses and past fire-blackened, contorted lorries like carya-
tids along the road.

And Anna saw Giustino again, Giustino who had been
Balestra, and Concettina and Emilio and Concettina's little
boy, and she saw the road by the river again and the soap
factory and Ippolito's seat and her own house and the house
opposite, where Amalia, all dressed as a widow, was furiously sweeping the garden.   And Mammina, too, was
dressed rather like a widow and had grown very old, with
grey hair and her face all wrinkled, and Emanuele said she
had become very mean and kept everybody hungry.   But
Concettina also had become mean, Giustino said, because
she had not understood that prices had increased since the
war.   You could scarcely recognize Concettina in the way
she dressed now, with coarse cotton stockings reaching to
her knees, and always a smell of sweat and a worried, bitter
face.   During the whole time of the Germans she and Emilio
had remained at Le Visciole and she had kept Emilio in

pyjamas all the time in his own room because she was afraid partly of the Germans and partly of the Partisans. Emilio no longer looked in the least like a calf and he was still pale and puffy from the time he had been shut up, and the black feather-brush which had once looked so gay on his forehead had lost its stiffness and its colour and hung rather to one side. He too had become mean and was always considering what to do to save money. And their little boy was dressed like a grown-up man with a tie and brilliantine on his hair, and Giustino said that Emilio and Concettina were a miserable couple and spent their whole time together wrangling and putting brilliantine on the boy's hair. Concettina never stopped talking about the terrible frights they had had at Le Visciole with the comings and goings of the Partisans and the Germans, the doctor with the hair like chicken's feathers was looking after the wounded Partisans and the Germans had seized him and he had died in Germany.

Anna asked Giustino if she too had changed much and Giustino said yes. She was fatter and she had a few grey hairs, Giustino said she had come to look like their mother in the portrait. The portrait was still hanging in the dining-room, but it had become darker with the years, it was rather difficult now to distinguish the frightened, tired features of the face. But the important thing was *not* to look like Concettina, Giustino said. As for changing, he himself was changed too and he no longer had any desire for anything. When he was Balestra he had been very happy, fighting in the mountains with Danilo, and Danilo had been extraordinary then, you couldn't imagine what Danilo had been like when he was a Partisan and called himself Dan. They had been great friends then, Giustino and Danilo, and when there was a pause in the fighting they remembered together all sorts of things which they thought they would never be able to have again, because they thought they were going to die. And since they thought they were going to die they lost all their shyness and told each other all kinds of things, and Danilo had spoken to him about himself and his wife and about how troubled he was because after the war, if he did not die, he would have to tell his wife that they could not stay together any more, he had another girl and they had had a child. And Giustino had told him not to worry because he, Giustino, would take over his wife. And they had laughed together over this but it had not been a nasty kind of laughter, it had not been the laughter of a couple of cynics, it had been a perfectly fresh, light-hearted kind of laughter. But after the liberation Danilo had made a speech there in the town, an important speech, and Giustino had stayed listening to him for some time, and the man who was standing far, far away and high up on the platform was someone he did not know, someone who was not in any way his friend. Certainly he didn't make at all a bad speech, said Giustino, and people clapped their hands loudly. In fact it had been almost too fine a speech, almost too well composed, with pauses and vocal explosions and even something to make you laugh now and then. Giustino had wondered all at once whether it was not perhaps a feeling of envy that he had, because he himself was not high up there on the platform amongst the flags but lost in the crowd of people listening. He had started thinking about a speech that he himself might have made if he had been high up there. A speech that was made entirely of words like the ones he and Danilo used to say to each other at night when they were going to blow up trains, and they had Germans all around them and thought they would be killed. He wondered why Danilo had not made his speech in the words of those days. Giustino had stayed listening for a bit and then had gone away, and he had heard the voice shouting and the voice had made him feel rather cold. And it seemed to him that Danilo was once again as he had been when he had come out of prison many years ago with a hat like a policeman's, and they had all sat round him and had hardly recognized him. For it was not at all easy to come well out of prison, said Giustino, just as it was not easy to win well or to speak true words in victory speeches. In the long run,

blowing up trains was much easier. But this was all nonsense and Danilo was a very good chap, there were few like
Danilo, Giustino said. When Danilo had come down from
the platform and had seen Giustino again he had asked him
why he had not come up on to the platform too and made a
speech, and he had asked him if his speech had been good
and Giustino had said yes.

Anna asked Giustino if he had really blown up trains and
Giustino said yes. Meanwhile Concettina arrived and said
that really Danilo had been very unattractive when he made
that grand speech from the platform, and besides, he had
not even thought of mentioning Ippolito who had died rather
than join in the war. Then Giustino said that Ippolito had
nothing to do with Danilo's speech and Concettina said that,
on the contrary, he had. Ippolito had died in order to show
that no one ought to make war. Besides, they had all of
them together kept those newspapers in the house, had
Danilo forgotten the time of the pamphlets and the newspapers, why not say what they had done against Fascism,
the whole lot of them together? And Giustino said they
had done nothing in the least extraordinary with those newspapers, and he and Concettina started quarrelling, for they
were always quarrelling now. And Concettina ended by
saying that Danilo was a disgusting person because he had
deserted his wife and had had a child by a younger girl.

When Concettina had gone, Anna asked Giustino why he
did not go and live with Danilo's wife now that she was left
alone. But Giustino said that he had no desire to take up
with any woman and the only desire he had was a stupid
one, the only desire he had was to be Balestra again and to
hide in the mountains and have the Germans all round and
blow up trains. However there were no more trains to blow
up and he must finish his course at the University and then
look for a job to keep himself going. He still went to see
Danilo's wife occasionally and they talked together about
Danilo and she was a very fine person and when she came
out of the foundry she knitted clothes for the child Danilo

had had by the other girl.   She no longer lived with Danilo's relations because they were too unkind, she lived alone in a little room and all that was left to her of her marriage with Danilo was the set of bottles and glasses on the chest-of-drawers.

Mammina sent for Anna to come to her drawing-room and she and Amalia wanted to know everything about Franz's death.   So Anna started telling the whole story, from the day when Franz had landed in the village square at San Costanzo with his suitcase.   Right up to the day when he and Cenzo Rena had died in that same village square. Amalia sobbed loudly into her handkerchief and in the end Mammina said it would be better if Anna stopped because Amalia was too much upset.   She sent Amalia off to her room to rest and told Anna she would like to go to San Costanzo some time and find La Maschiona and slap her face hard, for having told the German the way to the cellar.

They went out into the garden and Giuma came out with his wife.   Giuma's wife was very, very tall with a dress covered with little buttons and she had black spectacles which she wore over her eyes like a mask.   There was a tray with glasses of lemonade on the ping-pong table.   Giuma's wife started sucking the lemonade through a straw, looking all round the garden with an ironical, severe expression on her face.   Evidently Mammina did not like her much because Mammina kept moving restlessly in her chair and touching her necklace and her hair and in the end she said she must go to Amalia because Amalia needed a great deal of looking after, and so she made her escape.

Giuma talked and talked so as to make up for his wife's silence.   He was very elegant in a dark knitted shirt, closed at the neck, and a knotted handkerchief, and his lock of hair shook and danced on his flushed forehead.   You could see that he was not yet at all accustomed to having a wife and from time to time he turned in her direction to see if she was still there.   He turned in her direction with a look which

was a little frightened and shy, yet at the same time proud of
this long wife of his with her dark glasses and all her little
buttons.

It was only a few days since they had come back from
Switzerland, he said, and in a short time he would be starting
work at the soap factory. And his wife would help him and
together they were going into the question of children's
crèches and workmen's canteens. For the one thing that
had to be done in Italy was to set up model crèches in every
factory. He pulled out some American and Swiss magazines in which there were photographs of crèches with big
coloured balls and linoleum floors and lovely toy animals.
He had had many silly ideas in his life, he said, and had read
many silly things and there had been a moment when he
very nearly went over to the side of Karl Marx. He was in
Switzerland and he was very unhappy and he had a guilt
complex because he was living safely in Switzerland instead
of fighting with the Partisans in Italy. He had such a guilt
complex that he wanted to die. But he had met this girl
whom he later married, and she had taken him to a doctor
and had him psychoanalysed and so in a few days he had
been cured of his guilt complex because the doctor had
explained to him that it was not for everyone to be a Partisan
in Italy and risk his life and that he himself should stay
quietly where he was and then go back to Italy after the war
and make the soap factory into something fine. He turned
towards his wife and his wife nodded her head in agreement.
She had taken off her glasses now and you could see a pair
of little Chinese eyes and a large, ironical, curving mouth
with two or three drops of lemonade on a barely visible fair
moustache. And did she still remember Montale, Giuma
asked Anna. And he raised his hands and said : " Quando
udii sugli scogli crepitare—la bomba ballerina." But now
there had been real bombs and the *bomba ballerina* seemed
very, very small, very small and very far away, dancing and
crackling happily over those distant days.

The little girl went past across the lawn trailing a rope

behind her, and Giuma's wife asked Anna if it was *her* little
girl. And Anna said yes and Giuma had gone very red and
his eyes beat a retreat, but soon they returned to the little
girl, as she came slowly forward across the lawn, with her
long thin legs and her sharp, imperious face between the
locks of dry-looking hair. For an instant they looked at
each other in silence, the little girl and Giuma, they looked
at each other with intensity and distrust, and they laughed
with their wolf-like teeth. An instant, and then the little
girl went away again, trailing the long rope across the lawn.
Emanuele had now come downstairs, and he was all red and
sweaty because he had been asleep, they had no idea of the
life that he led in Rome, he said, he spent his nights at the
newspaper and during the day he had all kinds of meetings
and never could he spend an afternoon sleeping, in order to
sleep he had to come home. But in a short time he would
be giving up the newspaper and leaving Rome for good,
because he did not know how to produce newspapers. He
could produce secret newspapers but not newspapers that
were not secret, producing secret newspapers was easy, oh,
how easy and how splendid it was. But newspapers that
had to come out every day with the rising of the sun, without
any danger or fear, that was another story. You had to sit
and grind away at a desk, without either danger or fear, and
out came a lot of ignoble words and you knew perfectly well
that they were ignoble and you hated yourself like hell for
having written them but you didn't cross them out because
there was a hurry to get out the newspaper for which people
were waiting. But it was incredible how fear and danger
never produced ignoble words but always true ones, words
that were torn from your very heart. Giuma said how
pleased Mammina would be when Emanuele gave up the
newspaper and came home for good. Emanuele gulped
down a big glass of lemonade with a heap of sugar in it and
Giuma asked him if he had forgotten that sugar was rationed,
and anyhow it would make him even fatter than he was.
He told Anna to look what a double chin Emanuele had,

surely his newspaper and his politics might at least have served to take away his double chin. Emanuele still went into those fits of laughter that sounded like the cooing of a pigeon, but they were rather shorter and rather less shrill, and he had large dark circles under his eyes and no longer went limping backwards and forwards, he remained quietly seated and from time to time stared at the ground and his eyes filled with tears. And the dog, asked Giuma, what had become of the dog? But surely he knew, said Emanuele, surely he knew that the waiter had killed the dog and that it was buried at San Costanzo in the pine wood. He was angry that Giuma did not know about the dog. And Giuma told him it was his fault for never having explained to him exactly how things had gone with Cenzo Rena and Franz. And he said he wanted to go to San Costanzo to see the village square where Cenzo Rena and Franz had died. And they were all silent together as they thought of the ones who were dead, it was only Giuma's wife who had not known any of those who were dead, and she remained outside the thoughts of the others and sat smoking and looking round the garden. Emanuele called to Giustino over the hedge and Giustino sprang over the hedge with one bound and came and sat down and lounged about and smoked with them. And Giuma said he wanted to show his wife the whole of Southern Italy, and his wife might be able to do a great deal for Southern Italy, for instance if she went to San Costanzo she might have all sorts of ideas of things that ought to be done. And Emanuele puffed and snorted and said all right, let them go to the South and psychoanalyse the *contadini*. And Giuma's wife was offended and went away and Giuma ran after his wife. Evening was coming on and the sirens were sounding at the soap factory. Filthy soap factory, said Emanuele, utterly filthy soap factory, now he would have to go back and work in it again, and watch Giuma and his wife messing about with children's creches that they would never be capable of making work. What a catafalque of a wife Giuma had married, said Giustino, a real catafalque she was, and look at her dress with all those little buttons on it, he had counted the little buttons and there were fifty-six of them.   And they laughed a little and were very friendly together, the three of them, Anna, Emanuele and Giustino ; and they were pleased to be together, the three of them, thinking of all those who were dead, and of the long war and the sorrow and noise and confusion, and of the long, difficult life which they saw in front of them now, full of all the things they did not know how to do.

CPSIA information can be obtained
at www.ICGtesting.com
Printed in the USA
LVHW110430080722
723021LV00013B/95

9 781628 725087